RENNO—Unyielding, unconquered, unafraid, the great White Indian never retreated from battle, never surrendered in a fight, never weakened before adversity . . . but the time was coming to face a secret enemy—his divided heritage of the white man's world and Indian blood.

BETH—Passion made her the White Indian's bribe, but now the beautiful Englishwoman must accept the longhouse of the Seneca forever . . . or leave Renno for another man's arms.

MINGO—Destiny enslaved him to a cruel Dutchman; his prodigious strength doomed him to train as a gladiator, and staying alive meant killing on his master's command.

TANO—A brother's betrayal sold him into bondage, but now he could reclaim his kingdom if the White Indian rode into the heart of Africa to fight at his side.

BASTIAN VANDERRENNER—Evil guided this twisted slaver's heart; he killed for pleasure and for gold . . . and his fondest dream was the destruction of one man—Renno.

TOR-YO-NE—Ambition drove this fine young Senecan warrior to stride into Renno's village and stake his claim . . . to another brave's woman and to the title . . . Sachem.

The White Indian Series
Ask your bookseller for the books you have missed

The White Indian Series
Book XVII

SENECA WARRIOR

Donald Clayton Porter

Created by the producers of
**Wagons West, Stagecoach,
Abilene,** and **San Francisco.**

Book Creations Inc., Canaan, NY · Lyle Kenyon Engel, Founder

BANTAM BOOKS
TORONTO · NEW YORK · LONDON · SYDNEY · AUCKLAND

SENECA WARRIOR

A Bantam Book / published by arrangement with
Book Creations, Inc.

PRINTING HISTORY

Bantam edition / March 1989

Produced by Book Creations, Inc.
Lyle Kenyon Engel, Founder

ISBN 0-553-27841-X

Published simultaneously in the United States and Canada

Bantam Books are published by Bantam Books, a division of
Bantam Doubleday Dell Publishing Group, Inc. Its trademark,
consisting of the words "Bantam Books" and the portrayal
of a rooster, is Registered in U.S. Patent and Trademark Office
and in other countries. Marca Registrada. Bantam Books,
666 Fifth Avenue, New York, New York 10103.

PRINTED IN THE UNITED STATES OF AMERICA

O   0 9 8 7 6 5 4 3 2 1

The Dark Continent (Africa)

MILES

0 100 200 400 600 800

Niger River

FULANI EMPIRE

Zari

CAPE VERDE ISLANDS

SLAVE COAST

YORUBA

BENIN

Benin

Bight of Benin

Niger Delta

© BOOK CREATIONS INC. 1988

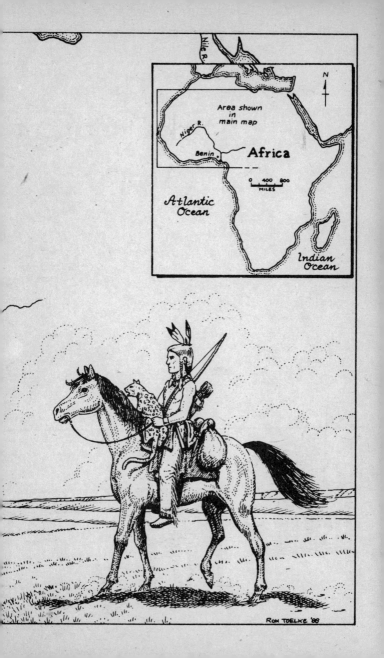

Area shown in main map

Africa

Niger R.

Benin

Nile R.

Atlantic Ocean

Indian Ocean

N

0 400 800
MILES

RON TOELKE '88

Prologue

All things that are good come from the Master of Life. So it had been since the dawn of time, when He subdued the Dark One, his opposite, his brother, the maker of evil, in a titanic battle and stood triumphant on a high place overlooking waters warming under the sun. Rolling emerald forests extended to the horizon. In snug valleys tender, green grass gave sustenance to the grazing deer and buffalo. The whole earth teemed with life. A soaring hawk swooped low to call out his respect.

The Master of Life was pleased, but something was missing. The orenda was not complete. Orenda, that most powerful of spirits, pervades all. Its essence enriches the earth, lives in the sky-reaching branches of the great trees, and directs the interrelationships of all animals. But in

1

the dawn of time, the Master of Life felt that it was not complete.

Orenda was made whole when He made the People of the Hill. Of five tribes he made them, placing the Mohawk in the east to guard his land from any who crossed the broad river. In the west were the Seneca; and in between were the Cayuga, the Onondaga, the Oneida.

All the People of the Hill were brothers. They built their longhouses of poles and sheets of tree bark, so they were warm in the time of cold. In the blessed time their land was sweet with growing things. Their prosperity inspired jealousy in the heart of the defeated Dark One. For revenge, the Dark One put anger and the lust for blood into the People of the Hill.

A Cayuga warrior, visiting in an Oneida village, was killed. A cry for retribution rose from the Cayuga council longhouse. The blood price was two for one, and the wail of loss rose from the women of the Oneida, so once again, in revenge, the war clubs were red with the blood of brothers. The Dark One was pleased.

Year by year, decade by decade, the lust for blood grew among the People of the Hill, and isolated blood feuds became small wars. From His high place the Master of Life saw His people bleeding themselves into impotence.

To a virgin maiden the Master of Life gave the gift of motherhood, and there was born Dekanawidah, He Who Was Holy, and to Dekanawidah was given a vision of five nations united as one under the Tree of Great Peace. To Dekanawidah came the Mohawk warrior Hiawatha, who became obsessed by Dekanawidah's dream.

Hiawatha set about spreading the good message of Dekanawidah's vision, paddling and portaging his white canoe over the great reaches of water, from the land of the Mohawks in the east to the land of the fierce

Senecas, the most skilled and warlike of the five tribes. Even there, in the cool forests near the great roaring river, orenda prevailed.

The five tribes once again clasped arms as brothers, and the elders of the nations met on a hill under the branches of the Tree of Great Peace, where they lit a fire to symbolize the union, while an eagle on the topmost branch of the great tree gazed sharply into the distance, alert to warn the new league of any danger. The rising smoke of the fire of peace sent the message to all.

Now the land of the People of the Hill was divided into five strips, running north to south, one section to each tribe. Over that land rose a spirit longhouse more than two hundred miles long. The power of the spirit longhouse was great, enforced by the orenda of the Master of Life.

As the seasons changed, from the time of the new beginning to the time when the great bear in the sky dripped blood to paint the leaves, the desire of the young warriors to count coup was satisfied in wars against other tribes, and the longhouse of the Iroquois was extended to reach from the rocky shores of the sea in the east to the Father of Waters in the west, from the cold of the northern forests along the Great Lakes to the more moderate, rolling hills of the Smoky Mountains in the south.

The white men who came called the Iroquois the Romans of the New World.

Chapter I

In the late afternoon of an October day a red fox, taking his ease and gnawing on the bones of a fat, juicy rabbit, was startled into flowing flight by the sudden appearance of his only enemy, man. The fox barked in fright, and his padded feet made scurrying sounds on the pine mulch as he trailed his bushy tail.

The man laughed. ''Go in peace, Brother,'' he said in the language of the Seneca.

When white men first came to the low, flat, wooded, often marshy areas along the lower Cape Fear River in what was to become North Carolina, they found that October was the kindest month. In summer, saturated tropical air covered the area, and August days were humid and torrid; but in October, ah, the skies cleared of vapor, and the lights of the sky were small blazes as large as teacups. Clean, fresh air with a hint of coolness poured across the river, moving southward and eastward down the funnel of the unexplored great plains of the midcontinent. Frost dulled the appetite of voracious insects that had, in the early days, done more than hostile Indians to bring bitter failure to Cape Fear's first settlers.

But October days could be a balmy glory, and the beauty of that particular day was not lost on the man who had crept so quietly into the brush-protected lair of the red fox. He expropriated the glade in the tall trees for his own musings, seating himself on the pine mulch with his back against a huge, long-needled evergreen. His mind was distracted, his thoughts so chaotic, he had no peace.

The wilderness skills with which the young man had moved silently through the forest were incongruous with his dress, for he wore tight-legged trousers, strained by the well-sculpted muscles, and a white shirt dampened with perspiration. He had at his belt a deadly Spanish stiletto in a beautiful wrought-leather sheath. Only his footwear spoke of his background, for he wore plain, sturdy moccasins of deer hide. Those moccasins had covered miles that day at a warrior's pace—that loping run just short of full speed—that was the hallmark of the Seneca warrior.

In spite of his seeming isolation in the deep forest, he was actually in the heart of white civilization. Just beyond the stand of virgin pines were the plantations, rice paddies, and fields of indigo, all clinging closely to the river.

He felt an emptiness in the forest, an absence of orenda, for the original inhabitants had long since been exterminated or driven west by the guns and sheer number of European settlers. The manitous, it seemed, were not present in those areas altered by the white-man's work. That was a sadness, and a warning he did not need, for he knew the history of the white man. He could name many tribes that no longer existed, children of common ancestors far back in the dawn of time, brothers who had suffered the brunt of the white-man's rapacity for land.

He lifted his face to the blue sky beyond the canopy of pine branches and spoke in the Seneca tongue. "Hear me, for I am alone and in doubt."

A crow cawed, drawing out the sound, signaling that it saw no danger, and the wind sighed almost inaudibly in the upper branches.

Desperation drove the young man to his feet. He vaulted a low growth of brush and swerved through the trees to break from the copse into cultivated land. With the speed of a sprinter he lengthened his strides until his body cried out in protest and his lungs sought a second wind. He found that reserve as he sped past a gang of gaping, black slaves and ran on into another line of trees beyond the fields. He catapulted over a stream, slowed his pace, and moved through thick underbrush.

At twilight he rested and listened to the soft sounds of the woodlands—the scratch of a squirrel's claws on bark . . . the evening chirp of birds. He had been running through a marshy area laced by waterways. Ahead, a lake formed behind a huge, ancient beaver dam. He chose a spot and built a small fire in the shelter of a massive oak whose branches drooped to the ground, unable to support the enormous weight, a full thirty feet from the tree's six-foot bole. Smoke made its way upward through the branches and the leaves, and as night settled, the fire became the only spot of brightness.

"Hear me," he implored. His eyes were closed, and he was envisioning the rolling, green hills to the west, beyond the mountains, where his Seneca dwelled among the Cherokee. "Hear me, spirits of my ancestors."

Now he saw in his mind's eye the original, northern home of the Seneca, in the sweet land near the great roaring river where winter snow lay as deep as a man's shoulders. He called upon the totems of his clan, the bear and the hawk, but there was no answer.

A full moon rising sent beams of light dimly through the canopy of the oak, and its brilliance dimmed the stars.

"Ghonkaba, Father," he whispered. "Come to me and advise me. Ja-gonh, Grandfather, hear me. Great Renno, white Indian, I am in need. I am Renno, son of Ghonkaba, son of Ja-gonh, son of the great Renno, adopted son of Ghonka. I am in need."

He had not eaten since leaving the home of his wife, Beth, in Wilmington, before dawn. He had drunk little—only enough to replenish the liquid he had perspired away. He would neither eat nor drink until he had his answer.

The night was long. He sat motionless as the moon faded in the west and the smell of early morning surrounded him. He had moved during the night only to keep the fire going. Around him the marshy wilderness came alive with the dawn's light. An oily, bedraggled-looking beaver began his work within fifty feet of Renno, gnawing anew on a partially cut sapling. With the sun came warmth.

"Hear me, manitous," he whispered, so softly that his words did not disturb a pair of wood ducks swimming at the edge of the lake.

During the day he gathered firewood. He greeted the night with gladness, for the spirits most often came to him in the night. To midnight and past he chanted his hymns. In the small hours, when the world was quietest, he felt a building of orenda, so it was no surprise to him when a manitou formed from the air in the dark shadows under the oak. The form was feminine; at first the features were indistinct. Then there was a glow, and his heart thudded as he recognized her pale hair and a face that lived in his deepest heart. He leaped to his feet. The manitou held up one slim, white, graceful hand to stop him, and he froze. She spoke one word, "No," but it was unquestionably the voice of his first love, his wife, and the mother of his children, Little Hawk and Renna.

He forced himself to sit, his heart filling to bursting. "Wife of my heart," he whispered.

"You are not alone," the manitou told him.

"I have never ceased to hunger for you, Emily." She laughed, and a thousand fond memories tore at him. "Was I not your wife? Did I not choose to be Seneca? Did I not live wherever you lived, to bear your children?"

"I am thankful," he whispered, for now he knew he would be with Emily in the Place across the River when the manitous called him.

"You are not alone," she repeated.

He leaned forward, hands extended desperately as the spirit faded, but she was gone, and in her place was only the lonely darkness and the distant sound of a whippoorwill, the cry of a soul lost in eternity.

What did it mean, this appearance of his Emily? It was true, of course, that a Seneca warrior was never alone; the spirits of all those who had preceded him to the Place across the River were with him, but did her message have a special meaning?

Actually he was not alone, for he had the flame-haired Beth, his wife, and his children. He had his brother, El-i-chi; his sister, Ena; and his mother, Toshabe. And he had his people, the clans of the bear and the hawk, Seneca who had followed his father, Ja-gonh, into the white man's War of Independence on the side of the settlers. They had left the ancestral homelands, those northern lands given to the People of the Hill by the Master of Life. It was, in fact, this basic conflict between his personal life and his duty to his people that had sent him running into the wilderness, searching for guidance.

For months he had been far away from the village his Seneca shared with the Cherokee. He felt a great need to be in his rightful place as sachem, at the head of his people. Guilt was strong in him, for he feared that it was self-indulgent to want to be with Beth, whose business and personal obligations kept her in Wilmington. He questioned his decision to travel to Jamaica with Beth, but perhaps that had been sanctioned by the manitous, for on that island he had met and vanquished his old enemy, the evil Hodano.

And in Jamaica the manitous had blessed him with a new friend, the giant Maroon named Mingo. Renno knew he should be on the way home, but word had come that his blood brother Mingo had been captured with his wife, Uanna, and their two sons, Tanyere and Little One, while returning to Jamaica. The Maroon warrior to whom Renno had sworn eternal loyalty was in chains, stolen by the slave trader Bastian Vanderrenner.

Mingo had fought bravely at Renno's side, and now Mingo and his family were slaves. To think of the proud Maroon chained was almost a physical pain in Renno's chest. Now Renno was torn between two great forces: his duty to his people and his sworn brotherhood to the Jamaican Mingo. For days he had been lost in indecision.

Letters from his family had reported that all was well with the Southern Seneca. Game was plentiful, and all those dear to him were in good health. One letter especially had lifted his heart, for his sister, Ena, the warrior woman, was at last with child. The manitous had answered the prayers of Ena and her Cherokee husband, Rusog. Renno longed to share Ena and Rusog's time of great joy.

"Hear me," he chanted. A light breeze rattled the leaves

of the oak over his head, and now another presence, misty and insubstantial, was here.

"Ah-wen-ga," he whispered, for it was his grandmother, but young and slim, the beautiful maiden who, like Renno, had traveled to far lands.

"Will you speak, Grandmother?"

The spirit remained silent, her dark eyes looking past him, into the distance. Sounds came, unidentifiable at first, then, as the din grew, Renno recognized the sound of battle, cries of desperation, anger, pain, the crackling of musketry, the shoutings of the captains. Suddenly all was silence.

Ah-wen-ga's spirit bowed her head as if in mourning and vanished.

"I do not understand," Renno called. His voice startled the lake's sleeping waterfowl, which, in protest, honked for a moment. "Help me. I need to understand."

He was sure that a warning had been given, but he burned to know more, to understand his duty and his course of action. If war was to come, his place was with his people.

"Spirits of my ancestors, explain this to me."

Now a tall, handsome figure glowing with internal light came to him, in the traditional fighting garb of the Seneca warrior, tomahawk in hand, blond hair gleaming, blue eyes piercing. The manitou towered over Renno, dwarfing him, and his breath caught in his throat, for he faced the spirit of the great Renno, the original white Indian, whose name he carried.

The words, not of sound, thundered into Renno's mind.

"Honor," the manitou said. "There will come a time when all that is left is honor. The vow of brotherhood is sacred."

The light of dawn added its glow to the gigantic figure, and the handsome, sun-bronzed face was smiling with approval and fondness. And then there was only the morning, the rattle of the oak leaves in the wind, the last, sated hoot of an owl that had hunted successfully. Renno rose, elation glittering fiercely in his bright-blue eyes, for now he knew. As always in times of crisis, the manitous had answered his pleas and given him guidance. All was clear: The vow of brotherhood was sacred.

Hunger assaulted him. He removed his clothing and bronzed and naked, entered the lake in stealthy silence, submerged, and swam underwater to seize the legs of a wood-duck drake. Within the hour he was tearing at the roasted flesh of the duck with his strong, white teeth, and his mind was, once again, covering watery distances.

Roy Johnson halted his horse atop a rounded knoll. To the east the blue haze hanging over the distant mountains illustrated, once again, why the range was called the Great Smoky Mountains. He was in no hurry to get back to Knoxville. Soon winter would come, and he was getting a bit too long in the tooth and thin in the blood to enjoy snow and sleet; but October was a good month, just right during the day. Deciding it was high time to eat, he dismounted and took from his saddlebag the lunch prepared for him by Toshabe back in the Seneca village.

Roy had enjoyed his stay with the Seneca. It had been a sort of vacation, and the only thing that would have made it more fun would have been the presence of his son-in-law—he still thought of Renno in that respect, even though Emily, his daughter, was dead—and the youthfully exuberant El-i-chi.

Well, he thought, there'd be time for hunts with Renno and El-i-chi. Knowing Renno, Roy didn't think he'd stay away too much longer, regardless of that Englishwoman Beth Huntington. Roy, unlike his wife, Nora, didn't actually condemn Beth for having married Renno. Renno was a good-looking young fellow, just the sort to attract all kinds of women—even if he did deny his white blood and proclaim himself to be Seneca, all Seneca, today and forever—but it was still painful to him to think of another woman's taking his Emily's place in Renno's life.

Toshabe had packed roasted venison, corn bread, parched corn, and for the sweet tooth, a nut-filled ball held together with sugar and flour. Delicious. He took his time eating, letting his gaze fall where it would—on the beauty of the forests, the imposing blue heights of the mountains, the scurrying of a covey of quail, and then the booming flight when the birds spotted him.

He reached Knoxville just after dark, resisting the temptation to spend one more night in the open. Nora hadn't been in the best of health, so his concern for her sent him into town, the horse's hooves raising puffs of dust on the dirt streets. There was a light in the window. He hailed, and Nora came to the door.

"I'll just put the horse away," he told her.

She was setting the table when he came into the house. A delicious aroma of something with beef emanated from a pot on the woodstove.

"Did you bring some venison?" she asked.

There'd been no embrace, no kiss, just an exchange of comfortable looks. They'd been married a long time, and each knew that the other was pleased to be together again.

"Too warm still," he answered. "Wait for the first cold spell, and then I'll go get a couple for the smokehouse."

"There's mail," she said.

"Ah." He sat at the table. "Anything from Renno?"

"Not a line." She went to the mantel and came back with an envelope. "Something *for* Renno, though."

He took the letter and whistled as he saw the masculine

scrawl and the name swirling in the upper left-hand corner.
"General Washington," he read.

"So it seems," Nora said.

"All the way from Virginia."

"Are you going to open it?"

"Of course not," he said quickly, in denial of his intense
curiosity.

"If it's important, there might be something you can
do . . ." she suggested.

"Renno'll be showing up most any day now," Roy said.
"He won't want to take the children across the mountains in
the wintertime."

Nora snorted. As far as she was concerned, the proper
place for Emily's children was with her, their grandmother,
now that their mother was dead, not traipsing all over the
country with Indians. "The man that brought the mail, a
trader, is going east to Charlotte tomorrow. Do you want to
send a letter, just in case Renno isn't on the way back yet?"
A wave of disapproval washed over her as she pictured
Renno there in Wilmington, North Carolina, with that
Englishwoman.

"Might do that," Roy mumbled, devouring beef stew so
hot that he had to roll it around in his mouth. "Ena's preg-
nant," he managed around the bite.

"I'm pleased for her." She was pleased, for if Ena had
her own child, maybe she wouldn't be so determined to keep
Renna and Little Hawk with her during Renno's frequent
absences from the village.

"Yep, old Rusog's like a newlywed. Can't do enough for
her."

"Roy," Nora said, sitting across the table from him,
wiping at an imaginary stain on the smooth, varnished surface
of the pine top, "I'd like for you to talk to Renno when he
gets back."

"Now, Nora . . ." Her concern for the grandchildren was a frequently discussed subject.

"Try to convince him to let at least Renna stay with us for the winter. An Indian village is no place for a little white girl at any time, much less in winter."

"Nora, Renno's longhouse is as snug as this cabin," he said. "Maybe more so. Especially when the mud chinks freeze and fall out so the north wind blasts in."

"But you'll talk with him?"

"Sure, sure," he promised.

He finished his dinner in silence while Nora moved off to sit in her rocker before the fireplace. For Roy's taste it was too hot in the cabin, but Nora had been noticeably sensitive to cold lately. He could always take off some of his clothes if it got too uncomfortable. He glanced at the letter from George Washington, picked it up, turned it over, and made his decision.

"You're going to open it?" she asked.

"Well, I was thinking that it might be important," he explained. "I don't think Renno will mind if I read it. If it's something important, I can make a copy and send it to North Carolina just in case Renno is planning to spend the winter in Wilmington—"

Nora shuddered.

"—and keep the original here, to hedge bets. My guess is that he's already on his way, maybe in the mountains this very night."

Nora couldn't contain her curiosity. She put aside her sewing and stood behind Roy's shoulder as he carefully opened the envelope and unfolded the letter.

My dear friend Renno,

I am reminded of your excellent report on conditions in the Northwest Territory following your last journey through those parts. I would that I had another representative

*there as keenly observant as you, for disturbing reports of
unrest and impending war waged by the tribes north of the
Ohio continue to reach my ears. I hesitate to ask you to
leave your people and your family, nor will I. If, however,
any of your people have traveled or plan to travel in the
lands of the Ohio, I would be grateful to know of their
observations. I am sure that you, old friend, know that
these are perilous times. In this young union of ours there
are many disruptive forces, and as you well know, we do
not have, at this moment, any organized military force to
send into the Ohio Territory, where, I am told, people are
dying from Indian attacks. Quite frankly, our information
regarding the state of affairs there is scant, and any
information you can add would be most helpful.*

The letter was signed simply "Geo. Washington."

Roy coughed and looked up at Nora. "He's not asking,"
he grumbled. "Like hell he ain't."

Nora was thinking that if Renno went off again soon, she
might be able to convince him to leave the children with her.

"They don't hesitate to call on Renno for help when they
need it," Roy complained. "And then they allow incursions
into the Indian lands."

"Perhaps you feel that we should give all this back to the
Cherokee," Nora said.

Roy frowned but didn't take up the issue. He busied
himself copying Washington's letter, sealed it in an envelope
addressed to Renno in care of the Huntington Shipping Company in Wilmington, then stored the original in his tin
strongbox.

He was up and about with the sun to find the trader going
into North Carolina. There was, of course, no organized mail
service between the states and the frontier settlements, so the
flow of mail had to depend upon chance travelers.

Roy thought he knew what Renno's response to Washington's letter would be: He would, of course, go, even if Washington hadn't asked him directly. His father had fought with Washington; Ena and he had been scouts for Washington's armies.

Roy didn't quite approve. He had no love for the people in the various states of the new union. They'd defeated John Sevier's and his efforts to form a new state, named after Benjamin Franklin, west of the Smoky Mountains. As far as he was concerned, they could stew in their own juices and leave him and his alone. Renno had his own concerns—his people and his children.

But, Washington had said, people were dying north of the Ohio. If enough of them died, maybe the politicians would forget trying to feather their own nests and vying for power long enough to realize that the bloody British were at work up there, still maintaining a foothold in America and trying to prove to the newly independent United States the folly of going it alone on a continent as wide as North America—a land still divided among the British, the Spanish, fierce indigenous tribes, and the new nation. Yes, Roy decided, Renno would go.

Renno crossed the Cape Fear River by ferry in the late afternoon. He had not slept more than three hours in thirty-six and had covered a great many miles at the warrior's pace, but he was alert—eager, even, now that the decision had been set to act. There were preparations to be made, and as the ferry slowly traversed the muddy river, his mind was busy as his eyes took in the activity around him: A coastal sloop was being hauled up the river by straining rowers in a longboat, and the docks on the eastern bank bustled as longshoremen offloaded the cargo of a schooner. From the western shore the sounds of shipbuilding rang in the clear air.

Renno was not deeply appreciative of towns, but as towns went, Wilmington was very pretty. Although the British general Cornwallis had wintered here, Wilmington had been spared the destruction of war. Prosperity had seen houses proliferating along the river bluff, back from the wharfside commercial district, and beside the running springs that emptied into the river.

The house that had been purchased by Beth and her father, Cedric, was visible from the river, and as the ferry drew closer, Renno could make out the forms of his stepsister, Ah-wa-o, the Rose, and his two children in the garden overlooking the water. He waved, and Little Hawk, spotting him with the sharp eyes of youth, performed a quick little war dance, waved his hands, and sent out such a whoop that Renno heard and smiled.

Renno found Beth in the cluttered study of her home, which she used as a second office for the shipping firm she had built against all odds into a considerable economic force in Wilmington. A woman in the maritime business was a novelty, and her success had not been accepted graciously by some who would have laughed and said "I told you so" had the business foundered.

Seeing him, she leaped to her feet, swept her full skirts from behind her desk, and threw herself into his arms. Then she frowned, looking into his blue eyes. "I've been worried. You left without a word."

"I didn't want to wake you."

"I forgive you," Beth said, brightening. "You have, of course, been in the woods."

A flash of memory showed Emily's face to Renno. She would never have questioned his going, but—he smiled at himself wryly—would he have crept away before dawn without telling her of his intention?

He held Beth at arm's length and studied her face. So unlike Emily she was, her hair fiery red, where Emily's had been pale; her eyes larger, a sparkling green; and her skin touched only slightly by the sun, in spite of just having spent considerable time in a tropical climate and aboard ship.

His serious scrutiny caused her to flush. "You're leaving, aren't you?" Her eyes misted, and she turned her face away.

"Yes, we're leaving," Renno verified.

A tear escaped her left eye to course down her smooth cheek, and she pulled out of his grasp to turn away.

"I knew," she whispered.

"I'll need a ship," he said.

Startled, she faced him. "A ship? Then you're not going home. You're going after Mingo."

"Yes." His knowledge of the world's geography was incomplete, although he was one of the most traveled men in America. He had seen the Bay of St. Lawrence and the swamps of Spanish Florida, the coastal plains of North Carolina and the dry, desert lands of the ancient Pueblo Indians in the Southwest. He had traveled by sea, from Canada to North Carolina and North Carolina to Jamaica. Africa, he knew, was across the Atlantic.

"Oh," she whispered, relieved, coming back to press into his arms. "Then we'll be together a little longer."

They had talked before of the possibility of his going after Mingo. The Dutchman, who had enslaved Mingo to be his bare-handed fighting champion, would probably be in Africa for months, gathering and loading a cargo of new slaves. But Africa! Immense, dark, savage. Even knowing that Vanderrenner's slave fort was on the Niger River delta between the Bight of Benin and the Bight of Biafra left a huge and wild area of possibilities.

"You've determined that this is what you must do?" she

asked. He nodded. "Then we must recruit men and arm them well. The *Seneca Warrior* will be back soon from Jamaica. She's the best armed—"

"No," Renno said. "No men. No army."

"Renno, a successful slave trader like Vanderrenner has allied himself with strong African tribes. He enjoys a well-fortified position. Why do you think people refer to Vanderrenner's headquarters as a fort?"

"For the reasons you just named, a shipload of men would not be enough to attack openly," Renno said. "No, I need only a ship."

"I will not allow you to go alone," she declared.

His face darkened.

"Forgive me for speaking so authoritatively," she said. "My concern for you only—"

"Would it be possible for one of your ships bound for England to take me to Africa?" he asked coldly.

"Yes, of course," she agreed quickly. "If that's what you've decided. I think we should talk about it further, however."

"So." Renno turned, leaving her to find that El-i-chi and their Cherokee friend Se-quo-i had joined Ah-wa-o and the children in the garden. Old Cedric Huntington was ensconced on the veranda, a blanket around his shoulders, watching as the two young warriors played stickball with Little Hawk and Renna, with Ah-wa-o calling encouragement to the children. The game broke up immediately, and two small, human projectiles launched themselves simultaneously at Renno, to be caught and hoisted, one in each arm.

"Do you come from the hunt empty-handed?" Little Hawk asked.

"This time I hunted wisdom," Renno responded.

"Is wisdom good to eat?" asked Renna.

"Renna is good to eat!" Renno said, biting his daughter's

neck playfully. She squealed in pleasured protest, throwing her arms around her father's neck and trying to bite him back until, with a laugh, Renno eased both children to the ground. "Run to your play. I will speak with El-i-chi and Se-quo-i."

El-i-chi, too long inactive, sensed a change in his sachem, his brother. El-i-chi was a blue-eyed, pale-skinned man in buckskins, light-brown hair long and gathered in the back. The shaman of the Southern Seneca, he was much the same size as Renno, although his running muscles were not quite so developed, and they shared a definite family resemblance in the face.

"Soon the mountain passes will be deep in snow," Renno began.

El-i-chi frowned. "We desert our blood-brother Mingo then?"

"The place for my children is with their people," Renno said. "You will take them there—you and Se-quo-i."

El-i-chi's eyes flared.

"Hear me," Renno said. "It was I, not you, who swore blood allegiance with Mingo. I will not risk the loss of both sachem and shaman to our people."

"I go with you," El-i-chi announced firmly, crossing his arms.

Se-quo-i, so young but wise beyond his years, smiled. "I will see that the children reach home safely."

"You left me behind when you went to Jamaica," El-i-chi pointed out. "This time—" He paused, for there was a dangerous look on his brother's face. Then, "Renno?"

Touched by El-i-chi's capitulation, Renno was smiling inwardly. Only to his sachem would the proud El-i-chi bow. And Africa was far away, and large, and unknown. "And Ah-wa-o?"

"She goes with Se-quo-i," El-i-chi said. "She is young.

There is the matter of getting approval from the council for a marriage between stepbrother and stepsister. There is time.''

This time Renno smiled openly. With El-i-chi, the choice between love and the chance of a good fight was the choice of youth.

Chapter II

Cedric Huntington, the former lord Beaumont, died in his sleep. He had enjoyed his last day—a day of fine weather, much of which he spent outdoors with the two lively youngsters he'd come to consider his own grandchildren. A servant, sent to awaken the old man, came running out of his room, face distorted, to break the news to the little group who were at breakfast.

Beth took it well, weeping in the privacy of her own room. Cedric had been ill for a long time, so his demise was not totally unexpected. Renno stayed at her side. Comforted by his presence, she worried more than ever that his trip in search of Mingo was ill-advised and could result in her losing him forever.

Little Hawk told Beth with great seriousness that she was

not to weep, for Granddaddy Cedric was now with Little Hawk's other grandfather in the Place across the River. "Isn't he, Uncle?" he demanded of El-i-chi.

El-i-chi looked toward the heavens for a moment, then smiled. "You were doing a good job of teaching him Seneca ways, Ne-wa-ah Os-sweh-ga-da-ga-ah," he confirmed, using the boy's full Seneca name.

The departure of Se-quo-i, the children, and Ah-wa-o was delayed until Cedric Huntington was interred with a full Christian ceremony. The minister's words of comfort rang out on a glorious October day, and Beth cast the first loose clods of earth atop the casket.

Renno hid his emotional pain at parting from his son and daughter behind an impassive expression. He took Little Hawk aside. "You will help Se-quo-i take care of your sister."

Little Hawk drew himself up and thrust out his boyish chest.

"I will be gone many months, and when I return, you will have grown this high." Renno held his hand inches above Little Hawk's head. "Then we will see if you can pull a proper bow, and we will begin your instructions for the hunt."

Little Hawk beamed. "I will see that no harm comes to Renna," he promised.

"Express my words of honor to your grandmother and to your aunt and uncle," Renno continued.

"And to Grandfather Roy and Grandmother Nora," Little Hawk reminded him.

"Them, too."

Renno, El-i-chi, and Beth accompanied the departing party across the river. Beth had arranged for a coach to take them westward, much to Little Hawk's disgust, for he disdained traveling as a white man. But soon the snows would come to the mountains, and by making the long trek across the state by coach, travel time would be shortened.

Renno stood for a long time, watching long after the coach had disappeared into the forest. Beth and El-i-chi respected his silence.

The *Seneca Warrior* had been loaded for days, having been ready to sail before Cedric's death. Beth arranged to leave her Wilmington firm in the hands of Captain Moses Tarpley, with advice, if needed, from Nathan Ridley, Renno's distant cousin. Nate and his wife, Peggy, had become close to Renno and Beth. Roberto de Mendoza, Beth's brother-in-law who preferred to be called Adan Bartolome, the name he had adopted during his short-lived days of piracy—had proved his responsibility by captaining one of Beth's ships. He would continue the trade voyages during Beth's absence, thus freeing Moses Tarpley for administrative tasks. He asked Beth and Renno to give his best, and his love, to his sister, Estrela, and brother-in-law, William, Lord Beaumont. It was also Adan's hope that Beth might soften, if possible, the telling of his attempt to extort money from William.

Oddly enough, on the day before the *Seneca Warrior* was to commence its Atlantic crossing in the season of tropical storms, mail arrived from England that affected Renno's plans. Letters from William excitedly detailed his involvement with a new organization, called the African Association, whose purpose was to promote increased trade with and exploration of the Niger River areas off the Bight of Benin.

"That's wonderful!" Beth exclaimed. "You'll be able to sail directly from England to the Niger River with men who know the area."

Renno interpreted the coincidence as a sign from the manitous that his mission was to be regarded with favor.

Although there was ever-increasing commerce between North America and Europe, an Atlantic crossing was never to be taken lightly. Billy the Pequot, captain of the *Seneca Warrior*, had advised all concerned to bring warm clothing, for a winter crossing was often very uncomfortable and quite uncertain.

The weather initially favored them as the ship rode the Gulf Stream current northward. As the bow pointed to the east, the ship rocked on a cold, turbulent sea where icebergs were sighted, and then battled the usual winter storms in the North Atlantic. Renno was a good sailor, having discovered during his previous voyages that sheer willpower could overcome the vile sickness caused by the ship's erratic motion. He imparted this advice to El-i-chi, who nodded grimly and summoned all his willpower, only to lose his stomach after a frantic rush for the rail. For El-i-chi it was a miserable trip, and only the thought of adventure and counting coup prevented him from praying to be taken to his ancestors. For days, even before the ship entered the worst storm area, he spent most of his time at the rail and ate nothing.

Billy the Pequot almost lost his scalp because of El-i-chi's seasickness. Billy had been at sea since he was eleven, first as ship's boy, then as one of the finest harpooners ever known in the whaling trade. But he could remember how, during his first voyage, he had been so sick that he had prayed for death. After El-i-chi had been sick for three days, Billy sauntered up to where the shaman clung to the rail, looking down with a pale face and gloomy expression into the white waves quartering into the *Warrior*'s bow.

"It's cold on deck," Billy observed sympathetically. "Maybe you'd be more comfortable below."

El-i-chi had tried lying down in his stuffy, cramped cabin, and the very thought of being closed in, away from the fresh air—the only thing, he felt, that was keeping him alive—made his stomach roil. He shook his head.

"The sickness will pass," Billy consoled.

"Everyone keeps telling me that," El-i-chi whispered.

"But there's a sure and instant cure," Billy ventured, his face serious. Two seamen, working nearby, looked up, grinning.

Hope surged up in El-i-chi. He looked at Billy expectantly. "A cure?" he croaked.

"Oh, yes. It's very simple," Billy said, still solemn.

"By the manitous," El-i-chi begged, "tell me."

"Well," Billy explained, "all you have to do is sit under a tree."

For a moment El-i-chi's face was blank, and then a look of such fury came that Billy saved his own life by taking a quick step backward, narrowly avoiding the swipe of El-i-chi's tomahawk. The two seamen roared with laughter, for no matter how many times a landlubber was caught by the old joke, it was still funny; but their laughter faded quickly as El-i-chi whirled, tomahawk at the ready.

"Hold! Hold!" Billy cried.

El-i-chi slowly put the tomahawk into its place at his belt, his colorless face still glowering.

"For a moment there you forgot the sickness, no?" Billy asked, and El-i-chi managed a weak grin.

Bastian Vanderrenner's ship had made a good crossing without having encountered a *huracán,* which made the southern portion of the North Atlantic exceedingly dangerous from midsummer into early November. The ship had only a light load of trade goods—life was cheap along the slave coast of West Africa—and she rode the equatorial countercurrent toward the nose of the dark continent, finding favorable winds through the zone of the doldrums. The Dutchman was thus hopeful that he would have his slave holds filled in time to reach the slave markets in Spanish Florida before spring.

The voyage was made interesting to the Dutchman by the

presence of two good fighting men: Tano, who had once been his champion, and Mingo, the Jamaican Maroon who had bested Tano. The Dutchman spent many pleasant hours watching the two men train. The threat of giving Mingo's wife, Uanna, to the crew for their pleasure guaranteed the giant's full cooperation.

Mingo had rightly assumed that Tano could teach him much about the skill of bare-hand fighting. During his stint as the Dutchman's champion, Tano's skills had forced the life out of the eyes of many men. Although Tano was smaller than his pupil, he was a veteran, trained by the Dutchman and the formidable Noir, Vanderrenner's lieutenant.

"Attack," Tano advised. "Always attack. The first blow is all-important. An unexpected first blow can take the fight out of a man. After that you toy with him, never letting him recover from the effects of the first blow."

Mingo had never had to engage in such tactics, for he had never been defeated. At first he refused to play Tano's game and always accepted his tutor's first blow. The punches dealt in training were not intended to maim or kill, but because it was not always possible to pull the force of the blow, Mingo quickly learned respect for Tano's power. On the day when Mingo finally sneaked in the first blow, Tano grunted from the force of it and then grinned.

"Ah, you learn," he commended.

The Maroon grinned back. "Not that I need the advantage, little man."

Mingo had never been in bondage before. His ancestors had escaped Spanish slavery and found a safe haven in Jamaica's convoluted, impenetrable Cockpit Country. Nor did he feel like a slave. His every waking thought centered on obtaining his freedom, and that of his family. There was, of course, no possibility for freedom while they were confined aboard a ship; in fact, the Dutchman had shackled him to a bulkhead in its stinking hold to teach him the penalty for obstinancy. But Africa was huge. There he would find his chance and grab it, and somewhere in Africa he would make a place for his family. It seemed too much to hope that he would ever be able to return to Jamaica.

Mingo was allowed to remain on deck as the ship closed on a low, dark landmass. Africa. Uanna and the boys were locked in the hold, where, on the return trip, hundreds of new slaves would be crowded. Had he been alone, he could have leaped over the side to swim for the shore. But he could not abandon his family, and, he realized, the Dutchman knew that.

At his side Tano grunted. "There were our ancestors born."

"Long ago. My blood is in Jamaica," Mingo told him.

"All our blood originated here," Tano said. "Do you smell it? The scent of Africa."

Indeed the air had become heavier, and there was a musty sourness to it—the reason for which soon became evident. The ship maneuvered into a waterway between rank growths of strange trees so dense that there seemed to be no way through them. Odoriferous mud flats made navigation difficult, so the ship was towed by longboats into a maze of merging waterways. The channel being followed by the ship narrowed and twisted.

After the slaver made a sharp turn around a jungly point, Mingo saw a wooden stockade on a slight rise. A signal burst boomed from the ship's bow, to be answered by a burst from the fort. A group of men came through the stockade gate and waved. Mingo's eyes narrowed in the deepening dusk as he recognized the gigantic black form of the Dutchman's right-hand man, Noir.

Soon the ship was moored to a wharf built across a mud

flat, and the red-haired Noir led a small group of men, mostly black, aboard.

"How goes it, Noir?" the Dutchman asked.

"Not good." Noir's scarred, sinister face turned toward Mingo. "You have taken the big one, I see."

"A bit of luck," the Dutchman explained. "Blown straight into my hands by *huracán*. I want you to work with him."

Noir nodded. "And the other?" he asked, indicating Tano.

"Chain him."

Noir nodded. He had been with Vanderrenner since the days of his youth, and he knew the Dutchman's mind. During the days when he was training Tano to take his own place as the Dutchman's champion, he had learned Tano's story and had shared it with Vanderrenner. Tano claimed to have the royal blood of Benin in his veins, having been sold into slavery by the oba of the city of Benin, his half brother, Eweka. If the story Tano had told Noir in confidence was true, Tano would bring a fine price when sold back to the ruler of the City of Blood.

At the rail Tano nudged Mingo and whispered, "Watch that one."

Mingo was fully aware that Noir's eyes were on him. He knew that Noir had once been a great fighter, before middle age and multiple injuries had lessened his strength. Tano had described Noir as having been the fiercest fighter of all, feared throughout the Spanish provinces of the New World, where men appreciated a vicious battle to the death.

"Although he is no longer champion," Tano whispered, "he can be deadly, and he has no fondness for those who have taken his place."

Mingo nodded. He could sense the hostility emanating from Noir, but he knew that if the occasion arose, he would have little trouble overcoming a man of Noir's age. He tensed when Noir sent a group of thugs toward where Tano and he were standing, but he was not their target. Tano was roughly seized, and steel cuffs, connected by heavy chains, were secured to his arms and ankles.

The Dutchman approached. "Now, Tano," he intoned, "you will see what happens to one who fails me and deserts me. You should never have escaped with the white Indian and Mingo. You must be punished for your disloyalty."

As the men started to drag Tano away, Mingo protested. "He is my trainer! My friend!"

"Speak when you are spoken to," Noir said harshly.

"You want me to fight," Mingo said. "I will fight better with Tano at my side."

Mingo had not noticed that the leather sash at Noir's waist was a lash. With one swift movement Noir had the haft in hand. The braided leather thongs cut across Mingo's back once, twice, before he was on the attack—only to come to a halt when a pistol ball whistled past his ear from a weapon that had appeared almost magically in the Dutchman's hand.

"Remember your place," Noir grated, flaying Mingo's skin with the lash once again.

"I leave this one in your capable hands," the Dutchman said, inclining his blond head toward the Jamaican.

"Take him," Noir ordered, and men closed in.

"My family," Mingo pleaded, barely holding his rage deep inside. There would come a time, he promised himself, when Noir was not protected by men with guns.

"Get them," the Dutchman ordered. "Place them in the guest house."

Uanna and the two boys, Tanyere and Little One, were lifted from the hold. Noir's scarred head turned. Although Uanna had borne two sons, she had a full, lithe figure. She held her head proudly, and her hair was braided into a complex and attractive pattern of small coils ornamented with beads and shells.

"Well, now," Noir said. The sound of his voice and the obvious lust in his eyes made Mingo's hair stand up on the back of his neck.

Vanderrenner laughed appreciatively. "Not for you, Noir. We must, after all, keep our new champion happy."

William Huntington had changed little since Renno had last seen him. His handsome face was a bit fuller and his body a bit heavier from good living, but he was still a powerful-looking man. His strong arms embraced Beth, and he warmly greeted Renno and El-i-chi with a Seneca arm clasp.

"We have much to discuss, old friend," William told Renno. "And I'm looking forward to rehashing old memories."

Renno smiled, remembering how well the Englishman had conducted himself during their long and dangerous expedition to the mountain of gold in the far Southwest.

England was cold, a damp, clinging cold unlike anything Renno and El-i-chi had experienced, seeping into the bones and prompting even El-i-chi to don the white-man's clothing and a heavy beaver coat that William brought along. The trip to Beaumont Hall was made in a handsome coach drawn by four spirited bays. Renno and El-i-chi were mostly silent, taking in the sights. In the quiet beauty of the English countryside, remnants of snow created dirty, frozen ruts through which the coach slewed and bounced. Where the snow had not been disturbed, it lay in melted and refrozen patches in the shadow of brush and trees. William and Beth grieved for their father but also managed to talk with great animation, catching up on events since they had last seen each other. William saved one bit of news for their arrival at the manor. There they were greeted tearfully and happily by Estrela, her usually slender form great with child.

El-i-chi looked up at the massive stone pile of the manor, his mouth agape. "You could house an entire tribe here."

William laughed. "I wish you had brought everyone. Plenty of room. I would love to see Rusog and Ena and all the others. You all must be famished, and I fancy that my Spanish wife has had something special prepared for you."

Indeed she had. The long table boasted pheasant and venison, good English roasted beef and Yorkshire pudding, mushy peas, potatoes prepared two ways, and a sideboard of sweets that El-i-chi attacked with great enthusiasm until, with a groan, he sank back in the ornately carved antique chair. "Renno," he moaned, "we must run away quickly, or I will become as bloated as a calving cow."

"As it happens," William said, "I plan to carry Renno off this very evening. There's a meeting of the African Association. I was afraid you were going to miss it. Men there can give you good information about the country you seem so determined to enter."

Had Renno not had previous experience with the type of Britisher who wore a powdered wig, tightly fitted trousers, ruffled shirt, and spoke prissily, he might have been disappointed upon meeting the members of the African Association. But he had faced such men in battle. Once, when he had been much younger and not yet wise, he had underestimated an effeminate-looking British officer and had almost died as a result. Such men had spread the British influence in America, Africa, Asia, and odd bits of land and islands worldwide. No, they were not to be underestimated. Their defeat by the Americans was, Renno believed, more a reflection on their politicians' stupidity and greed than on the lack of courage and fighting ability of the soldiers in powdered wigs and silken clothing.

Renno was not dressed as elegantly as the company, but in his dark, tight trousers, waistcoat, and gleaming white linen he presented an impressive picture. And William was silently amused when Renno, with a wink, affected a believable British accent.

"I say," a bewigged, paunchy oldster began, "I simply cannot fathom why good Englishmen such as yourself, Mr. Renno, chose to separate from your mother country."

At that, William had to turn away, muffling his guffaw in his kerchief.

The guest of honor was a sea captain recently returned from the Slave Coast. He referred to the fact that public sentiment against the slave trade was growing in England; in fact, the past year had seen the formation of the Society for the Abolition of the Slave Trade, which, he stated, would surely prevail in the near future, ending what had been, for some British subjects, a profitable venture.

He suggested that a far more honorable and potentially more profitable trade could be established with the black tribes of the Slave Coast, and British spunk and initiative could do the job. Although that area known as Yoruba along the Niger River had first been explored by the Portuguese— what area of West Africa hadn't, for that matter—the Dutch had tried to establish trading posts in the Niger Delta. The territory, the captain assured them, was still wide open for British exploitation. In fact, British ships had been sailing to the Bight of Benin for decades.

Renno listened with great interest, especially when the captain described the dark conditions of the Niger Delta—the pestilence-ridden jungle, impenetrable swamps, poisonous reptiles, crocodiles, and jungle cats that could, with fang or claw, kill a man. After the speech Renno made his way to the captain's side, waited patiently for his turn, and affecting his English accent, asked several questions about the populace in the area.

The captain, accustomed to eccentricity in his fellow countrymen, assumed that Renno was an Englishman who liked to wear his hair natural and long.

"Scurvy lot, the natives. It's the law of the jungle there, with the strong devouring the weak. The stronger tribes raid the villages of the weaker tribes, capture men, women, and children, and sell them to the slavers. I tell you, sir, that were it not for the cooperation—indeed, the rapacity—of the Yorubans themselves, there would be no slave trade. The slavers would not have the power or the resources to fill their holds with human cargo."

"What weapons do the natives use?" Renno asked.

"Anything they can lay their hands on—generally spears, clubs, and knives when they can get them. They'll kill or sell their brothers for a musket. They're a bloody lot, always engaging in petty, intertribal warfare. It's a way of life for them, what?"

Renno nodded, remembering that his own people once conducted intertribal wars. With the coming of the white man to America, various tribes took sides in the larger, more deadly wars brought to America by the Europeans, to avenge some long-past tribal bloodletting.

"They say," the sea captain continued, "that a powerful and splendid empire once existed in those rotting jungles, but I've seen no evidence of it—no heroic construction, no great works of art. I have been told that the city of Benin, which is all that remains of the so-called great Benin Empire, is an impressive, walled city, but I haven't seen it with my own eyes."

Renno was quiet during the ride back to the manor. In William's study he declined brandy. Beth joined them here, full of questions.

"There are possibilities that we should discuss," William pointed out. "If Renno is to take a ship to the Slave Coast, we might as well turn a profit from it, don't you think?"

"I think that is up to Renno," Beth answered.

"I am concerned only with getting there," Renno replied.

"Good, good," William said. "We'll load the *Seneca Warrior* with trade goods. The natives want guns, whiskey, cloth, and decorative items for their apparel. While you're accomplishing your purpose, Renno, we'll be trading for palm oil and ivory."

"When can you have the ship ready?" Renno asked.

"Two weeks, I'd say," William answered.

"Good," Beth said. "That gives us some time to see a bit of England, Renno."

He nodded, his mind far away, preceding him to the steaming jungles and swamps of the Niger Delta.

El-i-chi was enjoying himself. English foods were solid, without much adornment, but English sweets were an experience in themselves. Better, Beaumont Hall boasted a stable of excellent horses. One big bay stallion had, with some coaxing, agreed to do El-i-chi's bidding without the aid of a dinky little English saddle. Although William had been busy amassing the trade cargo for the *Seneca Warrior,* he had arranged for the estate's gamekeeper to instruct El-i-chi in the whereabouts and habits of some surprisingly swift grouse. The shooting was excellent. The gamekeeper needed time to become accustomed to a man dressed in frontier buckskins, but that was not an impossible hurdle to clear.

It took longer to convince El-i-chi to sample the resplendent array of William's clothing. They were of a size, and El-i-chi admitted that he was pleased when Beth exclaimed that he looked absolutely splendid.

Estrela warned with a smile, "Ah, Beth, we'll have to watch this one carefully, or he will break every heart within fifty miles."

The occasion for placing El-i-chi in formal wear was a

small dinner party, for those of William's business associates who would be investing in the *Seneca Warrior*'s voyage to the Bight of Benin. El-i-chi found them to be a stuffy lot, and he considered leaving the table to change into his comfortable buckskins. His boredom was allayed by the woman seated next to him, who, as the evening progressed with course after course and endless talk of investments, profits, and trade, began to capture his attention. At first, when he felt the gentle pressure and the warmth of her leg against his under the table, he thought that it was a mistake on her part and moved his own leg away, only to find that contact was reestablished immediately.

He had been introduced to the lady, but then he'd been introduced to a dozen other people. In experimentation he applied pressure with his leg on hers, and when the lady did not object, smiling at him prettily instead, he leaned toward her and said, "Forgive me. Your name?"

"Elaine, but you can call me whatever you desire or call *on* me at any time."

The drone of business talk continued around them, but El-i-chi now had ears only for this Elaine. He smiled. "Do people ever get up and leave in the middle of one of these affairs?"

She answered his smile. "There is always a first time for everything."

He started to rise, but she put a soft, long-fingered hand on his arm. "Not just yet," she whispered. "The gentlemen will retire to the study for cigars and brandy soon."

"I don't smoke cigars, and I don't like brandy," El-i-chi said.

"That's fortunate for us, isn't it?" she observed.

When the dinner party separated, El-i-chi noted with great interest that Elaine did not go with the ladies into the parlor. Instead she exited through a side door toward the gardens. He waited until the men, Renno among them, had filed into the study, then looked around guiltily and followed Elaine through the door. She was standing on a stone terrace overlooking the back garden, arms clasped against the chill. The sky was solidly overcast, and if El-i-chi had sensed such conditions back in his own country, he would have expected snow.

"You're cold," he said, coming to stand beside her.

"Very," she admitted.

He removed his coat and wrapped it over her shoulders. Snuggled into it, she smelled of the sweetness of flowers, and her blond hair reflected the lamplight coming through the window.

"Elaine," he said, liking the sound.

"Yes?" Her face—the perfect little nose, wide, sensuous mouth, and strikingly dark-brown eyes—was tilted upward.

"Who are you?" he asked, and felt stupid immediately.

She laughed. "I am a member of the privileged class."

"So," El-i-chi said, not quite understanding. To him everyone he had met in England seemed rich.

"A poor little widow, alone, with only the protection of my brother."

"Who is—?"

"He's the loud one, with the red waistcoat. Sir Joffre Jowett. He was seated at the end of the table next to William."

"Ah, yes." He didn't know where to take the conversation from there. Elaine shivered, and he said quickly, "We must get you in out of the cold."

"Or something," she suggested, moving closer to him. Before he could understand how it happened, she was in his arms. Her lips tasted of the sweet tarts that had been dessert, and her body was warm, soft, and pressed firmly against his. He felt himself responding, and she pushed herself away.

"Not here," she breathed.

"Not here what?" he asked, a bit stunned by the power of his attraction to her, his young blood hammering.

"Come to me tomorrow," she said. "And now we must go in. Scandal, you know."

El-i-chi didn't know, but he let her go, for he didn't feel that to do as he wanted—which was to seize her and taste those lips again—would be acceptable. He followed her in. She gave him his coat, smiled glowingly, and said, "Ten o'clock?"

"Yes."

Still not quite believing what had happened, El-i-chi joined the men in the study. As he entered, Sir Joffre Jowett was talking of the profits to be made from the African venture. Then the conversation turned to other subjects, the words passing over El-i-chi's head until Sir Joffre was talking again.

"Things are in a proper muddle at court," he complained. "German George has gone absolutely spare, you know."

William laughed. "Joffre, you'll have to speak proper English for our guests."

"Spare," Joffre repeated. "A shallow pate. Or to put it in plain talk, stark, raving mad."

This caught El-i-chi's attention. "The king is mad?"

"As mad as a hatter," Joffre confirmed. "There'll have to be a regency, of course."

"That means," William explained, "that a body of men to serve in the king's stead will have to be selected."

"And that's the problem," Joffre continued airily, "what with everyone wanting to be named. There are those who look upon the situation as a chance to increase the powers of the Parliament, and therein lies the trouble. I'm sure that you'll all agree that this nation has had all of the democracy it can stand and still exist."

El-i-chi made a small sound of disgust, something noticed only by Renno, who smiled inwardly.

"Politics," El-i-chi whispered to him. "The politics of the white man. Nothing more than men of wealth and power concerned with their own interests."

Then he closed off his mind, for he had more important things to consider. The white-man's politics were simple to understand. The actions of one rather beautiful white woman called Elaine offered greater challenges.

Chapter III

With Christmas only days away, the weather in Knoxville was surprisingly mild. The cords of firewood cut by Roy Johnson showed much less than the usual attrition, for the entire season had been warmer than any winter in Roy's memory. When Nora and he had ventured out of town to cut fir boughs and mistletoe to decorate the cabin, the sun was kind. The hills and mountains in the distance were clearly defined, devoid of the usual haze. The bright winter light caused Roy to squint as he looked up in search of the bunches of mistletoe.

Nora had always decorated the cabin for Christmas, even though Roy, only half teasingly, told her that she was carrying on a pagan custom; 25 December marked a festival celebrating the birth of the unconquered ''sun,'' not ''son.''

He enjoyed the ritual nonetheless, for the fir boughs gave a sweet scent to the cabin, which was often smoky from the fireplace, the cookstove, and the lamps. And the unmatched aroma of freshly baked breads made Roy's mouth water. Nora had been baking and making candy for days.

"Do you remember how much Emily loved Christmas when she was a child?" Nora asked now, as Roy sneaked a look inside the pie safe.

"I remember," Roy said.

"We'll have to teach the children all about Christmas and the teachings of Christ," Nora continued.

"You know Emily talked to Little Hawk about the Bible," Roy reminded her.

"I'm sure she did, but who has taught Renna?" Nora wiped her hands on her apron and walked to the front door, which was open, since the heat of the stove and the fireplace was a bit too much. "Roy," she whispered. "Oh, my God, Roy!"

His heart leaped, for she sounded as if she'd seen the end of the world. He moved quickly to look over her shoulder, and she raced away from him and down the steps, moving with speed he was amazed she possessed. Two bedraggled urchins were running down the dirt street to meet her, Little Hawk loosing the hunting yell of the Seneca and Renna straining every muscle to keep up with her brother. Ah-wa-o and Se-quo-i were not far behind.

The cabin rang with the sound of childish laughter. Little Hawk began to tell, in an excited voice, about his adventures with his father at sea and in Jamaica. Nora's face darkened to think that Renno would expose Little Hawk to such danger. Renna babbled about her pretty "mother," Beth, and the beautiful clothes that Beth had given her. The latter, at least, did not displease Nora.

Roy asked Se-quo-i about conditions in North Carolina.

He'd noticed that Se-quo-i's travel pack was especially heavy, and when the Cherokee warrior unpacked, Roy saw the reason: several heavy books. He raised one eyebrow. There was only one book in the Johnson cabin, Nora's Bible.

Se-quo-i agreed to stay through Christmas. The group had enjoyed a relatively easy journey through the mountains, he said, after leaving the coach that Beth had hired for them. There'd been only a little snow in the higher elevations. Still, it had been a long trip, and the children, although they denied it emphatically, looked a bit worn and tired. That condition was remedied quickly as Grandmother administered hot baths, cookies, cakes, candy, months of pent-up love, and warm beds.

On Christmas Eve a fast-moving weather change brought swirling, black clouds and before darkness, the first drifting snowflakes. Pleasantly full from a good dinner, the group gathered around the fireplace, and Roy, as he'd done when Emily was a child, read the story of the birth of Jesus from the second chapter of Luke. The old words rang with special significance on the eve of the birth of Christ, so Roy's eyes were damp and his voice hoarse when he finished.

Little Hawk nodded wisely. "I have always liked that story."

"Dear," Nora said, "it's more than a story, you know."

"Yes, I know, Grandmother," Little Hawk said. "I know that it has special meaning for you, as the manitous of my ancestors have for me."

Nora's face contorted, and she started to speak, but Roy took her hand quickly and shook his head.

In bed that night she turned to him. "Do you see? They're turning him into a heathen."

"Wife, tread easy," Roy advised. "Belligerent evangelism has turned more people away from belief than to it."

"I will not abide my grandchildren not hearing the true words of faith," she insisted.

"Then let them hear them, but with loving kindness. Actually, if you think about it, the Seneca are devout people."

Nora snorted.

"They recognize one Supreme Being," he said. "The Master of Life."

"And a host of ghosts and spirits and—"

"And not the saints, and the Virgin Mother, and the three heads of God?"

"Don't talk blasphemy," she hissed.

The household was up at dawn. It had snowed throughout the night. The streets were untracked. The trees carried a frosting of powdery snow. The sky was still dark, with more flakes to fall. For Christmas the Johnsons had gaily wrapped a pocketknife for Little Hawk and a doll that had taken many hours of Nora's time for Renna. For Se-quo-i, Ah-wa-o, and the Johnsons there were sweets and roasted nuts, and when Roy could get Se-quo-i alone, a glass of eggnog with something more potent than spices in it.

Roy refilled their glasses and lifted his to say, "To friendship, Se-quo-i. May our two peoples always live together in cooperation and prosperity."

Se-quo-i drank. Until that time he had put aside any questions about Renno and El-i-chi by simply saying, "They will come later." Roy, sensing that there was more for the telling, hadn't pushed it; but now Nora had Ah-wa-o and the two children in front of the fireplace, singing Christmas songs.

"I sent a letter to Renno," Roy began. "It was important, from General Washington. Do you know if he received it before you left?"

"He said nothing of it," Se-quo-i answered.

"Then he should have it by now," Roy said. "I imagine he'll be coming along soon."

"No," Se-quo-i said. "It will be many months." He told Roy, then, of Renno's plans.

Roy whistled. "Africa? He could be gone a year, even longer." He wasn't looking forward to Nora's reaction to this news. "Did Renno give you specific instructions about the children?"

"To take them home," Se-quo-i answered.

"And I suppose you're eager to go."

"I have been away too long," Se-quo-i confirmed. "I have work to do."

"There's going to be more snow," Roy said. "Rough traveling. The youngsters have just finished quite a trek. I'd be much beholden to you if you'd leave them with us. I know Toshabe will want to see them, too, and Ena. Tell you what: I'll bring them out myself as soon as spring comes—in a couple of months."

"This is not my decision to make," Se-quo-i said.

"Then I'll decide for you," Roy offered. "And I'll make it right with Toshabe and Renno."

Se-quo-i hesitated.

Roy pushed on. "After all, we're the children's grandparents. Trudging through the deep snow won't be easy for them. In good weather, it's only two days' travel to the village."

Se-quo-i nodded.

When Nora was told that the children would be staying, she was overjoyed. Ah-wa-o offered to remain behind, to help her care for them, but Nora said, "No, thank you, Ah-wa-o. I won't keep you from your homecoming any longer. I know you're eager to see all your folks."

The journey to the conjoining Seneca and Cherokee villages was, indeed, a difficult one. Snow came down in blizzardlike proportions, and Se-quo-i and Ah-wa-o had to break their way through waist-high drifts in windswept areas. The decision to leave the children in Knoxville had been, Se-quo-i concluded, a good one.

When at last the smoke of the chimneys and fires of the village were sighted, Ah-wa-o quickened the pace, then she ran ahead of Se-quo-i to burst into the longhouse of her father, Ha-ace the Panther, and her stepmother, Toshabe, with a glad cry.

Toshabe was pleased to see the Rose, who, she thought, had grown even more beautiful during her absence. But she could not resist looking past Ah-wa-o's shoulder as they embraced, seeking her sons and grandchildren. She saw only Se-quo-i, and fear filled her until Ah-wa-o explained with downcast eyes that Little Hawk and Renna were with the Johnsons.

"In this weather, perhaps that is for the best," Ha-ace said, seeing the stricken look on his wife's face.

"Perhaps," Toshabe agreed.

The children's absence, however, took first priority at the family gathering that evening. Ena's pregnancy had just begun to show, and there was a new serenity to her face—at least until she heard that her niece and nephew had been left in Knoxville.

"Their place is here," she said heatedly. "I'm sure that Renno would not have intended to keep them from us."

"Let us not start a new war with the Knoxville whites," Rusog said dryly, smiling fondly at Ena. He had always admired his wife's fiery spirit, but he also knew how to soothe her. "They will be here when the weather breaks."

"They should be here now," Ena said, hardly mollified.

The elders of the Seneca and the Cherokee gathered in the council longhouse. Although this was a man's affair, Toshabe and Ena sat with the elders to hear Se-quo-i tell of the journey to Wilmington and of Renno's adventures in Jamaica. The story was long in the telling, and the fire was replenished many times.

The men were especially interested in the secondhand account of the battles in Jamaica, when the black warrior Mingo was at Renno's side. And there was a general sigh when Se-quo-i ended the account with Mingo's capture and enslavement.

"Even now," he concluded, his voice pitched in the storyteller's singsong, "the sachem and his brother journey far to free the black warrior . . . or to avenge him."

Toshabe's face showed no expression, but her heart sank. She had known that her two sons were not coming home soon, but she had not guessed at the unimaginable distances involved or the dangers that they might face.

So as not to appear conspicuous, El-i-chi had donned white-man's clothing for the short ride into the city. He had some trouble finding the address, for the streets were like rabbit trails in dry grass—narrow, filthy, congested, and twisting—but finally he got the proper instructions from pass-ersby and approached Elaine's town house. A man took his horse and led it down an alleyway to the mews behind the residence. The butler brought him to Elaine. She was wearing a light-blue gown. The room was decorated in blue to compli-ment her skin and blond, unpowdered hair. Her cheeks had a touch of rouge, but her lips needed none.

"You're very punctual," she commented, nodding to dis-miss the servant. "What may I offer you after your ride? Something to eat? Tea?"

"Nothing," El-i-chi said, even though his throat and tongue were dry just from being near her.

"Nothing at all?" she asked, smiling up at him in open invitation.

"This," he said, moving to take her into his arms.

This was his first experience with a woman whom some would have called a lady of quality. Her willingness, her eagerness, and the swiftness of what happened next astounded him. He soon discovered that the frills and layers of an English lady's clothing came off in much the same way that one removed a buckskin skirt, if not quite as quickly. That this woman had unblemished, pale skin, never touched by sun, was a novelty. Her responses were much like those of the women he'd known and as passionate as those of his dead wife, if not as sincere.

It was late afternoon before Elaine left the huge, soft bed and coaxed El-i-chi to follow her to bathe and dress. El-i-chi was ravenous, but still in a sensual daze, he hesitated to mention it. Their conversation, to that time, had been limited to very few exchanged words.

"And now, my wonderful, savage lover," Elaine cooed as she adjusted the ruffles at his throat, "do we eat here, or will you allow me to show you off in public?"

El-i-chi laughed. "Whichever would produce food the more quickly."

"You, too?" she asked. "How thoughtless of me to starve you. The quicker way is to walk just a short distance, where a formal tea is under way at this moment."

"Tea?"

"Oh, there'll be food in plenty, not just tea."

She clung to his arm as they gained the sidewalk, laughing up into his face as a chill wind brought a blush to her cheeks. It was only a short walk, and then a liveried servant was admitting them to another town house and taking their coats. A babble of voices came from a great room, and El-i-chi caught glimpses of formally dressed women with a lot of shoulder and cleavage showing, men in afternoon wear, and servants weaving their way through the mass of people with trays of food and drink. Elaine led him into the room, snagged a passing servant, and said, "Just put the tray down here, please." Then both she and El-i-chi dived into the tasty morsels of food. She looked at him with her mouth full, her lips closed but smiling. He nodded in appreciation. His mouth was still full when a buxom dowager came sailing toward them, skirts sweeping the floor.

"Elaine, my dear," the woman enthused, "so sweet of you to come. And who is this striking fellow you have brought to us?"

El-i-chi, his mouth full, didn't realize he'd been brought to anyone.

"He has the most charming name," Elaine said. "Lady Smyth-Watson, this is my friend from America, El-i-chi."

"Absolutely charmed," said Lady Smyth-Watson. "You must tell us all about conditions in the colonies."

"Former colonies," El-i-chi corrected after swallowing quickly.

"Oh, dear, yes," Lady Smyth-Watson said. "You must excuse my lack of knowledge about such things." She turned to Elaine. "You won't believe, my dear, who is here. Lord Kinsley himself, don't you know. He's sure to be appointed to the regency. Come, I must introduce you."

"Come," Elaine said to El-i-chi.

"I am not yet finished," he said.

"Oh, come on," Elaine said rather impatiently. "You can eat later."

"I will eat now," El-i-chi said in a low, even voice, his eyes drilling into hers.

"Well, suit yourself." She turned to Lady Smyth-Watson. "Americans, it seems, are not to be easily impressed by a man who may soon be one of the most powerful men in the world.''

El-i-chi returned all his attention to the platter of little sandwiches and tidbits. He looked up when a shadow fell across the tray.

''I say, old fellow.'' A bewigged young man in gleaming white pantaloons and powder-blue waistcoat stood before him. ''I don't think we've met.''

''No.'' El-i-chi reached for another bite.

''You're from the New World, I hear.''

''Yes.''

''I'm quite interested to know how things stand there, now that the ex-colonies no longer have the protection of the Crown.''

''They stand,'' the shaman said. He gave up trying to eat, rose, and nodded. ''I am El-i-chi.''

''Odd. What sort of name is it?''

''My name.''

''Oh, jolly good.'' The young man laughed. ''My name is Edward. There's more to it, of course, about a half dozen other increments, but I suppose one name is good enough for a man, right?''

''Right,'' El-i-chi confirmed.

''I've never been to America, of course,'' Edward went on, ''but I understand that it's nothing more than a conglomeration of log cabins and clapboard villages. Am I correct?''

''Not exactly,'' El-i-chi answered. ''New York and Philadelphia are sizable cities. Not so large as London, of course.''

''I should think not,'' Edward said with a disdainful smile. ''There are those of us who still don't understand exactly why all of you went along with hotheads like Patrick Henry, Sam Adams, and George Washington. What did you hope to gain?''

"I think you would have had to be there to understand," El-i-chi said.

" 'Pose so," Edward agreed thoughtfully. "I say, are the Indians really as cruel and savage as we've been led to believe?"

"Oh, much worse."

"Do tell me!" Edward encouraged with a shiver of delicious dread. "Do they actually take scalps?"

"Oh, yes," El-i-chi said, "and more. You see, the white men have killed off a lot of the game animals, and there's nothing for the Indians to eat. So when they capture a white man, or woman, or child, they first fatten them on acorns, as one would fatten a pig—"

Edward gasped.

"And then they hang the person by his heels and slit his throat, as one does with a deer, to allow the blood to flow away so as not to give the meat a strong taste—"

"My word!"

"And you can guess the rest," El-i-chi said. "The haunch is the best cut, you know."

Edward's face was red. "You—you—haven't—ah—"

"Oh, yes," El-i-chi verified, showing his teeth in a mirthless grin. "Quite tasty."

Edward backed away slowly, as if to avoid contamination. El-i-chi, grinning wryly, went back to the tray of food and took a swallow of wine. It was not to his taste, but it was the only liquid available.

Edward had moved to join a group of several people in conversation. El-i-chi watched as first one startled face, then another, turned his way. He returned the stares until curious eyes turned away from him. He had eaten his fill when Elaine came sweeping across the considerable space that had formed around the chair and the table where he sat.

"What sort of nonsense have you been telling Edward?" she asked, laughing. "You've got him terribly upset."

"My apologies," El-i-chi said.

"You really are terrible, you know, telling him that you have eaten human flesh."

"Do you know for a fact that I haven't?" El-i-chi was enjoying himself thoroughly. He had always felt that many of the white-man's customs were artificial and pretentious, and never had he been presented with such a satisfying opportunity to play a joke.

"Of course you haven't," Elaine scoffed. Then she looked at him seriously. "Have you?"

"Only this afternoon I nibbled on delicious, white flesh," he whispered. "And that hunger is back in me."

She took a deep breath and released it with a sigh. "Yes," she said. "I will pay our respects to our hostess."

The regency crisis was dominating the attention of all the people with whom Beth needed to meet to establish free trade between American and British Caribbean ports. It was frustrating to keep an appointment with a trade official, only to find that he'd been called away from his office on urgent business. After several days of such disappointments she decided to forget the negotiations until things settled down. If the king's madness was only temporary, then sooner or later things would return to normal. If not, a state resembling normalcy would come with the establishment of a regency. Meanwhile, postponing her business gave her a chance to be with Renno.

The white Indian had been spending his time with William and members of the African Association, learning as much as possible about the land to which he would soon travel. William encouraged him to hire fighting men skilled with firearms, but Renno refused, repeating that it would be impossible to take enough men into West Africa to force the release of Mingo and his family.

He also politely refused William's offers to outfit El-i-chi and him with camping equipment, a variety of weapons, and foodstuffs. Renno had brought his primary weapons with him—the Spanish stiletto that he had taken from a dead man, his tomahawk, and to William's pleasure, the English longbow that had been William's gift to him when they first met. Renno asked for two muskets, four pistols, and powder and ball. William supplied those quickly. And, in a room used for storing and displaying mementos and items of importance from the past generations of the Huntington family, Renno saw another weapon that was added to his arsenal.

Beaumont Hall was a sprawling structure, its original wing dating back to the reign of William the Conqueror. Other sections had been added over the centuries. In the entrance hall and the display room were suits of armor, the sword used by the original Beaumont during the Conquest, family portraits, and odds and ends of jewelry, documents, presentation silver, and in a case by itself, a weapon that Renno recognized immediately as being of New World origin. Beth, who had taken him to the display room, noticed his interest. She lifted the glass cover of the case and placed into his hands a war club fashioned of solid, fine-grained maple, hardened by age and darkened by regular applications of oil to keep the wood from drying and splitting.

The head of the club was a round ball of five-inch diameter. Designed to impart more force to a blow, the handle curved back to the smaller grip of the club, which ended in the symbolic head of a bear, mouth slightly open.

"I had forgotten that," she said. "You know what it is, of course?"

"It's Seneca."

Never had Renno seen such workmanship. He knew that

the club was old, for not since the introduction of iron by the white men had the Seneca used wooden war clubs.

"Read the plate, here," Beth told him. "You won't believe it."

Renno bent to read the words aloud in the dim light. "Seneca War Club: Presented to Lord Beaumont by his good friend Renno, sachem of the Seneca."

And when he read the name, *his* name, the name of his ancestor, the original white Indian, the wooden club in his hand seemed to become heated and to snug its haft deeper into his palm. He strongly felt the presence of the manitous, and his expression made an impression on Beth.

"What is it?" she asked.

"Nothing," he said. "For a moment . . ."

"You felt something?" She had tried to understand Renno's closeness to the spirit world, but never having witnessed the appearance of one of Renno's manitous, she doubted.

"He reached across the years to me," Renno said simply.

Beth was silent. Then, on impulse, she urged, "Take it with you."

"It has significance to your family," he wavered.

"More to yours. It belonged to your great-grandfather. It might bring luck to your venture."

"Thank you," Renno said, lifting the club. Balanced perfectly, it could crush a skull with one blow. And he knew as he felt the warmth, it would bring more than luck, for it was a physical manifestation of the manitous. Finding it here, forgotten, was another sign to him that his mission was blessed by the spirits.

That evening Sir Joffre Jowett and his sister, Elaine, came to dinner. The party of seven dined well while Jowett recounted the stores he had purchased with William to load the *Seneca Warrior*.

Elaine sat next to El-i-chi. She pressed her warm thigh across the space between their chairs and took off her slipper to run her stockinged foot up and down El-i-chi's lower leg so that he had difficulty in concentrating on the good English roasted beef. Since that first day, they had been together almost constantly, much to Beth's amusement. Estrela, however, was dismayed because her strict Catholic upbringing was less forgiving of loose conduct than was Beth's more worldly Protestantism.

Beth faced Renno's impending departure with mixed emotions. She would be concerned for him, of course, but she had important business to conduct. Surely she'd be admitted to the presence of the minister of trade soon. With this on her mind she responded immediately when Joffre asked her about the progress of her negotiations.

"Everyone is so busy," she complained.

"Yes," Joffre said, "but things should ease soon. The king is reportedly regaining his senses. If so, there'll be a lot of disappointed people, but perhaps it will be for the best. At any rate, Beth, I'll be happy to assist you in getting in to see the proper authorities. I am not without influence, you know."

"Any help will be greatly appreciated," Beth responded.

"The *Seneca Warrior* will be ready to sail in three days," William remarked. "After Renno leaves, you'll have plenty of time to get on with your business."

Beth looked quickly at her husband. She already felt the pain of loss, and later, when she was alone with him in the privacy of their chamber, she wept small tears.

"Three days," she whispered, clinging to him. "I insist that you spend every minute with me. We have a secluded cottage on the shore. It's cold there this time of year, but it has a fine fireplace, and there's a woman in the nearby village who can come in and cook."

"Yes," Renno agreed. He had had enough of the hectic

social life of the manor and felt no desire ever to venture into the city of London again.

With the morning they were away. The cottage sat on a windy crag overlooking a gravelly beach, where the cold, gray breakers crashed onto the strand. Renno sat with Beth curled in his arms, the fire burning cozily.

"It seems that we're fated always to be saying good-bye," she whispered.

Renno was silent for a long time. "When we were alone in the forests and first found our love, I told you of my life and my duties."

"I know, I know," she responded. "And I have mine, too. But I promised that I would be a Seneca wife. Can you bear with me for just a while longer?"

He shrugged. "I see no choice."

She pushed herself up to look into his face. "We'll live in a longhouse, and I'll cook over an open fire. As long as I am with you, it will be fine."

He chuckled. "Maybe I'll build you a log cabin."

"I'm making so much money, we could build a splendid house."

"In the Seneca village?"

"We could use some of the money—there'll be mountains of it if I conclude this trade agreement—to better the life of the tribe."

"And if they choose not to live in grand houses?"

"Then let them live as they please," she said. "Doesn't there come a time when we must think of our own happiness?"

"I am sachem," he said.

She pulled away, frowning, and went to toss more wood onto the fire. She turned. "Let's not discuss the future—not for these three days. Let's just be Renno and Beth and pretend that we're back in the Canadian wilderness, running from enemies, and that we're all snug in our camp and there's only our love."

"A simple solution to our immediate problems," Renno agreed, holding out his arms.

At first El-i-chi didn't realize that he had a problem. He was besotted in sensualism, and he loved every moment with Elaine. Although he would have preferred to be alone with her, he did not object when she brought him to various fine houses in London to "show him off." It was only when he began to realize that she was making a determined effort to change him that he came out of his haze and noticed that he hadn't worn buckskins in weeks and that his knowledge of those English customs he considered effete was slowly increasing. When Elaine presented him with a magnificent wig, however, made of human hair and powdered to perfection, he felt his resentment rise.

"I take my own scalps," he grunted, pushing the wig away.

She gave him her big-throated laugh, deep, husky, and very sensual, and tried to position the wig on his head. "But we're having dinner tonight with a real Hanoverian prince, and you'll want to look your best, won't you, for me?"

El-i-chi's smile should have warned her. There was a hint of boyish mischief in it. "Of course. Leave it to me."

"There, that's a dear," she said, handing him the wig.

He took it with him, carrying it by a dainty ribbon attached to its box, and tossed it into the river as he rode toward Beaumont Hall. Renno and Beth were away. William was off somewhere seeing to the last of the loading of the *Seneca Warrior*.

Estrela asked him to take tea with her, and they sat in the great room, El-i-chi once again telling how Estrela's brother, having orchestrated his own kidnapping, had tried to collect ransom for himself from William and how he had, at last, decided that piracy was not for him. Estrela could not seem to hear enough about her brother—although William had not proved similarly amused by the scheme—and laughed in approval every time El-i-chi called him Adan. She rather liked the name.

"One day, after our son is born, William and I will visit in America," she said. "I don't know if we could come all the way west to your country, but perhaps you could meet us at Renno and Beth's house in Wilmington."

El-i-chi was about to say that his brother had no house in Wilmington, that Renno's house was with his people; but he did not, for he was fond of Estrela, and there was no need to hurt her or make her wonder, as El-i-chi often did, about the strange marriage of Renno and Beth. Loving a white woman, he thought, could be bothersome.

He smiled, thinking of Elaine. But he didn't love her. Their relationship was not like the one between Renno and Beth. Perhaps Renno would work out his marriage with the flame-haired woman who had been predicted by the manitous. As for his own liaison with Elaine, there was no problem working that one out.

He sent a note by one of the servants to tell Elaine that he would be a bit late and would meet her at the fine home where the Hanoverian prince was being entertained.

She sent a short answer: "How very nasty of you." He smiled.

He spent a lot of time in preparation, but when he came downstairs, ready to ride into the city, he was wearing not the formal togs of an English gentleman but the fringed buckskins of an Indian brave. His face was painted—El-i-chi, believing that a Seneca warrior must always be prepared to put on the paint of war or the paint of the dying, was never without a supply. A hawk's feather rose from his queued hair at the back of his neck, and at his belt he wore his tomahawk and his knife.

Dinner was just being announced when El-i-chi walked past a startled doorman to enter a room of magnificent dimensions filled with glittering, chattering people. A curtain of silence preceded him as he strode toward Elaine, who had been fretting over his lateness. When she saw him, her eyes went wide, and her face flushed with fury. Her expression was cold as he bowed formally before her and said, "My apologies for being late."

"What is the meaning of this?" she hissed.

"You wanted me at my best," he said mildly. "I am El-i-chi, of the Seneca."

"Damn you," she said.

He took her arm as guests started toward the dining room. Elaine had negotiated long and hard with her hostess to have El-i-chi and herself seated near the head of the table, near the guest of honor. His Royal Highness Prince Rupert of Hanover first saw El-i-chi in all his glory when he turned to sit down. He froze halfway into the chair. Those who had followed his lead struggled in vain to stop their downward momentum to wait for the prince to sit. Rupert was a young man, not yet twenty, and he'd found London society to be dull. Once recovered from the initial shock of seeing a wild Indian in war paint at the table, his pudgy face split in a wide smile.

"*Sehr gut,*" he approved, nodding at El-i-chi. Then, in heavily accented English, "Sir, are you being serious?"

Before El-i-chi could speak, Elaine said, "Your Royal Highness, may I present El-i-chi, chief of the Seneca, from America."

"My pleasure," Prince Rupert responded.

"Sir," El-i-chi said, "I am being misrepresented. I am not sachem. I am shaman of the Seneca."

"And that means?" Rupert asked.

"The meaning is difficult," El-i-chi replied. "Some would call me a medicine man; others might say I am a magician."

"Ah," Rupert said, nodding. "Show us some magic, then."

For this El-i-chi was prepared. Some of the magic tricks taught to him by old Casno, who had gone to the Place across the River, were handy. He held out his hand, palm up, made one quick movement, and his dagger was in his hand as if it had materialized from thin air. A gasp went around the table.

"A useful trick for a man of war," Rupert commented, sitting. The other guests followed. "Perhaps you would teach it to me?"

"There are other uses for a dagger," El-i-chi declared, stabbing into the roasted duckling on a sideboard platter and lifting the entire carcass for a large, satisfying bite.

Elaine went pale and looked as though she might faint, but the prince roared with laughter. Beckoning a servant to bring a duckling, the prince seized a table knife, stabbed his own duckling, and began to gnaw on it while he plied El-i-chi with questions. One by one, following the royal example, the other guests stabbed duckling. One lady of quality dropped her bird into her lap, and although she blanched with horror, she picked up the bird, put it back on her plate, and gamely tried to stab it again.

Hours later, back in her own town house, Elaine was cold and angry. El-i-chi shrugged, preparing to take his leave once he'd delivered her into the drawing room. But when he was in the hallway, she called his name and ran after him.

"Don't go! Not just yet," she pleaded.

"But you don't seem to fancy me at my best," El-i-chi said.

"Come," she said, holding out her hand. "I forgive you."

"Have I asked forgiveness?"

"No."

"We'll be leaving for Africa tomorrow. This is good-bye."

She smiled. "Then won't you make love to me just once more? We can save our differences for when you return from Africa."

"I think that our differences will be with us always."

"I fear so," she agreed. "But we do have one thing in common, yes?"

El-i-chi grinned. "Yes," he said.

Chapter IV

A Cherokee-Seneca hunting party ten miles north of the village sent a runner at full speed back to the house of Ha-ace and Toshabe. The young runner struggled through the remnants of the Christmas storm and breathlessly cried out his news when he had reached his destination. His message caused a stir.

"You are sure that they are Seneca?" Toshabe asked, having heard the young warrior's story.

"Of this there is no doubt. Would I not know my own people? Would I not recognize the tongue of my ancestors?"

Seneca. A large group of them, coming down from the northern homelands. Toshabe's heart soared. There would be news of friends and members of her clan who had not elected to join Ghonkaba in the self-imposed exile in the south.

"We must prepare places for them," she told Ha-ace. "Renno's house can be used, and we can take some into ours until they can build their own shelters. Food must be prepared."

It was not until late in the following day that the vanguard of the traveling group came into the village. The men and the women were laden with personal possessions, and the children looked tired, casting wide eyes around this strange new place. The elders of both the Seneca and the Cherokee were waiting in ceremonial dress. Ena's husband, Rusog, was the spokesman. In good Seneca he spoke the traditional greeting: "I thank thee that thou art well. Welcome."

"We have come in peace to join our Seneca brothers," said a tall, young man, strong of visage. His nose was a powerful statement on his proud, handsome face. Although he was bundled in furs, one could see that he possessed a splendid body with the long-muscled legs of a runner. "I am Tor-yo-ne. Do I have the honor of speaking with Renno, sachem of the Seneca?"

His expression did not change when he heard that he was indeed speaking with a chief, but of the Cherokee.

"We have heard many stories of Renno," Tor-yo-ne said. "He met with the sachem Cornplanter and the elders of the Iroquois when last he was in the northland. We have come, these people and I, to request that we be allowed to become part of the clans of the great Renno, for we can no longer live in peace and dignity in our own lands."

"I am Toshabe, mother of Renno."

That a woman spoke did not surprise the gathering. Unlike the Europeans, the Iroquois valued their women highly and assigned them important responsibilities. The fields, the homes, and the distribution of food were the provinces of women. Lineage was traced through women. If members of different clans married, the child of that marriage belonged to the

mother's clan. At the head of each family was a matron.
Women neither ruled nor governed but had great influence,
since the matron of the noble line named the new sachem
after the death of a chief. It was therefore no dishonor for
Tor-yo-ne to be speaking with the mother of Renno; in fact,
to him it was much preferable to speaking with a chief of the
Cherokee.

"We honor you, Toshabe," Tor-yo-ne said, bowing his
head.

"We are of a blood," Toshabe responded. "You are
welcome. We have food ready for you, and we will shelter
you in our houses until you can build."

"We have sickness among us," Tor-yo-ne warned. "Some
women and children have been made ill by the long trek in
the dead of winter."

Toshabe gave orders, and the women of the two tribes
went into action. Soon all the travelers were housed, the sick
receiving healing potions.

The leaders of the new arrivals met in the council longhouse with the elders of the two tribes. The standing of
Ha-ace in the Seneca tribe was solid. A senior warrior and a
pine tree, or elder, of the council, he spoke for Renno in the
sachem's absence. After the passing of the pipe he inclined
his head, inviting Tor-yo-ne to speak.

"Our homelands are the scene of great trouble," Tor-
yo-ne began. Because we fought with the British, much of
our traditional land has been taken from us. With each passing moon, more white men enter our hunting grounds, killing
not only for food but for pleasure. Our sachems no longer
rule—they obey orders from the white-man's government,
and many young warriors leave us to join with those in the
west, in what the white man calls the Northwest Territories,
to dance the dances of war and to paint war on their faces.

"When Renno was among us, he spoke of freedom and of

maintaining our traditional ways while slowly adapting to the ways of the Europeans. He has wisdom and the ear of the sachem of the whites, George Washington. For these reasons I have come, with these others, to join with the clans of Renno. Had we stayed in our own lands, we would have had to become the dogs of the white man or to fight against his cannon and his great armies.''

Many among the Seneca welcomed the arrival of over a hundred of their blood, for intermarriage with the Cherokee was diluting their smaller tribe. Many Seneca warriors were leaving the longhouses of their fathers to live with their chosen mates among the Cherokee; only a few Cherokee, marrying Seneca maidens, chose to leave their own tribe to live among their wife's clan. This new infusion of pure Seneca blood would ensure the survival of the tribe in the south.

''When Renno returned from his last trip into the northland, he said there would be war,'' Ha-ace confirmed.

''War will come, even here,'' Rusog put in. ''The whites are too many. Their fields are not only for feeding their own families but to feed and clothe the peoples of Europe, whose numbers we can only imagine.''

''War here?'' Tor-yo-ne asked.

''Here there is peace,'' Ha-ace corrected. ''We live in cooperation with the white settlers.''

''For now,'' Rusog persisted.

''And what says Renno?'' Tor-yo-ne asked.

''Renno seeks peace,'' Rusog said, ''but he would be the last to shy away from fighting to protect his own.''

''So I have thought,'' Tor-yo-ne said, satisfied. ''I look forward to clasping arms with him.''

''My brother is not with us,'' Rusog said. ''Nor will he be for many moons.''

Tor-yo-ne hid his disappointment and his question why this Cherokee called a Seneca "brother."

"You will be welcome in my own house," Ha-ace invited, "where your sister now rests among my own women."

Tor-yo-ne nodded. He had been honored when Toshabe singled him out, telling him that he and his family would stay with her. His family consisted of only his younger sister; their parents had died of the winter fever two years before. Uncles and brothers had died in the great white-man's war and in the clashes that arose now and then in the lands north of the Ohio, where more and more Seneca were migrating.

"Perhaps you, too, would like to rest," Ha-ace suggested.

The evening meal in Toshabe and Ha-ace's longhouse was a lively one. Ah-wa-o and An-da, Tor-yo-ne's sister, were of an age, and they had become instant friends. An-da wore one of Ah-wa-o's buckskin suits, and her face was freshly scrubbed. Her full name, An-da-ga-uh, meant Sweet Day, and it suited her, for her face, always smiling, perfectly proportioned, enlivened with a pair of snapping black eyes and expressive eyebrows, would make any day more pleasant. Until the arrival of An-da, Ha-ace had felt that his daughter, the Rose, was the most beautiful maiden in the territory. This An-da at least equaled Ah-wa-o, for she was a striking example of Seneca young womanhood.

Ha-ace remained mostly silent as Toshabe and Ah-wa-o asked An-da many questions about conditions in the northland and the people Toshabe remembered. There was an occasional sadness when Toshabe was told that Seneca of her own generation had gone to the Place across the River. It was impossible, however, to be sad for long in the company of two such beautiful girls, so animated, so lively, so quick to giggle.

Tor-yo-ne, too, was mostly silent except when a question

was directed to him. His frame, relieved of the furs, was sturdy, much like Renno's. He was a strong man—of body and conviction.

"The Sweet Day and the Wolf," Ha-ace murmured late that night to his wife, for Tor-yo-ne was named for the totem of his clan. "What changes will they bring into our lives?"

"Certainly An-da will attract her share, and more, of suitors," Toshabe whispered in reply. "The Wolf? Tor-yo-ne? His influence remains to be seen."

The *Seneca Warrior* had made a swift passage across the Bay of Biscay and past the coast of Portugal, from whose ports the early navigators had blazed the watery trail to the portion of West Africa that was the ship's destination. The *Warrior* encountered the same contrary winds and currents that had, in part, made the Portuguese explorations long and difficult, but Billy the Pequot was a skilled captain, capable of taking advantage of the slightest breeze. The *Warrior* rounded arid Point Etienne only slightly behind expectations, making for the Cape Verde Islands and reprovisioning.

El-i-chi had, at last, found his sea legs. Thankfully the weather was not cold, wet, and miserable, as it had been during the North Atlantic crossing to England. He became edgy as the wind brought a scent of land, however, and was the first ashore when the *Warrior* moored in Praia harbor on the island of São Tiago. He found the population of Praia to be mostly black and mulatto. The Cape Verde Islands had long been a collecting point for the slave trade, and the early Portuguese settlers had brought in black slaves to work their plantations.

Unable to understand the *lingua crioula*, the black's corruption of Portuguese, the shaman was soon content to go back to the ship to watch the taking on of fresh water, fresh broad beans and potatoes, and a variety of fruits that would make a welcome change from the ship's usual fare.

Now the ship sailed into tropical heat, much more muggy and oppressive than in the lowlands of Jamaica and far more uncomfortable than the dry heat of the southwestern lands of the Apache.

Luck had been with them in the Cape Verde Islands, for Billy the Pequot had encountered a Portuguese sailor who knew the Slave Coast and, indeed, could pinpoint the location of Bastian Vanderrenner's slave fort. It was he who called the course that put the *Warrior* off a coast of forbidding aspect. The jungle seemed to rise from the sea itself, with no intervening strands. Behind the dank, green line of vegetation, the land rose into hazy distances.

The Portuguese sailor directed the ship into the mouth of a sizable stream, which soon narrowed so that the ship seemed imprisoned in a convoluted, winding maze lined by huge mangrove swamps.

"From here we proceed with great caution," the Portuguese sailor advised. "The Dutchman has cannon." He shrugged. "But then you have cannon, as well, and more than he has at the fort. If your intention is to assault from the sea, however, I would ask you to lend me a longboat so that I may stay here to await the results of your actions."

"There will be no assault," Renno promised. "Tell me once more the layout of the fort and the nature of the surrounding land."

"See for yourselves," the Portuguese invited El-i-chi and him, gesturing toward the dense mangroves. "It is more water than land. No man can walk through such swamps."

"When will we encounter solid land?" Renno wanted to know.

"The island where the Dutchman has his fort is small. Any approach by ship or by boat would be observed."

"We can swim," El-i-chi suggested as Billy joined them. "If there is no land, we will walk on the peculiar roots of those trees."

The Portuguese sailor casually picked his teeth. "And if you don't drown, become a meal for a crocodile, or die from snakebite, you will die later of fever."

"You made your way through the swamps of Florida," El-i-chi reminded Renno.

Renno gazed at the forbidding swamp. "How close can we get in a longboat without being seen?"

"Another mile or two," the Portuguese answered. "But should you be caught by an outgoing ship—"

"We'll arm the crew," Billy declared. "This doesn't sound like a job for just two men, Renno."

The sachem shook his head. "How many men in the Dutchman's fort?" He had asked the same questions before, but the sailor answered without complaint.

"It depends. If he has men out in the jungles collecting slaves, a few—no more than six. If he has already made his collections, however, the place will be swarming with men."

"Two men to row the boat and bring it back," Renno decided.

"I will be one of them," Billy volunteered.

"No, your responsibility is this ship. Wait here until morning, no longer. If we have not returned, proceed to the ports where you intend to trade, do your business, and return to England."

"Bedamned if I will," Billy growled.

Renno smiled. "If this is a fool's errand, then it is my errand, and I am the fool. I will not allow my sacred bonds of brotherhood to damage Beth's commercial interests. Nor will I risk the lives of good men in a cause in which they have no personal part. You will do as I say."

"I'd rather be with you," Billy observed regretfully. "I

haven't had any excitement since we chased that whale in St. Lawrence Bay.''

Renno clasped Billy's arm, then the Pequot, resigned to Renno's preferences, went to order the final preparations.

Before dawn the longboat was pulling up the winding, narrow river. Dense clouds of voracious insects attacked, biting through the torrents of sweat that poured off the rowing men and dampened the buckskins of Renno and El-i-chi. Renno was traveling light: He had only the Spanish stiletto at his belt and instead of his tomahawk, the war club that had once known the hand of his great-grandfather. El-i-chi was similarly armed but with a tomahawk instead of a war club.

Renno pointed to an indentation in the solid vegetation of the shore, and the sailors eased the longboat into the maze of mangrove roots as far as they could, cursing quietly as they fought the stinging, biting insects. Renno led the way, climbing overboard to sink almost knee-deep in mud. ''Be here at dawn tomorrow,'' he told the sailors. ''Wait only until the sun is showing.''

El-i-chi pushed and weaved forward, wading in waist-deep water, sinking deeply into the mud. Ahead was a solid curtain of dirty green. A roar sounded from their left, and El-i-chi halted, his hand on his tomahawk.

''I have heard something much like that in Florida,'' Renno confided. ''The call of a bull alligator.''

El-i-chi cut through a curtain of vines with his tomahawk and pushed on, remarking that he had never seen such land, such adverse conditions.

Renno had survived the Jamaican jungles, the swamps of Florida, the deserts of the Southwest, the deep snows of Canada, but for him, too, this land offered the supreme challenge. Sweat poured from them, running into their eyes and stinging, and insects seemed to cloud the air. Although both men were in superb condition, soon they were panting with exertion as they struggled through mire that threatened to entrap them forever.

They had left the longboat with the rising sun. By the time the sun reached its zenith Renno estimated that they'd traveled only a few hundred yards, and the nature of the swamp had not changed. There was a deadly sameness—heat, air so thick with humidity that it seemed to drip water, and the feeling of being trapped in a green nightmare of clinging vines, thorns, and impassable, interlocked mangrove roots.

They took turns leading, for it was necessary, at times, to slash their way through a curtain of vines. El-i-chi's tomahawk was becoming dulled by its unaccustomed use as an ax. Such treatment of a fine weapon obviously grieved him, but he forged ahead. When he suddenly stood motionless, Renno sensed danger and stiffened as El-i-chi gave the soft, quiet warning hiss of a threatened beaver. He listened but heard nothing.

"Ease ahead slowly," El-i-chi whispered without moving his mouth. "To my front."

Renno pulled his foot from the deep mud and advanced, every muscle tensed, until he could see over El-i-chi's shoulder.

The reptile was huge, larger than the rattlesnakes of the Southwest, and it reared upward a full three feet from a rotting mass of mangrove roots, its neck flattened into a deadly hood. Its forked tongue was tasting the air not a foot from El-i-chi's face. That the snake was deadly was evident. Nothing that looked so evil could fail to be fatal. A gunshot would alert the Dutchman's fort, less than a mile away. But to delay action meant disaster, for the snake was clearly disturbed, swaying as if in search of a target for its deadly fangs. Slowly, slowly, Renno raised one hand and put it on El-i-chi's shoulder.

"At my signal, fall to your left," Renno whispered, hiding the sound and his lips' movement behind El-i-chi's head. He eased his feet into more secure footing, then pressed with his hand. El-i-chi, with all the quickness at his command, threw himself to his left, plunging into the rank, black water.

The snake struck, launching its powerful upper body forward. The razor-sharp Spanish stiletto caught the cobra just behind its hood at the full extension of the striking body, and the head fell, tongue flicking, into the water near El-i-chi, who splashed frantically to get away from it. The snake's writhing body slid into the water. Renno seized it by the tail and hyperextended his arm.

"Perhaps we should save this meat," he suggested as El-i-chi struggled to his feet. They had not brought food, for the short trip to the fort would be over, with or without success, in one night.

"I am not hungry," El-i-chi said, grimacing. "Nor will I ever be, for that."

"You ate rattlesnake with the Apache. . . ." Renno teased.

"For a senior warrior you can still move pretty fast," El-i-chi shot back.

Renno struck a playful blow to El-i-chi's shoulder and took the lead. Within an hour the ground became more firm underfoot, and they could move without sinking to their knees, although the growth and mangrove roots were still as dense as ever. The brothers halted when they heard a man's singing voice nearby, a chant in some unfamiliar language.

Renno moved forward cautiously, to see the Dutchman's island, which lay across a stretch of muddy water about a hundred feet in width. The singing man was sitting on a log near the water, a musket within easy reach. The fort itself was protected by a wooden stockade ten feet high with hewn, pointed tops and surrounded by a ditch filled with muddy water. There was no sign of the Dutchman's ship, but to Renno's relief, boats were tied at a long wharf extending into the river on the side of the island to his left. The man on the shore was the only guard visible, and no sounds of activity drifted from within the stockade.

Renno motioned to his left and led the way back into the mangrove swamp to a position from which they could see directly into the open gate of the stockade. A collection of thatched huts stood inside, plus one square, wooden building and a smaller enclosure, which, Renno guessed, was a slave pen. As he watched, two black men walked slowly across the open area from hut to hut, then disappeared.

"Let's do it now," El-i-chi urged, rubbing mosquitoes into a bloody mass on his cheek. "Before we are drained of all blood."

Renno reached down, came up with a handful of the odoriferous mud, and rubbed it onto his face and El-i-chi's, berating himself for not taking this simple precaution against mosquitoes earlier. El-i-chi caked his face, his neck, and his exposed hands with mud. Aside from the nuisance of the mosquitoes' trying to land in his eyes—the only area not covered with mud—he found life to be slightly more bearable.

For one hour, then two, Renno sat motionless on a mangrove root, peering into the fort. He saw and identified seven black men. When he saw no white face, he began to fear that the Dutchman had not come to this place, after all, and the trip had been for nothing. He tensed when a man of lighter skin emerged from a thatched hut, scratched his belly, and stretched in the sun. He was seedy, his hair lank, and his white-man's clothing was rumpled and soiled. He lifted his voice in command, and a black man sauntered through the gate to relieve the singing guard sitting on the log.

When the relieved guard went into the fort, El-i-chi turned to Renno. "No more than seven or eight. Why must we wait?"

"But how many are sleeping?" Renno asked. "How many are on the river in boats, to return without warning?"

El-i-chi grunted with frustration and tried to find a way to be comfortable on the mangrove roots. He did not question his brother's decision; he was accustomed to obeying orders from his sachem. He slept and dreamed of the coolness of the stream near the Seneca village, where he and Holani had cavorted and fought and loved. The face of the beautiful Elaine intruded into his dream, becoming a sensuous thing that awoke him, startled. Darkness was falling. Renno was in the same position as when El-i-chi had fallen asleep.

"They eat," Renno said.

Seven black men and the light-skinned man were gathered around a fire over which a haunch of meat was roasting. The aroma saturated the soggy air and made El-i-chi's stomach growl.

"No boats came?" El-i-chi asked.

Renno shook his head. "There are eight, and perhaps more there."

The light of a lamp came from high, barred windows in the square wooden building.

Now the light-skinned man attacked the roasting meat with a huge knife, cutting off hunks to be distributed to the black men.

"Don't eat it all," El-i-chi begged.

Renno smiled.

"Ah," El-i-chi breathed as the light-skinned man went into a hut and emerged carrying a large jug. The jug was passed around, and the men drank deeply. "That will make them sleep soundly."

The eating went on for almost an hour, the drinking even longer, and the black men staggered off one by one to disappear into the huts, leaving only the light-skinned man sitting by the fire, sipping now and then from the jug. When he cut several large chunks from the last of the haunch of spitted meat and carried them into the wooden house, El-i-chi tensed in expectation. But Renno waited. The man came out, locked the door behind him, then disappeared into a thatched hut. Outside the stockade, the new guard was seated on the ground, leaning back against the log and snoring loudly.

"You, there," Renno whispered, pointing to a spot opposite the gate. El-i-chi nodded. He followed Renno through the deepening darkness to the edge of the water and eased into it beside him, letting his body lay forward, to swim with only his head showing. While his strong strokes pulled him to the spot opposite the gate, Renno was swimming silently toward the sleeping guard.

When El-i-chi was in his own element, no man would have dared question his courage. There, in the bath-warm water of an unknown river, far from home, his muscles tensed, and he fought against the urge to draw up his feet lest they be taken by some many-toothed monster of the deep, of the sort they had heard bellowing during their trip through the swamp. But he swam on in silence, gained the shore, and found a position from which he could see without exposing more than his eyes. Renno's head was only a dark spot in the water near the point.

The white Indian crawled onto the muddy shore not twenty feet from the sleeping guard and slithered forward silently. When he was close enough to smell the rank stench of the native beer that the man had been drinking, he rose slowly and reached for the war club. It was fitting that this weapon, with its orenda coming from the man for whom he was named, should strike the first blow. He positioned himself, and the man snored on. With his arm raised, he paused. Because this black man might only be a tool, a slave of the Dutchman, Renno moderated the blow. The rounded head of the war club made a solid, thunking sound, and the force caused the man to topple sideways and lie on the mud. His breathing was slow and deep; he was alive. Renno picked up the guard's musket and checked its priming. His own pistols and El-i-chi's had been left behind, for they would be useless when saturated by swamp water. Musket in hand, he crouched and moved rapidly toward the shadows of the stockade.

Once there, he gave the hiss of a beaver. He did not know, as yet, the sounds made by the birds of this land, but the hiss carried just far enough to bring El-i-chi, also crouched, tomahawk in hand. Renno handed his brother the musket. Without extra ball and powder, only one shot could be fired.

They walked openly into the stockade. Obviously those within felt safe, for the gate had not been closed. Renno entered the first hut, where a man was breathing heavily and evenly. Renno backed out of the hut and found El-i-chi waiting.

"They sleep soundly," he reported. "Come."

El-i-chi followed Renno toward the wooden building. The front door was chained and secured with a heavy padlock. To force the door would make too much noise. Renno pointed toward the hut where the light-skinned man slept, and soon they were inside. A lamp was still warm. Renno brought a blazing stick from the dying fire to light the lamp. The hut was a sodden, stinking place, with filthy clothing and decaying food on the floor. The man with light skin was naked on a rank, blanket-covered cot. Renno stood beside him, positioned the point of the stiletto in the hollow of his throat, and clamped his hand over the man's mouth. He jerked into awareness but froze as the point of the stiletto stuck him as the result of his movement.

"Perhaps you will live," Renno said, "if you are quiet." He removed his hand from the man's mouth.

The man nodded silently, and his eyes widened with fear.

"The Dutchman?"

"Not here."

"A black man named Mingo?"

"Not here, either."

"Where?"

"Gone. Into the interior."

"Who is locked in the wooden house?" Renno asked.

"Mingo's woman and two boys."

"The key," Renno demanded, releasing the pressure on the knife.

The man on the cot had not noticed El-i-chi, who stood outside the lamp's glow. He thought that he faced only one man, so when Renno stepped back, the man's hand darted under his pillow and came out with a pistol, which was moving to point toward Renno's chest even as the sachem reacted. There was a flurry of movement and a sound of solid contact; then the pistol flew from the man's hand, and blood spurted from a severed finger as El-i-chi's tomahawk flashed in the lamplight. When a scream of agony reverberated, Renno struck the man a glancing blow with the war club to silence him. El-i-chi was already outside the hut, crouched and ready.

A black man clad only in a loincloth rushed from a hut, but before he could level his musket, El-i-chi's weapon blasted him in the face. Renno met the next two opponents. The first man's bones broke under the force of the war club, and the second man's chest was opened by the stiletto, steel on bone. Renno had not wanted blood, not from these two, but the choice had been theirs.

He ran toward another hut, catching a glimpse of a falling man as El-i-chi's tomahawk swished through the air and clobbered a black head with the rounded club to the sound of crunching bone. A musket ball zipped past his ear with the deadly sound of a close miss, and he hurled himself to the ground, rolled, came up running toward the point of the musket's flash, and propelled himself through the air to send the musket-wielding man to the dirt, where the stiletto tasted flesh again.

El-i-chi was at his side. The silence of death reigned in the stockade. "Are you whole?" El-i-chi asked.

"I am whole. You?"

"It was quickly over," he remarked, a cold grin on his face.

The light-skinned man was beginning to stir when they went back into his hut. His cot was soaked with blood from his severed finger. El-i-chi poured water from a pitcher over the man's head, and he groaned, opened his eyes, and screamed as he saw the blood gushing from the stump in his hand.

"If I were you, I would do something to stop the bleeding," Renno suggested mildly.

"Help me, damn you! I'm bleeding to death!"

"The key?" Renno asked.

"In my pocket."

El-i-chi picked up the man's trousers with the tips of his fingers, grimacing with distaste as he searched. When he held up the key, Renno tore a strip of cloth from a rotting blanket and wrapped it around the stub of the man's finger.

"You've killed me," the man moaned. "If I don't bleed to death, infection will get me."

"Perhaps not," El-i-chi said.

"I want the direction of the Dutchman's travel," Renno said. "His destination, the number of men with him."

"My God, I don't know," the man answered. "There are native villages scattered all through these damned jungles. But you can follow him—it'll be easy to see where he's been. He has many armed men. He'll stay out until he has a shipload of slaves."

"The Dutchman's ship?"

"Up the coast. It carried trade goods to Benin."

"Brother," Renno said, "do you believe this man?"

"Perhaps," El-i-chi answered.

"Then I think you might do something for him."

Renno took the key to the wooden house. He inserted it in the lock and swung open the door. It was dark within. "Uanna," he called, and threw himself to one side in the same instant, sensing a swift movement. A rough stick narrowly missed his head.

"Uanna," he said, "I am Renno."

The woman, clad in a ragged, baggy dress, came forward cautiously. Behind her Renno saw the boys, wide-eyed, each wielding a stick.

"Renno! Thank the gods!" Uanna gasped.

A scream of pain came from behind them, and Renno turned. Beside the fire El-i-chi was kneeling over the light-skinned man.

"Kill him," Uanna urged. "Kill him now."

"So bloodthirsty?" Renno asked her.

"He is Hassan, the Dutchman's slave master. He deserves death."

"Have you come to kill the Dutchman and free my father?" Tanyere, the older boy, asked.

"I have come," Renno confirmed. "Take your mother to the wharf and untie a boat to carry five."

"Five?" Uanna asked. "You came alone? You did all this alone?"

"There is my brother, El-i-chi."

"But Tano—" Uanna began.

"Tano? Where is he?"

"There," Tanyere answered, pointing. Renno saw nothing. Then as the boy took his arm and led him closer, he could make out a low mound, much like the rounded top of a storm cellar. "He is in the hole. He has been there for many days."

"To the wharf," Renno directed.

The two boys and Uanna moved toward the boats as Renno walked to the fire. There was a smell of burning flesh; El-i-chi had cauterized the stump of the Arab's finger, and Hassan was moaning in pain.

"Tano is here," Renno said. "I will go get him."

"What are we to do with this one?" El-i-chi asked.

"I have done you no harm," Hassan pleaded.

"Only because I intervened," El-i-chi reminded him. "If you live, you would tell the Dutchman we are here."

"No, I swear. I will go away. I will take one of the boats and go."

A Seneca warrior does not kill for the killing, nor does he slay a beaten enemy without reason. "We will take him with us to the ship," Renno decided.

He then ran to the low mound, found that the wooden door was secured only by a pole through brackets, pulled the pole out, and flung open the door. A stench of human excrement assailed him. "Tano?"

He heard movement from the pitch blackness in the hole, then a voice, weak and hoarse. "Who is it?"

"Renno. Come."

"Renno?" There was a scuffling sound and the rattle of chains. Renno leaped down and met Tano, taking his arm. The young captive smelled of filth and stale sweat. Renno half carried Tano up the dirt steps.

"The keys to your chains?" Renno asked.

"Hassan."

After Renno had used the key ring to open the padlock to Uanna's prison, he had tossed it into the house. He ran to retrieve it, then fitted the key into the cuffs one by one. Tano seized the chains and threw them to the ground. "I can walk," he assured Renno when the warrior took his arm. "I am even strong enough to kill the Dutchman and Hassan."

"The Dutchman is not here," Renno told him, slowing his pace to match his companion's, "and Hassan can be of use to us."

El-i-chi helped Hassan to his feet and steered him toward the wharf. Tanyere and Little One had a boat ready. Tanyere stood in the bow, and Little One, on the wharf, next to his mother, held the line. Renno and Tano were walking a few steps behind El-i-chi when Uanna suddenly hefted the metal anchor and crashed it down onto the Arab's skull. The sound of the blow and the limpness of the falling body as it splashed into the muddy water told Renno that Uanna had struck well.

"No one else will feel his lash," she hissed. "He had the cruelty to apply the lash to me and to my sons."

"I regret only that you deprived me of the pleasure," Tano told her.

Chapter V

A rank mist lay over the water. The stars were visible, but the fog and the darkness made it difficult to find the way downriver. Renno and El-i-chi, at the oars, tried to judge direction by their well-developed instinct and kept to the center of the waterway, away from the darker shadows of the mangroves. The river made two sweeping bends. At intervals, when he felt that they were nearing the position of the *Seneca Warrior*, Renno gave the hoot of an owl.

The ship loomed up out of the mist suddenly; Billy the Pequot was being cautious, for there were no lamps burning on board. While El-i-chi backed oars, Renno hooted twice. An answering hoot set them to bending their backs into their rowing, and the longboat soon thumped against the hull of the ship. Billy was standing at the rail. Willing hands helped

Uanna, the boys, and Tano aboard as Renno and El-i-chi climbed up.

"This is Mingo?" Billy asked, hopeful, when Renno stood beside him.

"No, this is Tano. But Mingo is alive," Renno answered.

"My friend, you stink of the swamps," Billy said. "And of blood."

"There were eight," El-i-chi explained. "They chose to fight."

"It will be safe to have light," Renno said. "The Dutchman's ship has gone to Benin. Have someone tend to Tano— clean him, feed him, and give him a place to rest."

Jumping into the sea, Renno and El-i-chi cleansed themselves and donned fresh clothing. In spite of protests that they were not sleepy, Mingo's two sons had been put to bed in the crew's quarters. Uanna was taken to the captain's cabin by Billy, where she ate with a gusto that brought a smile to Renno. El-i-chi was glumly scratching insect bites.

"We are in your debt," Uanna said between mouthfuls.

"There is no debt between friends," Renno told her. "What do you know of the Dutchman's plans?"

"Nothing. My sons and I were kept in isolation. Mingo was allowed to come to us at night. During the day he trained with Noir. They want to make him a killer. You came far, Renno, with only your brother. I will not ask you to do more. When Mingo returns to the fort with the Dutchman and realizes that his sons and I are safe, he will find a way to escape."

"Eat. Rest," Renno urged.

Uanna wiped her mouth with the back of her hand, then yawned hugely. "Your suggestions are good ones."

"And now?" Billy asked.

"Now you will go to do your trading," Renno said.

"What about you?"

"Our business here is not completed," Renno replied.

"You're going to try to find the Dutchman and Mingo?" Billy asked.

Renno nodded.

"My friend," Billy said, "you have done enough. The woman was right. You cannot be asked to do more. There will be an opportunity for this Mingo to free himself. This is a big country, and you know nothing of it."

"There is one who does," El-i-chi suggested.

"Tano is weak and wasted," Billy pointed out.

"He is a strong man who will recover quickly," El-i-chi said. He looked at Renno. "We came to free a blood brother, not only his wife and sons."

"So," Renno acknowledged. "We will sleep now."

The sachem and shaman were awakened by a knock on their cabin door. Renno pulled on his clothing quickly. Tano, scrubbed and in clean sailor's togs, gave him a white-toothed grin. "There is talk that you are going after the Dutchman. I ask only that no one kills him but me."

Tano had lost much weight in captivity. There was an unhealthy pallor to his face, and the whites of his eyes were red.

"You have been poorly treated," Renno observed.

"But I will not slow you," Tano promised. "I know this country. As a boy I hunted it, and I can speak the root language all tribes can understand."

"So," Renno said. "Rest today. Eat."

El-i-chi had heard. While he was dressing, a huge grin lit his face. "We go for Mingo, then?"

Renno nodded, reaching for his war club, to feel its reassuring warmth.

The day was spent in preparations: cleaning the pistols, sharpening the tomahawks and the stiletto, checking arrows for the longbow, seeing to fresh supplies of ball and powder for the pistols and the muskets, and finding weapons for Tano in the ship's stores. Tano assured them that they would be able to live off the land, so they could travel light, with nothing more than the weapons. Billy, seeing that Renno was determined to rescue Mingo, did not voice any more objections.

"The Dutchman has been gone for over two weeks," Renno said to Tano. "He could have traveled far in that time." He thought for a moment, then turned to Billy. "You have told me that it will require perhaps two months for you to visit the various trading locations. That should give us enough time. Two months from this day you will be back here, in this river. If we are not here, you will set sail for England."

"The search for slaves could lead the Dutchman far inland," Tano pointed out, "and in the jungles the travel is slow."

"Three months," Billy decided. "I will be back here in two, and I will wait another month if necessary."

Renno nodded in agreement, although he felt that if they had not returned after two months, they would not be coming back at all.

"Everything is ready," El-i-chi said eagerly. "We could travel some distance in what remains of this day."

"With the morning," Renno said.

A longboat put the three men ashore on the inland side of the river near the Dutchman's slave fort. A trail of sorts existed there, leading them over more-or-less solid ground— although they sank in the mud with each step. They had traveled no more than a mile when El-i-chi pointed toward the sky. Pillars of smoke were visible from the direction of the fort.

"I think that Billy has taken some revenge for the slaves that have been held there," El-i-chi said.

"I wish the Dutchman were burning with it," Tano growled.

"My friend," Renno said, "it is time that I begin to learn your language."

Tano looked at the sachem skeptically. "It took me many years to learn the English of the white man."

"It will help the time of travel pass quickly," Renno said. "Let us begin."

As the trail wound through a jungle that slowly gave more solid footing, it quickly became evident to Tano that Renno had a flair for languages. He was impressed to learn that Renno spoke Seneca, English, French, some Spanish, and several Indian dialects in various degrees of proficiency. El-i-chi listened as Tano gave names to the sky, earth, and jungle in the Edo language, but his patience was soon exhausted. He concentrated instead on setting the pace—slower than his liking out of consideration for Tano's weakened condition—leaving the language lessons to Renno.

Once they had negotiated the mangrove swamps along the river, the trail led through a jungle dense beyond El-i-chi's belief. Teak and mahogany trees reached for the gray, leaden sky. The jungle floor was congested by brushwood, thorny vines, and seemingly a hundred types of creepers. The air was hot, damp, and heavy, and their breathing was labored. There was an ever-present stench of rotting things . . . musty things . . . damp things. Rain occasionally filtered down through the jungle canopy, washing away their sweat and momentarily refreshing them. The trail wound among the huge tree trunks. El-i-chi found evidence of a hacked-out trail in the dying vegetation, but the jungle was already reclaiming the trail with new growth. Still, it was a relief to be away from the mangrove swamps, where the black and brackish water, at low tide, exposed mile after mile of stinking mud.

Tano chose a campsite near a tree that bore leathery nuts

about the size of a walnut. He gathered some and cracked them, offering the meat. "Kola nuts," he said. The taste was bitter. El-i-chi spat out his first bite, much to Tano's amusement.

"My friend," Tano said, "do you see how the kola nut splits neatly into parts? That is a symbol of friendship."

"If I can't be your friend without this," El-i-chi retorted, "then let us be peaceful enemies."

Tano left the weakly burning fire, to return with orange-colored palm kernels. "Perhaps these will be more to your liking," he told El-i-chi.

"In all this land is there nothing fit to eat?" the shaman demanded, rising, taking the English longbow.

"Soon game will be plentiful," Tano assured him, putting a staying hand on his shin. "But here the hunter often becomes the hunted, my friend."

"We will see," El-i-chi said, moving off the trail with difficulty into the mass of vegetation.

Renno chewed kola nuts. They had one advantage: After their bitter taste, water taken from the cavity of a tree stump tasted delicious. He smiled as he heard El-i-chi forcing his way through the undergrowth. In his own forests El-i-chi's passage would have been so silent that it would not have been heard twenty feet away. Gradually the sounds diminished into the distance, and Renno lay back, content to eat the nuts until better hunting conditions were encountered.

He awoke when his brother returned but dozed off again until the smell of roasting meat made sleep impossible. He sat up to join El-i-chi and Tano before the fire, where a small animal carcass was roasting on a spit.

El-i-chi looked at Renno and grinned. "There is hope for this place, after all. I saw signs of larger animals, but due to reasons I will not detail at this time—"

Renno laughed. His brother's face and hands were scratched from his battles with the thorns and the undergrowth.

"—our evening meal is porcupine."

"Porcupine is game for small boys," Renno teased.

"Then I will not ask the great Renno to lower himself to eat of it," El-i-chi retorted, removing the meat from the fire to slice it on a fallen log.

"For once," Renno said, taking out his stiletto, "I will forget my pride."

The meat was fatty and delicious. Tano told them that there were deer to be found in the jungle, but they were quite tiny. The bush pig was easier game, and tasty. In the absence of anything better, however, they could eat snails and tortoises.

"I think," El-i-chi observed, "that the taste of your people is as odd as that of the Apache, who eat rattlesnakes."

"In fact," Tano told him, "snake meat is quite good."

That night and for many nights thereafter as the trail meandered through the jungles, Renno added more and more Edo words to his vocabulary. He was able to carry on a rudimentary conversation within just a few days, much to Tano's amazement.

El-i-chi, with his love for a good, rousing tale, was more interested in hearing Tano talk of his youth in the city of Benin. He had been only thirteen years old when his half brother, Eweka, betrayed him, seizing power that was rightfully Tano's and selling him to the Dutchman as a slave.

"Because I owe you a great debt," he said, "I accompany you, to help. Because I owe a different kind of debt to the Dutchman, I go, to see the blood run from his body in death. And then I will travel to my city, to Benin, where there will be more blood—the blood of my half brother and those who support him."

"Twice has my brother freed you," El-i-chi teased. "Will we have to come to your rescue in Benin, as well?"

Tano glared at him, then his look softened into a smile. "When I am in my rightful place as oba, you will be welcomed in my city. We will feast, and you can have your choice of women."

"Of the last, I have enough," El-i-chi said, thinking of his liaison with Elaine and his love for the Rose, Ah-wa-o. "Tell me more about your city."

"Once the empire of the oba included this entire coast, all of the delta of the Niger, and far to the east. The royal line, of which I am the heir, is descended from the Edo people—a race apart, with a language that is different from all other African tongues. But slowly, because of cruel obas like my half brother, the people revolted, protesting the sacrifices of men, women, and children."

"Sacrifice to what?" El-i-chi asked.

"To the oba. To the most powerful of the gods of Benin."

El-i-chi was puzzled. "But you were oba."

"And I have not felt like a god these last years, but as a slave, killing men with my hands for the Dutchman," Tano admitted. "My people believe that when the new yams are harvested, it is the oba who safeguards the crops. To make the earth fertile, the oba's body is sprinkled with human blood. This is decreed by Osa, who created all. But the laws of the Creator were altered by the greedy obas who came before my father. They secluded themselves in the great palace, away from their subjects. The people began to question and to blaspheme against Osa, the Creator, and against his son, Okoku, the god of rivers and the sea, and to follow Ogun, the god of war."

"What did the obas do when the rebellions began?" El-i-chi asked.

"Unable to lead, the obas ruled by terror," Tano answered, "instilling the fear of being chosen as a sacrifice for

the ceremonies that the oba created. Our city became known
as the City of Blood. One by one, the people broke free to go
their own ways—the Ibo, the Itsekiri, the Ijaw, and the
Yoruba—leaving the oba to rule only a small portion of what
had once been a great empire. Now the oba was the giver of
life and the giver of death to only a few, and thus my father
came into a kingdom greatly diminished. Dreaming that the
royal line of Benin could once again rule a vast empire, he
sought to soften the policies established by his predecessors.''

"He sounds like a wise man," El-i-chi commented.

"But others did not want to give up the power they held,
even if that power was confined to a very small area," Tano
continued. "My half brother, who was the high priest of the
Order of the Hand—a powerful group of men, the king's
bodyguards and other elite warriors—had my father killed. I,
being so young, could do nothing." He shrugged. "On the
day I was sold into slavery, two hundred people died by
sacrifice to celebrate Eweka's victory."

This was incomprehensible to El-i-chi. He spread his hands
in question and looked at Renno. Renno made no comment.

"And so, once again, the oba was the great one, controlling life and death. He was the Child of the Sky, to whom we
pray not to fall and cover us; he was the Child of the Earth,
whom we implore not to swallow us."

El-i-chi lifted his tomahawk and tested the recently honed
edge with his thumb. "Perhaps, Renno, after we have freed
Mingo, we can take a hand in Tano's return to Benin. I
would like to see if this Eweka, this great god, can control
life and death when death is delivered by a Seneca blade."

The next day's march gave Renno the first indication that
he was indeed on the trail of the Dutchman. He was leading
the way. The path had become wider, and there were signs of
frequent travel. The jungle was just as dense, the weather as
warm and humid, but there was a different smell in the

air—the stench of death. He reached a clearing where the jungle had been slashed and burned. A cultivated field had been trampled, and across the field two huts stood amid the smoldering ruins of others. An old woman, digging with a stick in the field, saw the three men emerge from the jungle, and she hobbled away, crying out a harsh warning.

Renno approached the destroyed village with his musket at the ready. The old woman had disappeared. There was no other sign of life.

"He has been here," Tano said. He stepped forward and called out, "We are friends. Do not be afraid."

An old man with a livid bruise on his cheek came out of hiding in the jungle to stare warily at the two white men armed with muskets.

"Who has done this to you?" Tano asked.

Renno could understand some of the old man's answer, catching the word *slaver* and getting the idea that the recent raid on the village killed some of the warriors while capturing others.

"It is the way of Vanderrenner," Tano said when the old man had finished speaking. "He takes all the able-bodied people from the age of ten and kills many of the others. There are only a handful left—the old and the very young."

"There is nothing we can do here," Renno said grimly. What he could do was find the Dutchman and those men with him who had ruined a village.

The trail now led directly toward the north, and twice more in that day they came upon villages burned by the Dutchman and heard the same account from the few survivors.

The practices of the slavers were not unknown to the Idahs whose small settlements were scattered throughout the jungle. Village sites were chosen for their remoteness, in the depths of the protecting jungle. Men and women cut down trees, burned the underbrush, and planted their crops. When the land was depleted, the villagers moved on to clear another site, and if the gods favored them, the slavers' raids bypassed them. Such luck was not to be for a small settlement several miles north of Renno's position.

An early morning mist rose from the sodden earth and clung thickly to everything. An elder rose just as the sun was beginning to burn through the mist. As it rose over the jungle, the old man tensed, poised to flee. He took two steps before a musket ball burned into his flesh between his shoulders, severing the spinal cord.

The sound of voices raised in terror and in threat awoke Sokata, a young girl just coming into the bloom of womanhood. At first she thought that she had been having a nightmare, but as she wrapped her gay, red skirt around her, she realized that something terrible was happening. Into her mind flashed all the stories she had heard about slave raids.

In that village Sokata was the most fair, the most desirable. Already six men of this settlement and others from far away had made their offers to the man she called her father. She was long limbed, narrow waisted, large breasted, with hips that, the women said, were perfect for bringing sons. Until that misty morning her future had been bright, for she would become the first woman of a chief. Now she could hear her world crashing down around her. The blasts of muskets gave way to the terrified shrieks of women and the bawling of children. There had been only thirty warriors in the village, and they were armed only with spears.

Sokata's father leaped from his bed beside the woman Sokata called mother and seized his spear. He had not even cleared the door before a musket ball struck him on the bridge of his nose and he tumbled heavily backward into the hut. His wife wailed in anguish and fell to her knees beside him.

Sokata leaned down, took her mother's arm, and urged, "Come! We must hide!"

There was the madness of loss in her mother's eyes. Sokata's words fell on ears that did not hear, and try as she might, she could not pull her mother away.

My mother is old, she thought. *They will not take her.*

There was a back way out of the hut, which Sokata had secretly fashioned herself in the mud-thatched wall and had hidden with her bed. Often, when her mother and father were sleeping, she had used the exit to meet one young man or another under the stars to play the sexual games that Yoruban girls enjoy while still protecting their virginity. Now she shoved the pile of bedding aside and crawled through the opening in the wall. She reached back, yanked the bedding into place to hide the opening, then looked fearfully around. There were gunshots and cries of pain, the shouts of the invaders and the wailing of women.

Sokata's hut bordered on the jungle, with only a narrow, cleared area between its protective stockade of cut, entangled thorn bushes and the trees. She had created a way through the piled thornbushes, too, and she crawled through it quickly, not daring to look back lest some devil, some slaver, be on her trail. When she gained the protection of the trees, she scrambled to her feet and raced to a small clearing where she had trysted with the boys of the village. No one was there. She waited, heart pounding, until, after what seemed to be years, the invaders' voices could be heard no more. Only the wail of women broke the wary silence.

Sokata crept back to watch from concealment. One blond, white man and a group of blacks had chained together all the able-bodied survivors of the village. A huge, red-haired black man struck out with a lash as a young woman protested—the sound a wet, terrifying snap as her black skin opened under the cutting blow to pour blood. Sokata saw ten-year-old boys and girls chained in the line. Horrified, she backed into the jungle but could not tear her eyes away as the black man with the red hair lifted a wicked blade and slashed downward onto the nape of the neck of a kneeling, weeping woman. With a shock of pure terror Sokata realized that she'd just witnessed her mother's death.

Stunned, she could only stand and watch as the chaining was completed, and with lashes the slavers started the line moving. At that moment a young warrior burst from the jungle, spear raised, screaming the war cry of his tribe. The young man's spear impaled one of the black slavers toward the rear of the coffle. The slaver fell, and the young warrior rushed on, a knife his only weapon. The white man raised his musket and fired, and the young warrior's legs seemed to deflate, although he continued the running motions as he fell and until his life ended.

Sokata could not comprehend the words of the white man, but the anger in his voice was clear. What happened then she would never forget. The price extracted for the death of the black slaver was the life of everyone left in the village. Old men, women, and young children were dragged, screaming, from the huts and put to the blade and the club. Then, with all dead, the white man led his lieutenants and the stunned, silent villagers, chained into one long line, into the fading mist.

There was only silence. Sokata crept out and knelt beside her mother. The black man's blade had almost severed her neck. Inside their hut her father lay still, with large, blue flies crawling into his wound and drinking the blood.

There were no tears, no wails of mourning. The young girl rose from one knee to stand and look out over the village. She gathered her belongings, then systematically searched the other huts, which the slavers hadn't bothered to loot or burn.

She found copper beads, which she strung around her neck, and a cook pot, which she tied to a leather thong and lashed, with other items—clothing, some food, and a pouch of water—to her back.

For one long moment she stood on the edge of the site and looked back, a strange, small smile on her face; at last she was free. She had been in that village since she was ten years old. She had been adopted by the childless man and woman whom she had called father and mother. Long ago she had been taken by Idah warriors during a battle in which her real parents were killed. She was Beni, and now she was free to find her way back to her own people.

Renno had positioned himself in the fork of a tree above a game trail. He sat motionless, bow in hand, and listened to the strange, early-morning sounds of the jungle. He had left camp at first light, rousing only El-i-chi with his quiet movement. El-i-chi had looked at him questioningly with one eye, then had gone back to sleep when Renno motioned him to be still. El-i-chi would have his laugh later, Renno was thinking. For weeks he, Renno, had eaten without complaint the fare recommended by Tano: tortoise and monkey and a variety of odd birds. He craved honest red meat, roasted in its own juices and flavored with the salt that he carried so carefully in his travel pack.

He sensed the approach of an animal, then saw a flash of dull color. It took all his training and skill to send the arrow winging to enter the neck of the dwarf antelope. It was a clean shot, and the antelope died without suffering. Renno quickly purged the carcass and carried it across his shoulders to the campsite, where Tano sat chewing on nuts and El-i-chi, still a bit sleepy, leaned against a tree. When the shaman saw that Renno had not returned empty-handed, he leaped to his

feet with a whoop and immediately set about skinning the
antelope. Soon the delicious aroma of roasting meat was
overpowering the dank stench of the jungle.

Thus was El-i-chi in high spirits as the day's march began.
Tano, too, was happier. He had begun to fill out after his
near starvation, and he had put away prodigious amounts of
the antelope meat. He carried a haunch of cooked meat
wrapped in jungle leaves as they traveled, so the midday meal
was also filling.

Renno was in the lead when odd sounds from ahead froze
him: first he heard a metallic clanking, then mournful keening. He doubled back and motioned for Tano and El-i-chi to
take cover. From the dense foliage came a black man in white-
man's clothing, musket in hand. Renno motioned to El-i-chi
to let the man pass. Then a swarthy white man, followed by
the chained captives, came slowly down the trail. Renno
waited as the head of the slave coffle passed. Some of the
captives' necks bled from the cruel bite of the slave collar.
Others showed the marks of the lash.

A cold fury built in Renno as he remembered the devastation in the three villages that had felt the Dutchman's power.
Still he waited; he wanted to see Vanderrenner's face—and
he wanted the blond slaver to see him—before the Dutchman
died. And he searched for Mingo as the mournfully chanting
coffle passed. But there were only three more armed black
men at the rear of the line of slaves. They, plus the white
man in the lead and the scout, totaled five.

Renno motioned El-i-chi forward, his target the scout
armed with a musket, who would hurry back at the sound of
trouble.

"The Portuguese is mine," Tano whispered. Renno nodded. Tano, musket at the ready, moved toward the trail.
Renno edged through the trees, made his way around thick
undergrowth, and came up onto the coffle from the rear.

The signal came from Renno—the roaring, fighting challenge of the totem of his clan, the bear. And even as he roared out his anger, three arrows flashed so quickly that the first man had not yet breathed his last, the arrow from the English longbow deep in his chest, before the other two were dying. Renno heard the crack of Tano's musket and from up ahead, El-i-chi's victory cry.

The slaves, stunned by the suddenness of the attack and not knowing what had happened, cowered in silence.

Tano came back to join the white Indian and told the captives: "Do not be afraid."

Five men had died on the trail, but many more had been killed in the villages attacked by the Dutchman. To Renno, simple justice had been done; each man had the right to live, to grow his crops, and to hunt for game on his own ground. No man had the right to enslave others.

Tano had removed the key ring from the pocket of the dead Portuguese. "Go home," he said to the slaves as he unlocked the collars. "You can go home now."

A babble of talk broke out. Women fell to their knees to kiss Tano's feet. He stood tall and proud and accepted the adulation as if it were his due.

"Maybe he is a prince," El-i-chi conceded, coming from down the trail with a dead man's musket in his left hand, his own musket slung over his shoulder.

A young woman, bare-breasted, full in the hips, covered only by a tiny loin patch, came to talk excitedly to Renno. Renno couldn't understand her words of gratitude. He told her to go home, but she fell to her knees, and Renno had to step back to prevent her from kissing his feet.

"Watch Tano and see how a prince does it," El-i-chi suggested with a laugh.

"These people say that they will go with us because we are gods and they need our protection," Tano translated, breaking away from the women thanking him. "This one here is their chief."

Renno nodded toward a man of middle age, who stood proudly while blood ran down his back from the open wounds of a lash. "Tell him," Renno requested, "that we travel fast and far and that they must go back to their homes. Tell them that the Dutchman will not harm them again."

They left the freed group behind, their own trail leading northward. They skirted another ruined village—more dead, keened by weakened, frightened survivors. They moved at the warrior's pace along a route that had been well traveled. It was not possible, however, to track the Dutchman and his men, for footprints were erased by daily, torrential rains. They moved onward through the downpours, and three days later they encountered another slave coffle. To facilitate the handling of slaves, the Dutchman was apparently sending them back to his fort in groups of thirty to fifty, under a small guard. It became evident that his policy of murdering all opposition was deliberate, to create in his wake a temporarily safe corridor for the passage of his slave coffles. This time four of the Dutchman's lieutenants died, all black, with Tano taking grim pleasure in killing two of them.

Renno, using his growing command of the African root language, closely questioned the freed slaves about how many men were with Vanderrenner. He received unbelievable answers, for the people reported as many as one hundred, or more, all armed with muskets.

To his pleasure he was told by several ex-prisoners that, yes, there was a giant black man with the Dutchman—a man who did not take part in the killing and the chaining but who seemed to be guarded himself by the dreaded red-haired Noir, a name that was well-known in the land, a renegade Yoruban who took his brothers into the white man's slave pens.

To know that Mingo was alive gave strength to Renno's legs. He set a pace that challenged the weakest of the three, Tano, to the utmost. But the Beni, with good food, freedom, and his burning desire for revenge, was looking better; there was meat on his ribs and fire in his eyes as he matched the warrior's pace without complaint.

Sir Joffre Jowett found many reasons to visit Beaumont Hall. He and William were allied both in business ventures and in the African Association. He came alone after the departure of the *Seneca Warrior* for the Bight of Benin. His sister, Elaine, had secluded herself, refusing to attend even the most gala London parties.

"She says," Joffre told Beth and Estrela, "that she needs rest."

Estrela cast a disapproving look at Beth, who smiled knowingly.

"Actually, Beth," Joffre explained, "you are the reason for this visit."

Truthfully this flame-haired woman, being wasted on an American savage, was the reason for most of Sir Joffre's visits. He could have conducted his talks with William in the city or by correspondence. But Sir Joffre had been favorably impressed by Beth's extraordinary talents and courage. He had heard from William about the great gold hunt, involving a long trek across America's wilderness to a haunted mountain. To win for himself a woman who had killed men—even American wild Indians—was an intriguing prospect. He had no doubt that he, the cream of English aristocracy, could wean her away from her Renno; if he couldn't do it immediately, the extended trip to Africa would solve the problem for him. He was certain that everyone had seen the last of Renno, his brother, and Beth's ship. Spanish privateer vessels roamed the seas, and although peace officially existed between Spain and England, it was often broken in the far sweeps of the oceans when there was a chance for booty.

"How can I serve you?" Beth asked politely.

Joffre smiled, imagining several ways that were, as yet, unmentionable. "It is just the opposite. I have come to offer my services to you. I wish to assist in your efforts to conclude the trade pact you seek."

"How kind," Beth responded warmly.

"The king is in his castle once again," Joffre continued, "and I think that now is a good time to strike. If I may offer, I can arrange meetings for you with very important men who can help you." Jowett, a bachelor, spent much time at the court of King George III, and he willingly used his connections to further business propositions.

"I would be deeply appreciative," she said.

"It remains only to be done then," he said. "When will it be convenient for you to come into London?"

"I am at your convenience," she replied.

"Tomorrow, then. I shall bestir myself first thing tomorrow morning to make appointments for you, and I shall personally escort you to them tomorrow afternoon."

When Joffre was gone, Estrela looked doubtfully at Beth. She had never been overly fond of Joffre. He had a disrespectful way of looking at a woman. Early on, after coming to England as William's new bride, Estrela had had to treat Joffre coldly to turn his attention away from her to other, more eligible women at several social events.

"Do you actually need his assistance?" Estrela asked.

"I will gratefully accept help from any source," Beth answered. "This matter is of too great importance to be selective." Then she laughed. "Don't worry, Estrela. There are men like Sir Joffre the world over. They think that all they have to do is look at a woman, and she immediately falls into the nearest bed.''

"Beth!"

"I can handle Joffre," Beth assured her. "You see, I have become quite the businesswoman. I can use men and discard them as skillfully as any man exploits a woman."

Chapter VI

Each day the march began when the first light filtered through the jungle canopy and the lush growth became visible through the morning mist. Usually Renno took the lead to set the pace. Each day he hoped to hear the movement of many men in front of him, but the Dutchman had left the coast long before the *Seneca Warrior* had reached the Niger delta, and although the Dutchman's movements were slowed by his raids, he was still far ahead.

On one steamy morning, with the day's heat building early under lowering skies, Renno was moving forward at a slow trot, bow slung over his shoulder, musket in hand, and all senses alert. Twice now they had been stalked by the leopard—a man-killing cat, according to Tano. Jungle animals were not the only danger; in a land riven by intertribal wars and devastated regularly by slavers, men killed first and made identification of the victim later. Thus, when Renno detected a movement in the dense growth along the trail a few yards to his front and saw in the mud and detritus of the trail the fresh imprint of a human foot, he halted, sought cover, and signaled El-i-chi and Tano to approach quietly.

Renno pointed toward the spot where he'd seen the motion and made the sign of man. Before Renno could stop him, Tano leaped forward, crouched, and using the jungle for cover, moved to approach the spot from the rear. Because Tano was moving, Renno motioned El-i-chi to wait. Renno himself had his bow ready, arrow nocked.

Tano, skilled at moving in the jungle, made only the slightest sounds. Then, suddenly, there was a great thrashing in the undergrowth. El-i-chi leaped forward, his tomahawk at the ready. An unidentifiable wail rose from the brush, and Renno leveled his longbow for action, fearing that Tano had encountered a dangerous animal. As he ran forward, however, a rolling ball of mixed humanity burst out of the brush and onto the trail. Renno saw the flash of thigh and breast and heard Tano screeching in Edo.

El-i-chi, wide-eyed, halted near the struggling pair and lowered his tomahawk. Tano was locked in combat with a sturdy-limbed young woman doing her best to scratch out his eyes with her fingernails and to bite his nose with her gleaming, white teeth.

"Tano," El-i-chi intoned calmly, "if you need help, just call for it."

A wail of rage and anguish came from the girl. She actually managed to roll Tano onto his back so she was atop him, striking him in the face with her open hand.

"This man," El-i-chi observed with a straight face, "is a champion. I am sure he can overcome one girl."

Tano flipped his opponent off, then pinned her to the

ground. She fought him fiercely, her short skirt hiked up to reveal strong thighs. "If you, my friend, want to try your own luck with this she-leopard," Tano grunted through clenched teeth, "you are welcome."

"Perhaps you should have used your musket," El-i-chi said as the girl almost freed herself, leaving a deep scratch on Tano's cheek. "Or I can lend you my tomahawk."

"Enough!" Tano yelled to the girl in Edo. "Cease your struggles, or I might harm you by accident."

The girl was still, her chest heaving with exertion, her eyes wild.

"You will not be harmed," Renno said in Edo. "Let her up, Tano."

Tano released the girl gingerly, leaped to his feet, and moved out of range of her claws.

"You are alone?" Renno asked.

"You will have to kill me," the girl threatened. "I will not be a slave."

"There will be no killing," Renno assured her. "Nor will you be a slave."

"Your tribe, girl?" Tano asked.

She drew her shoulders back. "I am Beni."

Tano laughed. "Then you are a long way from home."

The girl looked at him. "You speak with the accent of the city."

"Yes," Tano confirmed. "As do you."

"I am Sokata. I have escaped from the tribe that held me captive and am on my way to Benin, home."

"You will never reach Benin alone," Tano warned. "Not even though you fight like a leopard."

"I can try," she said stubbornly.

Renno questioned the girl, with Tano's help when he could not find the Edo words. The Dutchman had passed through her village two weeks before. She had not seen a big black man of Mingo's description—only a white man and blacks who killed and enslaved. Tano was interested in what the girl knew about Benin.

"I was ten," she recalled. "It was the dry season, the time for war, when the crops were in and the young men were idle. The Idah warriors were in the field, marching toward the city to avenge a past defeat. The drums sounded, and the court officials with their white wands of office called for war, so the young men came in from the farms and villages. There was much celebration in the streets. The soldiers drank and danced far into the night. Then the gongs rang, and the oba came out to give the order for war."

"Eweka?" Tano asked.

"It was he," Sokata verified.

"He went to fight?" Tano wanted to know.

"No, he sent his general, Esigie."

"As I thought," Tano said. "Eweka has never had the stomach for fighting. He prefers to let others do his killing and dying."

"My father was captain of a group of fighting men," Sokata continued. "My mother and I followed the army, carrying food for my father. The battle was far from the city, and it did not go well. My father was killed. My mother, badly wounded, sent me running back toward the city, but Idah warriors took me. The man who seized me was childless and adopted me as his daughter."

"How are things in the city?" Tano asked. "Do the people support Eweka?"

"How can they not?" she shot back. "The preparations for war are sanctified by the sacrifice of many people. The god-oba is the giver of life and death. To anger one of his people means death."

"Eweka's dream of regaining the empire, then, has not been realized," Tano said.

"Every year it was becoming more and more difficult to turn back the attacks," Sokata said. "The oba blamed the people, calling them cowards, and punished failure with blood."

"And you want to go back to a place like that?" Renno asked.

"It is my home," she said simply.

"What are we to do with this one?" Tano asked in English. "If she survives the jungle itself, any man who encounters her will seize her. She would not be treated so kindly if she was captured by men of the jungle again."

When El-i-chi saw that Renno was considering the matter, he said, "She would slow us."

"Shall we leave her here to be eaten by a jungle cat or to be used by the first men who encounter her?" Renno asked. Then he turned to Tano. "What do you suggest?"

"She is young and strong," he pointed out. "She could probably keep up. She might even be useful. She could gather food and cook for us."

Renno nodded assent to Tano.

"We go to the north," Tano told the girl, who had followed the conversation with her eyes. "When we are finished, I go to Benin. If you wish, you may accompany us. Then I will take you to the city with me."

The girl looked thoughtful, and then she smiled at Tano. "You are a noble man," she declared. She rose, went into the undergrowth, and emerged with her pack.

Her cook pot rattled when she walked, so that Renno had Tano muffle the sound by wrapping the pot in cloth. Throughout the day she maintained the pace without complaint, trotting at the rear of the single-file group, and when Renno called a halt with the darkness, she opened her pack and had a fire going within minutes. She disappeared into the jungle and returned almost immediately with tubers, which she washed in water taken from the pocketlike leaves of large plants. In the late evening El-i-chi left the trail to bag a small bush pig. The smell of the roasting meat caused Sokata to lick her lips and swallow often, and when it was ready, she ate ravenously.

At midmorning the next day another slave coffle came down from the north, with the same results as the previous encounters: The guards were killed swiftly and mercilessly; the confused, tired, battered slaves loudly praised the bravery of their liberators. The people told Renno and Tano a disturbing story: Soon after the Dutchman's party had decimated the village, a group of well-armed northerners, Fulani tribesmen, had happened onto the site. After a night of revelry the Dutchman had disappeared with the Fulani onto a trail leading north, leaving his lieutenants with instructions to escort the small coffle of slaves to the coast.

"Why did he negotiate with the Fulani?" Renno asked an old man who liked to talk.

"I heard the white man speak to the Fulani of ivory," the old man reported.

"Ah," Tano said, understanding. "The Fulani are fierce fighters who raid other tribes for slaves, which they trade for guns and whiskey. But the white ivory of the elephant is worth more than the black skin of slaves."

"How far are the Fulani lands?" Renno inquired.

The old man waved his wrinkled, pink-palmed hand. "Far away. The moon comes and goes many times."

"Not moons," Tano told Renno, "but many days' march."

"Then we must move swiftly," the white Indian declared. "We must catch him before he reaches the Fulani lands."

They encountered no more slave coffles. After days of travel the rain forest gave way to open plains. The country was as new to Tano as it was to Renno and El-i-chi. In his youth Tano had heard tales of far northern lands where the grass grew as high as a man's head and where low, thorny trees grew in scattered patches.

When the jungle thinned, the heaviness of the air lessened, much to everyone's relief, and the number of miles traveled in one day increased dramatically. They came to a wide, shallow river where armored crocodiles slept like logs in the sun, and across the river, in an open grassland with scattered trees, hunting was no longer difficult. Many antelopes roamed there, and Renno's longbow was the ideal weapon for providing meat for the night camp.

The sachem believed that they were not far behind the Dutchman. Under a pale-blue sky and a blazingly hot sun, Renno set a warrior's pace. They passed a site where the Dutchman's party had camped. The fires were cold and rain had washed away most signs, but the heaps of antelope bones and the number of fires indicated that many men had slept there. Against such numbers Mingo's rescue would have to be accomplished by guile, not force.

El-i-chi was now in the lead, setting the pace. They saw the first of the many odd animals they would encounter. A huge bull rhino grazed peacefully in their line of march. Small birds perched on his back. El-i-chi halted in amazement.

"A bull with a horn and armor," El-i-chi marveled.

"He looks formidable," Renno observed.

"Tano," El-i-chi asked, "is it good to eat?"

"I have never heard of anyone eating rhino," Tano admitted.

"I don't think I care to find out," Renno commented, guessing that the tough, armored hide would turn an arrow and make the use of a musket doubtful. "If you care to try . . ."

El-i-chi grinned. "He is too big. There would be too much wasted meat."

"He intimidates me a bit, too," Renno confessed, also grinning.

El-i-chi struck the pose of a stoic Indian, arms crossed.

"My brother knows my heart well," he intoned. Then, in a proper English accent, "Actually, old boy, the only reason I don't take the beast with m' tomahawk is that I wouldn't know how to go about skinning the blasted thing."

They gave the grazing rhino a wide berth, moving in an arc and coming back onto the Dutchman's trail to the north. Now the path led through trees. It was almost sunset, so Renno looked for a likely campsite. Game trails branched off the main path, an indication, he had learned in the past few days, that water was nearby. He led the way carefully down a game trail and smelled the water before he saw it. Many animals came to the water holes during the night, so it was not a good idea to camp on the water. He chose a grassy glen among the trees. Sokata started a fire and was soon on her way to the water hole with her pot.

"I think it would be best if someone went with her," Renno suggested. El-i-chi was just starting to rise when they heard Sokata cry out. Renno seized his longbow and was moving before El-i-chi and Tano could grab their weapons. He heard a low, angry snarl from ahead as he raced down the game trail. He skidded to a halt to see Sokata, frozen, pot in hand, just ahead of him. Then he saw the animal—a sleek, powerful leopard crouched not ten feet in front of her, its huge teeth exposed, a threatening growl rumbling from its throat.

"Back toward me slowly," Renno whispered, but the girl was too frightened to move. The leopard tensed at the sound of his voice. "We mean you no harm," Renno said to the leopard. "Sokata, move!"

He had the bowstring pulled. The leopard was tensed, and he could see the bunching of muscles in its powerful haunches. Renno crept forward and had gained Sokata's side when the leopard charged. Sokata hurled herself into the deep grass along the trail while Renno let his arrow fly. He had hunted much, and he respected the swiftness and the ferocity of the wolverine, the wolf, and the giant cats of the Southwest; but never had he encountered anything as fast as the leopard. His arrow grazed the cat's shoulder, leaving a gash that oozed blood even as the cat launched itself.

He had time only to seize his stiletto before the weight and the momentum of the cat bowled him over. He could smell the cat's heated, carnivore breath as he landed, his hand driving the stiletto upward into the animal's belly. And then the wind was knocked from him with the cat's weight atop him. There was a scream of pain and rage in his ears as his blade twisted in the animal's entrails. Great claws raked down his chest, drawing blood, but his arm pumped even as the cat drew back one heavy paw for the killing blow. Renno's blade struck deep into a spot just behind the cat's foreleg. He avoided the swipe of the deadly claws and twisted the stiletto to find the cat's heart. With one final blow that left deep, angry wounds on Renno's shoulder, the leopard went limp on the man's chest.

El-i-chi came pounding down the trail and hauled the heavy cat off Renno. Then the sachem was helping him, pushing the cat aside, and standing, so El-i-chi, obviously much affected, could see that some of the blood was the leopard's. But Renno had not come out of the encounter unscathed. The cuts on his shoulder were deep, those on his chest were bleeding profusely.

Tano and El-i-chi helped Sokata and Renno to the campsite. Sokata, at last recovering from the shock, took charge. She began to stanch the flow of blood by pressure and then, after venturing back into the foliage, to cover the wounds with a leaf. As she worked, she talked, Tano translating for El-i-chi. The Seneca shaman took a leaf and smelled it. It had a spicy, herbal scent. Already familiar with the herbs and leaves used in healing by his teacher, old Casno, El-i-chi memorized the look and the smell of this African leaf.

"He has lost much blood," Sokata said. "We will have to rest here until he regains his strength."

"We will move with the first light," Renno announced. The potions applied by Sokata seemed to be relieving the pain, but the ground tilted and spun under him. He lay back, closed his eyes, and slept.

He was awakened by an odd sound from the game trail. He sat up, and the movement sent pain through his chest and shoulder. El-i-chi was crouched, weapons in hand, beside the smoldering fire. Renno gingerly grasped his longbow and joined him.

"Sleep," El-i-chi told him. "I will handle this."

But Renno followed his brother down the trail. The moon was full, and in its soft light they saw movement beside the leopard carcass.

"Scavengers," El-i-chi whispered.

Renno saw the moon's light reflected in yellow eyes, and he readied an arrow for his bow, knowing now how swiftly a leopard could move. But the sound that came from the animal beside the dead leopard was a soft mewling. Renno edged closer. Moonlight showed him a leopard cub, not yet a yearling, lying beside the dead animal.

"She was a mother with young," Renno said sadly. "Perhaps she chose to fight because this one was near."

Tano had come up behind them. "The cub has not yet learned to hunt. It would be merciful to kill it."

El-i-chi raised his musket. Renno, sensing fear and puzzlement coming from the young leopard, put a staying hand on El-i-chi's arm. "If the cub is to die, let it die by the will of nature."

El-i-chi lowered the musket, and the men returned to the campsite.

Renno could not sleep. Down the trail the leopard cub was still mewling pitifully, as if urging its mother to rise. It was true, he thought, that the cub would die without its mother to provide for it. He felt a sadness, and quietly, without waking the others, he moved to the fire and took the remainder of the evening's meat from the spit. He moved down the trail and approached the cub, which snarled.

"Be at peace, Brother," Renno whispered in Seneca. "Perhaps you will die, but tonight you will eat." He moved to within a few feet and tossed the meat-covered bone to a spot near the leopard. The cub snarled and tensed itself to flee, but the smell of the meat tempted it. It moved forward, and when Renno went back to the camp to sleep, the cub was gnawing on the bone.

The white Indian was awake with first light. He was so stiff and sore, he knew that any plans to follow the Dutchman's trail today were impractical.

"You must rest," Sokata told him. "Three days, maybe four, and then the soreness will be bearable."

Renno fell asleep almost immediately and remained so until Sokata woke him for the midday meal. The meat El-i-chi had provided was fresh, red, and rich in heated juices. Renno forced himself to eat, although he wanted only to sleep again. When he awoke, he could not identify at first the sound that had disturbed him, then he heard a chorus of squawks and the snarl of a leopard.

"Vultures," Sokata told him. "They are after the carcass of the leopard. The young one tries to protect it."

Renno considered helping the young leopard, but he was asleep again almost immediately. Later that evening he went down the trail, walking carefully to hold his shoulder steady. Jackals and hyenas were fighting over the carcass. The young leopard was not visible.

"Brother," Renno called. His voice prompted the scavengers to withdraw, snarling and yelping. He noticed a movement in the grass, and there was the cub. Renno tossed scraps from the evening's meal to the leopard, then stood guard against the scavengers.

With the second day Renno felt better. Having slept for almost thirty-six hours had apparently given his body time to begin repairing the damage wrought by the leopard. The wounds were scabbed, with no sign of infection. Renno slept little and ate well that day, spending his time questioning Sokata and Tano about the city of Benin and the power of the oba.

After dark the leopard cub ventured to the edge of the clearing and lay there, the smell of roasting meat making its nose twitch. It was a male, Renno determined, a sleek, handsome animal, still a bit awkward in youth; but its movements already hinted of its adult power. Renno spoke to the cub quietly, holding out a chunk of meat. The animal, nervous, made growling protests, but slowly, slowly, it crept forward. Renno tossed the meat when the cub was within a few feet.

El-i-chi had his musket in hand, ready for anything.

"No," Renno said. "He is young and frightened." He held out another piece of meat, and the animal, his hunger honed to a fine point by what he'd already been given, came forward to take the meat from Renno's hand. The sachem extended one hand. The animal drew back and bared his fangs in a snarl but allowed Renno to touch his head.

"Renno is a god from beyond the sea," Sokata whispered.

"It is true," Tano confirmed. "He has great magic."

"He is Renno," El-i-chi added. "In our own country he talks to the totem of our clan, the great bear."

After consuming several more hunks of meat, the cub, belly full, moved gracefully back into the trees. Renno went to his bed of grasses and leaves. Soon he was asleep.

"Tell me," Tano said, "of the bear that Renno speaks to."

Embellishing the tale only a bit—the black bear of America was not really as big as a rhino—El-i-chi told how he had once seen Renno calm a man-killing bear by speaking to it and calling it brother. This led to other tales, for Sokata and Tano seemed to be insatiable. As Tano kept the fire burning, El-i-chi told the story of the creation of the People of the Hill by the Master of Life, and of the great Iroquois League, which was the power of the Northeast until the coming of the white man.

"The Master of Life," Tano mused. "For the Beni he is Osa, who created all."

"Once all men lived in the sky," El-i-chi said, not yet willing to give over to Tano. After all, as shaman of his people, he was the keeper of legends and the teller of tales, and he had not performed his duties for a long time. "The sachem of all people had a daughter of great beauty, but she became ill, and no shaman could cure her. But one shaman dreamed that if the sachem would cut down the magic corn tree, which fed all the people, his daughter would be cured. When the sachem sent men to cut down the tree, a warrior warned, 'This tree provides the only food we have, and it is not the will of the Master of Life to have it cut.' So the warrior pushed the young girl through the hole that had been dug, and she fell down, down, toward the center of the world, which in the dawn of time was only water, with waterfowl swimming on it and flying above it.

"The waterfowl saw the girl falling and pitied her. They came together to form a solid mass on which the girl landed. She avoided falling in the water, but the birds grew tired and asked the great turtle to hold her for a while. Even this was not a solution, so the toad dived to the bottom of the sea and brought up earth, forming an island atop the shell of the turtle.''

"A big turtle?" Sokata asked.

"The great turtle," El-i-chi said. "And on this island lived the first people.''

"Ha!" Tano did not know whether to believe.

"Tell us more," Sokata requested.

"Soon," El-i-chi promised. "Now we sleep.''

Renno was awake with first light, and before the sun they were moving at a pace that Tano and Sokata would have thought impossible for a man so recently mauled. Tano had repeated that it would be best to kill the cub rather than leave it to starve and become prey for the jackals and hyenas, but Renno said no. At first the cub trailed behind them, but then it disappeared into the trees. When night came and they camped, however, a purr at Renno's back made him turn to see the cub lying near him, waiting expectantly for his meal.

"So, Brother," Renno remarked, "you are now one of us.''

"He eats more than we do," El-i-chi complained.

"He has growing to do," Renno said as he tossed the cub meat. "Here, Ese, this is for you.'' The name he had given the animal meant, in Seneca, *thou or you*.

Upon his return to the Cherokee village Se-quo-i had greeted his relatives, paid his respects, and made his report in great detail to his chief, Rusog. Then, with winter making it cozy in the log cabin he had constructed for his mother and himself, he concentrated on the books he had carried back from Wilmington. It had long been accepted by the male members of Se-quo-i's clan that the young man was different: White-man's blood flowed through his veins, and he could speak the white-man's language and read the magic marks that they put on paper. The work he did in silver and in wood also set him apart as a creator of beauty, thus to be spared the everyday duties of the Cherokee warrior. Because the clan of Se-quo-i's mother was numerous, there was never a lack of fresh venison in their pots.

Se-quo-i had set himself to understanding the system behind the white-man's writing. As the weeks passed, he could often be heard emitting odd sounds as he took the white-man's words apart and reduced them to their components. When he began to analyze the individual sounds of the Cherokee language, his mother often thought that the spirits had moved into his head and that he was becoming one of those blessed by the spirits. Se-quo-i only laughed and tried to explain to her that one day, when he knew more, he would commit the Cherokee language to paper and therefore would be able to preserve the history, legends, and traditions of his people.

His mother snorted. "Some of the tall tales told by the old ones are not worthy of preservation."

Thus, with the time of the new beginning near, when winter was having its last victories and there was a smell in the air to indicate that new life was just below the cold surface of the ground, Se-quo-i ventured back into the world from his isolation to discover that things were odd in the Seneca village. He was already aware of Ena's discontent with having her niece and nephew spend the entire winter in Knoxville with their grandparents; the rebelliousness he found among the young warriors of the Seneca, however, came as a surprise to him.

Se-quo-i's first hint of unrest came during a visit to the Seneca village to see Ha-ace, Ah-wa-o, and Toshabe. He was met by the handsome young war chief from the north, Tor-yo-ne, accompanied by a group of young men.

"You have traveled with the sachem," Tor-yo-ne began.

"I have," Se-quo-i confirmed.

"And you have told all of his great adventures and bravery in faraway lands."

"That is true," Se-quo-i said.

"So," Tor-yo-ne said, turning to the assembled young warriors, many of whom were not newcomers, "we hear of the sachem, but we do not see his face. If Renno is sachem of the Seneca, where is his face?" Tor-yo-ne turned to Se-quo-i. "When can we expect the return of our sachem? Today? Tomorrow? Next moon? Never?"

"Perhaps he is dead," a young warrior suggested.

"No," Se-quo-i said immediately. "Renno will return."

"Today? Tomorrow?" repeated Tor-yo-ne. "These are times of peril for all Seneca. In the north the war clouds gather while we wait here, living on the generosity of the Cherokee, while the lands and homes of our people are threatened."

"The Seneca and the Cherokee are brothers," Se-quo-i reminded him.

"True, there is peace and goodwill," Tor-yo-ne agreed, "and we are grateful to our Cherokee brothers for letting us exist on their land."

"These are Seneca lands as well," Se-quo-i pointed out.

"Is that a Seneca longhouse?" Tor-yo-ne pointed to a log cabin built by a Seneca family. "Where are the lakes that have been the water roads of the Seneca? Where is the sound of the great, roaring river that flows through our lands?"

Se-quo-i left Tor-yo-ne addressing a growing crowd of young warriors and went to find Ha-ace and Toshabe in their longhouse. He did not mention what he had just heard.

After the evening meal, with the two maidens Ah-wa-o and An-da engaging in giggling and private talk, Toshabe spoke.

"You two," she said, "take your giggles into the open air

and bring firewood.'' The two young women scurried out, relieved to be away from the quiet talk of the adults.

Toshabe looked at Se-quo-i seriously. "I saw you with Tor-yo-ne."

"Yes," Se-quo-i said, still unwilling to admit to Renno's mother that anyone dared question the sachem's absence.

"You heard him question whether or not Renno will return?" she asked.

"He will return. Before the leaves turn red, perhaps."

"And in the meantime Tor-yo-ne stirs our young warriors into restlessness and urges them to leave their home to join the questionable venture in the north," Toshabe complained.

"His appeal is only to the young ones," Ha-ace said. "Pay no attention."

"When do we start paying attention?" Toshabe wanted to know. "When he leads most of the young warriors to the north? When he takes away all our best hunters?" She sighed. "That, however, is not your worry, Se-quo-i. I have other things to discuss with you."

Se-quo-i nodded respectfully.

"It is Ah-wa-o," Toshabe said. "As you may know, she has had no lack of suitors."

"I've been—" Se-quo-i started.

"I know, you've been cooped up with your books," Toshabe said. "The girl is acting strangely, and I thought that perhaps you could enlighten me as to the reason. Tell me honestly, as a friend of my sons, what transpired during the journey to Wilmington. What happened between my daughter and my son to make her talk only of El-i-chi, El-i-chi, El-i-chi?"

Se-quo-i shifted uneasily. "Of that I would prefer to let El-i-chi speak."

"He is not here to speak," Toshabe said. "You know that they are, in the eyes of the tribe, brother and sister."

"But in blood . . ." Se-quo-i faltered.

"My son, then, saw Ah-wa-o as a woman while she was away," Toshabe said, and Se-quo-i nodded.

Toshabe looked at Ha-ace grimly.

"I assure you, Toshabe," Se-quo-i said, "that both El-i-chi and Ah-wa-o acted properly."

"He is a shaman," Toshabe said. "The brother of the sachem. Is it not enough for them to journey off to the far reaches of the earth to leave the leadership of the Seneca to a newcomer?"

Se-quo-i, thinking that it would be good to have Toshabe and Ha-ace prepared, said, "Renno has told them that he will do his best to relax the tribal taboos and that he will speak in favor of their marriage."

Toshabe was a traditionalist. She had seen the great power of the Seneca nation—indeed, of the entire League of the Ho-de-no-sau-nee—lose land and power. She had watched them be split into factions by the white man's war. And now one of the most basic foundations of tribal life was to be violated by her own son. She closed her eyes and voiced a prayer to the manitous for guidance and deliverance from the problems that faced her in the absence of her sons.

Chapter VII

Although Bastian Vanderrenner had never traveled far north, he was no stranger to the Fulani. He had dealt with representatives of Zangara, the Fulani chieftain, on several occasions. Like other powerful tribes, the Fulani engaged in the slave trade. Their raiding parties went into the jungles of the south, where centuries of intertribal warfare had weakened the people. Unlike the Dutchman, the Fulani did not slay indiscriminately, but they did what was necessary, which meant killing the many who dared to fight them, then taking captives to be sold to the white slavers.

When Vanderrenner had first encountered the Fulani party in the jungles, he had assumed that this was just another slave-raiding expedition and had made his standard offer for any captives that the Fulani had taken. He was surprised to

120

learn that they had not raided for slaves and that their destination had been his own fort.

The delegation was headed by the chief's number-one son, Chigi, a sturdy, tall, gaily bedecked young man of twenty years. After a long night of dancing, drinking, and the casual use of a few of the female slaves taken by the Dutchman and not yet sent back toward the fort, Chigi told Vanderrenner that the great chief Zangara requested that the Dutchman come to the Fulani city of Zaria for an important meeting.

"Zaria is far," the Dutchman objected, "and there are no slaves to be had in the lands of the Fulani."

"Is Vanderrenner interested only in the black gold of slaves and not the more valuable white treasure?"

The tall, blond trader lifted his cup, filled with a bitter African beer, to hide his excitement. Chigi, he knew, was speaking of ivory, that ultimate wealth from Africa, a commodity that was almost worth its weight in gold.

"I go," he assented, "but only to honor the king, your father, not in hopes of gain."

During the trek the Dutchman played up his disinterest, always assuring Chigi that he had no great desire to trade for ivory. It was during the trip that he learned the reason for Chigi's long journey into the jungles of the south.

"It is not whiskey or cloth we want," Chigi explained. "We want guns of the white man."

"My friend Chigi," Vanderrenner scoffed, "guns are hard to come by, and they are costly. It would take many slaves to pay for enough guns to arm your people."

"But I do not speak of slaves," Chigi reminded him.

"The Fulani have never dealt in ivory," the Dutchman said. "The Fulani are warriors, not killers of elephants."

Chigi remained silent, but from the members of Chigi's travel party there came hints of a tribal treasure—a mountain of ivory collected over the decades, the king's own hoard, heretofore untouchable. By careful probing when Chigi was under the influence of potent rum, Vanderrenner learned why the Fulani now considered parting with the ivory.

"Two dry seasons past," Chigi said, "Eweka, oba of the City of Blood, sent his army to the north. The Beni had not raided our lands for years, so they took us by surprise. They killed many and carried off others—men, women, and children. One of the women was my father's favorite wife, and two of my father's sons went with her."

"But the Fulani are brave. They have horses, and your blades are capable of extracting revenge," the Dutchman said.

"The city of Benin has high and strong walls," Chigi explained. "No army has yet breached the fortifications, and the oba's personal army, although small, is a force to be respected. No, to take Benin, to kill the oba, and to make the Beni pay for our dead requires guns. For this we have come to you."

"Then," Vanderrenner said, "out of my love for your people, out of my friendship for you, Chigi, and your father, the king, I will help you."

William Huntington, Lord Beaumont, was a man fully content with life. His land and title dated back to the time of the Norman Conquest. He had a beautiful wife, and the initial shock of a peer of England's having married a Spanish woman had long since dissipated. In fact, Estrela had charmed everyone she had met since coming to England with William, and before her pregnancy had confined her to the manor, they had always been a couple in great demand.

Just after William's return from America, Sir Joffre Jowett had taken him aside. "A bit of fiery Spanish blood will be good for the tired, old blood of England," the man had approved, thus sealing a friendship that eventually expanded into a mutually profitable business association.

William had few regrets. He had mourned the death of his father, for he had loved the old man in spite of the compulsive gambling. William had forgiven his father for that, because as a result of his father's bringing the family to the brink of financial ruin, William and Beth had gone to America, followed an ancient map to a mountain of gold, and had found their loves. William was proud that he had restored the Huntington estate to prosperity.

One of his few regrets was that he had not been free to accompany Renno to Africa. He marked the slow passage of the days, and then the weeks, on a calendar, and often, at night, he dreamed that he was with Renno there on the dark continent. He thanked God that he had met such a man, who would travel half a world to fulfill a pledge of brotherhood. Not a day went by that William didn't send up a prayer for the safety of Renno and El-i-chi.

The voyage of the *Seneca Warrior* to the Niger delta would determine future action in expanding Joffre's and William's trade ventures in Africa, but William's chief concern was the safe return of Renno and El-i-chi.

During the first days after the *Warrior* had sailed, he had expected Beth to be morose, but she accepted Renno's departure as an opportunity to pursue her own business ventures. William knew that his sister loved Renno, but he couldn't quite understand her lack of worry or concern. For a long time he did not see much of her. She was staying in the Huntington town house in London for convenient access to the various government offices.

With the year still new, William took the carriage into London and presented himself at the town house, only to be told that Beth was out. He went in search of Joffre, with no success. Joffre's office secretary knew only that he had had

an appointment with "Mistress Beth Huntington." William
had his own business to transact, so it was dusk when he
returned to their town house. Beth was at her bath. He poured
himself a glass of sherry and waited. She came into the room
in a warm, ornately embroidered dressing gown and kissed
him on the cheek.

"Sorry I wasn't here earlier," she said.

"I imagine you've been busy."

"Incredibly," she said, beaming. "At last, William, I
was able to see the minister of trade."

"And?"

"He's a pompous old fraud," she confided, "but he was
impressed with the requests from the governor of Jamaica to
allow Huntington ships to trade freely there." She accepted a
glass of wine that William offered, sat down, and smiled at
him. "Are you going back to Beaumont tonight?"

"No. It's a little late. I told Estrela that I would probably
spend the night here. I thought you and I could have dinner. I
don't see much of you these days."

"Oh, I am sorry. . . ." she said.

"Previous engagement?"

"Business," she replied.

"I could tag along." He raised his right hand. "I promise
I won't open my mouth while you're charming whomever."

She looked at him appealingly. "It isn't that I don't want
your company."

"Not to worry," he said. "I shall dine all alone, not
missing your company at all, so you really don't have to feel
sorry for me."

"You're terrible," she said, laughing, rising to kiss him
on the cheek. "I must get dressed now."

When she emerged dressed in a striking blue gown adorned
with the proper amount of jewelry, William realized anew
that she was one of the most beautiful women in England.

"I will come to Beaumont very soon," she promised. "We can have a nice, long talk."

"Yes," he encouraged. "Estrela asks about you constantly. She's quite lonely there. I, for one, don't believe in secluding a woman simply because her stomach is protruding a bit." He smiled. "In fact, I find Estrela's beauty to be enhanced by her approaching motherhood, but she says that she'd be embarrassed to be seen in her condition."

"I'll come soon," Beth repeated.

A servant stood in the doorway. "Your carriage, madam."

"Must go." She kissed William on the top of the head and swept out, a tall woman who moved with confidence, a woman to turn any male eye.

William tarried over his sherry, sighed, rose, and decided that he would dine at a room favored by his friends—an exclusive place where the prices kept out what Sir Joffre called riffraff, meaning any Englishman without a secure fortune and a title. Deciding not to bother the servants, he took a carriage through a night of light rain that threatened to freeze.

Well-known at the dining room, he was greeted with great respect and shown immediately to a table that afforded privacy. The chef did well with a duck, and William used the time alone to make a long-delayed business decision.

The decorously quiet dining room was arranged in such a way that he could see only two other tables. He recognized a government minister, a peer who was a power in the House of Lords, and a Royal Navy captain in full uniform, all with their ladies. He lingered over brandy, reluctant to return to the town house so early. He was in the process of declining more brandy when he heard a familiar laugh, low and throaty, and looked up to see Beth passing his alcove on the arm of Sir Joffre. He was looking down into her face with an expression familiar to William, who had seen Joffre working his male charms on women before.

Anger flushed William's face. Self-control kept him seated. He had known that Joffre was using his influence to help Beth, but she was solid minded and honorable. Surely their engagement was innocent; perhaps Joffre was putting her at table with someone in the government who might be able to help her.

His anger faded, but then he glanced back to see Joffre and Beth alone at a table for two, Beth smiling across at Joffre, and he leaning forward, talking in a low voice. William left the room in a hurry, so as not to be seen. Then he felt angry again. Why was he concerned with not being seen? After all, he was not the one dining alone with a person who was not his spouse.

At the town house he dallied over his preparations for bed, drew on a dressing gown, walked into the parlor, paced, and took down a book only to find that he could not concentrate. He was in a proper stew when, two hours later, Beth was admitted to the house and swept through the dimly lighted parlor, not noticing him.

"Beth," he said, his voice harsh. She started, then turned.

"William! You're not in bed?"

"Obviously not," he answered.

She moved toward him. "If you can't sleep, I'll get you some warm milk."

"Thank you, no," he said icily. "Did your business meeting go well?"

"Yes, thank you."

"Good, good."

"And you? Where did you decide to dine?"

He didn't answer for a moment. He hated unpleasantness, and he felt guilty for suspecting her, but it was heavy on his mind. "Joffre and I favor the same place," he said, waiting for her reaction.

"Oh, dear." She came to sit across from him. "So you saw me alone with Joffre."

"I was not spying on you."

She laughed. "Still looking after me, eh?" She leaned forward and touched his hand. "I think that is very sweet of you, William."

He was silent but disapproving.

She sighed. "My dear, I know what Joffre is. And perhaps our dining alone did look rather suspicious."

He shrugged.

"He pays court to me. That's his nature. But he knows that I am a happily married woman."

"You've told him that?" William asked.

"Not in so many words," she answered. "In actions, yes." She frowned. "Concern is one thing. Suspicion is another."

"There are certain proprieties," he pointed out.

"Oh, nonsense," she said heatedly. "If I had observed the niceties all my life, I would never have learned to shoot a musket and a longbow. If I had always been the proper English lady, I wouldn't have had the courage to go to America with you, and I would never have met Renno. If I had observed all the proprieties, there wouldn't be a Huntington Shipping Company in Wilmington." She rose and looked down at him. "Of course Joffre wants to seduce me."

William felt himself blushing. People just didn't talk about such things.

"But I assure you—if you need assurances—that he will not succeed. I've handled men like Joffre before, and I've gotten what I wanted from them, without giving more than a smile in return."

"With Joffre that's a dangerous game," William said.

Beth's face softened. "I know what I'm doing. Soon I'll have the trade compact in hand, Renno will be back, and we'll be off for America." She bent to kiss him. "Satisfied?"

William was filled with misgivings, but he nodded and kissed her. "What will become of you and Renno?"

"Ah," she said. "Now there is the question. I do love him, you know."

"Of course."

"He's the most fascinating, devastatingly handsome man I've ever known."

"But?" William asked.

"Aye, there's the rub," she confessed, sitting down again. "I could live with him in his own country and be ever so happy. I really wouldn't mind not having servants. After all, a Seneca wife has only two or three changes of clothing, so there's not much washing. Cooking is simple. We could build a log cabin, like some of the Cherokee had done when we were there, and it would be all snug and warm in the winter and open to the air in the summer—"

"Beth, are you trying too hard to convince yourself?" William asked softly.

He was astounded when, without warning, she burst into convulsive sobs. He was paralyzed for long moments, and a great sadness washed over him. Great changes were inevitable in the marriage of his sister and his friend. He could not envision Renno's leaving his people to live with Beth in Wilmington. He knew Renno, his sense of duty, and identity as a Seneca—all of which combined to make it impossible for the sachem to throw off his responsibilities. And sadly, William knew his sister. She had been brought up with all the amenities and had reason to be proud of what she had accomplished in the man's world of business.

"You are greatly troubled," he said, moving to take her into his arms. "I wish that I could help you."

Her sobs diminished. "Oh, how I wish someone could help me." The anguish in her voice told him that his fears for Beth and Renno's future were well-founded.

"Harry," Nora Johnson called, standing on the porch of the cabin in Knoxville. "Oh, Harry."

The day was glorious, all blue and bright. The always unpredictable weather of the region was presenting a fair face after a dreary time of cold, days-long rain. The streets were awash in mud, and Roy would have to hitch up the buggy so she would not drag her skirts through the mire, although the church was less than three hundred yards away.

"Harry," Nora called again. "Harry, I can see you. Why don't you answer me?"

"Maybe it's because his name isn't Harry," Roy Johnson suggested from inside the cabin. "Try calling him by the name his parents gave him."

"The name given to him is not a proper name for a respectable white child," Nora complained, but in momentary defeat she called, "Little Hawk, come in. It's time to get ready for church."

Little Hawk had been investigating the depth of the mud in the street. He held his moccasins in one hand and was tramping in the cold, oozy stuff with no little delight. He had, of course, heard Nora calling. More than once he had protested politely that his name was not and had never been Harry, that he was Little Hawk, or if his grandmother wanted to be totally accurate about the matter, she could call him Ne-wa-ah Os-sweh-ga-da-ga-ah.

"Just look at you," she chided when the boy stopped at the bottom of the steps and made an unsuccessful attempt to scrape the mud off his feet. "You're going to catch your death."

"Grandmother," he said, "I am fine. My feet are not at all cold."

"Come in this house immediately and get washed up," Nora ordered. Renna, dressed prettily in a little white outfit, giggled.

"Why can't you be as nice as your sister?" Nora demanded. "Look at her, the perfect little lady, and she got dressed all by herself."

"Come on, boy," Roy said kindly. "I'll help you get ready." He took Little Hawk to the washstand and used a rough cloth to scour his face and ears and neck, then put the washbasin on the floor so that Little Hawk could clean his feet. Nora had sewn clothing for the boy, a proper Sunday-go-to-meeting outfit of trousers, shirt, and jacket. Since he was in the midst of a growth spurt, the clothing was too tight, making him feel that he could not move without ripping seams. He suffered the discomfort with dignity, however, and helped Roy hitch the horse to the buggy. He was allowed to take the reins, although it made Nora nervous, as they drove to the church.

The log building was filled to bursting, for the traveling preacher who was to hold the service was known far and wide for his ability to give Old Ned to all sinners. Renna piped up in her sweet, childish voice on the opening hymns. Little Hawk took the time to look around and wonder why these people trussed themselves up. The women wore so much clothing that if they ever had to run from a bear or an enemy, they would be carrying so much weight that they wouldn't have a chance. The men wore high collars that made their faces red, as if they had difficulty breathing.

The first part of the itinerant preacher's sermon interested Little Hawk. He remembered the story of little David from his mother, and he could imagine himself facing a giant—in his mind the giant was Chickasaw, and six feet tall—with only a sling, whatever that was. But then the preacher found his second wind and began, with great shouting and hair pulling and sobs of anguish, to be very much against transgressions in any form and to bring down the wrath of the God of the prophets on the sinful heads of all the congregation.

"Poor sinners," the preacher warned, "you, like the Children of Israel, have erred through wine. You have erred through strong drink."

Well, Little Hawk was thinking, *he* hadn't, but Grandfather Roy occasionally took a nip from his jug.

"And you, like the drunkards of E-phra-im, will be trampled under the just foot of the Lord."

Little Hawk lost his concentration after about the tenth sin and the tenth promise of being cast in the lake of everlasting fire, roused only a bit when the preacher promised that the Lord would send serpents and cockatrices to bite and punish all sinners—which, apparently, included everyone, even children. He tugged on Roy's sleeve and whispered, "What's a cockatrice?"

"*Shussh,*" Nora hissed, giving him a solid pinch on the arm.

The people around Little Hawk squirmed in delicious agony under the castigations and condemnations, crying out, "Amen" and "Praise the Lord." Mercifully, sleep came to dull Little Hawk's senses. It was not deep enough to make his head loll but caused his eyelids to be heavy. The sweet, warm sense of rest enveloped him, so the preacher's voice became a dull roar, like a distant waterfall.

"I hope you were listening well," Nora said after the handshaking and exaggerated friendliness following the church service. "I do so want all my loved ones to be with me in heaven when the Lord calls me."

"My mother is in the Place across the River," Little Hawk said.

Nora gasped. "Didn't you hear one word about what the preacher said about blasphemy?" She looked at Roy helplessly.

"Don't be too heavy with the boy, Nora," Roy advised.

"Heathens," Nora croaked, on the verge of tears. "They've made my grandchildren heathens."

"Not me," Renna said.

"No, darling, not you," Nora agreed.

The only good thing about Sunday was lunch: fried chicken and mashed potatoes and biscuits hot from the oven. Little Hawk had been allowed to take off his Sunday clothes and was now comfortable in buckskins. Renna had kept on her Sunday dress and was very careful not to drop food on it. Afterward both Little Hawk and Renna helped clear the table, and then it was quiet time for the adults, who sat in their chairs before the fireplace and nodded, then dozed. Little Hawk climbed the wooden ladder to the loft that was his sanctuary inside the cabin. Because of the steepness of the ladder, Nora rarely came up to his sleeping place. Here he kept his collection of interesting rocks, a few arrowheads that, according to his father, were the work of brothers who had lived on the land long before the coming of the white man or before Ghonkaba had led the Seneca to the south, the small bow that had been a gift from his father, and dead bugs pinned to the cabin's wall.

He was trying to imagine how wide the Atlantic Ocean was and wondering when his father would come back, when Renna crept up the ladder. "They're both asleep."

"So," Little Hawk said, trying to sound like Renno.

Renna brushed her skirts under her and sat down on the edge of Little Hawk's bed. She gazed at the largest in her brother's bug collection for a moment and asked, "Is a cocka—cocka—whatever it was that the man with the loud voice said was going to come and bite us like a spider?"

"I don't think so," Little Hawk said. "I'd think it would be much bigger and much more fierce."

"I don't want it to bite me," Renna said with a little shudder.

Not only had Little Hawk promised his father to look after Renna, he was fond of her. He patted her on the leg. "Don't worry. That monster is a thing of the white-man's god, not of ours."

"It'll bite only white people?"

"Sure."

"But Grandmother says that we are white."

Little Hawk sat up straight, crossed his arms, and did his best to put on a stoic face. "We are Seneca."

"But—but—"

"Don't worry," Little Hawk soothed. "I will protect you from all the bad things that this god of the white man sends against his people."

Renna shivered. "I don't want to be tossed into a lake of fire."

"You won't be," Little Hawk promised in Seneca. "Soon we will go home, to be with our people. Perhaps we'll be in time for the feast of the new beginning."

"The false faces scare me," Renna admitted.

"Because I am son of the sachem, I will wear a false face. You need not be afraid of me, for I will scare away all the dark spirits and keep you safe."

"Little Hawk," Renna said after a time. "Grandmother says that our mother is in heaven."

"Our mother is in the Place across the River, with our ancestors," he said. "Our mother was Seneca."

"But Grandmother says we are white because our mother was white and our father is mostly white."

"We are Seneca," the boy repeated, his voice rising. "Our mother was Seneca, and she is in the Place across—"

"Little Hawk!" Nora yelled sternly. "I will not have you filling Renna's head with that heathen nonsense, that evil blasphemy. If I hear one more word of it from you, I will thrash you within an inch of your life."

The look of a young eagle came into Little Hawk's eyes. "You will have to catch me first," he whispered, so Nora could not hear.

Roy, too, spoke in a whisper so that the children could not hear. "Nora, don't be so harsh."

"I will not have it," she hissed.

"It is one thing to teach them our ways," he said. "Renno agrees that they should know about the world of the Seneca and our own. To try to drive it down their throats—"

"I will not hear blasphemy against our Lord," she persisted.

"You will adhere to our agreement with Renno," Roy said, his voice forceful. "You will remember that they are Renno's children, not ours, and you will act accordingly."

He didn't like speaking angrily to her, for her health was deteriorating with each passing week. He knew how much she loved the children, but he suspected that it was unhealthy for her to view Renna as Emily, reborn. Their daughter was dead, and he was going to see to it that Emily's choices of living with Renno and becoming a Seneca were not dishonored by anyone—not even an ailing wife.

When Little Hawk prepared for bed that night, he arranged his clothing very carefully for easy access in the dark. He gathered the most valuable of his personal belongings in a pillowcase and tied them into a pack. He took the knife he had received for Christmas, the best of his rocks, the arrowheads, and his spare moccasins. He left behind all articles of clothing that bore the influence of the white man.

He had to fight sleep, pinching himself to keep awake.

Roy and Nora stayed up—Nora reading the Bible by lamp-light, Roy dozing in his chair—until it seemed to Little Hawk that his grandparents were going to see the dawn before going to sleep. When at last he heard Roy's banking the fire and Nora's getting ready for bed, he relaxed, and his eyes closed of their own accord. He did not know when the glow of the lamp disappeared as the Johnsons went into the side room that was their bedroom.

He awoke with a start, fearing that he'd slept all night, but it was dark in the cabin and there was a chill in the air. He gently placed his feet on the floor, dressed in his buckskins, and pushed his feet into his moccasins. He had a deerskin robe, heavy and warm, that Nora didn't like him to wear, and he carried it in one hand, his bow and quiver of arrows in the other. His pack was tucked under his arm as he eased down the creaking ladder.

The ladder to Renna's loft was near the fireplace. He left his belongings beside the front door and climbed up, pausing now and then to be sure that the even breathing from his grandparents' bedroom was not disturbed. He knelt beside Renna's bed, put his hand over her mouth, and began to tickle her nose. She moaned, and then her eyes flew open, and a gasp was muffled by his hand.

"Quiet," he whispered. "Renna, be quiet." He removed his hand.

"Little Hawk?"

"I am going home."

In the darkness he heard her catch her breath.

"You are not to worry about me. I know the way, and it is not far. In the morning, when they find that I am gone, you do not have to lie. You may tell them that I told you good-bye and that I went home."

"But—"

"Shush, be quiet," he whispered. "I will tell our people,

Grandmother Toshabe and Aunt Ena, that they are to come
for you. Would you like that?''

"Oh, yes," she said. "But we can come back and see
Grandmother Nora and Grandfather Roy, can't we?"

"Yes, but we will be at home, in our father's longhouse,"
he said. "I go now."

"Little Hawk?"

"Yes?"

"I'm going to cry."

"So," he said, squeezing her hand. "Cry quietly."

Downstairs he eased the door open just wide enough to
slip through, and then he was outside in the late-night darkness. The blue sky of the day had given way to a night of
gusty winds and scudding clouds that sailed past a half-moon.
In the darkness the mud of the streets was a cold, delaying
nuisance. When he gained the open fields outside the town,
he was moving at a trot. The footing was also bad in the
fields, and his feet were soaked. He could feel cold entering
his toes, but he ran on, and then the forest closed around him,
and he trod silently on a layer of pine needles. He found the
trail without any problem. The way was west. The lowering
moon pointed the way.

When Ena had finished her morning chores, she straightened, hands at the small of her back. This son of Rusog's was
going to be a very big man, she thought, for already her
stomach distended hugely, and when she bent, there was an
ache in her back. Rusog was away, hunting. The weather was
fine, blue and clear. She had opened their lodge to air it, so it
was as chilly inside as it was outside. She threw a blanket
around her shoulders and emerged into the day.

A group of small children whooped past, and she smiled.
In only a few years her own son would be stalking imaginary
game and playing the young warrior with the boys of the

village. Then she frowned and was resentful, for they reminded her of Little Hawk. She shrugged mentally. Renno would be back before the coloring of the leaves. Roy would bring the children home soon; the time of the new beginning was not far away. Already preparations were being made for the celebration.

She walked the short distance to Se-quo-i's log cabin. Rusog had not yet adapted to the white man's way, and her own dwelling was the traditional Cherokee lodge, a state of affairs that had suited her until now.

Se-quo-i was at work, writing with a quill pen. He put the pen aside and said in Seneca, *"Nyhah-weh Ska-noh,"* meaning, "I thank thee to know thou art strong."

"Good morning, *gayah-da-sez,"* Ena answered, calling him friend. "Don't let me interrupt your work."

"I welcome interruption," Se-quo-i told her. "The pot is hot for tea."

"Thank you. Tea would be welcome."

Se-quo-i started toward the fireplace, where a teapot hung over the fire on a hook.

"Let me," Ena offered. "A cup for you, as well?"

"Thank you."

"How goes your work?" she asked when they were seated across from one another on wooden benches in front of the fireplace and cradling mugs of tea.

"Slowly," he said. "The Cherokee language does not lend itself well to analysis. The sounds mean one thing at one time and something different at another." He laughed. "But you didn't come here to have me bore you with that."

"I have been thinking of taking a trip into Knoxville," Ena admitted.

"Is that wise, in your condition?"

"I am Seneca."

"The children," he said. "I have often berated myself for leaving them."

"You did no wrong. But now it is time for them to be where they belong."

"I would, of course, be glad to accompany you," he volunteered.

"I may call upon you. Let us see when Rusog comes back from the hunt."

Se-quo-i nodded. "Perhaps there will be mail in Knoxville."

"Perhaps." She was thinking angrily, *Renno, you should be here*.

Se-quo-i was silent for a long time. Ena, too, mused. Then, "Tor-yo-ne has taken most of the young Seneca warriors westward, did you know?"

"Yes," he replied.

"It is not enough that he dominates the hunt; now he takes young warriors in search of coup against the Chickasaw."

"It has always been thus," Se-quo-i pointed out.

"But there has been peace between the Chickasaw and us," she said, her eyes flashing. "I have asked Rusog to speak to the elders of both tribes, to advise them to stop this raiding into Chickasaw lands."

"What does Rusog say?"

"The same as you. Thus it has always been. But by the manitous, that does not mean that it should be that way forever. The Chickasaw have stayed in their own lands for years now, and so it should remain."

"This from the warrior maiden?" Se-quo-i asked with a laugh.

"I would not hold back from a just war, or a war in defense of that which is ours," she retorted.

"I know. Forgive me my jest."

"One day we might have to fight for our homes, for our lands," Ena said. "But not against the Chickasaw."

Se-quo-i knew full well what she meant. "I pray that it does not come to that."

Ena rose. "Thank you for the tea. I will let you get on with your work."

Enjoying the sun, she walked up the gentle slope into the Seneca village to hear and see children at play, just as they had been in the Cherokee village, and to take in the good aromas coming from cook pots. At the longhouse of her mother, the two young maidens Ah-wa-o and An-da were airing bedding, taking advantage of the fine weather. They greeted her with respect. Ah-wa-o asked politely if she could feel the baby, and Ena obligingly lifted her deerskin shirt to bare the bulge of her stomach. The baby kicked, and Ah-wa-o laughed in delight.

"He will be a strong warrior," Ah-wa-o predicted, "like his father and his uncles."

Toshabe hailed her daughter from inside the longhouse. Ena said she felt like walking for a while and started away. Ah-wa-o followed.

"May I talk with you, Ena?"

"Your company is a pleasure," Ena told her.

It took Ah-wa-o some time to bring up the subject that was constantly on her mind. She skirted it, speaking of Renno and El-i-chi in one breath, but Ena knew that it was El-i-chi that the girl wanted to talk about. Ena cooperated by describing El-i-chi's recklessness and his bravery as a young boy.

Finally Ah-wa-o had gathered enough courage. "You have guessed, I think, that the feeling between El-i-chi and me is more than the love of brother and sister."

"My advice," Ena said, "is to return to that state and forget anything else."

Ah-wa-o's face expressed her pain.

Ena continued. "But I, too, am a woman, and I remember how it was when I was young and first saw Rusog."

"Renno will speak for us," Ah-wa-o said. "Dare I ask that you lend your support?"

"You ask much, little Rose," Ena said. "You know the customs."

"I am of the deer clan," Ah-wa-o remarked. "And El-i-chi is of the bear. Deer can marry bear."

Ena laughed. "If that were all, little Rose, if that were all."

"Things can get so complicated," Ah-wa-o complained. "We are told that all members of the deer clan are brothers and sisters, whether they be Seneca, Mohawk, or one of the other tribes. And I am told that not long ago a deer of the Seneca could not marry a deer of the Mohawk. But that old custom has been broken."

"So why not break with custom further and have sister marry brother?" Ena asked.

"Not blood sister and brother," Ah-wa-o pointed out.

"Ah, but open the door, little Rose, give blessings to the marriage of sister and brother by marriage—to you and El-i-chi—and what follows?"

Ah-wa-o was crestfallen. "I knew that the old ones would not agree, but I had hoped—"

"I have not said that I would not speak for you," Ena said. "There is time for that decision. We will speak of it again when Renno and El-i-chi return."

Ah-wa-o was much troubled. It was evident.

"There is more you wish to say?" Ena asked.

"It is Tor-yo-ne," Ah-wa-o confided. "He pretends to come to the longhouse to see his sister, but if Toshabe is not there, he speaks to me and tells me that I will be his. He is very insistent. If I could tell him that I am betrothed to El-i-chi—"

"Not just yet," Ena warned. "Go slowly with this. Give Toshabe and the other old ones a chance to mull it over, to come to yet another break with tradition. Since we have come south we have been forced by circumstances to leave many of our customs behind. Now Seneca and Cherokee marry. To marry into a tribe not of the Ho-de-no-sau-nee is something that would not have happened in the homelands. Give it time."

"But Tor-yo-ne—"

"A true Seneca would not force his attentions where they were not welcomed," Ena said.

"I have told him that."

"And he ignores you?"

"Yes," Ah-wa-o answered.

"Then perhaps another should speak to this Tor-yo-ne," Ena said grimly.

Chapter VIII

When Renno first entered a Niger delta coastal swamp in search of Mingo, he had no way of knowing that the journey would bring his group through swamp, jungle, and plain for a distance of almost five hundred miles. The Dutchman's trail led them into a land of thickly treed hills rising to heights of two thousand feet. Renno and those with him made their way through vegetation-clogged valleys and crossed great and small rivers. There was still an alien feel to the air, exacerbated by unfamiliar smells and sounds that they had never heard. On the broad plains studded with low-growing trees they saw an abundance of animal life—some odd, some dangerous. They paused to marvel at the awesome giraffe and, in spite of the danger and the fierceness of the animals, to admire the powerful, carnivorous lion and the swift cheetah. The foursome ate fresh meat regularly on the plains—waterbuck and hartebeest.

The first encounter with that largest of African animals, the elephant, made a lifelong impression on both Renno and El-i-chi. The sachem crept forward in the lead, through chest-high grass toward a copse of trees from which came crashing sounds and an occasional blare like an out-of-tune horn. Tano and Sokata had told them that the source of the noise was a herd of elephants and that it would be best to pass the copse from a safe margin, but the Seneca warriors had never seen an elephant and were not content to miss the opportunity.

They stood shoulder to shoulder and gazed with awe at four adult elephants and a young one, the adults reaching high with their odd, flexible trunks to rip formidable limbs from the trees. Suddenly a huge bull, skin sagging in heavy wrinkles, tusks long and discolored with age, sensed the presence of intruders. He turned to face them, ears forward, and blared a sound of alarm.

"I think, Brother," El-i-chi suggested, "it would be wise to start thinking of escape."

Renno had never seen such magnificence. "The Master of Life outdid himself," he whispered.

"Was he here?" El-i-chi asked.

The bull elephant took quick running steps, trunk outstretched, ears flapping.

El-i-chi tensed to run for his life. "The Master of Life gave his people the good sense to know when they are overmatched. Will you join me in ignominious flight, Brother?"

"Hold," Renno said.

The elephant made another abortive charge. Renno, right hand up and palm out, stepped forward from the cover of the trees. The elephant trumpeted a challenge.

"Peace, Brother," Renno said in Seneca. "You are strong and beautiful."

The elephant trumpeted once again, stood his ground for a few seconds, and then, with a great breaking of wind and the plop of elimination, turned and walked back slowly and heavily toward the other animals.

El-i-chi was laughing so hard that he had to bend over. "Thus, Brother, has he spoken to you."

Travel was much easier in the grassy plains. In the mornings Renno set a warrior's pace, slowing to a walk as the heat intensified. The great herds of grass eaters reminded him of the buffalo in the land of the Comanche. It was a harsh land, a land of heat and distances, but it was fruitful. There was such a multitude of game that, he suspected, the land could have nourished great tribes of many people, and yet, after days of travel in the grasslands beyond the hills, they had only seen animals.

The trail of the Dutchman's party was easy to follow now. There had been no rain, and the Dutchman's campsites showed undisturbed, dead embers of their fires and the clear tracks of unshod horses. This last concerned Renno. The Fulani who had joined the Dutchman to the south, in the jungles, had been walking. The presence of horse tracks meant that more Africans, mounted, had joined the group.

Renno became more cautious, scouting ahead himself to look over the next rise or sending El-i-chi in his turn. The plains extended endlessly to the north under a sky that blazed with the coppery heat of the sun. One-third of the ninety days he had allowed himself had been used up, and still the Dutchman was ahead of them.

"Long ago," Tano said, "the Beni fought these Fulani. The army of the oba outnumbered them greatly, but the Fulani had horses and could move swiftly to hit a weak point of the Beni lines with deadly suddenness. The oba, it is said, claimed a great victory, but the Fulani lands remained Fulani."

It was evident to Renno that both Tano and Sokata were

nervous. There was no real shelter here on the plains. What would he do if the group was attacked by a large force of mounted Fulani? At night when the others slept, he prayed to the manitous but felt only a deep loneliness, as if he were too far away from everything that was Seneca, as if the spirits of Seneca warriors could not find him on that wide, grassy plain.

"Tano," he said, "you say we are in the land of the Fulani. We are few, and this should not be your concern. You have your own destiny. Take the girl and retrace our steps. Go to your city."

Tano was clearly tempted, but he shook his head. "Mingo was my friend, too, and I owe a great deal to you and your brother. I am with you. The girl can make her own decision."

"I go where Tano goes," Sokata declared.

Renno had noted that Tano and Sokata were constantly together. They marched side by side during the day and slept near each other at night. He nodded.

On a day much like all the days since they had left the hills and the jungles behind, they marched down a grassy valley. Renno had scouted ahead and had seen only expanses of grass, grazing animals, and the endless vault of the sky. In the heat of midday, his eyes constantly searching the skyline of the rolling ridges above the narrow valley, he saw four horsemen coming over a ridge. They were impressive figures in flowing robes of various colors, wound turbans, long capes, and ornately decorated, loose trousers. The horses were bedecked with silvered harness.

"El-i-chi," he hissed.

The shaman saw to his priming. The horsemen paused on the ridge top, and their voices, a rhythmic singsong, drifted into the valley.

"I see no muskets," El-i-chi remarked.

Renno raised his hand in the universal appeal for peace. The chanting from the ridge top continued.

Tano came to stand beside Renno. "There," he said, pointing. On the opposite ridge four more Fulani horsemen had appeared. They shouted across the narrow valley to the others and were answered.

"I ask only that I be allowed to die guarding your back, my friend," Tano said.

"We have reinforcements," El-i-chi said grimly, his musket ready.

Ese, the young leopard, had come stalking silently through the tall grass.

"Thou," Renno said, "go." But Ese lowered himself into the grass, disappearing with his natural talent for concealment.

"We come in peace," Renno shouted, holding up his hand, but the calling back and forth across the valley did not abate, and with a shrill cry the Fulani charged, sending their handsome horses plunging down the slopes.

The Africans were armed with long, curved, bladed weapons that reflected fire from the sun as they were brandished over the heads of the charging riders. El-i-chi's nervousness was evident when he fired his musket too soon and missed. Renno held his fire. The shaman started to reload but soon saw that the horsemen would be on him before he had rammed the ball home. He put his musket aside and drew his pistols.

One horseman riding down from the west was outdistancing the others. Renno brought his musket to his shoulder and, without seeming to aim, fired. The horseman tumbled from his animal. The horse ran on toward them.

Now the four riding down from the east were within pistol range. El-i-chi's two shots killed one. Renno fired toward the east and did not wait to see the fallen Fulani hit the ground before he whirled and shot one of the riders coming from the west. The man toppled from the saddle, and then the Fulani were on them.

A screaming Fulani, his face twisted with rage, chose Renno as his target. It was now four against four, with one of the defenders an unarmed girl. Renno stood his ground, his Seneca war club poised, the haft giving a reassuring warmth to his hand. He saw the Fulani lean toward him, and as the curving arc of the blade came toward his neck, he leaped high, swinging his body to one side to avoid the whistling slash of the blade, and wielded the club with all his strength, even while he was in midair. The club half buried itself in the Fulani's forehead, and Renno was rolling as he fell to avoid the flanks of the charging horse.

El-i-chi met the first of the remaining two riders from the east with a mighty toss of his tomahawk that embedded the steel blade in the rider's throat and sent him tumbling into the grass, blood spurting. El-i-chi, falling, narrowly avoided being decapitated; the hooves of the horse of the remaining rider from the east thundered dangerously close to the shaman's head as he rolled aside. The horseman jerked his animal around and with a shrill yell bore down on El-i-chi again. Tano, meanwhile, was trying to prime and load El-i-chi's fallen musket with hands that would not obey his wishes.

Renno was dashing about in a tight circle, the surviving Fulani in his area trying to guide his horse closer, in order to strike a fatal blow.

The white Indian timed his movements to be on the rider's left side, so the Fulani would have to strike across his own body with his curved blade. Renno danced in dangerously close, war club at the ready. The Fulani prematurely shrieked victory and let loose a murderous slash that Renno avoided, and before the rider could recover, Renno launched himself to grapple with the rider and haul him off the horse. The men

landed with the Fulani underneath. Renno, with the hot blood
of combat surging in his veins, smashed the turbaned skull
with the club.

El-i-chi was being hard pressed by a rider more skilled
than the one who had just faced Renno. The shaman was
darting back and forth like a cornered mouse, with the rider
gradually closing in. Renno drew his stiletto, but before he
could throw it, there was the blast of a musket, and the last
surviving Fulani was driven forcefully forward over his horse's
neck, then tumbled limply to the ground. A horse neighed in
fright, and the animals bolted.

All was silence. A vulture appeared overhead, to be joined
within minutes by a dozen others. The smell of death, Renno
thought, carried far on these African plains.

"Well done, Tano," El-i-chi panted.

"They were eight," Tano said in amazement, clutching
the still-smoking musket. He grinned broadly, his teeth a
white slash in his sweat-dripping black face. "*Eight.*"

"They fought well," Renno remarked. "El-i-chi, the horses.
Tano, you and the girl take cover there." He pointed toward
an indentation in the grassy floor of the valley. "No fire. If
we have not returned by the time the sun goes down, move to
the shelter of that ridge and conceal yourselves."

Having reloaded their weapons, the brothers set off at a
run in the direction of the last sighting of the bolting horses.
They ran a mile, climbed a long, low undulation, and looked
down to see five of the horses grazing peacefully near a herd
of hartebeests. The brothers crept through the grass slowly
until they were within a hundred feet of the horses. Renno
whistled softly, and the heads of two of the horses jerked up.
One took a few steps in their direction. Renno nodded to
El-i-chi, and they rose together. A horse snorted and trembled, poised to run, but halted when Renno whistled again.

"Easy," Renno told El-i-chi. With horses under them

they would soon overtake the Dutchman. He walked forward slowly, hand outstretched, whistling and talking softly in Seneca. As he neared a horse that was tossing its head and snorting nervously, he crooned, and the horse allowed Renno to seize a dangling rein. El-i-chi, too, had succeeded. He was mounted even as Renno threw himself astride the animal and began to collect the other grazing horses.

Tano and Sokata were lying side by side in the deep grass, having pressed down a bed in the manner of animals.

"I had prepared myself for death," Sokata confided, showing Tano a knife that she had carried hidden in the folds of her skirt. "I would not have been a captive of those men."

"We live," Tano said.

"For how long?"

"Don't concern yourself," Tano soothed. "You were given the chance to go back."

"To be eaten by a lion," she said scornfully. "Or to be taken by the first tribe encountered."

"You made your choice," Tano reminded her.

"When the Fulani come again, stay by me," she pleaded.

"I will fight alongside Renno and El-i-chi."

"You fought well." Her smile was genuine and warm.

Tano had not been unaware that this Beni girl had youthful charm. He nodded.

"If we live," she said, "and if you do, indeed, regain your rightful place in our city . . ."

"Yes?"

"I will ask nothing more than to be your slave," she whispered.

He reached for her, pulled her to him, and let his hands learn, in that way that was allowed by their customs, the full curves of her body. "Perhaps I will make you first wife, in charge of all my other wives."

Her eyes widened. "You would do that?"

"We will see," he said, losing himself in enjoyment of her body but respecting her status as a maiden.

Tano did not hear the approach of the horses until they were quite near. He jerked himself into a crouch, reaching for his spear, ready to battle against Fulani horsemen. But it was Renno and El-i-chi, riding easily and leading three horses.

The brothers had found the horses to be spirited. Not knowing the Fulani riding habits or the commands to give the horses, the first portion of the ride back to camp had been interesting. Both men were good riders, however, and soon, by trial and error, they had learned to control the horses well enough.

With Tano and Sokata it was another matter. Tano's first attempt at mounting a horse resulted in his being pitched head over heels into the grass. He rolled to his feet, shook his head in a dazed way, and said, "If it is all the same, Renno, I will walk."

"Courage," El-i-chi urged, boosting Tano back onto the horse.

Sokata too took her falls, but she showed determination, yelling angrily at the horse after being thrown twice and sawing on the reins until, finally, she managed to stay on the horse's back in spite of its spirited prancing. In consideration for the new riders Renno set the pace at a walk. They covered a good distance before darkness forced them into camp, the horses tethered nearby to graze.

Ese, the leopard, almost cost them the horses when he quietly stalked into camp, coming from downwind so the horses didn't immediately catch his scent. When they did, as Ese was gnawing the bones of the day's kill, the mounts bolted, hobbling as fast as they could with their front legs tied together with leather thongs cut from El-i-chi's spare buckskin shirt. Renno and El-i-chi chased them down and tethered them at a greater distance.

"I think, Brother, that your Ese will be a great problem anytime he comes around," El-i-chi observed. "If he should appear suddenly while we're riding, it could result in serious injury for Tano and Sokata."

Day by day, week by week, Ese had been growing. He had filled out well and now moved with only a hint of playful awkwardness. Being a nocturnal animal, he did not create the problems El-i-chi envisioned during the day, but each night he entered the camp and took his meal. Gradually the horses began to accept his presence, although each night the first scent of the carnivore caused them to blow and stomp nervously. Each night Ese arrived later and later, for in spite of sore rumps and various bruises, Tano and Sokata were becoming adept riders, and the pace was now swifter, leaving Ese greater and greater distances to cover when he awoke from his daytime sleep to catch up with the party in the cool of the evening.

"The spirits have blessed you," El-i-chi said, alluding to insanity, when Renno announced that he was going to teach his horse to carry both him and the leopard.

"He is indeed sunstruck," Tano agreed. "The leopard is the natural enemy of the horse, and not even so great a warrior, with such amazing magic, can persuade a horse to carry the leopard."

At first it seemed that El-i-chi and Tano were right. El-i-chi, however, admitted that not even he, with all the magic and skills of a Seneca shaman, had Renno's uncanny gift of communication with animals. No, El-i-chi would not have predicted failure, although he doubted.

Neither Ese nor the horse thought too much of the experiment. The leopard allowed Renno to lift him, but when Renno tried to put Ese on the horse's broad rump, Ese jerked out of Renno's hands and the horse began rearing. Ese, with a disgusted snarl, disappeared into the grass. Days later, however, with many more miles behind them, the horse, although snorting wildly, accepted the burden of the leopard with rolling eyes and prancing feet, and thus a man from the faraway New World rode a Fulani horse across the African plain, with a yearling leopard lolling peacefully behind him.

"He is of the gods," Sokata breathed.

"Indeed, he has great magic," Tano agreed.

The Fulani's destination was in the semiarid north. Zaria was a cluster of stinking mud huts shimmering under the burning sun, the site made habitable only by the presence of a natural spring, which fed a watering place. Date palms waved their fronds in the dry breezes. As the Dutchman entered the city, shrouded women stopped to stare, and naked urchins followed the group as it wended through dusty streets to the local chief's residence, where the king was a guest, a mud-brick structure only slightly more grand than the poor mud huts that extended in all directions without much semblance of order. A half-starved dog growled, then fled in fear. Goats shared the dirt streets with men in flowing garments and chattering children.

Zangara, king of all the Fulani, was a three-hundred-pound man. His bulk was swathed in fine silk, and a gold necklace that Vanderrenner estimated to weigh at least two pounds was almost lost in the folds of fat that made the chief appear to have no neck, only a great head that blended with the mass that was his torso.

"Our dealings in the past have found you to be fair," Zangara told him. "Thus I have sent for you."

There were the usual ceremonies. Warriors danced and brandished weapons, chanting what they would do to their Beni enemies. A cow was roasted over a huge fire, and the beef was a welcome change of diet for Vanderrenner. He drank his share of native beer, gifted the king with a full bottle of rum, and saw almost the entire bottle consumed in one swig without any obvious intoxication. The immense weight of the king, he thought, had soaked up the rum as if it had been only a thimbleful. After the ceremony Vanderrenner found two nubile girls waiting in his tent to tend him, wash him, feed him, and perform other services that Vanderrenner did not scorn.

It took two days of talk and entertainment and feasting for the king to introduce the subject of the ivory. With great ceremony he heaved himself up from his throne, fashioned of hardwood from the jungles to the south and decorated with the skulls of fallen enemies. It had been carried here from the Fulani's capital city because it comfortably accommodated Zangara's bulk. People dropped to the ground, prostrating themselves, as the royal entourage made its way from the chief's abode to a large, specially constructed mud building guarded by big-boned, well-armed warriors. The heat had accumulated inside the windowless room, so the space was like an oven.

But the Dutchman wasn't thinking of the heat. Here, piled neatly in great rows as high as his head, was a fortune in ivory. He saw tusks of a size that he had never encountered, and he had trouble controlling his reaction as the king waddled down one aisle after the other between the rows of piled elephant tusks.

"The king's treasure is impressive," Vanderrenner commended.

"I have thought long and hard," Zangara said, "before deciding to sell the treasure of my father and my father's father. But the Beni must be punished, and to do so my warriors must be armed with guns. You will give me one musket for each tusk, Dutchman."

"The king is my friend," Vanderrenner said, "and the king is a wise man. So the king must realize that the price he asks is far too high."

Actually, a musket for an elephant's tusk was a ridiculously low price, but Vanderrenner knew that the king's first demand was merely an opening for the negotiations. The group went back to the chief's home. The walk had exhausted Zangara, so he went to rest, a group of women hovering around him to shoo flies off his royal body.

When the bargaining started again, Vanderrenner said, "Great King, the bail of a musket will kill a man. Thus one shot, one ball, is worth one man, is that not true?"

"It is true that one shot from a musket, properly aimed, can kill a man," the king agreed.

"Thus, it is safe to say that a musket is worth one man," Vanderrenner concluded. "Although I can buy slaves for much less."

The king waited, sensing that the Dutchman was ready to make his first offer, which would not be taken, of course.

"And who is the first among all men? Zangara, king of the Fulani," the Dutchman continued. "And so we have established our measure for the worth of the ivory. For each amount of ivory equal to the weight of the great king Zangara, I will give one musket with enough power and shot to kill many enemies."

"But," the king pointed out, "since Zangara is first among all men, he thus stands alone, and to measure value by his unequaled majesty would not be a true measure. For even a boy-child, taught how to aim a musket, can kill a man. Thus you will use my youngest son"—he pointed to a slim boy of perhaps ten years—"as the unit of measure. One musket for each matching of the weight of my son in ivory."

Vanderrenner was tempted to say yes immediately. He wanted that ivory, and the sale of it in Europe and in the Far

East would equal the profits made by a dozen voyages with his holds filled with slaves. But he knew that the king was enjoying the bargaining and that haggling was half the pleasure of doing business.

"Am I to be beggared by my friend the king of the Fulani?" Vanderrenner protested, wringing his hands. "Is the price of our friendship to be my undoing?"

The king was silent and motionless in his huge throne.

"Will not the muskets be used by Fulani warriors?" Vanderrenner pressed. "Will not the men killed be warriors? Thus the measure should not be a boy who is not yet a warrior but the weight of one of the king's finest fighting men."

The pleasant sport of negotiating went on for the rest of the day. It was evening before the Dutchman had an inspiration. "Great Zangara, we are within this much"—he held his thumb and finger up with the pads a fraction of an inch apart—"of striking a bargain that will be fair for both of us." They had narrowed the unit of measure down to two warriors, who stood stiffly at attention in front of the throne. One was six feet tall and weighed approximately two hundred pounds. The other was shorter, and lighter by fifty pounds. "I ask the king to let the gods decide which warrior will be the unit of measurement."

"I am listening," Zangara said, intrigued.

"You have seen the big warrior I have brought with me," the Dutchman said. "He is my champion, from an island far across the great sea. He fights with no weapons but his hands, his teeth, and his feet. Let us pit my champion against the strongest and bravest of your warriors. If my man wins, we will use the larger warrior as the unit of weight in our business. If your man wins, then the smaller."

The king's eyes gleamed from between folds of fat. He had seen the stranger, and he was indeed big but of mild

demeanor. He obeyed the orders of another of the Dutchman's men, the red-haired one called Noir, without question.
One who submitted so meekly to another man's underling
could not be much of a man. On the other hand, there was a
warrior called Sardic, a man of small brain and huge body, a
man who was always at the fore in battle, a man who, alone,
could lift a cow upon his broad back. He thrived on fighting;
in fact, at that very moment Sardic was confined to his hut
and guarded by six armed men as punishment for breaking
the heads of three warriors in a brawl over a woman.

"You have appealed to my sporting instinct," the king
said. "It will be so."

Mingo had memorized every bend and landmark of the
trail northward. At first he had felt almost at home, for
although the animals were odd, the Jamaican jungles were
similar to those in Africa. He considered running away, for
he was, at times, loosely guarded. Apparently the Dutchman
and Noir felt that the threat of death to Uanna and his sons
would keep him under control.

So Mingo bided his time, prayed to his old gods each
night to keep his family safe, and vowed to the dieties and to
himself that he would not die before killing the Dutchman
and Noir if any harm had come to his family during his
absence.

In Zaria he was housed in an odoriferous mud hut, but he
had plenty to eat and fresh water. Sneering, Noir offered to
share one of the Fulani women loaned to him for pleasure and
had laughed with great amusement when Mingo refused.

"Take what you can get, Jamaican," Noir advised, "for
if you dream of the smooth thighs of your wife, you must
remember that I, Noir, will part those thighs when we return
to the fort."

Noir was near death then without realizing it, for Mingo's

hatred rose up in him, and he had to use all his control to keep from breaking the older man's back with his bare hands.

Late that night Noir came and woke Mingo. "Tomorrow you fight," Noir said. He extended a hunk of meat. "Here. Eat. Be strong."

Mingo accepted the meat. He knew that he had to keep up his strength and be ready for action.

"I have seen the man you will fight," Noir went on. "He is a bull—larger than you and stronger but stupid and probably slow. It is important that you do not kill this one quickly. I want you to make it look as if he is winning and that it is a good fight. Understand?"

Mingo nodded. He had been dreading this time, when he would have to kill a man whom he had never met and who was not his enemy.

The day started with wild ceremony, for the king had declared a holiday. Warriors arrayed in their finest danced in the streets, and the city's beer inventory was quickly threatened. The people of the city greeted Mingo with jeers and hisses as he was escorted by Noir to a central square in front of the chief's mud-brick residence. The Jamaican wore only a loincloth, and his muscles rippled impressively as he walked.

The king's throne had been moved to a wooden pavilion shaded by a bloodred canopy. The square was thronged by the entire population of Zaria and by others who had come in from neighboring villages. A small area in the center was clear. Bastian Vanderrenner came forward to instruct Mingo.

"Noir has told you what is required?" the Dutchman asked.

Mingo nodded.

"Stay away from him," the Dutchman warned. "He is strong. Pull your blows at first. I want this fight to last at least an hour—if the big Fulani has the stamina to stay on his feet that long."

Mingo saw his opponent. He was, Mingo estimated, about six and a half feet tall. He had arms the size of a man's thighs, and his thighs were like tree trunks. His muscles were well developed, and as women trilled and men shouted, he advanced toward Mingo with the shuffling gait of a caged lion. He would be slow, Mingo believed, and based his actions on that.

The king signaled the beginning of the fight with a wave of his pudgy hand. He was leaning forward eagerly, his fat face wreathed in an expectant smile. Sardic and Mingo stood face-to-face. The people were screaming as Mingo lanced out, intending to strike the giant Fulani in the stomach, to test his softness. He was caught completely unaware as Sardic moved with the speed of a striking snake. A giant fist thudded into Mingo's face, and he felt his nose give and blood spew even as he stumbled back, dazed, to land heavily on his rump in the dust.

Chapter IX

T wice in three days Renno's little group was forced to detour around Fulani villages built beside water holes. The group would pass inspection from a distance, for they had taken clothing from the dead Fulani warriors—although El-i-chi did not at all like the feel of the turban on his head—and they rode Fulani horses.

The Dutchman's trail was being lost in a profusion of other tracks, but it seemed logical that the well-traveled way led to Zaria, and that the Dutchman's long trek could have but one objective, to meet with the Fulani king.

"You plan to go into Zaria?" Tano asked, incredulous. "With your white face, how can you expect to live?"

"So," Renno acknowledged.

El-i-chi laughed and shook his head. Renno's noncommittal response meant one of two things: Either he had a plan, or he had not the slightest notion of what he would do.

That afternoon they passed through an arid plain. The dry season had parched what vegetation there was, and grazing animals were few. The foursome made do with the water carried in their Fulani waterskins, which they had taken from the fallen warriors, and for food there were the leftovers of the previous day's kill. Tano and Sokata ate well, but both Renno and El-i-chi chose to fast, for the meat had become slightly rancid. Ese had to be content with light rations, since there were only tidbits left when Tano and Sokata finished eating.

The leopard, his appetite only partially sated, was restless. He lay near Renno for a while, and then slinked into the darkness. This was not unusual. Ese dozed well while lying across the rump of Renno's horse and came into his own at night.

Oddly enough, the nights were cool in that sun-blistered land. Renno had chosen a well-concealed campsite, and it was not necessary, he had concluded, to mount a guard. He slept well but awoke before dawn with the vague awareness of having been disturbed by a sound. He lay absolutely still. He heard the far-off and eerie cackle of a hyena, the whisper of a light breeze in the dry grass, and the deep, even breathing of his three companions. But then the sound came again, a coughing, snarling roar. A lion. *Poor hunting here,* Renno thought sympathetically. He dressed quietly and was checking his pistols when the roar of the lion came again, this time close at hand.

They had seen many big cats during the long trek and had avoided them. The lions of the plains had been content to leave them alone if the favor was reciprocated. Once, from a distance, they had witnessed lionesses making a kill, and their power was impressive. As long as this lion close to the camp minded his own business, Renno would do the same. But the roar came again, with a quality Renno had not heard before. He tensed when he heard the howling, fighting challenge of a leopard and looked around quickly to see that Ese was not in view. He seized his longbow, bent to tap El-i-chi on the shoulder, and pointed in the direction of his departure, leaving El-i-chi to follow.

Renno had just climbed a bank from the hidden campsite when he heard the mingled snarls of lion and leopard. He broke into a run. Ese would be no match for a lion. He was not yet fully grown and even in adulthood would be much smaller than a lion.

The light was increasing so that he could see well. In a hollow not a hundred feet below him, a huge male lion was crouched, tail lashing angrily, poised for a charge. Ese, blood staining his smooth coat at one shoulder, was crouched defensively a few feet away, fangs bared in a hissing snarl. The arid ground was torn in one small area between the two animals where a clash had occurred.

"Ese," Renno called softly.

The leopard's ears twitched, and he cast one quick glance in Renno's direction, and that moment of inattention sent the male lion charging with impressive speed. Ese sidestepped and lashed out at the lion with a forepaw, landing a blow on the lion's flank that would have felled a hartebeest. The lion slid to a halt, raising dust, and leaped at the leopard again.

Renno ran down the slope, yelling. His intent was to scare the lion away; he had no desire to take part in this fight. Perhaps, he thought, the lion was merely protecting his hunting grounds against an intruder. He halted twenty paces away, for the lion showed no intentions of running. Instead, the beast whirled to face this new challenge, loosed a rumbling roar, crouched, tail whipping the dust, and without further warning came at Renno, its mouth open and huge, yellow fangs dripping. Renno unslung his bow, drew an arrow, and in one smooth motion notched and drew. The arrow flew to meet the charging lion in the chest, penetrating deeply. The lion's charge faltered, then its legs became rubbery, and with the huge, gaping jaws just inches from Renno's feet, it fell to twitch out its life.

Renno felt sudden sadness. The lion's death was reason for regret, for he had been a magnificent animal. From the depths of the white Indian's memory came a few old words, which he had heard from Emily: "Also he went down and slew a lion in a pit on a snowy day."

"You are much like this mighty man of King David's," she had told him, "for you have, like Be-nai-ah, done many acts, and you are honorable among your peers, as was Be-nai-ah."

Why was Emily so much in his thoughts of late? Because her spirit had come to him, he concluded, to remind him of her pale beauty and how much of his heart she had occupied. This line of thought brought Beth to his mind, and he could picture her in England, her flame-red hair with every strand perfectly in place, her green eyes laughing.

At a sound he whirled, but El-i-chi had made the sound deliberately, knowing that it was dangerous to approach Renno from the rear without warning. Behind him came Tano and Sokata.

Ese approached the lion with care, sniffed at the blood, then sat to lick the wound on his own shoulder. Renno bent to see that the injury was shallow. "I think, little one," he said to Ese, "that you should pick your opponents with more care."

Tano, looking at Renno, whispered to Sokata. "See what he has done now!" He ventured forward. "It was a great lion. We will take the hide for you, Renno, and dry it, so that you can use it to keep you warm on cold nights back in your own country and to remember your triumph here.''

"No,'' Renno said. One did not kill an animal to brag about one's triumph. One killed to eat or in protection of self, or as in this case, for the protection of a brother.

"The scavengers will have him,'' Tano protested. "The skin of a lion is—''

"No,'' Renno said forcefully. "Come. It is time we were moving.''

It was midmorning when El-i-chi, riding in the lead, trotted back to report that a large party of Fulani horsemen were coming to intercept them on the road. "So,'' Renno said, considering a course of action. Now there sprang into his mind a decision, which seemed to be a gift from the manitous.

"There is a ridge to the left,'' El-i-chi suggested. "If we ride hard, we can be behind it before they are in view.''

"No,'' Renno said. "Sooner or later we will have to meet and deal with the Fulani. Let it be now.''

Little Hawk had no difficulty in finding the well-traveled trail that led to the west and to his home. Just out of town the trail led through virgin forest. The winds of that cold, disturbed night sang in the treetops like the spirits of warriors who had died in shame. At first Little Hawk moved at the warrior's trot, but he knew that he was not yet a warrior like his father, so he could not keep up the pace throughout the night as Renno could have done. He slowed to a walk as the sounds of the wild night became more intense—the wind howling and odd cracks and creaks coming from the dense forest around him.

"I am Little Hawk, and I have the blood of sachems,'' he loudly announced. "Spirits of my grandfather, spirits of my ancestors, be with me.''

The son of Renno could not be afraid of the dark or of being alone in the forest on a night that threatened snow; and the son of Renno was not afraid. Perhaps a bit on edge, a bit cautious. He was not afraid of the howl of the wind or of the dark spirits. He was merely being alert, just in case wolves should appear, although usually wolves stayed far from the habitats of man. He was just a boy, but he was a Seneca, the son of Renno. Had not the manitous predicted that he would be a great sachem? Therefore, he would not be taken by dark spirits on this black, windy night, for if that happened, how could the prophecy be realized?

As he trudged onward, sleet stung his face and rattled through the trees. His wet feet became more and more chilled, and he had learned enough of the art of wilderness living to know that something should be done about that. He veered off the trail, found a secluded clearing among the trees, struck fire with his flint, and soon had a cheery blaze going. He felt better. He removed his moccasins and hung them to dry, then snuggled into his one blanket and slept. When he awoke, the light of dawn was coming. He put on his dried moccasins and after listening carefully, ventured onto the trail and went at the warrior's pace until he was panting with exertion. He drank deeply from a stream that had ice around its banks, then leaped over it without wetting his feet. He knew that with the morning Grandpa Roy would be after him. Renna, when asked, would tell her grandparents Little Hawk's intentions. So as he marched, he listened, knowing that Roy would come on horseback, and Little Hawk would hear the horse long before Roy could see him.

It started to snow before midday. He was leaving clear tracks in the new snow that quickly covered the ground, but he was not concerned. The snow was falling hard enough to cover the marks of his passage. Roy, at any rate, would stick to the trail, realizing that Little Hawk knew the way well enough not to get lost. The boy estimated that by riding hard, Roy could catch him by early afternoon, but it was difficult to approximate the time with heavy clouds obscuring the sun.

He moved off the trail to rest and wait until the falling snow had obliterated his tracks. He made his way through the trees, parallel to the trail, moving to a point where he could see the track now and then. Had there been a sun, he could simply have traveled toward it as it fell in the afternoon sky, but even the most experienced warrior could be misled and could lose his sense of direction in a heavy snowstorm.

The snort of a horse alerted him. He crouched out of sight behind a tree and watched Roy, bundled into furs and a snow-covered blanket, ride by—a white specter on a ghost horse. The snow was deep enough to muffle the sound of the horse's hooves. Little Hawk waited for a half hour, then went back to the trail. For a while he could see the tracks of the horse, then only the smooth cover of the snow.

Ordinarily it was easy to follow the trail toward the Seneca village; much travel had beaten down the layer of pine straw that covered the ground. But with the snow the passageways between the large trees looked much the same. Several times Little Hawk found his way blocked by underbrush covered with a shroud of snow, telling him that he had gotten off the trail. He found his way back to it each time, but his progress was slowed. As the dim light began to fade and the snow continued to fall, he was circling back through the trees, moving around underbrush, in search of the trail once more.

With dusk closing in around him Little Hawk knew that he would not find the trail until morning. He picked a spot in the shelter of a deadfall, then dug and brushed away the snow from a small area with his hands. He cut sticks with his pocketknife and fashioned a tent with his blanket, one end weighted with rocks to anchor it to the trunk of the fallen tree, the other draped over upright sticks, thus forming a snug retreat. He dug dry twigs from under the log and soon had a fire blazing. After eating one of Nora's biscuits and a chicken leg taken from the Sunday leftovers, the boy stumbled around in total blackness to cut pine boughs and shake the snow from them to layer a soft bed. Soon he was protected from the snow, enjoying a fire and a full belly.

He slept. Snow piled onto the blanket, and it sagged but did not fall. The snow acted as insulation, so he was warm. When the boy awoke, the blanket was pressing down around him from its burden. He emerged from his shelter in a flurry of snow to see that the flakes were no longer falling—but it was very cold. He shook off his blanket, ate snow for water, and began to search without success for the trail. There was a lightness to the clouds now, and when he saw a glow that was the morning sun to the east, he put his back to it and blazed his own way through the forest. By traveling away from the trail, he rationalized, he would not be discovered if Roy decided to turn back.

He finished the last of his food at what he estimated was midday. The going was slow, for he had to break his way through six inches of snow that, in more open areas, was piled in deeper drifts. The temperature stayed below freezing, so there was no melting. He could not estimate how much longer his trek was going to take, because he had to make his own way through the forest, circling and pushing through dense areas of underbrush, so snow fell down his neck in a frozen cascade.

Late in the day he caught a glimpse of the sun in broken sky and was pleased to see it directly in front of him. He had been moving west all that day. Sooner or later he would cross the trail again or would reach a recognizable landmark. Hunger was his only concern, and that problem was solved when he came upon rabbit tracks. He followed the tracks, crawling through thick growth, until he saw a hole, a darkness in the snow. He thrust his hand into the hole, felt warmth and softness, seized it, and drew forth a squealing rabbit. He ate half of the little animal before it was cooked to his preference, roasted the rest a bit longer, and stored it strung high in a tree away from his camp—he did not want a hungry bear rumbling around his blanket-tent in the middle of the night searching for the origin of the delicious smell of the cooked meat.

The boy started his second day's travel with great confidence. The clouds were thinning, and now and again he saw the sun, so he could aim his nose straight west. He saved the remainder of the rabbit for his evening meal and sucked out the marrow, extracting every last morsel of goodness before burying the bones in the snow. He had not found the trail again, but late in the day he had crossed a stream and was sure, although he did not recognize that particular section of it, that it was the last creek before the village. He was becoming an old wilderness hand now and made his tent and built his fire quickly and efficiently. With the morning he estimated that he would reach some Cherokee or Seneca habitation before the day ended, so he didn't concern himself with food, although there were rabbit tracks in the snow.

The sun shone in the afternoon, but the air was still cold, the going hard. His legs were sore with the effort of three days' trudging through snow that sometimes reached his calves, but he ignored the soreness and pushed onward, for there was, in the distance ahead, a hill with a familiar profile. In proof, he heard, to his left, the sound of voices speaking Seneca. He moved quietly toward the sounds, creeping from tree to tree. Then he spied a group of four Seneca warriors on what was obviously the trail. He was ready to make his presence known, when he realized that he didn't recognize any of the young men.

"This is a fool's errand," a warrior complained. "To go seeking a boy who had not the good sense to stay on the trail."

They were, Little Hawk realized, talking about him. So Roy, having reached the village and finding that Little Hawk was not there, involved others in a search.

"Tor-yo-ne," one of the warriors said, "the boy is the son of Renno. To find him would put the sachem in our debt."

"Should the sachem not return," Tor-yo-ne pointed out, "this boy will be next in line."

"My longhouse is warm," another said. "Let the friends of Renno conduct this search."

"No," Tor-yo-ne said. "We will continue. But it is useless to stay on the trail. We will go into the forest."

Little Hawk tensed. He felt a certain indignation, having heard his father discussed in a disrespectful way. His pride rose. He was not lost! He had left the trail, but he was within a short distance of the village now. He would not be carried home as a lost boy; he had traveled the distance alone, he had made his camps and had fed himself. He would enter the village on his own, for he was, as the warriors had noted, the son of Renno.

Within a mile he was on familiar ground. Not even the snow cover could disguise areas where he had played and hunted squirrels with his small bow. He circled around the village, smelling the smoke of the fires and the good aromas from the cook pots. He crossed the swimming creek by walking on stones and came up to the village. Approaching darkness helped him proceed unseen, although he saw people were moving among the longhouses and log cabins. He hid himself not far from his grandmother's longhouse and waited until it was dark and no one moved. The boy approached the longhouse silently from the rear. Light came from within, and when he stood beside the front door and peeked through a tiny crack, he saw Toshabe and Ena, Ena's stomach protruding hugely, kneeling beside the fire. He opened the door and stepped in.

"I thank thee that thou art well," he said in Seneca.

The two women looked up, startled, then both broke into wide smiles.

"Who found you?" Ena asked, rising slowly to run to him in waddling haste. He suffered her embrace.

"I was not aware that I needed finding," he responded, his face expressionless.

"But—" Ena began, then spread her hands. "Everyone is in the forests looking for you. Just what in the name of the manitous did you think you were doing, Little Hawk?"

"I was coming home," he answered simply. "I am Seneca."

"Ena," Toshabe said quietly as Ena started to speak again. She rose and embraced Little Hawk. "I thank thee that thou art well, Grandson."

"As for those who look for me," Little Hawk continued, "was it I who sent warriors off on a fool's errand?"

"I will prepare your food," Toshabe offered. Tears of love wetted her cheek, so she turned away to wipe them surreptitiously. Little Hawk was indeed his father's son. He would tell his story in his own time, and she was eager to learn why he had decided to take such a drastic measure, why he was so intent on coming home. She asked only one question. "You decided to leave the trail?"

"The trail disappeared in snow," Little Hawk explained, seating himself by the fire and accepting the bowl of steaming venison stew from his grandmother. He spoke calmly and saw no need for further explanation. He *was* Seneca. He had found his way, in a snowstorm, through miles of forest.

"Ena," Toshabe said proudly, "please inform the others

that the son of Renno has come home and needed no help in getting here.''

Roy came back to the Seneca village late on the night of Little Hawk's homecoming to feel both relief and anger when he discovered that the boy had made the trip through deep snow without being able to follow the trail. His anger had soon dissipated, to be replaced with a grandfather's pride. ''You are Renno's son,'' he told Little Hawk. In a way, Roy felt, Little Hawk's solitary journey had been a rite of passage, the boy's first step toward manhood. ''But you have given *me* and your grandmother Nora great cause for worry.''

''For that I am regretful,'' Little Hawk apologized, ''but my blood called to me, and so here I am.''

There had been no question of punishment. Had anyone attempted to punish Little Hawk or to reprimand him too severely, they would have been face-to-face with two female Seneca wildcats named Toshabe and Ena.

Some of the young warriors, mostly those who gathered around Tor-yo-ne, had grumbled about the useless night spent in the snowstorm, but for most, Little Hawk's journey was a subject worthy of a small smile, and many predicted that his adventure would become, as the seasons passed, a legend of the tribe—how one small boy had felt the call of his people and had proved his own blood by overcoming severe obstacles.

Roy went back to Knoxville in haste to let Nora know that Little Hawk was safe. The scene there was tearful and loud, with Nora demanding that Roy go right back to the village and fetch Little Hawk.

''He would only run away again,'' Renna said.

''What if he had taken *her*?'' Nora cried out, and the thought was so horrible that it weakened her, put her to bed, and left Roy to do the cooking.

*　　　*　　　*

Mingo shook his head to dispel the dizziness. The giant Fulani warrior was airborne, feet coming directly toward his face. Mingo rolled, thrust out one hand, seized Sardic's ankle, and tugged. The Fulani grunted and crashed to the ground with such force that dust flew high around him.

Slow, is he? Mingo snorted. The man had moved like summer lightning. *Make it a good fight, eh?* He would be lucky to survive one more blow like the one the Fulani had delivered. He scrambled away as Sardic bounced to his feet and closed on him. He flicked out his left hand, and the Fulani's head jerked back as Mingo's fist found an eye. The strike had not been a heavy one, but it jarred Sardic. Now he became more careful, stalking Mingo with his hands high and huge fists clenched. Mingo bobbed, moved in under a round-house swing that would have hurt badly had it landed, and sent a tattoo of punches into the giant's belly. The muscles there were hard; it was like hitting a tree. A glancing blow bounced off Mingo's shoulder, and the force of it numbed the Jamaican's right arm for a moment as he backed away to gain time.

Mingo no longer heard the roar of the Fulani warriors or the trilling cries of the women. He knew that he was in a battle for survival. He ventured in, sent a right and a left to the Fulani's face, and felt the might in the African's right hand as a blow landed on the top of his ducking head. His punches seemed not to bother Sardic. He figured that his best strategy would be to let the big man tire himself with his swing—for Sardic's fists were thrown with impressive swift-ness, each one delivering a potential knockout, each missing narrowly as Mingo ducked and weaved and hammered the giant's midsection with his iron-hard fists.

He thought briefly of Tano, who had been a master at the strike-and-run technique. Tano had often tried to best Mingo with it during their hours of training. He had learned much from the faster, smaller Tano, and now he was applying it.

"Close and fight like a warrior," the spectators jeered. "Stop dancing."

Once Mingo saw Noir's face over Sardic's shoulder, and Noir offered a gesture of approval. *The fool,* Mingo thought. *He thinks I'm toying with this big African when I'm fighting to keep my head from being knocked off my shoulders.*

Sardic landed a punch to Mingo's cheek that rendered his vision hazy. The Jamaican's legs felt rubbery for a moment, and he had to retreat rapidly. Jeers erupted from the spectators. He managed to survive until his head cleared, and then, thinking that it was time for him to deal some damage, he darted in, using his stiff fingers in a serious attempt to puncture or gouge one of Sardic's eyes. He missed narrowly but left bloody fingernail marks. The Fulani was infuriated. He bellowed in rage and rushed into a flurry of fists that jarred Mingo, forcing him back.

"Now, Mingo!" Noir called in English. "You have put on a good show."

"That's easy for you to say," Mingo grunted. He thought at least one of his ribs might be broken.

The African, his mouth open, gasping for air, came in a bull-like rush, arms flailing, and Mingo fell back, close to the spectators. A Fulani warrior thrust out his spear and tripped Mingo, who fell heavily and rolled. But Sardic was on him, his massive weight driving the breath from Mingo's lungs. Huge arms closed around Mingo, and he could not breathe. His struggles were futile as he tried to break the viselike hold. He felt himself being lifted, and then Sardic was standing, arms in the small of Mingo's back. The big man had the power to snap his spine.

In desperation, his strength ebbing, Mingo butted his head into Sardic's face and felt the big nose squash under the impact. As the Fulani roared with rage, Mingo opened his mouth, took in a mouthful of bloody nose, bit down with all his strength, and felt his teeth cut flesh. At the same time he jumped from the African's grasp and lifted his knee to drive it into Sardic's genitals.

The strength drained from Sardic, and Mingo fell to one knee, weak and dazed, as the African clutched at his genitals. Mingo found the strength to rise and threw himself feetfirst, driving his callused heels into the African's belly. With a grunt of pain Sardic collapsed, and Mingo kicked him, hard, in the temple. The Fulani's eyes closed, and he lay still, except for the rapid rise of his chest.

Mingo stood panting over the fallen man.

"Kill! Kill!" chanted the Fulani, for they had been disgraced by Sardic's defeat.

The Dutchman looked at the king, who was no longer smiling. The king hesitated, then gave the signal. His thumb pointed down.

"Kill him," Noir ordered Mingo.

Mingo stood, chest heaving, his arms hanging at his sides.

"Kill him!" the Dutchman demanded.

Mingo raised his head and looked at Noir, then at the Dutchman. "If you want this man who fought so bravely to die, then *you* will have to kill him."

"The king will have your head for disobeying," Noir warned.

"He'll have to fight me for it," Mingo declared as Sardic began to moan and tried to rise. The Jamaican faced the king. "This man is brave. He is a match for three, four, maybe more warriors. He has fought well. I will not kill a brave man."

A hush fell. The Fulani had not understood Mingo's English words, but they knew that he had spoken in a raised voice to the king. The king looked at Vanderrenner. With a shrug the Dutchman translated Mingo's words. The king's face darkened, then the fat folds of his face rippled in a laugh.

"Dutchman," the king enthused, "I will give you five warriors' weight of ivory for this man."

"It grieves me to displease my friend the king," the Dutchman responded, "but this man is not for sale."

Mingo leaned, grasped Sardic's arm, and helped him to his feet. The Fulani's nose was mutilated, and he could barely stand because of the pain in his genitals. Four men came forward and took Sardic's arms.

"You're lucky to be alive, you fool," Noir hissed, coming to Mingo's side, "and I'll warrant you get a few lashes for disobeying the Dutchman's orders."

The murderous look in Mingo's eyes caused Noir to take a quick step backward before he recovered and blustering, led Mingo toward the mud hut where they were quartered.

Renno's foursome sat their horses atop a rise. A quarter mile away, over twenty mounted Fulani warriors were approaching at a trot.

"Why does he laugh?" Sokata asked Tano, nodding toward El-i-chi. "Surely we will die now."

"He laughs, I think," Tano said, "because he said he was supposed to be the one who does magic."

"I do not understand." Sokata's voice quivered with fear.

"Nor do I," Tano confessed, "but there is much about these brothers that I do not understand."

El-i-chi was laughing at the simple brilliance of Renno's strategy. It had taken a bit of doing, but the sachem had positioned Ese in front of him on the horse. The leopard's legs sprawled down the leather of the stirrup supports so his claws could not scratch the horse.

Now the approaching Fulani were near enough to see just

what it was that made a double load for a horse—a leopard almost full grown, a wild thing of the jungle, and a white man. The two warriors in the fore of the group jerked their horses to a halt. A babble of amazement erupted from the group, with a pointing of fingers.

"They have seen," El-i-chi said, "and they do not believe their eyes."

The group's two leaders edged forward. One of them called out a greeting, which Renno answered. The excited Fulani moved forward until their horses caught the scent of the leopard.

Now El-i-chi had another reason to laugh, because the Fulani warriors suddenly had their hands full, dealing with some twenty bucking, panicked, squealing horses. Finally two men staggered from the dust cloud. The others, some filthy from being thrown, had run away. Several riderless horses were galloping back toward Zaria.

"Who is this man of great magic?" one of the Fulani asked in Edo.

"A man also of peace," Renno replied. "I have heard that your king has a great treasure. I come to trade."

"Already the trade is done," the warrior said. "A musket for the weight of a large warrior in ivory."

"Then I am sorry," Renno said, "for I am sure that the Dutchman did not offer a price as great as what I would have offered for this treasure." This much he had formulated while waiting for the approach of the Fulani. His objective was to get into the city and to weaken the king's confidence in the Dutchman by offering whatever price was necessary for his ivory.

The two Fulani conversed in their own tongue quietly but with excited gestures, then the spokesman advanced a few steps. Ese obligingly opened his mouth, yawned to show his great teeth, and made a growl of protest. The Fulani stepped back a pace before speaking. "A man of such great magic will be heard, I am sure, by our king."

"I am willing to offer one musket for each tusk of the elephant," Renno added, to seal their access to Zangara.

The Fulani's eyes widened. "It will be my honor to escort you, man of magic. Come, if it pleases you."

"No," Renno said. "To greet your king in these garments would not show respect. We have come far this day, and we will rest here the night. With the sun we will come."

"I will go to inform the king of your arrival."

"That is not my pleasure," Renno told him. "I wish to be a pleasant surprise for your king. You and your men will camp here, near us."

El-i-chi prepared to defend himself when he heard Renno issue imperious orders to the Fulani, but he relaxed when the warriors obeyed in deference to this man of great magic.

"It will be my pleasure to be your guard of honor," the Fulani responded, inclining his head.

"We are to sleep, with all of them so near?" Sokata asked, incredulous, when El-i-chi was preparing a haunch of meat for the spit. He had killed a tender young buck.

The Fulani had encamped not over a hundred feet away, but because of Ese, their recaptured horses were tethered at a greater distance. The leopard stalked around the fire, sniffing the winds, gazing haughtily in the direction of the Fulani now and again, and yawning to show his teeth.

"We have a splendid guard," El-i-chi said, casting an eye at the carnivore. "Sleep without concern."

When the meat was ready, Renno extended an invitation to the Fulani warriors. Only four accepted, and they walked close by Renno's side, for Ese was keeping his yellow eyes on the newcomers. The meal was a nervous one for them because Ese lay near, waiting for the tossed bones and hunks of meat that comprised his main meal. The warriors departed quickly.

"We will alternate guard," Renno said.

"I'll take the first, until midnight," El-i-chi offered.

"My brother would not like to awaken at midnight and relieve me?" Renno asked with a wry grin.

"Renno, you know you're better at staying awake in the early morning hours," El-i-chi protested.

"But then you must need the practice," Renno said. "I will guard until midnight."

El-i-chi was asleep immediately. Renno sat before the fire, feeding it twigs and branches. Ese left for his nightly prowl. The Fulani camp was quiet. Overhead the stars blazed, huge and distant in an alien sky. Half his mind was alert; the other half wandered far, to the familiar areas where the stars were those of his ancestors. And as if from the stars themselves, there came the voice of Emily:

"Hurry . . . Hurry . . . Hurry . . ."

He had never before had a vision of the manitous without first praying and fasting. He had never heard a spirit voice in the presence of others, even if the others were sleeping. His eyes searched the night sky. He prayed silently, asking for more information, but there was only the cough of a lion in the distance and the sharp cry of a jackal.

He awakened El-i-chi at midnight. Ese was back, and Renno saw the cat settle down, his sides heaving, a contented rumble coming from his chest, beside the shaman.

"Thou, Ese," El-i-chi whispered as silence came to the camp again. "You must keep me awake." As if in response, the leopard ran a tongue like the burrs of a chestnut over El-i-chi's hand.

Chapter X

An honor guard of Fulani warriors, straight-backed in
their saddles, preceded Renno's party into the city of
Zaria. The returning Fulani were treated with indifference by
the people in the streets, for armed parties of warriors were
always coming and going from the village, but as the first ten
warriors rode past, a hush descended and all faces were
turned.

Renno's preparations had exhausted the emergency stock
of paints that El-i-chi always carried with him. His face and
Renno's were painted in the patterns of a Seneca messenger.
They wore only breechclouts and moccasins and a leather
sash to hold their weapons. They rode, heads high, faces
impassive, through the dirt streets.

Behind them came Tano, Sokata, and the balance of the

force of Fulani warriors they'd encountered on the plain. A mass of the people of the city followed them in awed silence toward the central square, which, only the day before, had been the scene of the fine battle between Sardic and the Dutchman's big warrior.

Bastian Vanderrenner was eager to get under way toward the coast with his treasure in ivory. He was being feted once more, however, by King Zangara in celebration of their agreement. The heat of midday had passed, although it was still torrid. Zangara lounged under a canopy, Vanderrenner reclining near him on a pallet of skins. Both men looked up when mounted warriors rode into the square, hailed the king with great shouts, and announced the arrival of an important visitor. The Dutchman was not impressed, for during his stay in Zaria two other so-called important visitors had come— local chiefs from outlying villages, paying their tribute to the king. Vanderrenner, therefore, applied himself to a fine cut of beef cooked exactly to his liking and looked up again only when he heard the king grunt in amazement.

"By the devil's beard!" the Dutchman exploded, for now the warriors had fanned out to give way to Renno and El-i-chi, who rode toward the royal pavilion with proud, erect carriage and stoic faces. "You!"

Ese, made nervous by all the people and the enclosed feeling of the city, was spitting and growling. Renno's hand was on the leopard's head, and he whispered to Ese to be calm.

The king was astonished to see a pale-skinned man with a painted face riding a Fulani horse with a leopard perched in front of him. He struggled to his feet, his mouth agape.

Renno pulled his horse to a halt and waited in silence.

The leader of the escort ran forward and threw himself to the dirt in front of the throne. "Great king," he cried, "here, from far places, is a man of great magic who would talk with you, with your permission."

Zangara sat, dismissed the warrior, and gazed at Renno, who lifted his right hand in the sign of peace.

"I greet you, Zangara, king of all Fulani. I salute you, great bull elephant." He had learned the proper form of address from the Fulani warriors.

"You may dismount," Zangara invited, speaking, as had Renno, in the root language of the area's tongues.

Renno did so, tapping Ese on the back. The young leopard leaped lightly to the ground to crouch at Renno's feet. El-i-chi stood slightly behind and to Renno's right.

It was then that Tano came into view. At the sight of him Vanderrenner's jaw dropped and his eyes bulged. There was no need to tell him that circumstances at his slave fort had changed in his absence.

"I am told," Renno said, pointing a finger at the Dutch-man, "that this man has cheated you, offering a price for your royal treasure so small as to be insulting."

Vanderrenner tensed. "This man, great king, is a liar and a thief!"

The fat, massive face of the king turned first to the Dutchman, then back to Renno. "Your charge against a longtime friend of the Fulani is a grave one."

"Great king," Renno said, "I, Renno, sachem of the Seneca in the lands across the seas, offer you one musket with a supply of powder and shot for each ivory tusk."

A gasp went up from the people crowded around the pavilion. Vanderrenner's face went ruddy with rage. The king moved his head slowly, slowly, and looked at Vanderrenner from his hooded eyes.

"The man is mad!" Vanderrenner sputtered. "Ask him to show you this great store of muskets, for no such number of muskets exists in all of Africa."

Renno was at a disadvantage, for he could not understand the Fulani that was being spoken between Vanderrenner and the king. He waited, arms crossed.

Zangara looked at Renno. "Where are the many muskets you promise?"

"Where are the muskets of the Dutchman?" Renno countered.

The king turned to ask the Dutchman the same question.

Vanderrenner heatedly replied, and Renno knew that the Dutchman was defending his honor.

The king, bemused, looked back at Renno. "I know where the Dutchman's muskets are."

"My ship awaits at the mouth of the Niger," Renno stated. In that he was truthful, although he feared that by the time he could return to the ship, Billy the Pequot would have long since traded the muskets for African goods and produce. He would cross that bridge when he came to it. He was not interested in the king's ivory—only in finding Mingo, freeing him, and returning him to his family aboard the *Seneca Warrior*.

"One musket for each tusk?" the king asked.

"That is my offer," Renno confirmed.

"Food and drink for these newcomers," the king ordered with a wave of his hand. "I will consider."

Awestruck, young, bare-breasted women escorted Renno, El-i-chi, Tano, and Sokata to a mud hut. Ese, at first, was reluctant to enter, but he was teased inside by the offer of meat from Renno.

"El-i-chi," Renno said, "see if they will allow you to walk in the town. If so, try to locate Mingo."

El-i-chi went to the doorway, stepped out to face no fewer than six Fulani warriors holding curved weapons. They politely insisted that he stay in the hut.

"There are six," he reported to his brother. "We can take them quickly, by surprise, and then find Mingo."

"And the hundreds between us and the plains?" Renno asked.

"I don't like being cooped up, under guard," El-i-chi complained.

"Patience," Renno advised, sitting down.

Zangara had summoned his chief juju man, an ancient witch doctor who wore the skin of a hyena and the desiccated fingers and ears of men and women who had, for one reason or another, displeased the great king.

"You heard?" the king asked.

"I heard, my king," the juju man replied.

"The Dutchman has been fair with me in the past," Zangara said, "paying for slaves."

"But never before has so great a treasure been involved. Slaves are easy to come by. A man is worth far less than one tusk of the elephant."

"He bargained hard," the king mused. "Until the coming of the man who tames the jungle cat, I had thought that the offer was fair. Now I am ill at ease."

"There is this to consider, great King," the juju man proposed. "All white men are liars. They will promise to deliver the moon and hang it permanently over your village, but they do not deliver. There is a test to see which of these white men should get the tusks."

"Yes," the king agreed. "There is a test. You may go."

The Dutchman had sought out Noir. "What is he doing here, five hundred miles into the interior of Africa?" he seethed. "And with Tano! We'd better get back to the fort and find out what happened there."

"Perhaps he does have magic," Noir suggested, having seen Ese riding on the horse.

"The devil he does!" Vanderrenner snarled. "It's a trick!

An animal trainer's trick! I have seen lions and tigers in the same arena in a circus. He has no magic. He is only a man, and he can die just like other men.''

"For the price of four bottles of rum, I can hire Fulani to go into their hut and kill all of them," Noir offered.

"Not yet," the Dutchman said. "To kill him now would cost us, for we would have to match his offer of one musket for each tusk. First we must discredit him, proving to the king that he is a madman, then talk sense to Zangara to lower the price for his ivory." He was silent for a moment. "Be ready, Noir. Have our pistols ready. No matter where we are, if I give you the signal, shoot both Indians, and be sure you kill them both with the first two shots."

A warrior entered the hut where Renno and the others were waiting. Ese snarled, and the man backed out quickly. He stuck only his head in and spoke in Fulani, then gestured.

"I think the king has made his decision," Renno said.

He checked his weapons and felt the constant, reassuring heat from the haft of the war club. El-i-chi's face was grim. While Sokata was obviously agitated, Tano tried to match the calm of Renno and El-i-chi.

A great crowd lined the square before the king's pavilion. Vanderrenner was no longer in a place of honor on the platform but stood on the ground in front of the king. The old juju man rattled a skull filled with pebbles as Renno led the way forward, Ese at his side.

"This one," the king said, pointing to Vanderrenner, "says that you are a madman, that your only intent is to discredit him, and that you cannot deliver the muskets you promise."

Renno started to speak and was silenced by a wave of the king's hand.

"This one," the king said, pointing to Renno, "says that

the Dutchman has tried to cheat me. Who, then, are we to believe?"

A murmur rose from the crowd.

"Believe our old friend!" a man yelled.

"The painted one has much magic!" someone else yelled. "Listen to him."

"Thus it is," the king declared. "We cannot be sure without invoking the will of the gods. This question will be answered in the time-honored way of the Fulani." The king paused. "The two white men accused of lying will face each other in combat to the death."

A whisper of anticipation swept through the crowd.

"Dutchman," the king asked, "is this to your liking?"

"Very much so, great king," the Dutchman said, grinning viciously.

"And you, man of magic, are you in agreement?"

"I am," Renno answered.

"As for weapons," the king said, "no muskets. With the white man's musket there is only a quickness that could confuse the gods."

Renno nodded. "Let the Dutchman, then, choose his own weapon."

"All right," the Dutchman agreed. "And let this liar choose his own weapons."

"This, then," Renno said, hoisting the curved war club over his head. "And this," he said, showing the ornate Spanish stiletto.

"So be it," the Dutchman agreed. He turned to the king. "Great Zangara, I claim the right of the accused to be represented by a champion."

"He doesn't want to face you himself," El-i-chi whispered.

"That is your right," Zangara allowed. "You may call your champion." To Renno he said, "Do you also substitute a champion?"

"I am my own champion," Renno announced. "And I am disappointed that the Dutchman has not the courage to face me."

The Dutchman turned to Noir. "Get Mingo."

The pitch of excitement was escalating in the crowd. Some women were dancing in place, and warriors were swaying, making a rhythmic drone through their noses. Noir returned quickly with Mingo at his side. When Mingo saw Renno and El-i-chi, his step faltered and his eyes widened. But at a small gesture from Renno, he remained silent as he came forward to stand before the pavilion.

"Arm your champion, Dutchman," Zangara ordered.

"Great king," Renno said, stepping forward, "This is yet another example of the Dutchman's dishonesty, for he would have me fight a slave who is my property, a slave stolen from me far away on the oceans by the Dutchman, a slave who has come to mean much to me." He had considered telling the king that Mingo was his blood brother but had decided that Zangara would understand better if he said that he owned Mingo.

"Dutchman, is this true?" the king asked.

"It is another lie of this cheater," Vanderrenner said. "This man, my champion, was no man's slave. He was a freeman in Jamaica until I took him and trained him."

"You," Zangara said, pointing to Mingo. "Whose man are you?"

"My master is there," Mingo said, pointing to Renno. "It is true that the Dutchman took me from my rightful master by force."

The king's face clouded with anger. "I tire of these endless lies! You, slave," he said to Mingo. "Will you fight this man who calls himself your master?"

"Great king," Mingo said, "I respect this man, for he has been kind to me. I could not raise a weapon against him."

"We cannot doubt the black man's bravery," the juju man declared, "for he fought well against Sardic, who, I am sure, is far stronger than this pale-skinned one."

The king made his decision. "Dutchman," he ordered, "fight your own fight or name another champion."

Quickly Noir stepped forward. "I will fight this foreign one."

A cheer went up from the spectators. Noir's scarred face was impressive, as were his height and his powerful muscles.

Mingo bowed toward the king. "Your permission, sire, to be champion for my true master."

The king frowned. "But this man, Noir, is your friend, is he not?"

"He helped steal me and my family away from our rightful place," Mingo said. "It would be just to allow me to kill him."

"I fight my own battles," Renno said.

Mingo came to stand beside Renno. "He is dangerous."

Noir was selecting his weapons, borrowing a Fulani spear and scimitar. He whirled the blade over his head skillfully, the razor-sharp edge hissing.

"Zangara," Renno requested, "grant me this. It is agreed that the result of this combat will determine who speaks the truth, the Dutchman or me. Let it also decide the rightful ownership of this man, Mingo."

The king looked toward the Dutchman, who shouted, "He puts my property at risk without risk to anything that *he* owns! Is that fair?"

"What say you to that, man of magic?" Zangara asked.

Before Renno could answer, Tano stepped forward. He stared directly at the Dutchman and said in a great voice, "This man, Renno, is also my master. I will be Renno's stake."

The Dutchman laughed. "An ex-champion, beaten, against

the finest fighting master in the world? How is that fair, great King?''

''I, too, will be at stake,'' Sokata volunteered, stepping forward to join Tano.

The Dutchman heard the king hiss in appreciation of Sokata's beauty and knew that he should not protest further. He nodded.

''To the death,'' Zangara commanded, motioning the combatants forward.

A silence fell as Noir crouched and began to stalk Renno, who was armed with his wooden war club, the Spanish stiletto at his belt. Noir brandished the black-tipped spear expertly, prepared to use it as a lance. Renno, watching Noir's leg movements, let him close. When he saw the big man coil for a lunge, he stepped easily aside, and his club hissed through the air as the spear tip passed close by his side. But Noir recovered quickly, and Renno's killing blow struck only air.

Twice more Noir closed on Renno, and twice more Renno avoided the stabbing lunge of the spear. Noir realized that Renno was too quick to be killed by using the spear as a lance, so he gave ground. Renno, sensing what was on Noir's mind, did not follow; instead, he backed away until twenty paces separated them.

He saw Noir's arm tense, watched the spear being drawn back into throwing position, faked to the left, and leaped to the right, but Noir had been feinting, and the spear was still firmly in his hand. He feinted again and again, analyzing Renno's reactions, and then he threw the spear with surprising quickness just as Renno lunged to the side, having anticipated the direction of Renno's evasive movement. There was a mass intake of breath from the spectators as the black-tipped spear flew hard and true toward Renno's torso. At the last second Renno dropped to the ground. The spear whistled

over his head and fell just short of the spectators. He quickly
moved to the spear and snatched it up. A cheer rose from the
spectators, who expected to see how skilled this pale-skinned
one was with a Fulani weapon. But Renno broke the spear in
half over his knee and tossed it aside.

Now Noir was armed only with the curved blade. Renno
walked forward, war club at his side, his eyes drilling into
Noir's. He leaped back as Noir lunged and the curved blade
sought his belly.

"You think to kill me with a wooden club?" Noir laughed,
advancing swiftly. As the wicked blade slashed the air, it was
a metallic blur reflecting the sun. "This little man," Noir
roared, playing to the crowd, "would kill me with a stick of
wood."

Renno's teeth showed in a grim smile. He ducked under a
fearsome, arcing slash of the scimitar and swung the club
low, where it made contact solidly with Noir's thigh. The
impact staggered the larger man, and he fell back, holding the
scimitar at the ready.

"Do you have more respect now for this stick of wood?"
Renno inquired mildly.

Noir snarled and attacked, although he favored the leg that
had just been struck. Renno, going for the kill, leaped inside
the reach of the blade as it passed over him and was swinging
a killing blow at Noir's head when, with a grunt of effort, the
huge black man caught him on the side of the head with the
scimitar's backswing. Renno would have died had the razor
edge been properly positioned, but in his haste Noir had
turned his wrist. It was enough, however, to cause an explo-
sion of pain in Renno's skull and to dim his eyesight for a
moment. He backed away quickly, shaking his head, and fury
toward himself roared up in him for underestimating his
adversary.

"You scorn my war club," he said as Noir bore in toward

him. "So." He stuck the war club in his belt and drew out the stiletto, its good Toledo steel blade gleaming in the sun.

There was a roar of appreciation from the Fulani, for the man of magic faced a long, curved blade with only a short dagger.

"So you want to die more quickly," Noir said, leaping and lunging to send the point of his scimitar at Renno's chest. Almost disdainfully, Renno parried the long blade with the stiletto. The clash of steel on steel rang out. Noir swung with all his force, but the white Indian pulled in his hard-muscled midsection to let the blade pass within a fraction of an inch. Then with a wild roar—the fighting challenge of an enraged bear, a sound never heard by the Fulani—Renno leaped before the blade, probing and darting in, tempting Noir to strike, but avoiding the strike when it came, for he saw that Noir's arm was getting weak, that the blows no longer smote the air with their initial force.

"Old man," Renno taunted, standing insultingly motionless, the knife lowered beside his thigh, "it seems almost cruel to kill you, since you are so overmatched."

Noir roared his own rage and attacked, the scimitar slashing powerfully. And then with one quick movement Renno closed in, and the blow aimed at his neck faltered in midair as the Spanish stiletto tasted blood. One quick slash, and the blade bit deeply into and across the front of Noir's neck, severing the arteries. Twin spouts of blood gushed forth, the scimitar dropped from his hand, and the big man sank to the dust.

The gathered Fulani stood motionless, silent, stunned by the suddenness of Noir's death. And then there was a roar of approval. The king rose with great effort and raised his hands for silence.

"The gods of war have spoken," Zangara proclaimed. "Man of magic, your offer is accepted."

*   *   *

Bastian Vanderrenner had seen his hopes of a fortune bleed into the dust with Noir's lifeblood. And not only were his plans for great financial gain foiled, his very life was at stake; in spite of Zangara's claims of friendship, the fat man was the sole dispenser of life and death in his lands, and the gods "had proven" the Dutchman to be a liar who was trying to cheat the king out of his ivory treasure. During the tumultuous cheering of Renno's startling victory, Vanderrenner surreptitiously signaled his men to start working their way toward the city gates. He knew that his best chance for survival was to flee. Vanderrenner was prepared for departure, having purchased fine horses that were just outside the gates in the care of his own men.

What the slaver needed was a diversion while he made it safely to the gates. As Renno stood, stiletto at his side, his head bowed toward Noir's corpse, he seized his opportunity. He drew his pistol and took careful aim at Renno's heart. His finger tightened on the trigger.

The king was holding up his hands for silence. The pistol barked, but in that instant before the Dutchman's finger curled, a streak of movement raced toward him. He heard a snarl and saw, as the pistol boomed, the great, gaping mouth of a charging leopard.

Ese leaped directly into the path of the ball, which took him at very close range in the softness of his underchest. He was dead in midair, his heart punctured. A great cry of dismay went up as the leopard fell heavily.

Vanderrenner was fleeing, as were the men who had come with him, knocking aside women and children in their desperate escape.

"Dutchman!" Renno thundered as he set off in pursuit. El-i-chi and Tano raced after Vanderrenner's men. The shaman quickly cut down one man with his tomahawk, then caught another, knocking a musket aside as it fired. The ball narrowly missed him, and he buried his blade in the man's forehead.

Tano used his pistols to kill two of the Dutchman's men just as they were about to gain the gate. El-i-chi bellowed a war cry as three of them turned to face him. One of his pistols spoke, and a man was falling even as El-i-chi threw the tomahawk to lodge itself in another man's nose, driving bone shards into the man's brain for an instant death. The shaman threw himself to the ground and rolled as a musket ball spewed up dust within inches of his face, and then he was on his feet, knife in hand, closing to drive the blade deep and upward through the man's diaphragm.

Renno lost sight of the Dutchman in the crowd but pressed on toward the gate. As he sped down the narrow alleyways he saw nothing and heard only the roar of the crowd and two shots from behind him. His pounding feet slid in the slime of dumped household refuse, and he fell, skidded on the dirt, then leaped to his feet and ran on.

Vanderrenner saw Renno dart across an opening, so he adjusted his route of escape, approaching the city walls at a point where a palm tree grew close to the mud barricade. Chest heaving with exertion, Vanderrenner climbed the tree, swung to the top of the wall, and called out to one of the men watching the horses to bring his personal mount to a point under the wall. The men, having heard the shots from inside the city, were ready. The Dutchman vaulted directly into the saddle, kicked the horse into motion, and galloped to the west, quickly rounding a corner of the wall.

A Fulani woman had been killed by a wild shot fired by one of the Dutchman's fleeing lieutenants. She was placed in the square before the chief's home, and mourners surrounded her body and wailed. El-i-chi, Tano, Sokata, and Mingo came to stand before the king.

"The hirelings of the man who would have cheated you are dead," Tano said, translating for El-i-chi. "The man of magic now seeks the Dutchman himself."

"Go," the king ordered, "and tell your master that the Dutchman must be taken alive."

El-i-chi and Mingo went in search of Renno. At El-i-chi's request Tano stayed with Sokata. Mingo spotted Renno near the gate.

"He must still be inside Zaria," Renno told them. "He could not have beaten me to the gate."

"We'll find him," Mingo vowed. He had taken the scimitar dropped by Noir. "This blade thirsts for the Dutchman's blood, but first, what of my family?"

"Safe," Renno assured him, "aboard the *Seneca Warrior*."

"The gods are kind," Mingo breathed.

Fulani warriors joined the search, and soon Renno was convinced that somehow the Dutchman had slipped out of the city. He went back to the square and knelt beside the dead leopard. In Seneca he said, "Ese, thou wast sent to me by the manitous, and thou hast given thy life for me. Thou will not be forgotten, and in the Place across the River, thou shalt be greeted by one whose name I bear. Give him my honor for me, Brother, and await me there."

The king had the dead Fulani woman carried to her home. The other bodies were disposed of without similar consideration. The warriors gathered in small groups, and soon a dance of victory and war began, the men pleased to have witnessed such great events.

Renno and El-i-chi were given food and beer. Tano, Mingo, and Sokata were taken to slave quarters, and at first Renno was going to protest; but the purpose of his long journey had been accomplished, and it would only be a matter of time before El-i-chi and he and their "slaves" were on the trail back to the coast, where the *Seneca Warrior* would, he hoped, be waiting.

There were enough days left to make the trip at a comfortable pace, for only six weeks of the agreed-upon three months had expired to that date. The king was endlessly curious, and Renno left it up to El-i-chi, speaking English to Tano for translation to the king, to tell of their faraway home and of the great deeds of Renno of the Seneca. Only once did Renno smile, when El-i-chi, with youthful exuberance, told the king how his brother, the man of magic, had killed thousands of wild men and giant serpents in the far western deserts of their native land.

As evening came and the inventory of native beer decreased, the dancing was a thing of beauty as young girls joined in. The warriors forgot war and leaped with pure joy—joy of life, of the night, and of an exciting, memorable day. The king, at last tiring, showing no sign of intoxication although he had consumed gallons of beer, said that he would retire.

"This, my servant," he said, indicating the old juju man, "will show you to your quarters here in the chief's residence, where you are my honored guests. Nothing will be denied you."

The juju man rose, snapped his fingers, and pointed to four young girls dressed only in short loin coverings. Giggling, the girls followed as the juju man led Renno and El-i-chi through a maze of mud hallways to a spacious, airy room.

"For you," the juju said in the root language Renno could understand. He showed stumps of rotted teeth in a drooling grin and pushed the girls into the room ahead of the brothers.

"We thank you," Renno responded. "However, it is the command of our manitous, of the ghosts of our ancestors—"

"You communicate with the ghosts of your ancestors?" the juju man asked, eyes wide.

"It is their command that we keep ourselves pure for them," Renno said.

"I've never heard of that command," El-i-chi muttered in Seneca.

"And it is against the wishes of the ghosts of our ancestors for us to share a room with females," Renno added.

"How do you speak with these ghosts?" the old man wanted to know.

"Through prayer and fasting," Renno answered. He entered the room and gently escorted the puzzled young girls out the door, closing it behind them and in the face of the old man.

"Do we go tonight?" El-i-chi asked the sachem.

"No. To do so would see the entire Fulani nation on our heels."

"You have promised hundreds of muskets," El-i-chi said. "There were no more than two hundred on the *Warrior* originally, and Billy will have done his trading by the time we get back to the coast."

"We will talk of that tomorrow," Renno said, removing his weapons and placing them beside a bed of hides laid on a wooden pallet. "Now I sleep."

Rusog listened with an impassive face as Ena described her talk with Ah-wa-o and Ah-wa-o's complaint that the young war chief from the north, Tor-yo-ne, persisted in paying court to her in an overbearing manner when she had made it clear that she had no interest in his advances.

"It is time that I spoke with this Tor-yo-ne," Rusog agreed.

"You must tell him that Renno and only Renno is sachem."

"Renno speaks for himself," Rusog told her.

Ena trailed behind as Rusog walked up the slope toward the Seneca village. He carried no weapons of combat—only his knife in his belt, which was always with him, for it was not only a weapon but a useful tool. A group of young Seneca warriors had just returned from a successful hunt, and a crowd was gathering to help divide and distribute the meat. Rusog saw Tor-yo-ne there, standing with his hands locked behind him, a handsome young man, tall and straight and strong. After the venison was distributed, Rusog walked to stand beside Tor-yo-ne. Only those young warriors who had been on the hunt with Tor-yo-ne remained. Ena remained at a distance.

"It is necessary that we speak," Rusog began.

"It is an honor to speak with the chief of the Cherokee," the young warrior said.

"You are young and strong and a mighty hunter," Rusog commended. "All agree that it was good that you came with the people who followed you to join forces with your Seneca brothers."

"You honor me with your praise," Tor-yo-ne said.

"In the spirit of friendship and brotherhood between the Cherokee and the Seneca of the sachem Renno, I speak," Rusog continued. "I speak of the maiden Ah-wa-o, who is of my blood, being the daughter of my wife's mother."

Tor-yo-ne's face flushed with pleasure. Rusog saw by the young warrior's expression that his mission had been misunderstood. Tor-yo-ne obviously thought that the chief of the Cherokee had come to make marriage arrangements. There was nothing to do but forge ahead.

"She knows that Tor-yo-ne is a great war chief, but her heart is with another, and she does not welcome Tor-yo-ne's advances."

Tor-yo-ne's face froze.

"Then let the Rose tell that to Tor-yo-ne," he hissed.

"She is young and shy and modest, and she does not want to inflict hurt on you," Rusog explained.

Tor-yo-ne laughed. "Nor could she."

"Then it is settled," Rusog said, extending his arm to be taken, he thought, in a clasp of friendship. Instead Tor-yo-ne stared past him and kept his hands locked behind his back.

"To be rejected is enough. To be told of this rejection by a man who is not a Seneca is an insult," he grated.

Rusog's blood flared. *This young buck needs teaching*, he was thinking. "I offer the hand of friendship," he said, but to Ena's ears his words were a warning, cold and hard, and there was a harshness that she recognized as Rusog's fighting voice.

"This Seneca, unlike the great sachem Renno, does not need a Cherokee for a friend," Tor-yo-ne said, his voice full of contempt.

"So be it," Rusog said, controlling the urge to show this young cub why it was desirable to have a Cherokee for a friend and not an enemy. "Come not to me in time of need, Seneca."

"That day will never come when I need to call upon a Cherokee for aid," Tor-yo-ne retorted.

"Crawl back to the woman who gives you orders, Cherokee," taunted one of the young warriors, a newcomer of Tor-yo-ne's group who had heard it all.

Rusog whirled, and the knife at his belt appeared in his hand. "Try me not so severely, young one," he warned.

"If there is a challenge, Cherokee," Tor-yo-ne said, "it comes not from this young one."

"From you, then?"

"If that is your wish."

"It is," Rusog answered, crouching, giving Tor-yo-ne time to draw his own knife.

Ena was just running forward when, with a cry of dismay,

An-da emerged from behind a longhouse and threw herself between her brother and Rusog.

"Are you a mad dog?" she asked Tor-yo-ne. "Are you so ungrateful for the hospitality of our brothers and their allies the Cherokee that you would strike a blow against the chief of the Cherokee?"

"Stand aside, An-da," Tor-yo-ne fumed.

"Before you strike this man," An-da said, "your blade must pass through the flesh of your sister."

"Rusog," Ena said, standing beside An-da, "the girl is right. And this wild young one is not worth the price we would pay if you fought him—for of course you would kill him. Both of you, think."

Rusog's features relaxed almost imperceptibly. "This woman who does not give me orders but whose advice I value—for she has the blood of sachems and the great Renno—and your sister have saved your life." He put his knife back in its sheath, pushed both An-da and Ena aside, and took a step forward to lock his eyes on Tor-yo-ne's. "Renno is sachem of the Seneca."

An-da seized Tor-yo-ne's arm and clung to it, looking up pleadingly.

"My blood is now cooled," Tor-yo-ne said, turning to walk away.

"I would have killed him," Rusog growled as Ena and he walked back to their lodge.

"I know," she said. "Damn you, Renno, where are you?"

Chapter XI

The time of the new beginning came in the Seneca village, but the celebrations did not have the unrestrained joy that was usual for one of the most important Seneca festivals. The people seemed happy; the false faces were works of art and sometimes truly frightening; food was plentiful; and the elders' orations were full of wisdom and heartening words. But the schism that had been created by Tor-yo-ne was there, evident in the groupings of the people.

"This one," Tor-yo-ne whispered to a group of young warriors as Ha-ace was speaking, "is not of the royal line, and yet by default he is acting as sachem."

Tor-yo-ne's agitation was becoming more and more distressful to An-da, who, through her friendship with Ah-wa-o, had become fond of Toshabe and Ha-ace and many other

Seneca who had welcomed the newcomers. An-da had always been so proud of her brother, and since the death of her parents, he had been both father and mother to her. Such were his strength and bravery that no one dared slight An-da.

She was standing near her brother, beside Toshabe and Ah-wa-o, as Ha-ace took his turn at oration. She, like all the Seneca, loved to hear the older, wiser ones speak and enjoyed hearing the ancient legends, the praise of the Iroquois customs, and the stories of the power that had once belonged to the League of the Ho-de-no-sau-nee. An-da felt that Ha-ace was a fine Seneca orator. That Tor-yo-ne snickered and talked to his young followers during Ha-ace's oration made her angry. When Ha-ace had finished speaking, she pulled Tor-yo-ne aside.

"To show disrespect for a senior warrior of the Seneca does not become you," she said.

Tor-yo-ne frowned, but she was not frightened. He had never struck her, and she knew that he loved her. "You overstep your place," he growled.

"No, I do not. Sometimes one can be blind to his own mistakes, and for you to talk and laugh with your friends while a senior warrior speaks is a mistake—believe me."

"I give Ha-ace the respect he deserves as a senior warrior," Tor-yo-ne said. "But when he acts as sachem, he seeks honor that he has not earned."

"Oh, Tor-yo-ne," An-da pleaded, near tears, "why can't you be at peace with these good people?"

"Because," he retorted, "we are a leaderless people, stagnating when we should be making plans to counter the inevitable invasion of the whites into our lands. There is no sachem to guide us."

"But Renno—"

"I do not deny Renno's greatness or his right to lead,"

Tor-yo-ne interrupted. "I only try to make the others see that Renno is not here, that he may very well be dead."

"No," An-da said, shaking her head vehemently.

"Go to your little friends, An-da," Tor-yo-ne said.

She walked slowly, praying that Tor-yo-ne would cease his efforts to force the Seneca to choose a new sachem. She would not allow the suspicion that Renno was dead to enter her mind. She had never seen Renno, but she had heard so much about him that she felt that she knew him. She could picture him in her mind from the descriptions of Toshabe and Ah-wa-o—tall, with a body of perfect proportions, blond-streaked, light-brown hair, and utterly beautiful.

"I saw you talking with your brother," Toshabe said when An-da rejoined her.

"I share his shame," An-da said sadly. "I spoke to him of his disrespect."

"Little one," Toshabe soothed, "Tor-yo-ne's actions are his own, and you share no blame for them."

"It is hard for me to bear," An-da said, "when he speaks of the possibility of—of—"

"Of Renno's being dead?" Toshabe finished.

Toshabe was a woman of great experience. She had been married to Ghonkaba, who had been one of the finest judges of human nature that she'd ever known, and she had learned from him. She knew that words alone did not always express a person's true feelings, and she knew how to watch for other signs—for the lift of an eyebrow, the tilt of the mouth. For example, when An-da spoke of Renno or asked to be told one of the many tales of the sachem's bravery, a musing expression melted over her face, and the glaze of dreams came into her eyes.

To analyze An-da was not difficult; she was young, and the fires that led to mating were burning hotly in her. She had not yet chosen, although she suffered no lack of suitors. The girl had yet to experience that burning passion with which a woman knows that the man standing before her is the man for her; thus she was creating in her own mind the image of that man. In An-da's case she had chosen Renno as a dream object.

"Renno is not dead. The man who can kill Renno has not yet been born. He will come back," Toshabe promised. And then, in the same tone, "He will come back with his wife, who has hair the color of flame and is white, and to his children."

At the mention of Renno's wife, An-da's arched brows pulled together for a moment, confirming once again Toshabe's feeling that An-da was romanticizing Renno and building up the potential for hurt. "An-da," she instructed, "it is the time of the new beginning. Soon the sap rises in the growing things." She laughed. "And in the young." She made a hidden motion toward two young warriors who were studying An-da with great interest. Both had quite often been seen around the longhouse when An-da was present. "As witness those two," she added.

"They are young and foolish," An-da complained.

"They are at least two years older than you," Toshabe said. "There will come a time, An-da, when you will choose, and to choose wisely, you must become familiar with the available selection. Run along. Talk with those young, foolish ones and with many others. Get to know, and be able to recognize, the differences among men, so when the time comes to select your husband, you will be wise in their ways."

"I have no interest in such childish games," An-da scoffed.

Toshabe sighed. It was not the first time that a young maiden of the tribe had dreamed of Renno, and when he returned, he would be able to handle the situation without insult to An-da.

With spring Renna became the subject of conversation in the Johnson cabin in Knoxville.

"You know that I have promised to take her to the village with good weather," Roy said to his wife.

Nora was up and about but weak. She had been losing weight steadily for some time, and her once lush figure had vanished. Now she was stick thin, and her face was gaunt. She had aged, Roy observed sadly, and so quickly. He feared for her, and this concern was the only reason why he was not already on the trail to the village, for he, like the Seneca who were roaming the woodlands, felt the call of the new beginning.

"I'll have to take her soon," he said.

"A few more days," Nora pleaded. And because of her illness, Roy procrastinated.

Ena did not have the luxury of procrastination. Soon her time would come, and before she went into confinement for the birth, she was determined to have Renna in what she considered to be the child's rightful place.

"I am going to Knoxville," Ena told her mother.

Toshabe knew better than to issue a direct order to her willful daughter. Once Ena would have obeyed without question any command that came from her parents, but now she was a woman and the wife of a respected chief.

"There are two reasons why it would be best that you not go into Knoxville. The first one is obvious," Toshabe said, eyeing her daughter's midsection. "The second is that you are not known for your diplomacy in situations demanding tact, as this one would."

"The time for tact is past," Ena said.

"So we come full circle." Toshabe smiled. "We are back

in the time of our ancestors, when the great Ghonka raided a white settlement and kidnapped a white child.''

Ena laughed. "Mother, that is a farfetched comparison, and you know it. I'm not going to kidnap Renna. I plan only to bring her home.''

"You will go, no matter what I say,'' Toshabe said, "so I will go with you.''

"No,'' Ena responded. "Your place is here. As Renno's mother and chief matriarch, you are needed here to keep the peace, to see that this troublemaker from the north doesn't get out of hand.''

"What does Rusog say?''

Ena laughed. "You know Rusog.''

"Yes,'' Toshabe said, resigned. "What Ena wishes, Ena gets. Sometimes I think he goes too far in pampering you.''

"Ena gets what Ena wants only when it fits into Rusog's life,'' the young woman retorted. "You, of all people, would not make the mistake of thinking Rusog a man ruled by his wife. There are warriors and there are warriors, and then there are men like Rusog and Renno.''

"Of course,'' Toshabe said. She was counting on her fingers. Ena was huge.

Ena, seeing her mother's fingers moving, said, "No, I have not miscounted. There is plenty of time for me to go to Knoxville and back. The walk will do me good. Strong babies come from strong mothers.''

Ena was ready at first light next day. She would travel light, carrying only a bit of food and, of course, weapons. She was enough the warrior, in spite of her pregnancy, to feel undressed without her tomahawk and pistol, although she did leave behind her musket. Rusog was waiting outside when she emerged from the house. With him were two young Cherokee warriors.

"These will accompany you,'' Rusog said.

"I am not making up a war party," Ena told him. "I do not need these two."

Rusog's face was set. She sighed and resigned herself to being burdened with the two young men. "So," she said. "I will be back in no more than five days."

Rusog nodded. He wanted very much to talk her out of this trip, but that had already been tried. He wanted to go with her, but with the unsettled situation in the Seneca village, he felt that he should be in his place; Tor-yo-ne's continual agitation could explode into violence. He knew that Ena was capable of taking care of herself; she was as much at home in the wilderness as any man. Her pregnancy did not concern him, for the days were not too far past when an Indian woman, feeling the pangs of approaching birth, would simply fall out of a traveling column, squat beside the trail, give birth, and then catch up with the others.

"Well, then," Ena said, turning to face the east. She saw Se-quo-i hurrying toward them, dressed for travel.

"With your permission, Rusog," Se-quo-i said, "I will go with Ena."

"Good," Ena said. "You two, go back to your business. Se-quo-i is all the company I need."

"It is good," Rusog said, eyeing Se-quo-i's weapons. Both he and Ena were fond of Se-quo-i and respected his bravery and ability to fight, in spite of the time he spent with books and squiggles on paper.

Soon the village was left behind. Se-quo-i let his companion set the pace. They walked easily through a forest coming to new life. For Ena it was good to be away from the house and the village, in the wilderness that she loved. It was exhilarating to hear the birds, to feel the fresh breeze, and to smell the new, green growth. And it was good to feel her son—of this she was sure—kicking and plunging about inside her womb, as if he were determined to exercise his tiny limbs and to be strong and vital when his time came.

In the Fulani society, time meant little. Two days went by before Renno had an audience with Zangara, whose strength had apparently been sapped by all the excitement. When the sachem was invited to join Zangara on his platform, his strategy was already formulated. The plan was not without risk and he had included Tano in the planning. Because Renno's scheme involved the revelation of Tano's true identity, the young black was understandably nervous. The truth could result either in his swift death—for Beni and Fulani were deadly enemies—or his seizure by the Fulani to be offered for ransom to his half brother, the oba Eweka.

Renno sat cross-legged now on a pile of skins while the king heard several disputes among members of his tribe and dispensed his wisdom and justice in a great voice.

"My ship awaits," Renno said when Zangara turned to him. "Now we must work out the details of the exchange."

"My people will transport the ivory," Zangara offered. "And they will bring the muskets back."

"There will not, of course, be enough muskets aboard my ship to complete the trade," Renno said. "I beg the king's patience while my ship returns to England to get the proper number of muskets."

"This will take long," Zangara protested.

"The seasons will turn before the ship is once again in the waters of the Niger," Renno said.

"And meanwhile, the Beni, our enemies, will grow stronger," Zangara growled. "Perhaps, after all, I should have dealt with the Dutchman."

"The Dutchman, too, would have had to sail away to a place where muskets are made, for you yourself heard him say that so many muskets did not exist in Africa. In that, and that only, did he speak truth.''

"How many muskets will there be on your ship?" Zangara asked.

Renno shrugged. "When I left the ship, I did not know of your treasure. My men were instructed to trade the muskets for palm oil and valuables. It may be, great King, that all the muskets have already been sold." He was tensed, ready for an angry reaction. But he had become acquainted with the attitudes of these people, and he hoped that the African disregard for haste and indifference to time would prevail. He sighed in relief when the king spoke.

"The ivory will stay in my warehouse until your ship returns."

"That is fair," Renno agreed. "Now, great King, it is time that I left, to go to my ship so that it can sail as quickly as possible for your muskets."

"So be it," the king declared.

"And yet . . ." Renno said, starting to rise but lowering himself again.

"Yes?"

"May I tell the king a story?"

Zangara nodded with alacrity.

"I came to Africa for two reasons," the Seneca said. "First I came to gain back my property—the slave Mingo and his family. But there was another reason, which, I think, will interest the king."

"My ears are open," Zangara said.

"You know and have met in battle the Beni oba Eweka."

"I have met Eweka's men in battle."

"You know that Eweka is a bloody king, that he rules by fear, and that many are put to the ax and the knife in sacrifice to the Beni gods."

"So it is said."

"And so there is great discontent in the city and terrible fear among the tribes who live next to the Beni. In fact, when the Fulani send men to the coast to trade, do they not often have to fight their way through Beni war parties?"

"This is true," Zangara confirmed.

"Would it not benefit the Fulani to have allies in Benin?"

The king snorted in derision. "That is beyond the power of even the old gods."

"Perhaps not," Renno said. "Here is my story: Some time ago, when the old oba died in Benin, he had a young son named Tano, who was the heir to the throne. But he also had other sons, not born to his first wife, who were ambitious. One of these covetous sons was the chief priest of the powerful Order of the Hand. This half brother of Tano seized power by force and sold the rightful new oba into slavery."

The king leaned forward with great interest.

"I, Renno, freed Tano from slavery, from the Dutchman."

"The big man?" the king asked.

"Tano," Renno called, motioning. A very anxious Tano came forward and bowed his head to the king. "Before you, Zangara, is the rightful ruler of the city of Benin. Tano has learned the wisdom of the white man as well as the wisdom of Africa. Speak, Tano."

"Great King," Tano began. "This I have learned from the white man: They are many, and their weapons make the finest African warriors appear as vulnerable as children before them. Their purpose is to keep us fighting among ourselves. The white men encourage our tribal wars and arm us against each other, for if we bleed off our strength and lose our finest and bravest warriors fighting among ourselves, we are easy prey for the slavers. They care not for us but for slaves and ivory, and the products of our land and our soil."

Zangara was nodding.

"With my friend Renno, I go to Benin," Tano continued.

"There I will kill my half brother and assume my rightful place. As oba I will offer friendship to all my neighbors and halt the tribal warfare that makes us weak. United, we can stand against the white man's incursions, for eventually they will come to our lands not to trade and not to raid for slaves but to stay and build their houses and their cities and plant the fields."

"The white man cannot live long in our land," Zangara pointed out. "The old gods have given the white man the fevers and sickness that kill."

"So it was once in my own country," Renno interjected. "Our people were many, and we were strong. When the white man came he was few and weak, but he had cannon and muskets against our arrows and flint blades. At first he died of the fevers and the cold, but he continued to come in great numbers, and now many tribes of my people no longer exist."

Zangara frowned. "Why do you tell me all this, man of magic?"

"Because, Zangara, I would ask your help in restoring Tano to his throne," Renno answered.

"When we have muskets, we will kill Beni," the king proposed.

"*Now* is the time to strike," Renno urged. "It would be easier if we had many muskets, but we do not have them; however, Tano will find support in Benin. He will rally Beni of goodwill to his side, and there will be only a few—Eweka's private army—who will fight. Beni will kill Beni, and Tano will be elevated to his rightful place with or without your help, Zangara. But with your help, the act can be accomplished with more speed, and then you will have an ally on the throne in Benin."

"And the muskets?" Zangara wanted to know.

"When my ship returns to the Bight of Benin, the muskets will be in her."

"I will consider all this," Zangara proclaimed, making a sign of dismissal.

Lord Beaumont would have to wait for an heir to his title. Estrela gave birth to a healthy, six-pound girl who combined her mother's beauty with her father's coloring. Estrela came through the birthing well and was soon sitting up in bed, having a delightful time deciding, with William, what names would be given to the red-faced, squalling little bundle that lay beside them on the bed. Both parents advanced many possibilities but finally came to a compromise that, said William, put a heavy burden on the child.

Their daughter was to be christened Ena Estrela Elizabeth Huntington, in honor of the three women he admired most.

Beth had, of course, been present for the delivery, and she'd been a source of strength to William during the ordeal of waiting. But two days after the birth she was going back to London.

"I do wish you could stay," Estrela said, "but I understand that your introduction at court is very important."

"That it is. Besides, you are now the expert on child care," Beth said. "One cannot teach what one has not done."

"One day you'll have your own child," Estrela predicted. "A boy who has Renno's strength."

Beth felt a momentary sadness. She had never conceived— perhaps because she had so often been separated from Renno, perhaps because it was not meant to be. She smiled wistfully. "Someday," she agreed. "Your Ena Estrela Elizabeth can be his mentor and his friend."

"But you'd better hurry," Estrela warned, "if you want to have the first boy in this family."

Beth flushed both outwardly and inwardly, for Estrela's

suggestion had reminded her of the passion she felt in Renno's arms. "Now I must go."

"William has told me that you're certain of getting a trade agreement," Estrela said.

"Nothing is certain in this country until I have the documents in hand, signed and countersigned by all the proper people," Beth responded. "But yes, it seems that everyone who matters is now in agreement." She smiled ruefully. "And I've only had to pay bribes to nine different people, ranging from clerks to men whose names would be familiar to you."

"Come back soon."

"Of course." Beth bent to run one finger wonderingly over the downy softness of the tiny girl and to kiss Estrela on the cheek. As she rode away from Beaumont Hall, she felt a quick ripple of excitement, for being presented at court would enhance her status and help her business endeavors in the long run. Of course, she had to admit that she was going because she was curious, and blast it, for her pride. German George, King George III, was not exactly a social lion, and the ball that would follow on the very night of her presentation to the king and his court would be one of the few social occasions when the king and his family would be present.

Joffre was waiting for her at the town house. He rose when she came into the sitting room and advanced quickly to take her hand and brush it with his lips.

Control yourself, she thought when the touch of his lips sent a sensuous shiver through her. And as Joffre rambled on, detailing their schedule, she was thinking, *Renno, Renno, you have been gone far too long. It was you who taught me the uses of my body, the joy of love, and now, in your absence, my body mistakes my fondness for this man, who has helped me so much, for my love for you.*

She dressed and was taken to the palace, where, amid stiff

formality, she was presented as an astoundingly successful businesswoman whose shipping company was of great benefit to the Crown.

"Very impressive, Lady Huntington," said the pudgy, splendidly dressed, well-powdered man on the throne in his heavy German accent. "Will you be with us on this evening?"

"If it pleases Your Grace," Beth said with a little curtsy.

"Save a dance for me," the king requested. "I have heard of the American Indian who is your husband and would like to know more about him."

When it was done, she laughed about how seriously she had taken it, how nervous she'd been beforehand, and how quickly it had been over. "Will he really dance with me?" she asked after rejoining Joffre.

He shrugged. "I pray not, for I want every dance for myself."

"Don't be selfish, Joffre," she teased. "Let me be able to say that I have danced with the king of England."

She did dance with King George. He was heavy on his feet and mostly silent, and his breath smelled sour. She also danced with other men—peers of the realm, young and old—for in the dress that she'd had made for the royal ball Beth stood out as the most beautiful woman present. And she danced with Joffre, very much aware that he was a handsome man. She felt acutely sensitive to his slightest touch in a manner that would have concerned her had she not been so excited by her first royal ball.

"You belong here," Joffre intoned. "Not in some dingy warehouse office in a far and primitive land."

"My office is not dingy."

"It is shameful to waste your beauty on colonials." He smiled.

"Ex-colonials," she reminded him.

She was pleasantly tired when, with the departure of the king and the royal family, the orchestra played the final number and people began to leave the ballroom.

"I am famished," Joffre said. "Dancing is heavy work."

"If I've overtired you, I'm sorry," Beth teased. "There were other men who were eager to relieve you of your heavy duties."

"That I know too well." He laughed. "But now, food, food."

"Exactly," she said. "Food."

She had been to his spacious town house many times. There were always servants present, and she and Joffre were, after all, business associates; moreover he was an old family friend. She had never been in the town house so late, however. Only the butler was awake. He had prepared a tray of light food and delivered it quickly.

"That will be all," Joffre told him. "I won't keep you from your bed any longer."

With murmured thanks the butler retired. Beth found that she was ravenous and that the cockles and liver pâté were delicious and the wine a fine vintage. She was not at all sleepy, the excitement of the day and night still in her. When Joffre suggested that they take a midnight stroll in the garden behind the town house, she agreed. The night was pleasantly cool, and she was comfortable with only a lace shawl over her shoulders. Joffre guided her politely, his hand on her arm.

"Ah, the roses are beginning to bloom," she enthused as a delicious fragrance wafted to her.

"I'm rather proud of my roses," Joffre confided, plucking one and putting it in her hand. She sniffed it. "But their beauty fades when compared to yours," he added.

"Ah, our Englishman," she said, "so skilled with pretty words."

"You're English. English born, English still."

"I haven't renounced my citizenship," she said, "but—"

"I know, you're married to an American. Tell me, is he considered a citizen of the United States?"

"No, he is chief of an Indian nation."

"Nation, my dear?"

"So it's called," she explained. "Tribe. Joffre, he's an honored man, a friend of the most powerful men in the United States."

"I know. Yet he lives in the wilderness in what—a tepee?"

"No," she answered. "In a house."

"A proper house?"

"It is not a house of stone, not a massive pile like our manors."

"I see." He stopped and pulled her to face him, his hands on her arms.

"William says that you were always different," he said, "competitive with him, that you can shoot both rifle and bow as well as he."

"Better," she confessed, laughing.

"Beth," he said seriously, "haven't you had your adventure? You made a trek that most men would not have survived—two, actually. You see, I know the stories well, for I've pumped William about them. It must have been quite satisfying, since we English treat women as fragile things. You've proved that you can survive the worst that nature and savage tribes could thrust at you, then proved that you can outdo most men at business. But is that all you want out of life?"

"I have a very satisfactory life, thank you," she said.

"Your life should include great balls, such as the one tonight. You should travel to Paris and be extravagant at the Parisian dressmakers' shops, and to Venice, where the gondoliers would vie to have the honor of transporting you. You should be surrounded by beautiful things, not a wilderness.''

"Joffre—"

"No, let me speak," he interrupted. "These past months, my dear, have been both joy and torment for me—joy from being near you, feasting my eyes on your beauty—but a torment, knowing that you belong to another."

"Joffre, you go too far."

"I will say only one thing more: I pray, for your sake, that your Renno will return."

She gasped. To think otherwise was criminal.

"And yet, Africa . . ." He paused, and she could find no words. "I am one of the richest men in England, and my life would be complete if you should, in the future, allow me to take care of you, adore you, and surround you with the luxury you deserve."

It was, she knew, a contingency proposal, dependent on Renno's death, and anger flamed in her. "My husband will return. Now it's time that I go home."

But later, alone in her bed, her anger gone, she remembered the heady feeling of dancing and of being the focus for all eyes. She had so enjoyed the light repast after the ball. No liver pâté on the frontier, in a Seneca village. No roses, either. As she fell asleep, a repeating phrase lodged itself in her mind as she drifted away. "You belong here. . . . You belong here."

After consultation with his juju man, Zangara had made his decision. "Fifty men will carry tusks to your ship as a gesture of friendship," he announced. "Fifty will guard them. Two hundred warriors will go with you to Benin."

Thus was it settled. The balance of the ivory would be transported to the coast when next the *Seneca Warrior* came to the Bight of Benin with muskets for the Fulani.

"You will go to the coast with the ivory bearers," Renno told Mingo.

"Where Renno goes, there go I," Mingo said with stern formality.

"I have not saved you from the Dutchman to have you killed in another man's fight before you rejoin your family," Renno retorted.

"Nevertheless, I go with you, and if you try to prevent this, my friend, we must see who, after all, is the stronger." He grinned widely. "Although I will not kick and bite and scratch, as I do against larger opponents."

"If you want to remain the undefeated champion," El-i-chi advised, "don't try your good fortune, Mingo."

Now the city of Zaria was at their back. The group with ivory had already left them, arrowing toward the ship. Renno, his brother, and friends were mounted on good Fulani horses, and two hundred mounted Fulani warriors led by the king's son Chigi followed in a body. The trip back to the coast would be made in about half the time that it took them to reach Zaria. Then the manitous would decide the outcome of the venture at Benin, and there would still be time to join Billy the Pequot aboard the *Seneca Warrior*.

The sturdy horses carried them ever southward. There was work enough for El-i-chi and a contingent of warriors to kill enough game to keep two hundred ravenous travelers in fresh meat. Chigi often joined in the hunt, and El-i-chi gradually picked up enough Fulani words to have rudimentary conversations with the king's favorite son. The world was a wide place, El-i-chi knew, and filled with odd peoples. It was splendid to travel and see new lands and different peoples. The coming adventure at Benin would provide great stories as the years passed, as his children and grandchildren sat beside campfires or, he thought wryly, before a fireplace in a white man's house. Not for one moment did El-i-chi doubt that Renno and he would live to see Tano on his throne and return to their own country. And that last thought fired his blood, for home meant Ah-wa-o. She would be the mother of the children who, in later years, would tell and retell their father's adventures in Africa.

Chapter XII

The early Portuguese explorers who had pushed their frail ships past the hump of West Africa had been driven by the desire for prestige, gold, ivory, and personal riches. Being good Christians, however, there had been another inspiration for their dangerous travels: For centuries European Christians had awaited the discovery of the Kingdom of Prester John, a land ruled by an all-wise and righteous priest who, before the Second Coming of Christ, would join in one final, decisive holy war against the Muslims. It was believed that this paradise on earth, the Kingdom of Prester John, lay in the depths of the Dark Continent, guarded by the catoblepas, creatures whose heads were so heavy that their faces were always bent to the ground—which was, it seemed, a gift from God, since one glance from the eyes of a catoblepa was fatal to a mere mortal. There, too, were the blemmyae, whose eyes were in their chests, and the troglodytes, who lived in holes in the earth and survived by eating snakes.

In 1472, before Columbus first sighted an island in the Western Hemisphere, Ruy de Sequira came to a land of black, brackish water and dismal mangrove swamps. Rain fell in torrents that had no end, the mud flats stank, and insects made life a torment. The air was steamy, the sky was gray, and one's clothes were always wet. There, on the banks of the Benin River, the Portuguese saw black men naked to the waist with embroidered cotton kilts covering them to their knees. The natives wore round helmets of leather and basketry. Showing brightly against their bare chests were ornaments of red coral.

The leader of those black men who came to the Portuguese ship in canoes wore a heavy coral rope at his neck, and ornaments of carved ivory hung from his waist, along with decorative items of finely worked bronze. He also wore bronze anklets and bracelets and carried a white staff. It was apparent that his word was law. He was the oba of Benin, absolute ruler, giver of life and death to his people, and ancestor of the current oba, Eweka.

The *Seneca Warrior* was only the most recent of a long line of ships that had come to the Benin River to trade the products of European civilization for blue cotton cloth, ivory, kola nuts, and coral beads, for the skins of leopards and civet cats, and for the glands of the civet cat, which provided the strong, acrid aroma that gave body to perfumes.

Billy the Pequot was also offered slaves in exchange for the cargo of the *Warrior*, an offer he politely refused. He was content to load the *Warrior* with nonliving things, palm oil first on his priority list. To his pleasure he filled the holds of the *Warrior* without having to let the Beni merchants know that he had two hundred muskets available for trade; it would have been difficult for the ship's captain to explain his reluctance to put two hundred muskets into the hands of the oba's people. Billy was no moralizer, but he had heard stories about Benin, the City of Blood, and had seen the cruelty of the supervisors who drove the bearers bringing cargo to the ship. The casual lack of concern for human life was displayed clearly when a porter fell into the river and was attacked by a huge crocodile. The supervisor's laughter continued long after the porter, screaming in agony, was dragged under the black water. No attempt had been made to save him.

Billy stocked the *Warrior*'s larders with African yams; huge, earthy-looking potatoes covered by a coarse, gray skin; with squash, pumpkins, and deliciously hot peppers. The captain and his crew ate fresh okra, both boiled and fried, until everyone's stomach protruded. Billy found that he was not particularly fond of fried plantain, a bananalike fruit that had a starchy, mouth-drying taste. He welcomed freshly killed game—the small deer of the forests, bush pigs, and porcupine—but left the eating of the bush rat, snails, and tortoises to others.

The chief negotiator for the Benin merchants was of royal blood. The prince spoke enough English to boast of the greatness of the Benin Empire. Since Renno could not be expected back for weeks, Billy was in no hurry to leave the Benin River, and when Prince Ogane invited him to visit the city, he agreed.

Billy considered Benin society to be well organized, and it was evident that the oba's power extended into the jungles. When the prince's traveling party stayed the night in a native village, families were unceremoniously turned out of their huts to give the travelers shelter. Even on the jungle trails the organization was evident, for there were regularly spaced rest stops where jugs of water and drinking shells awaited travelers. Nearer the city the party passed through cleared areas where the farms were many and close together, the fields protected from flooding by levees and drained by ditches that extended into the distance.

The fabled wall of the City of Benin was a mound of earth twenty feet high and as thick, protected from the outside by a thorn-choked moat.

"Thousands of men worked to build this protection," Prince Ogane bragged. "No enemy can penetrate it."

The gates were guarded by the oba's soldiers, gleaming swords held under their left armpits. Inside, a dirt street forty yards wide was busy with people going about their daily chores. Chickens, goats, and children ran among the throngs. Broad streets led away from the entrance highway, dividing the town into sections. The houses that lined the surprisingly refuse-free streets were built of red mud and roofed with thatch. The red-mud walls of the houses had been lovingly polished until they gleamed.

"There is the house of one of royal blood," Prince Ogane said. "Only we are allowed to build to that height. The oba's palace is, of course, much higher."

Billy was a guest in one of Prince Ogane's several houses. Yams, fish, and soup flavored with palm oil and peppers were served on wooden platters. He saw examples of the art of the old empire, images in bronze, done quite nicely. The sea captain was not knowledgeable about art, but some of the older pieces appealed to him. In the house's shrine odd, African gods were worshiped. There were human figures of bronze and ivory on the altar, plus images of snakes, animals, and birds.

He was amazed to learn that most of the living area of the Beni house was open to the elements. Rainwater was drained into a pit in the courtyard and then away from the house through a pipe made of a hollowed palm-tree trunk. He slept in an open room on a woven mat laid over an earthen bench and awoke with the morning mist soaking his coverings and his clothing.

In the busy market he saw women dressed in gay colors, bearing huge burdens on their heads. The market offered ceramic pottery, leather items, and works in brass; but all ivory, slaves, skins of leopards, bronze, and coral were the oba's and the oba's alone.

The approach to the oba's palace was through several heavily guarded gates. It seemed to Billy that most of the space inside was taken up with shrines, each with its own courtyard. Most of the shrines were in honor of the oba's ancestors, and many had beautiful, ancient bronze heads on display. Ogane paused at one particular shrine, the Altar of the King's Hand. The Beni believed that the power to accomplish great or small tasks and especially to be fearsome in war came from within a man's hand. Atop the bronze altar two warriors squatted beside a symbolic figure of the oba. The circular, drumlike altar base had been carved with figures of gods, warriors, and past obas.

"I am of the Order of the Hand," Ogane said proudly. "We sit at the oba's right, and from his power we are strong. We guard his health, for only if the oba is healthy is the kingdom safe."

The oba's residence boasted a tower sixty feet high, adorned by a huge copper snake. Heavy pillars supported room after room in which bronze plaques told the history of the Benin Empire. Since all bronze and ivory belonged to the oba, the palace was filled with the works of the casters of bronze and the carvers of ivory.

Billy paused before a plaque that showed the oba as a god, swinging two leopards by the tail. Two older men, wearing coral necklaces and anklets and bronze and ivory bangles paused to look at Billy with overt curiosity. He was told that they were members of the oba's council and that the adorning items of their regalia were gifts from the oba.

"When will I be allowed to hold a conference with the oba?" Billy asked.

The prince made a sign of worship. "The god oba comes out of his dwelling only on very special occasions. You will not be allowed to speak with the god, but you are still fortunate, for you will be allowed to see him."

It was the time, Billy learned, for the blessing of the crops. The ceremony was scheduled to begin that morning, so the city was buzzing with activity. At midmorning the palace gates opened, and there issued forth a cavalcade of the oba's guards and servants, followed by men with drums and gongs and musicians with various types of horns, flutes, and fifes. There were women shaking calabashes, gourds into which seeds or pebbles had been inserted.

A hush fell over the throngs when the oba himself appeared. He was an obese man, six feet tall, and from his pointed crown of coral to the cotton skirts that hung to hide his feet—this custom had been originated by a previous oba who, according to legend, had had fish for feet—he was resplendent. Coral necklaces extended from his chin to his shoulders. His huge torso was decked with masses of bronze and ivory pendants, and his arms were laden with ivory and bronze bangles. In his hand he carried the white wand of office. He was supported on both sides by palace retainers naked to the waist; at his side walked two strongmen wearing only bronze anklets and carrying ornately carved swords—the wide-bladed Beni *ada*—and odd knives that, Ogane said, were *eben*, ceremonial execution knives.

As the oba passed, a moan went up from the crowd. Billy looked at Ogane questioningly. "The executioner," Ogane explained, indicating a huge warrior surrounded by younger men carrying the *ebere,* odd weapons much like flattened spears.

And around the entire procession leaped and cavorted dwarves, almost-nude women, and deaf-mutes kept by the oba for his amusement.

"The god's wives," said Ogane as a group of women began to pass.

The oba's wives wore coral pieces worked into their ornate hairstyles, necklaces, armlets, and anklets, and copper rings on their fingers. Their faces were painted with white and yellow clay. Their dresses were of fine cotton made into almost dizzying patterns by the use of different colors.

Billy did not have to be told that those who followed the women were soldiers. The officers, wrapped in red cloaks, were mounted on horses. They wore fur-trimmed caps and necklaces of animal teeth. The soldiers were very impressive— bare chested, strong, young, armed with spear and bow, and carrying the ornate Beni shield. Billy did not need to ask about the hundred men and women who were being escorted by the soldiers, for they were gagged and had their arms tied behind their backs.

"They who will, this day, go to serve their master," Ogane explained, nodding toward them.

So many? Billy thought.

"Theirs will be the good death," Ogane continued, "for with their blood the oba will be repurified, and with their blood the god will bless the crops and make them fruitful."

The ceremony took place in the great square. The oba, seated on a portable throne, nodded for the sacrifices to begin. A man whose hands were bound and whose mouth was gagged securely was shoved forward by soldiers. The executioner attacked him with a bronze club, and within moments the victim was lying in the dirt, brain matter oozing from his broken head. The executioner decapitated the corpse with one of the odd bronze weapons, and a murmur of approval surged up from the crowd.

"This man," Ogane said, "has gone to join Olokun, the god of wealth and fertility."

The priests were now draining the victim's blood into a bronze pan. When the pan was half-full, the holy men approached the oba with much bowing and scraping, then delicately dipped their fingers into the hot, sweet-smelling blood to sprinkle it liberally over his clothing. The oba, the giver of life and death, sat with his eyes forward and allowed himself to be covered with blood as a roar of approval went up from the crowd.

"Now the crops will be plentiful," Ogane predicted.

One by one a hundred victims went to their death. The manner of execution varied, and in each case the victim seemed calm, willing to die without question. Death came by sword or spear, by knife or club, but the finale was always the same—the neck of the victim severed, the head displayed to the crowd, the blood collected. Women sang. Priests chanted. The oba sat fatly on his throne, his garments drenched with blood, his gaze to the distance, never looking at the victims. As the day drew on, Billy was surfeited with death, sick to his stomach from the reek of the blood that poured out in torrents. When at last he was led away from the square by Prince Ogane, the entire city seemed to have the stink of blood, the stench of death.

Now Billy had only one goal, to be away from the City of Blood, to get out of this place of senseless murder. He quickly concluded his trading, made ceremonious farewells to his host the prince, and then felt the breeze of motion on his face as the *Seneca Warrior* made for the open sea.

Billy had no knowledge of the early Portuguese explorers or their hope of finding the Kingdom of Prester John; but had he known, he would have said that instead of an earthly paradise rich in gold, the Portuguese—and he, centuries later— had found only sodden air, gray skies, biting insects, and a society where the value of a human life had totally been debased, a society whose past greatness had, most probably, been nothing but a myth. There was no gold, only bronze. There was no Eden on earth, only a rain-soaked jungle. There was no holy, all-wise ruler, only a blood-drenched, obese oba who sent his soldiers into the city after the blessing of the crops to enforce a curfew, cutting down any who had the bad luck to be on the streets.

Billy did not know that at that very moment Renno was traveling south, with Benin as his destination and the deposing of the oba his intention. Had he known, he would have stayed there in the Benin River to warn Renno that Eweka's rule was buttressed by a well-trained and heavily armed personal army kept happy by gifts, drink, and women.

Renno was soon to learn that the city's soldiers were not afraid of a fight. El-i-chi was scout on that day. The party had been traveling for weeks and had come back through rolling, wooded hills into the fringe of the jungle. El-i-chi saw the Beni troop, forty strong, from a safe distance and, dismounting, crept forward. He saw strong black men who carried elephant-hide or woven, oblong shields and handled their spears and bows as if they knew how to use them. A short, broad-bladed sword swung from the left arm of each Benin soldier. The group was taking a break, eating, drinking, talking, and laughing.

When the troop of forty soldiers took up the march again, they moved with lithe grace, following a red-cloaked officer who carried a battle standard of bronze topped by a carved bird of prey.

El-i-chi thumbed the cutting edge of his tomahawk, esti- mating the strength that would be required to send the blade through the leather helmet of a Beni soldier. Flaps from the helmets came down to protect the ears, and the material looked tough. He decided he'd better wait to find out. He rejoined the column and informed Renno and Chigi that there were Beni ahead.

"Now it begins," Chigi said warily.

"It is time to fight now?" El-i-chi asked.

Renno grinned. Was his brother, at last, learning patience and transcending the youthful desire to count coup and attack the enemy whenever and wherever he appeared?

"My brother is concerned that word of our coming might get back to the city," Renno told Chigi.

"El-i-chi states that there are only forty," Chigi said. "We can be certain that not one lives to carry the message."

Renno nodded. It would not do to have an armed Beni force to their rear. He went ahead to survey the area. The Beni troop was apparently a routine patrol, moving northward slowly, not expecting trouble. He positioned his own forces and the Fulani warriors around an opening in the forest where the tall grass grew thickly. "Let no man move until the Beni are well into the clearing," he instructed Chigi, who grimly passed the orders along to his group leaders.

The Beni marched into the clearing as if they owned the earth, and indeed they had owned that portion of it for centuries, with incursions into it punished by arrow and blade and spearpoint. When the time was right, Renno gave the signal, the roar of a bear, and before the Beni soldiers could make sense of the situation, the Fulani were among them with their great, curved blades. El-i-chi, whooping, led Mingo and Tano into the fray.

When it was over, the dead were piled deeply. Renno had stood back with Sokata, for there were more than enough Fulani to do the job. To Chigi's embarrassment, more Fulani than Beni were dead. Almost sixty of the two hundred men had gone down before the weapons of the greatly outnumbered Beni, and many more had been wounded.

"They fought well, those," Mingo commended, coming to stand, panting, beside Renno. Blood not his own stained his skin.

"They were members of the oba's own army," Tano told them, having examined the shields of the fallen men.

"And how many of these can we expect to find in the city?" Renno asked.

"In my father's time, there were two thousand men in the Order of the Hand," Tano replied.

Chigi, also breathing hard from the ambush, had come up in time to hear. "We cannot fight two thousand men like these."

Renno eyed him and saw a coward. "We have known that we would not be able to take a fortified city—not with two hundred men, not with two thousand."

"Will the man of magic spirit us over the walls and into the oba's bedchamber, then?" Chigi asked.

"Once in the dawn of time," Renno said, "when there were many heroes, a queen was stolen, and a great empire organized to rescue her. Unfortunately, they found the walls of the city, a city called Troy, to be too strong and the defenders too capable. So a wise man built a huge horse of wood, placed soldiers inside, and left it, seemingly as a gift, for Troy's defenders. Thinking that they had driven off the attackers, the defenders took the wooden horse inside the walls, accepting it as tribute from the defeated enemy. In the dark of night, the soldiers came out of the wooden horse and with guile opened the gates that had been too strong to open by force. The city fell and was burned."

"That is a fine story," Chigi said. "The man of magic, then, has a plan to defeat the city of Benin by guile?"

"So," Renno said, moving away to take a closer look at the fallen Beni. Fulani men were busy looting the corpses of weapons and ornaments. He went among the Fulani, taking stock of the numbers of men who, because of their wounds, would be of no use or limited use. He found that no more than one hundred warriors would be at full strength the morning after the battle with only forty Beni soldiers.

El-i-chi found him standing alone, staring southward toward the dense jungle.

"Just what is this plan that will use guile instead of force?" El-i-chi asked.

Renno's face relaxed into a wry smile. "The manitous have not yet revealed it to me."

"Man of magic," El-i-chi said, imitating Chigi's thick accent, "I have not lost confidence in you, but I must admit that my confidence is being strained. Take a Fulani off horseback, and he is no match for those who died this day."

"But El-i-chi is the match for any number of Beni," Renno said. "So I have no doubts."

Sususu, one of the many wives of Eweka, oba of Benin, had marched dutifully in the parade of women. She did not rate a position near the front to watch the good deaths, for she was not among the comely women in Eweka's collection. She had become a wife of Eweka because her father had been a friend of the old oba and because Eweka had honored his father's pledge even after the old oba's death. The one night that Sususu had spent with Eweka had produced a son who had grown tall and strong and was sly enough to remain in Eweka's favor from the time he was a winningly friendly toddler. It was a source of pride to Sususu to know that her son, Prince Ogane, now a young adult who bore a proud, old Beni name, was trusted enough by Eweka to be his chief trade representative.

Curfew had come to the city, and the oba's men were in the streets, slaying anyone encountered, when Ogane came to his mother's quarters in the palace for his weekly visit.

"Today I saw you," Ogane said. "You were far to the rear. Others who have less honor were before you."

"My position is of no concern," Sususu said. "I saw you, my son, and your place was near the oba. For that I am thankful."

"It is possible to be placed too near the oba," Ogane said. "Two of those who died the good death today were of the court."

"But it is an honor to die thus," Sususu pointed out.

"Would you feel the same if I were given that honor?" Ogane asked.

Sususu's heart lurched. "But you are his son."

"Where, then, is Narawa, the first son, who was next in line for the throne of Benin?"

"I thank all the gods, my dear, that you are not in line for the throne." That was Sususu's way of acknowledging that being perceived as a rival to Eweka was dangerous. Narawa was not the only son of Eweka who had mysteriously ceased to exist. One day Narawa was in the city, a proud, strong young man. The next he was gone, and no one seemed to know what had happened. His body had not appeared in the death pits, but that did not mean he was alive; many corpses were transported after the sacrifices to be made a part of the levees in the fields or to help fill in marshy places on the roads to and from the city.

"There are times, Mother, when I wish that you had been a simple countrywoman, and I, your son, a man who works his fields in peace far from this City of Blood."

"Hush," Sususu warned. "Such talk is blasphemy."

"Against the god?" Ogane asked.

"He has ears," Sususu whispered.

"Even here?" He looked around his mother's well-furnished rooms. They were airy and open.

"You have position," she reminded him. "You do valuable work and are not a danger to him. Be happy. Take the gifts he gives you; take the women and enjoy their charms. For me it is enough to know that you are my son and a man among men."

"A man who cringes in the presence of the god," Ogane admitted. Suddenly he laughed and seized his mother to lift her considerable weight from the floor and whirl her around. "But that is enough seriousness! Tonight we feast and drink— just the two of us."

Sususu had cooked his favorite dishes and had obtained a large jug of beer. The meal was a pleasant one, and they talked of small things—of the new crops and the woman who was the current favorite of the oba—how she was courting disaster because she dared to be too familiar with the god. It was growing late, and both were feeling the effects of the beer when there came a call from outside the rooms. Ogane reached for his short sword and tiptoed to peer into the darkness.

"Ogane."

He heard his name hoarsely whispered and recognized the voice as Baro's, a young man of royal blood but not in the oba's direct line.

"You must not go out at this time of night," Sususu told her son.

"It's only Baro," he reassured her. "I will speak with him. I imagine that he has been caught unawares after the curfew because of calling on a wife not his own."

Ogane stepped into the darkness, and Baro seized his arm.

"You did not come," Baro hissed.

"I told you that I wanted no part of it," Ogane told him. "Now, Baro, it is late, and if you're caught in the streets—"

"You were needed there tonight, Ogane. We had counted on you. We cannot succeed without you."

"I am not sure that I favor your success," Ogane said. "He is god, after all."

"Who depopulates the city of its finest men with his continual bloodlettings," Baro seethed. "There are rumors, Ogane, that the Fulani are arming to attack us."

"There are always such rumors," Ogane scoffed. "Year after year there are such rumors, and yet, when the Fulani come, we kill them."

"Who? With what?" Baro challenged. "He has, in his fear of his own people, disarmed most."

"Baro, I remind you that I am one of the oba's own, and when it comes to a fight with the Fulani, we will fight and prove victorious."

"As oba, my friend, you could change much."

For the first time it had been spoken. For months Baro and others had been hinting, testing for Ogane's convictions. The words sent a chill through Ogane, and he clamped his hand over his friend's mouth. "Never, *never* say such a thing again."

"Ogane, with you, with your help, we can rid ourselves of this bloody monster," Baro pleaded. "There is not another, among all the oba's sons, who could win the support of the people. You must—"

"I must go back to my mother, now, this moment, for this is the night of the week that I promise her, and you are depriving her of that time."

"Think, Ogane. Think!"

"I have done so much of that that my head aches from it. Although I will not sleep at my mother's house tonight, there is a bed here for you. You are welcome."

"I can make it home," Baro replied, and was gone, a dark wraith moving through the night.

"And what said Baro?" Sususu asked when Ogane was seated again, beer bowl cradled in his hands.

He smiled. "It was a woman, as I had thought."

Sususu put her hand on her son's arm. "You don't have to be cautious with me. It is time you know that it was I who planted the idea in Baro and in the others."

Ogane gasped, then coughed on his beer.

"My son, once we were great. Our empire extended forever, and obas knew how to govern and to improve the lot of the people while protecting them against the raids of wild tribes. My father never tired of telling me of this past glory, and he himself tried to convince Eweka's father that the killing of one's own people could only be divisive. To be great again, the city of Benin must extend benevolent protection to the people of the jungle villages and work for the good of all."

"You walk in quicksand," Ogane warned.

"But you can lead us all through," Sususu urged. "What did you tell Baro?"

"I told him that I wanted no part of it."

"And what did he say to that?"

"He asked me to think," Ogane said.

"Yes, think," she said. "Now I will give you something more to think about. Do you remember Sokata?"

Ogane jerked his face toward his mother.

"The love of your childhood, the sweetheart of your youth. Do you remember how her voice tinkled like brass bells when she laughed?"

"Sokata is dead."

"Or wife to a jungle man, slaving in the fields. How did she come to such a fate?"

Ogane was silent.

"I will tell you. Her father displeased the oba. He was too well liked, too powerful, and too rich. So the oba organized a war party and sent it, undermanned, to certain destruction at the hands of Idah warriors.''

"How can you know this?''

"Because when I was younger and more comely, the man who arranged the massacre was often in my bed.''

Ogane's jaw dropped.

"I was in no danger because of that,'' Sususu said. "The oba, your father, had no use for me. The point is, Ogane, that Sokata, her father, and her mother were sacrificed as surely as if they'd felt the executioner's blade on their necks. Now will you think upon Baro's words?''

Ogane drained his bowl and weakly held it out for more. His mother had asked if he remembered Sokata. Not one day went by that he didn't think of her—so young, so beautiful, so full of life. He had only been a boy when Sokata's father fell in battle. Her body had not been recovered with those of her parents, and it was assumed that she'd been captured by the Idahs. A boy could do nothing about that, for the jungle was large and the Idahs many. But a boy could remember. And now he had been told the painful news that the girl he loved had deliberately been sent to her death or into slavery by the oba.

"You will not have to wield the knife yourself,'' Sususu softly whispered. "You might be asked to arrange the circumstances, but your hands will not be soiled by your father's blood. Then, once he is dead—''

"And the others? All the sons of Eweka who stand before me in line for the throne?''

"That, too, will have been arranged,'' she answered.

So the oba was to die, along with many sons. The idea was too overwhelming for his beer-dazed brain. He shook his head. "I will think,'' he said as he slipped out the door, "but not tonight. Tonight there is a nest of wild bees in my head, and I just want to go home.''

*　　*　　*

Renno stood hidden in trees and looked out across culti-vated fields to the high, thick mud walls of Benin. Chigi, on another path, had also moved to the edge of the jungle to look at the city. Women worked the fields; groups of travelers carrying goods moved up the main road toward the city; armed soldiers were visible atop the wall and at the gates. At his side El-i-chi grunted.

"The moat is deep," Renno remarked.

"There's one way in," El-i-chi said. "The gate."

"I have no wooden horse in which to smuggle Fulani warriors into the city," Renno said, "and no surprise force to rush in when the gates are opened."

"So," El-i-chi said soberly, "we have seen this City of Blood, and now it is time to tell Tano and Sokata that they will be happier in the land of the Fulani or with Mingo and Uanna in Jamaica."

Renno, without comment, led the way back to the small advance camp in the midst of the jungle where Tano, Mingo, and Sokata waited.

"The walls are strong," Tano said when Renno, El-i-chi, and Chigi sat down before the small fire.

"It will take the might of the Fulani nation, and mus-kets," Chigi said. "But my friends, this trip has not been wasted, for now I know the country, and I have seen the walls of Benin. I can tell my father and his war leaders the difficulties we will face."

"I go into the city," Tano decided. "I do not ask that you, my friends, go with me."

"I go with you," Sokata told him.

"Somehow I will penetrate Eweka's stronghold, his pal-ace, and I will kill him," Tano vowed.

"What happens to you then?" El-i-chi asked.

Tano shrugged.

"Revenge is not complete if one dies in its accomplishment," El-i-chi said. "Come back with us to our homeland. We have noticed, Tano, that you and Sokata have become close. The two of you come with us, or Mingo and his wife will find a home for you in Jamaica."

"There is a place for my little friend," Mingo boomed, slapping Tano on the shoulder.

"My place is there," Tano said, pointing toward the city.

"Perhaps we will not die," Sokata ventured. "There were those, my father among them, who thought that Benin should be rid of Eweka."

"Your father is dead," El-i-chi said.

"But there were others. I remember them. Some will be old now, but they could tell us if there are still people who would like to see the city freed of Eweka's tyranny. I will go into Benin and seek out those I remember." Sokata rose as if to put the thought into action at that moment, only to be caught around the ankle by Tano.

"Your idea is worthy," he said, "but you will not go alone." He pulled her to sit beside him. "Give us this night, Renno. If we are not back or have not sent word by midday tomorrow, go to your ship and sail back to your own people, for we will be dead."

"I am not good at waiting," Renno said, rising.

Tano cast a stricken look at El-i-chi, who was as puzzled as he.

"A party of three—two men and one woman—from the outlying villages, coming to see the great city . . . ?" Renno suggested.

"But your skin is white," Tano objected.

Renno bent, took charcoal from the fire, rubbed the back of his hand, and held it out. "I will be one of you."

"Unless it rains and washes off the charcoal," El-i-chi

said, amused at himself for thinking that Renno would give up on a goal.

Sokata, giggling, helped to blacken Renno's skin and hair. She insisted on covering his entire body. "Do not squirm so," she admonished. "When I was only a child, I bathed my uncle's boy-children."

"Do not squirm so, Renno," El-i-chi teased in a high-pitched voice, guffawing as Sokata reached into private places and rubbed vigorously with charcoal.

Renno would not have passed close inspection, but from a distance his skin was as black as Tano's. When he was dressed in a kilt, taken in one quick raid by Tano while Renno was being blackened, he was passable, Tano admitted, if they went into the city just at dusk, as planned, and were not caught there in the daylight.

"You cannot, of course, carry firearms or the longbow," El-i-chi said. "Or the club of our ancestor."

Renno hid the Spanish stiletto under his kilt, hefted a Beni spear and short sword, and felt naked without either toma-hawk or club. He started to hand the war club to El-i-chi for safekeeping, but the club grew hot in his hand. He nodded, as if speaking to someone or something unseen. "I will take the club," he announced. He pulled El-i-chi to one side.

"Is it just curiosity that inspires you to see this City of Blood?" the shaman asked.

Renno smiled. "There is that." He put his hands on his brother's shoulders. "I will tell Chigi to rejoin his warriors and to take them back to the land of the Fulani. You and Mingo will wait tonight, through tomorrow, and until the sun rises after another night. It may be that we will not be able to return tonight, and if not, we would have to hide during the day. If I am not back by dawn of the second night, go to the ship. And then home."

"I would not abandon you," El-i-chi said, his chin set firmly.

"This I order as your sachem. Our people must not be left leaderless. We will not have two of Ghonkaba's blood die in Africa. You will go when I have told you to go, and you will hurry back to our people and take your place as the heir of Ghonkaba."

"It will be so," El-i-chi agreed.

Chapter XIII

Renno waited until the road leading to the city's gates
was clear. He clasped El-i-chi's arm and said, "You
are on your honor," to remind him of his promise to leave at
the appointed time, even if Renno had not returned. El-i-chi
nodded. The sachem stepped out into the road with Sokata
and Tano, and the three started walking quickly toward the
city, for it was growing late. The sudden darkness that followed the sun's setting would soon be upon them, and with
darkness the gate would be closed. They overtook a small
group of hurrying Beni, merged with them, and passed through
the gate without incident.

"Things have not changed," Sokata said, looking around.
"Come, this way."

Renno was memorizing every aspect of the city as they

strode down the wide, main street, turned, and entered a neighborhood of mud-brick dwellings. The city was large, and there were many people, but only a few of the oba's uniformed soldiers were in evidence. As darkness came, the houses showed cheery lights, and there was the aroma of food cooking. Sokata was setting a fast pace. When she came to the corner of a narrow street, she paused.

"That was the house of my mother's brother, my uncle," she said, pointing to a red-mud house that was like all the others. "Perhaps you should hide here, in the shadows, for it has been many years, and although the city has not changed . . ." She paused, but Renno knew what she was thinking. "Soon the soldiers will be patrolling the streets. They kill without asking questions."

"Go," Renno urged. "Be careful. If your uncle no longer lives in the house, say that you have made a mistake and come back here quickly."

The girl ran down the street and disappeared from view when she went into the entry area of the house. Renno heard low voices, and then there was silence. The minutes passed. No longer were there people on the streets. A dog barked nearby.

"She has been gone too long," Tano grated. "I'm going after her."

"Wait a few more minutes," Renno said.

They stood without talking. Renno, the war club in his hand, tensed when he heard footsteps approaching from the direction of the main street. He placed a warning hand on Tano's shoulders, but Tano, too, had heard.

Now Renno could hear the voices of the men who were approaching. "Four soldiers," he whispered, drawing Tano back as far as possible into the shadows of a mud house, his club ready, the stiletto in his left hand. The oba's guards passed the sheltered alcove, talking in low voices. One laughed as they rounded the corner. Again all was quiet. It was minutes longer before Renno heard the sound of bare feet running and saw Sokata emerge from the darkness. He made a hissing sound, and she came to them.

"Quickly," she whispered.

They ran down the street and into the house of Sokata's uncle. He was an old man, his kinky hair white with the honor of years. He led them into a room without windows and lit an oil lamp, then picked it up and held it next to Tano's face, leaning close to examine the young man's features.

"Yes," he declared. "You have the face of your father."

"This is my uncle Xeno," Sokata said.

"My niece's father spoke against selling you into slavery," Xeno said. "For that he is dead."

"I have come to set right all the past wrongs," Tano announced, standing very erect, his chin high.

"And to do this you have one young girl and one warrior from far away?" Xeno asked, chuckling. Then he sobered. "But great things have begun from less. Are you hungry?"

Tano shook his head. "Only for news of conditions here. Sokata said that when she lived here, there were those who would see an end to this oba's excesses."

Xeno nodded. "There are still those who would welcome a change."

"Would they rally to the true heir to the throne?" Tano asked.

The old man shrugged. "They would rally with greater enthusiasm if the heir to the throne had an army to match that of the oba."

"No army is needed," Tano said. "When Eweka is dead, the army will cast its support to the victor."

"Or to one of the oba's many sons," the uncle retorted.

The old man sat down, put his chin in his hands, and was

silent for a long time. When he looked up, his eyes were hard. "Show me your loins."

Renno was puzzled by this, especially when Tano unquestioningly removed his kilt and bared himself. He lifted his genitals aside and spread his legs, putting one foot flat on the tabletop. There, on the inside of his thigh, high up, was a scar, white against his black skin, the outline of a leaping leopard. Renno was amused by Sokata, who had initially turned her eyes away from Tano's nakedness and then had stared in fascination at the mass of flesh held aside in his hand.

The old man leaned close to examine the work. He nodded. "If one dared, he could have the royal emblem cut into his skin thus, but this is the work of the royal juju, for there is his secret mark. You are indeed a firstborn heir to the throne of Benin." He fell to his knees, and Tano, a bit uneasy, put himself back together and helped the old man to his feet.

"You will help us, then?" Tano asked.

"May the gods help us all," Xeno said fervently. "You will eat now. The streets are not safe in the early night, but after midnight, the guards relax and drink beer. Then we will talk with others."

When the time came, Sokata was left behind in her uncle's house as Xeno led Renno and Tano into the night, moving with great care from shadow to shadow until, ahead, there was a taller residence—the home of a man of royal blood. Xeno stood before a door and made a small sound, and within seconds the door was opened. Inside, in a windowless room, a lamp was lit and Renno saw a strong man who was introduced as Baro.

"Show him," Xeno told Tano, and the ceremony of showing the leaping leopard high inside Tano's groin was repeated.

"We played together when we were children," Baro said, bowing to Tano.

"It was the old oba's wish that this one, this Tano, follow him to the throne," Xeno said.

"Those who stand with me now will be at my right hand when I am in my deserved place," Tano promised.

"Since the disappearance of the first son," Xeno said, "no man save Eweka wears the leopard."

"It is so," Baro confirmed. "But what of Ogane? He is the key to our plans, for only he can gain access to the palace."

"I have found Ogane to be sensible," Xeno said. He sighed. "But when great power is at stake, even a sensible man can lose his bearings."

"Without him we are helpless," Baro said. "Let me talk with him. Wait here, and I will go to him."

"Hold," Xeno said, then turned to Tano. "What I am about to suggest will be dangerous."

"I will listen," Tano said.

"Ogane is a lesser son of the oba. Of all Eweka's sons he is the most honorable, and for a long time we have been trying to enlist his participation in our plan to rid Benin of Eweka. Ogane has been reluctant, and it is my guess that in his heart he does not wish to be oba—especially at the expense of one who is his father. As I have said, it is impossible to predict the actions of any man when great power and wealth are at stake, so I propose to put you face-to-face with Ogane. He does not wear the royal leopard. If he is the man I think he is, he will accept you as the rightful heir."

"And if not?" Renno asked.

Baro shrugged. "Then perhaps we will all be dead."

"Before we go further, I would know more of this Tano,"

Xeno requested. "I know that Ogane would be a good man on the throne; I know nothing about you."

"As a child I questioned my father about the practice of sacrificing the best citizens of our city and our country," Tano offered. "Since being sold into slavery, I have traveled far and have seen the works of the white man and known his system of government." He held up one hand. "The white man cries freedom for his own but enslaves men of black skin. Yet many whites are wise. I would combine the wisdom of the white race with the traditions of our people. If it is necessary to appease the gods with human blood, that blood would be the blood of captured enemies, not our own people. No more would Beni be sold into slavery for some small offense against the oba. I know that I could not change everything overnight, but by trade with the whites I would improve the lot of all Beni citizens. I would extend the protection of the army of the city to the outlying villages and thus begin to reconstruct the empire of our ancestors."

"Well said," Xeno approved. "What say you, Baro?"

"Words come easily," Baro said.

Tano drew his knife, held up his arm, and made a short slash. Blood welled up. He smeared his blood onto his forehead. "By this blood oath I bind myself to you, Xeno, and to you, Baro. I swear by the royal blood of Benin that I will heed your advice, that the wanton killing of Beni will cease, and that I will do all in my power to be fair to all."

Xeno placed a finger in Tano's welling blood and made a mark on his own forehead. "By this royal blood I ally myself with Tano, rightful heir to the throne of Benin."

Baro proudly took the blood oath.

"And what stake has this warrior who blackens his skin in a not-too-successful attempt to look like a Beni?" Xeno wanted to know.

"The stake of friendship," Renno answered.

"To this great chief I owe my life and my freedom," Tano explained.

"And what army does this great chief command?" Baro asked, hope surging up in him.

"We are three who stand beside Tano," Renno replied.

Baro's hopes collapsed. "Three," he repeated, then shrugged. "But then it is best, if we are to accomplish this deed, to do it from within. Let us go to Ogane."

The deserted streets awaited them. They clung to the shadows, pausing at each intersection to peer cautiously in all directions. Once they had to detour around a block of red-mud houses to avoid a four-man patrol. The soldiers were drinking beer as they strolled. Renno felt the haft of the war club emanate heat, but killing the four would alert the oba and would not substantially reduce the odds.

The white Indian had moved often in the night without sound—in the wilderness in the midst of enemies, in the strongholds of the British in Canada—but he experienced a different sensation that night in Benin . . . a heavy presence, as if the spirits of all those who had poured out their blood in that city were crying for vengeance. He considered asking Tano if he, too, felt their presence, but the young African showed no sign of being aware of anything more than the need for stealth.

The man they had come to see, Prince Ogane, was in his bed. A young, lithe woman from his father's harem lay at his side. He was sleeping so soundly that the girl woke first at Baro's callings and shook Ogane's shoulder. He didn't bother to pull on clothing but padded naked to the doorway, where Baro revealed himself.

"Prince Ogane, we must see you."

"Go away," Ogane said. He drew close. "I am not alone, you fool!"

"Rid yourself of the woman," Baro whispered.

"That would rouse her suspicions. Go to the back of the house and await me in the kitchen. It may take some time, for I will have to wait until the woman is asleep."

Baro and Xeno huddled side by side, squatting on the kitchen floor. Tano leaned against a wall. Renno, club in hand, stood poised to attack. When he heard movement in the house he hissed at Tano, who came to stand at his side.

"It is he," Baro verified when Ogane tapped a signal and then joined them in the dark room.

"Who is with you?" Ogane asked.

"We must have light," Baro said.

"The storeroom," Ogane suggested.

The storeroom was redolent of rotting yams, but it was windowless. An oil lamp was lit. Ogane looked at Renno and Tano. "I do not know these men," he said, regretting that he was weaponless.

"Know this man by this," Xeno said, lifting Tano's kilt. Tano displayed the sign of the leopard. Ogane gasped and took two quick steps backward.

"Who is this imposter?" Ogane demanded.

"No imposter, Prince," Xeno said. "The mark of the royal leopard bears the secret mark of the juju man of your grandfather."

Ogane stepped close to Tano, holding the lamp. "There was such a one," he recalled. "My mother has spoken of him. Like many of the heirs to the throne, he disappeared. His name was . . ." He paused, his brow wrinkled in thought.

"I am he. I am Tano."

"It is true," Baro confirmed.

No one spoke then, for it was obvious that Ogane was

deep in thought. After a long time he sighed. "It is you whom I will serve." He went to his knees.

"Rise, Nephew," Tano said, taking Ogane by the shoulders.

"If it is to be done, it must be done quickly," Ogane declared. "Perhaps we shall all die."

"If so," Xeno said, "we only hasten the inevitable, when Eweka turns on us one at a time."

"That is true," Ogane agreed. "Oba Tano, you must wield the weapon that sheds Eweka's blood."

"I have lived only for that for many years," Tano said. "But I have been away from the city for a long time. I am told that only you can gain access to Eweka. On your strong shoulders, then, lies the weight of responsibility. Put me in Eweka's presence with a weapon in hand or within reach and leave the rest to me."

"The act must be done in the palace," Ogane decided, "for the oba has made his last public appearance for some time. For months now he will stay secluded with his women and his fools."

"We must plan carefully," Baro said unnecessarily.

"There is only one plan possible," Ogane pointed out. "First Eweka must die, and then we will see if those who are loyal to me in the Order of the Hand will respect my wishes."

"But the other sons of Eweka—?" Xeno asked.

"Only three are ambitious," Ogane answered, "and they do not wear the royal leopard at the groin. Those loyal to me will see to them. There is danger there, for by issuing orders to kill them, I expose our secret."

"Some risk will be necessary," Xeno remarked. "Pick only those men you trust. I think I can speak for Tano when I promise that they will be rewarded by the new and rightful oba."

Tano nodded.

"Tomorrow I will speak," Ogane said. "Have you a good place to hide our oba and his friend?"

"My home," Xeno answered.

"Good," Ogane said. "You will hear from me, or you will receive a visit from members of the oba's guard. One way or the other you will know before nightfall."

The group reached Xeno's house without incident. The old man was visibly agitated and not willing to retire to a sleepless bed. Sokata, however, was soundly sleeping in the next room. Xeno seemed to want to talk, so Renno and Tano accepted his offer of native beer. Renno set the bowl aside, but Tano drank deeply and then, with a grin, reached for Renno's bowl.

"We have to depend upon most soldiers' loyalty to Ogane," Xeno said, "although there are those who are so tightly tied to Eweka and who have shown such great cruelty to the people of the city, they will have no choice but to fight for their lives. If Ogane commands enough loyalty and sufficient men to offset Eweka's dedicated followers, then our plan will succeed. If not . . ."

"Will there be a way for me to be at your side?" Renno asked Tano.

"That would be far too dangerous," Xeno cut in. "It will be difficult enough for Ogane to get just Tano into the palace."

"Then I will stand ready to fight at the palace gate," Renno decided. "And I will have two others with me." He had thought for a long time before deciding to fetch El-i-chi and Mingo, but he had a feeling that the plan to overthrow Eweka would work, and El-i-chi would want to be part of it. Then, too, he knew of no other man he would rather have by his side than his brother, and Mingo was worth ten warriors in a fight. "Tell me how to get over the wall to the outside, and the three of us will reenter the city before morning, if possible, or by the gate as soon as it is morning.''

"It would be best to come back tonight," Xeno advised. He brought Renno a strong rope and gave directions.

Following Xeno's instructions, Renno made his way once again through the silent streets without encountering soldiers. A tree grew next to the wall not far from Xeno's house. He climbed out onto a bough that extended almost to the wall, checked carefully that there were no guards about, secured the rope to the tree, and leaped to the wall. It was a dark night, and a man would have to be next to the rope to see it lying across the wall and hanging down to the ground twenty feet below.

A tunnel had been cut through the thornbushes that grew in the moat, and the white Indian managed to get through and into the cultivated fields with only a few scratches. Then he melted into the night, moving as a shadow, and entered the jungle. But even that near the city, the jungle's night sounds were eerie. He felt his way toward the site of El-i-chi's camp and as he neared, made the sound of a cooing dove until it was answered.

El-i-chi awaited beside the embers of the fire. "You're alone."

"All goes well," Renno reported. "Tano has found friends inside the walls." He grinned at El-i-chi. "I didn't think that you'd want to miss tomorrow's fight."

El-i-chi showed his teeth in a wolfish smile. "When do we go?"

"Now," Renno said, retrieving his bow from the campsite.

"The night is made for sleeping," Mingo grumbled.

"Sleep on, then," El-i-chi taunted. "You are better at fighting with your hands than killing with weapons anyway."

"This cub," Mingo, eyeing El-i-chi, told Renno, "will one day nip at my heels once too often."

"My brother has not yet learned that some words are best left unspoken," Renno said. "But the choice is yours, Mingo. Your family awaits you aboard the *Seneca Warrior*. I will not tell you that tomorrow's events are without danger."

"I think that Uanna would enjoy having some of the trinkets that, I am told, adorn the Benin nobles," Mingo said, rising and looking to his weapons.

The rope was still in place. After listening for a long time, Renno scaled the wall, waited, and signaled with a jerk of the rope. El-i-chi, then Mingo, joined him. They started toward Xeno's house. Already it was growing light in the east; they had to get off the streets quickly. They were nearing Xeno's neighborhood when their way was blocked by the approach of a four-man patrol. Renno pulled back into the shadows to wait until the patrol had passed, but Mingo's foot contacted a rain barrel, knocking it over.

The soldiers came on the run, swords in hand. Renno pushed El-i-chi ahead of him down a narrow alley, only to find the far end blocked by a wall that was too high to scale. The Beni soldiers were charging down the alley.

"Quietly," Renno cautioned, hefting his club. El-i-chi's tomahawk was in his hand. Mingo had come to favor one of the curved blades of the Fulani. "Now!" Renno said as the soldiers came within a few feet of them. He leaped from the shadows and sent the club whistling—a deadly surprise from the darkness. El-i-chi's tomahawk split the skull of a second man, while Mingo's blade came close to decapitating the third. Even as his man fell, Renno whirled to silence the fourth, but before the club could deliver a blow, the man screamed hoarsely, his voice reverberating in the closed alley.

Renno ran toward the mouth of the alley, the others at his heels. Four-man patrols were converging from two directions.

"The fighting has begun before we wanted it," he told El-i-chi and Mingo, securing his bow over his shoulder.

"There are only eight," El-i-chi said brightly.

"If we are separated," Renno began, adding directions to Xeno's house. By that time the soldiers were on them. Renno faced four; Mingo stood with El-i-chi. A Beni short sword flashed toward Renno, and he twisted aside after sending the club to the man's belly. The blow folded the Beni, then the strike to his head came within split seconds. Renno leaped to avoid the thrust of a sword as he lashed in under the blade with his stiletto. Behind him he could hear grunts of effort and the dull thuds of El-i-chi's tomahawk. The two Beni who remained to face Renno drew back, then rushed together, swords hissing through the air. Renno broke a skull as he leaped over a slashing blade and spun in the air to take the remaining man in the temple with his backswing.

El-i-chi and Mingo now faced one man each. Renno looked around quickly. From down the street, trotting in timed cadence, came a group of no fewer than ten soldiers.

"Quickly," he urged, even as El-i-chi's tomahawk slashed a throat and Mingo's blade went six inches into a Beni stomach.

"Must we fight the whole Beni army alone?" El-i-chi groaned, turning to stand by Renno's side to face the oncoming troop.

"We must finish this before dawn," Renno warned, drawing his bow to cut the odds by two before the onrushing Beni were within sword's reach. Oddly enough, the Beni soldiers did not shout or cry out. They bore in silently, three dying quickly. But still there were five against three. For a moment Renno was severely tested by two expert swordsmen before he evened the odds with a great blow with the spirit club. His heart sank when ten more soldiers came rushing down the street.

"Kill and run," he ordered, using his stiletto to take down the other man facing him.

Mingo led the way. Renno had to push El-i-chi into motion. "Go!" El-i-chi shouted as they entered a narrow alley. "I will hold them."

"We go together," Renno said, but El-i-chi jerked out of his grasp and turned to face the oncoming Beni. Renno leaped to his side and sent arrows winging from the English longbow until it was time once again to sling it over his shoulder and use the hand-to-hand weapons. The alley was narrow; no more than three men could face the brothers at once, and the club, knife, and tomahawk took a fearful toll until more Beni soldiers came rushing down the street.

"Too many, Brother," El-i-chi said. "Go, and give my honor to all our people."

Renno realized that he and El-i-chi were going to die in this narrow alley in an alien city. He wished he had not brought El-i-chi into the fight, but now it was too late. His sense of honor and respect for friendship led him into danger, but this time he would not be the only one to pay the consequences.

"Let us show them how a Seneca warrior dies!" Renno shouted, then the alley was filled with the roar of a great bear as he leaped forward to engage the Beni.

The weather had held during Ena and Se-quo-i's walk to Knoxville. They arrived on the outskirts of town at dusk, with the evening star burning brightly. Ena had showed no signs of distress, setting a swift pace, as if she did not carry the weight of a son inside her. During the trip they had talked of many things, including Renno and his continued absence, Se-quo-i's work with words, and the troublesome situation in the Seneca village, which was exacerbated by El-i-chi and Ah-wa-o's disregard for Seneca tradition and taboos. As they entered Knoxville, Se-quo-i promised to teach Ena's son to read and write.

She led the way up the porch steps to the Johnsons' front door. A light glowed in the window. The door was quickly opened by Roy. "Ena!" he cried. "And Se-quo-i! Welcome, welcome. Nora, look who's here."

But it was Renna who greeted them next. Ena was puzzled when she saw the little white girl in frills and lace, and then she realized that it was her niece even as Renna was throwing herself into "Uncle" Se-quo-i's arms.

"No greeting for me?" Ena smiled.

It had been many months since Renna had seen Ena. Snuggled in Se-quo-i's arms, she peered into Ena's face. Se-quo-i whispered in the child's ear, then Renna broke into the most beautiful smile Ena had ever seen.

"Auntie Ena!" she cried, reaching out to be taken in Ena's arms.

With her face showing only sternness, Nora had risen from her rocking chair and faced the visitors. "Ena," she said coldly. "Se-quo-i."

"Ena, so long a trip in your condition?" Roy marveled. "You must be tired. Sit, sit. Nora, can you warm up what was left from dinner?"

"I can manage," Nora said.

"And how's that miracle boy who calls himself my grandson?" Roy asked as he pulled his own chair around for Ena.

"Ready to explore all of North America alone," Se-quo-i said, laughing.

"I fancy," Roy responded with a chuckle. "Toshabe and all the others?"

"All are well," Ena said, not wanting to reveal the tribe's private problems to a white man, even a friend such as Roy.

Soon there was food on the table. Se-quo-i ate eagerly. Ena nibbled. She had not mentioned to Se-quo-i that her stomach had been queasy during the last day of the trip.

"So what brings you in?" Roy asked.

"They've come, of course, to take Renna from us," Nora said.

Roy coughed. "As a matter of fact, I was planning to bring Renna along in a few days."

"We have saved you the bother," Ena said.

Nora's voice was bitter. "Has anyone thought to ask this child what *she* prefers? Has anyone even wondered if she would be better off in a decent home with God-fearing people than in a Seneca longhouse?"

"Now, Nora," Roy warned.

"I miss Little Hawk," Renna said.

"Oh, my darling," Nora croaked, near weeping.

"Don't cry, Grandmother," Renna piped. "I'll come to see you often, I promise."

"We have, of course, become quite attached to her," Roy explained apologetically.

"I'm sorry," Ena said, "but her place is with her own people."

"We *are* her people!" Nora shot back, her voice rising. "We are more her people than you! She is of my own daughter's blood."

"I must respect my brother's wishes," Ena said. "He wants both of his children to know and love you and to learn your way of life. But remember, it is his wish that they know the traditions and life of the Seneca, as well."

"You're going to have your own child," Nora shouted, hysterical, "and yet you come to steal away my only joy in life!"

"Nora, that's enough," Roy said, his voice full of concern. He rose, lifted a weakened Nora from her chair, and guided her to her bed in the next room. "You'll have to forgive her," he said when he returned. "She hasn't been well, not well at all."

"Roy, I'm sorry," Ena said. "I didn't know that she was

so ill." She thought for a moment, biting her lower lip. "If it weren't for—" She put one hand on her stomach. "If it weren't for this, I would stay to help for a few days."

"That would be kind of you," Roy said. "There's a doctor in Knoxville, Ena. You could have the baby here. Nora would love to help care for it."

"There was a doctor here when Emily gave birth to Renna," Ena said. "No, Roy, I will not put myself into the hands of your doctors. The childbed fever is unknown among Indians who live away from the towns and the white doctors. My son will be born in his own lodge, with a Seneca midwife and my mother in attendance."

"Yes, I see," Roy said. "I have often wondered if the sickness that strikes women after birth would have taken Emily from us if Renna had been born in the Seneca village. I can't blame you, Ena. But can you stay just a day or so?"

"I will," Ena agreed. "I must admit that the trip tired me." She laughed. "If men, Seneca and white, had to bear this burden for one month, there would be more understanding of women's contribution."

Roy laughed. "I'm sure. Like carrying a ten-pound watermelon strapped to your belly, eh?"

"Or twenty," Ena replied.

"Auntie Ena is going to sleep with me," Renna declared.

"And Auntie Ena is ready," Ena said.

"Yes, you go on, Ena. Se-quo-i, there's Little Hawk's bed up there."

Se-quo-i, who did not share Renno and El-i-chi's disdain for alcohol, folded his arms across his chest. "Ugh! Injun think white man offer firewater first."

"White man be glad offer big Cherokee firewater," Roy said, grinning. "Give white man two seconds to break out jug."

*   *   *

Ena did not sleep well. For some time now her midsection had been too bulky for comfort. She awoke several times with her legs cramping, and try as she might, she could not get comfortable. In desperation she spread a single blanket on the floor and lay on her back with her knees bent and feet flat on the hardwood surface. Toward dawn she fell into a deep sleep, to be awakened by Renna's voice from the room below.

"But what's wrong with Grandmother?" Renna kept whining.

"Hush, child," Roy said. "Your grandmother isn't feeling well. I've sent Se-quo-i for the doctor."

Ena struggled to her feet, dressed quickly, and went down the ladder.

"Coffee on the stove, Ena," Roy said. His face was creased in worry.

She nodded toward the closed bedroom door and raised her eyebrows in question.

"It came on her in the night," Roy explained. "I'm afraid she's in a great deal of pain."

"I'll go in to her," Ena offered.

"I'd appreciate that," Roy said, "but let's wait for the doctor, if you don't mind."

The doctor came running down the street alongside Se-quo-i and closeted himself with Nora in her room. He came out a few minutes later. "See you a minute, Roy?" he asked in a low voice.

"These are my friends," Roy responded. "It isn't good with her, is it?"

"It's bad," the doctor told him. "You know that I've suspected internal canker. Well, looks like I was right—more's the pity. Canker broke loose during the night, I guess. She just vomited blood."

"She vomited during the night," Roy said. "I didn't see

any blood, and she said she was all right and went back to
sleep."

"Is there anything I can do?" Ena asked.

"Looks like the best thing you could do is take to your
bed, woman," the doctor advised. "When are you due?"

"Not for another month," she said.

"Well, either you misfigured, or you're going to have
twins," the doctor said. "If you feel all right, it wouldn't
hurt to keep cool compresses on Nora's forehead and maybe
hot cloths on her stomach where the pain is. Truth is, Roy,
there's not much anyone can do, except wait—and I have to
say this—for the inevitable."

Roy felt a great surge of grief. He had to leave the room
hurriedly to keep from embarrassing himself. Nora had never
been the strongest of women, but she'd always managed to
rise up from all her other illnesses. Then, in this past year,
she'd gone downhill rapidly. He could almost see, day to
day, the aging in her face. Now he had been told that his wife
was going to die. All hope had been taken from him. First he
had lost his daughter. Soon his wife. He strode away from the
house, letting the breeze evaporate the tears that rolled down
his cheeks.

It took Nora a full week to die, a week of agony that was
beyond the reach of the laudanum that was administered in
ever-increasing doses by the doctor. She tried to be brave, but
as the end neared, her moans and screams terrified Renna, so
Ena took the child to the home of a neighbor who had a girl
Renna's age. The presence of a playmate cheered Renna, so
Ena was freed to help Roy tend the dying woman. It was a
terrible task, for Nora had been reduced by the canker inside
her to the status of a baby.

"Thank God," Roy said when Nora had breathed her last.
Ena was in the room. "I don't think I could have stood
seeing her suffer any more." He folded his wife's hands with

a loving touch, closed her eyes, and weighted them with pennies. Only then did he turn. There were tears on his cheeks. "Did you hear what she said? Could you understand her last words?"

"No," Ena said.

"She said, 'Now they will both be Seneca.' "

"I'm sorry that she could not die in peace," Ena said.

"But I think she did. I think she accepted it, at the end."

"I came at a bad time to get Renna," Ena acknowledged. "If I had had any idea—"

"Now don't go blaming yourself. She was dying. Don't you even think that your coming hastened the end, because Doc has been saying for months that it was only a matter of time."

"Thank you," Ena said.

"Ena, I don't want you to stay for the funeral. Take Renna and go. I want the child to remember her grandmother alive and loving her—not stiff and cold in a wooden casket."

"If that is your wish," Ena agreed.

"I think that's best. A child doesn't understand death, and to see people crying could affect Renna forever. When I'm through this, I imagine I'll be out your way."

"You will always be welcomed," Ena assured him. A sudden surge of pain caused her to gasp and bend.

"What's wrong?" Roy asked. He was thinking, *It's the baby. All this has sent her into premature labor.*

But she straightened. "It's nothing. Just a spasm. The young warrior was, most probably, playing stickball."

But there was a feeling of urgency in her. She helped Roy tidy up Nora's bedroom, and then grim-faced, silent women from the church arrived to do the washing and laying out of the corpse. Ena went into the room when they were finished, to see Nora's face pale in death, at peace now. They had clothed her in her nicest dress.

With the light of the rising sun the party of three was under way. Ena set a pace to match Renna's short legs. The girl was alternately concerned about her grandmother and excited by the prospect of the trip and of seeing Little Hawk, Ah-wa-o, and Grandmother Toshabe.

"When will we come back to see Grandmother Nora and Granddaddy Roy?" Renna asked as they left the town behind them.

"Renna," Ena said, "your grandmother Nora has gone far away."

"I know," Renna said with the innocence of the very young. "She's gone to the white-man's heaven. But when will we come back to see them?"

"Soon," Ena said. "Soon."

Chapter XIV

Renno fought as he had never fought before. Many times he had been outnumbered; many times he had faced what seemed to be insurmountable odds, but never had he confronted so hopeless a situation. The Beni attackers had to climb over the bodies of their dead comrades as Renno's ancient war club sang a song of death. At his side El-i-chi labored mightily at the business of killing. Mingo was with them, but due to the narrowness of the alley, he could not stand side by side with the brothers.

More Beni warriors came running down the street.

El-i-chi gasped as he swung his tomahawk after dodging a spear thrust. "Renno, go. I beg you, go."

The sachem did not bother to answer. He was lashing out with club and knife. A sword whistled past his head, striking a glancing blow with the flat blade. The impact gave new fury to his attacks.

"Mingo!" El-i-chi called. "Take Renno and find safety while I hold these black wildcats."

Mingo, although a practical man, would not have hesitated to stand to the end beside his allies. But El-i-chi had made a courageous and honorable decision, that his brother should live. He stepped forward and used his bare fist to strike a stunning punch to the base of Renno's neck, then caught the white Indian's sagging body.

"We go," he said, snatching up the war club. "The spirits will welcome you, my friend."

Now El-i-chi stood alone, his tomahawk cutting a deadly swath in the silent attackers. Mingo threw Renno across his shoulders and ran. Rounding a corner in the dim, early-morning light, he heard pounding footsteps, ducked into an alley, and with some difficulty remembered Renno's instructions on how to get to Xeno's house. From behind him he heard the roar of a fighting bear, and then Beni soldiers ran past to close on El-i-chi's position. Mingo ran on, gained the entrance to Xeno's house, and was admitted.

Sokata, seeing that Renno had been hurt, came forward.

"He is only stunned," Mingo told her.

Sokata looked over the Jamaican's shoulder. "El-i-chi?"

Mingo's eyes filled as he shook his head.

"Bring him," Xeno said. "Put him on this bed."

"We killed many," Mingo growled, "but they came by the dozens."

Xeno was worried. The incident would alert the oba and raise many questions. He considered contacting the others to call off the plans; but when he looked at Tano, he felt great despair, for the young man was the hope of Benin. To do nothing would mean that Eweka's cruel reign would continue until he died, to be replaced by one of his sons who had been taught by the tyrant.

"Sokata," Xeno said, "the others must know. A woman can walk the streets without notice. Are you brave?"

"I will do what is necessary," she promised.

Xeno gave her careful directions as to how to reach Baro and Prince Ogane. She left, eager to see her childhood friend again.

Mingo stood beside the bed where Renno lay. The Seneca came back to consciousness with a rush, sat up, war club raised, and shook his head to focus his eyes.

"You are among friends," Xeno said.

For a moment Renno couldn't remember, and then a wail of grief poured from his throat, for in an instant he remembered what had happened. He had been fighting at his brother's side, and then blackness, and now El-i-chi was not in the room.

Mingo put his huge hands on Renno's shoulders to hold the sachem on the bed and was amazed at Renno's strength as he threw Mingo aside and bounded to his feet. He was heading for the door when Mingo caught and held him in his strong arms, only to have Renno twist free and face him, club ready, eyes blazing.

"My friend," Mingo pleaded.

Renno lowered the club. "Tell me."

"Your brother is a brave man, a great man," Mingo said. "He chose to have you live, to complete this task here, and then to go back to lead your people. When you grieve for him, remember that."

"How did I come to be here?"

Mingo decided that a small lie was the better part of wisdom and valor. "A Beni landed a blow."

"And you ran, taking me with you?" Renno's expression was so dangerous that Mingo took a step backward.

"Only because El-i-chi begged me to do so," Mingo answered. He knelt at Renno's feet. "If my blood brother thinks that I ran from fear of the Beni or fear of death, then strike."

Renno bent and helped Mingo to his feet. The Jamaican had never seen such pain on the face of a man as he saw then. And that pain was replaced by a promise of death that prompted Mingo to thank all his gods that he was not a foe of this man who turned without speaking and walked out of the room.

The only place for privacy was the storeroom. Renno went there, closed the door behind him, and in total darkness, he lifted his tearstained face. Then he began to chant in Seneca, a low, rhythmic mourning for the dead. As his voice grew louder, the sound escaped the storeroom and filled the house.

Renno longed for the cool, tall forests of his homeland, for the freedom to run far away from any other human being, to chant out his grief, and to implore the manitous to welcome the spirit of his beloved brother to the Place across the River. He was sitting on the floor, legs crossed, voice low, and head bowed when Mingo opened the door.

"Sokata is back," Mingo said.

"So," Renno acknowledged.

"I have seen both Baro and Prince Ogane," Sokata said from behind the giant Jamaican. "Ogane said to tell you that the bird of death is in flight. When the gongs sound the time for the morning sacrifice in the public square, the bird will alight. Baro's group will take the palace gate when the gongs sound. He requests that you and yours, Renno, join the fight there; the issue will be decided at the gate, when it becomes known how many soldiers will fight or side with Ogane."

"That gives us only a little time," Xeno said, moving into the storeroom. "I have been giving thought to your appearance, Renno."

Indeed, by that time the tears of grief and the sweat of exertion had caused the charcoal on Renno's face to run.

"You cannot hope to pass for a Beni in the light of day," Xeno told him. "Therefore, you will become a priest." He produced cotton garments and an ornate woven helmet from which hung a veil and cowl of mesh. Renno donned the garments.

"Now no one can see the white skin," Mingo said, satisfied.

"Then we must go," Xeno said.

Renno felt a pain in his heart as he and the others passed the spot where El-i-chi had been abandoned. The bodies had been removed, but the dirt street was muddy with blood. People walking past seemed unaware of the blood; no soldiers were in evidence. Renno paused at the site, and his hand clenched on the haft of the club under his cloak. The weapon throbbed warmly. Renno's eyes narrowed, and the fire of revenge burned up in him so brightly that, for a moment, he trembled.

"We must hurry," Xeno urged.

The route to the palace gates led them through the public square. Already crowds were gathering for their morning's entertainment.

"Soon this will end," Tano promised.

"Quickly, Tano," Xeno said. "Ogane waits for you. You must be inside before the sounding of the gongs."

The palace gates lay ahead. As the men neared, the procession for the sacrifices came through. The little group moved to one side. First a squad of Beni soldiers marched out, leather shields held at precise angles and weapons gleaming. Behind them came musicians, but not nearly so many as had been present at the blessing of the crops. Behind the musicians came more soldiers, escorting six men, bound and gagged, to be sacrificed that day.

Renno's heart stopped for a moment, and a joy so great that it was almost pain made him want to whoop, for the second man in the queue of the sacrifice victims was El-i-chi. His head was bloody, but he walked strongly, his eyes searching among the spectators. His glance passed over Renno, unrecognizable in the garb of a priest, but lingered on Mingo and Tano.

"By the gods, he lives," Mingo whispered.

"Tano, get on with your mission," Renno said. "Mingo and I will join those in the square."

With Mingo at his side, Renno paced the procession moving toward the square. His priest's garb made a way for them through the crowd, for to offend a priest of the Order of the Hand was not a wise thing to do in Benin. In the plaza the priests did not seem to be in a hurry to begin the sacrifices. The manner of the executions was to be different that day. Soldiers bound the victims securely to posts anchored firmly on the platform. A leather band over their foreheads held the back of their heads tightly against the posts, exposing their throats. El-i-chi submitted to this indignity without protest, for he saw Mingo standing with an oddly dressed man in the front ranks of the observers. When El-i-chi's eyes rested on the veiled figure for a moment, Renno gave the hunting cry of a hawk. El-i-chi acknowledged by raising his eyebrows. Those around Renno looked at him oddly, then edged away.

Xeno and Tano walked through the main gate without being challenged, but at an inner gate, four of the oba's bodyguards made passage impossible.

"Where are you, Ogane?" Xeno whispered desperately as they neared the gate.

At the last minute the prince appeared. He spoke to the guards and extended his hand, indicating that Tano and Xeno were to be admitted.

Ogane led them in silence past tall columns. They passed bedecked nobles and lovely, lithe women going about the morning's business, then reached a passage. "Move swiftly," Ogane warned, ducking into the passageway. He led them at a run through a maze of corridors and halted before an almost hidden door, where two Beni warriors stood guard. They stiffened at Ogane's approach.

"They are with us," Ogane whispered to Tano and Xeno. "Through this door are the oba's private quarters. He will probably be breakfasting with a few of his senior advisers and some women."

"Guards?" Tano wanted to know.

"Just fools and deaf-mutes," Ogane replied. "They should give us no trouble." He walked to a window and looked up at the sun. "Soon the gong will sound. Come."

The doorway led into a courtyard with the customary rain pit in the center. A roofed balcony extended in a U shape. Ogane led the way, staying in the shadows under the roof. Music floated from an open room on the opposite side. When they reached that side unobserved, Tano peered into the large room: Eweka, bundled into his regalia even in the early morning, sat like a huge toad in a great chair while two shapely young girls, naked to the waist, attended him. Two older men sat on the floor in front of the oba's chair, their attentions on their food. A dwarf was cavorting in the center of the room, and other dwarves and several deaf-mute servants stood in various locations. Two musicians were in an alcove behind Eweka.

Again Ogane glanced at the sun. "Soon," he whispered.

Tano's hand tightened on the haft of a Beni short sword.

In the square the broad-shouldered, bare-chested executioner lifted the ceremonial weapon and tested it, making it sing through the air. He stepped to a victim tied to a post and

in slow motion practiced the killing stroke. The blade stopped
with the razor edge pressing against the victim's throat.

"Remember," Mingo whispered to Renno, "Ogane's men
will tie a red cloth to their helmets."

Renno grunted. He was watching two bored priests who
stood near the two huge brass gongs mounted over the altar of
sacrifice. Each held a round-headed striker. "When they raise
their strikers," he told Mingo, "give me a bit of room here."
In anticipation of the sacrifices, the jostling spectators were
closing in around Renno.

When a priest emerged from a mud building and strode
regally across the square, the crowd's din faded. This was the
officiating priest, who would give the signal. He walked to
stand in front of the six victims, lifted his hands, and chanted.
The executioner ran his fingers along his blade and smiled
humorlessly. Then, after a long time of chanting, the officiating holy man turned and signaled.

Renno tensed.

The priests at the gongs raised their strikers.

As the mallets made contact with the brass gongs, Renno,
in one motion, shed his cloak, threw the helmet to the
ground, drew an arrow, and sent it winging to impale one of
the guards at the sacrifice area. His next arrow pierced the
thick throat of the executioner. Then as screams of surprise
and terror made a hysterical mob of the milling crowd, he
expended his last three arrows, reducing the number of soldiers in the square. The guards brandished their weapons and
tried to ascertain the source of the deadly arrows as Renno
ducked into the crowd. Then as six soldiers spotted him, he
roared the challenge of the bear and moved swiftly, Mingo at
his side, to meet them. He left his longbow on the ground and
leaped to the attack. The war club was hot in his hand, and
his stiletto stole fire from the sun. The sound of the gongs
was still reverberating throughout the city.

"To El-i-chi," the Seneca ordered as he and Mingo rushed forward. One hissing swing of his club and a thrust of Mingo's curved blade cleared a path through the soldiers, and the two men sprinted forward and up to the sacrificial altar. Renno fell to his knees behind El-i-chi and in one slash freed his hands. Another slash and El-i-chi's head was cleared of the leather thong, and he was clawing the gag from his mouth. Mingo gently underhanded a Beni sword to El-i-chi, which he caught by the hilt from midair, giving voice to a great cry of triumph.

The panicked crowd trampled women and children while Beni soldiers surged forward, cursing and striking out to clear a path.

"For a spirit, Brother, you are quite lively," Renno said joyously.

"The dead will be piled higher than in that alley," El-i-chi vowed. "I don't take kindly to being bound and gagged."

They formed a triangle to protect their backs. As the soldiers moved in, the grim business of killing began with thrust, counterthrust, and the deadly hissing of the war club. A troop of soldiers came rushing through the diminishing crowd, leaping over the moaning women and children, to surround the brothers and their friend. Bodies accumulated quickly, so the soldiers had to walk on the fallen to meet their own deaths at the thunder of the war club, the thrust of Mingo's curved scimitar, or the lash of El-i-chi's sword.

"I see no red banners on their helmets," Mingo grunted, looking for Ogane's allies.

"This time," Renno growled, "we win or die together."

At the sound of the gongs from the plaza, Ogane and Tano stepped into the large room where the oba was peacefully enjoying his breakfast. The cavorting dwarf saw them first and squealed in surprise. Then Eweka lifted his heavy head, his eyes piglike in their folds of fat.

"How dare you violate my privacy, Ogane—" He fell silent, mouth open, for Tano was moving forward, a sword at the ready. "You!"

"My brother does not seem pleased to see me," Tano seethed.

"I was merciful," Eweka said, struggling to his feet and frantically looking around as if searching for help. "I could have killed you. Instead, I allowed you to live."

"As the white man's slave," Tano shot back. "Brother, can you still lift a sword, or has your love of eating made you as weak as a woman?"

"There is no time for this," Ogane warned.

"Ogane, kill this man!" Eweka ordered.

"I am the servant of Tano, oba of Benin," Ogane declared.

"You!" Eweka shouted, waving his flabby arms, naked save for his royal bangles, at the dwarves, the two old advisers who cringed on the floor, and the deaf-mute servants. "Protect your oba!"

"Give him your sword, Ogane," Tano said.

Ogane stepped forward, drawing his sword. Eweka cringed back until, with a swift motion, Ogane reversed the sword and offered it to Eweka haft first.

Eweka's piggish eyes narrowed. "I will show you who is oba," he threatened, waddling forward to swing the sword wildly. Tano danced to one side, grinning. Already Eweka was panting. He took another swing and almost fell.

"I will be merciful," Tano offered. "I will give you a quick death." He lunged, and his sword disappeared up to the hand guard in the softness of Eweka's midsection. He fell heavily as Tano jerked the sword out, the blade dripping blood.

"Be certain, my oba," Ogane suggested.

Tano lifted his sword, and the blade rang on bone as he severed Eweka's head. He speared the head on the end of his sword and held it high. "Go," he commanded the silent old advisers, the dwarves, and the women. "Tell everyone that Eweka is dead and that Tano sits on his rightful throne."

Beni warriors were accustomed to moving forward in disciplined ranks and overwhelming the enemy with sheer numbers. They fought with coordinated spear thrusts from behind a wall of shields. Now those in the square faced three instruments of death positioned to protect each other's back. The footing was slippery because of blood as the three strange warriors gave final lessons in death to those who came within reach. Worse, the Beni in the front ranks could hear the sounds of battle from the palace.

One Beni drew back, nervously looking over his shoulder. An officer struck him with the flat of his sword and ordered him back into the fight, but others were now drawing back.

Renno stood with his club poised, his muscular chest heaving with exertion and battle fury. He roared a challenge, causing a few soldiers to step back, but the officer rallied the men to advance in a wedge.

"This one is mine," El-i-chi declared. "He captured me." The shaman leaped forward, parried a thrust of the officer's sword, lunged to drive his tomahawk into the hollow of the officer's throat, and was back in his place in the triangle even as the officer fell.

It was the giant Jamaican who pointed out a new danger: Another officer had led a squad of archers on the run into the square, and he was positioning them, twelve abreast, at fifty paces from Renno and his two allies. The officer shouted orders to the men surrounding the threesome to draw back and give him a clear field of fire. One by one the fighting soldiers heard the orders and retreated.

Renno looked around, desperately seeking a place to take cover from the barrage of arrows that would come within seconds. The square was empty of people, and the nearest buildings were over a hundred feet away. Not even Renno could outrun a flight of arrows.

Tano ran through the palace corridors with Eweka's head on his sword. Ogane, behind him, could hear fighting at the main gate and hoped that his men had remained loyal and that any dangerous rival among Eweka's sons had been silenced.

Tano burst into the dim light of a sun obscured by clouds that formed the daily rain. He halted a few paces from Baro, who was involved in the melee at the gate. Old Xeno joined them. Beyond, across the plaza, Tano could see Renno's group still fighting but threatened by a squad of readied bowmen.

"Hear me, men of Benin!" he bellowed with all the power of his lungs. "Behold Eweka!" He lifted the head high. A sudden hush fell as the grunting opponents separated and looked at him. More than half the soldiers wore red banners on their helmets. He brandished the head. "There is no need to die for a dead tyrant! I, Tano, oba of Benin, welcome the allegiance of all who bear me no ill will."

"He bears the sign of the royal leopard!" Ogane shouted as Baro moved to his side.

Even those who had been fighting for Eweka knew Ogane and Baro as men of honor who stood up for the common soldier.

"Join me, soldiers, in honoring the rightful oba!" Baro shouted. "Sheathe your weapons."

"Traitors!" A strong, young man, sword in hand, rushed from a building. "Traitors! Kill all traitors and this imposter and his dog Ogane."

"That is Gudan, son of Eweka," Xeno said. "His blade

is red; that means that the two who were sent to kill him are dead instead.''

Baro moved toward Gudan threateningly, but Tano put out a restraining hand. He thrust his sword, heavy with Eweka's head, into Ogane's hand, then took Ogane's sword and moved toward the panting young man who faced him with hate-filled eyes.

"You are of my blood," Tano began. "Do you choose to live and honor me as oba or to die with your father?"

Gudan's answer was a scream of rage as he lunged forward. His onslaught caused his adversary to fall back momentarily, but then Tano's experience and quickness gave him the edge. "You can choose to live," he repeated, still on the attack, but Gudan leaped forward. With a casual swipe of his blade Tano cut Gudan's throat, then turned to face the soldiers. "Are there others who doubt that I am oba?"

"Show them," Xeno encouraged.

Tano bared himself and lifted one leg to let all see the royal leopard. Soldiers who had sided with Ogane began to make bows of obedience, and soon all others followed.

Tano raised his sword. "Those who still fight in the square are my friends! Place a red banner on your helmet and follow me!"

A blade left a thin line of red from its passing tip on Renno's chest. He feinted with his stiletto, sent home a killing blow with the club, and twisted to the side to avoid the thrust of a Beni spear. Beside him El-i-chi grunted with effort as he jerked his sword from a falling body just in time to parry a new attack.

"This is hard work," El-i-chi complained as another Beni warrior fell.

It was evident to Renno that unless help came soon, his threesome would be overwhelmed by sheer numbers. But the greater danger came from the squad of archers, still waiting for a clear field of fire; those Beni who were closely engaged had not heard the screams from the officer to fall back. Renno fought grimly, although his arm ached from killing and the war club was slick with blood. Still the Beni came.

"No use," Mingo gasped as he stabbed into the belly of a Beni soldier with his bloody scimitar.

A roar of new voices erupted, and Renno saw a great mass of soldiers running toward them from the direction of the palace.

Mingo, too, saw. "Speak to your manitous for me, Sachem," he requested, "when you reach the Place across the River."

"We will sail west together, alive," Renno said, for he had seen the red banners streaming from the helmets of the approaching soldiers.

"I see Tano, Xeno, and Baro," El-i-chi yelled, slashing the throat of one last soldier before the supporters of the new oba fell upon the soldiers from the rear.

The fight ended quickly. The surviving adversaries in the plaza immediately lost interest when they faced men they knew, their comrades in arms. Ogane and Baro took command and organized the soldiers in ranks to face Tano, Renno, El-i-chi, and Mingo.

Tano grimly looked over the square, counting the fallen. His dark, sad eyes turned to Renno. "I knew, my friend, that you were a great warrior, and your brother, as well. And from personal experience I know Mingo's strength. But this!"

Xeno, noting Tano's silence, let his eyes, too, fall upon the dead.

"Great Oba," Xeno said, "may this be the last time that the square of Benin runs with the blood of our own people."

"It will be so," Tano vowed.

*　　　*　　　*

Beth had been counting the days, the weeks, then the months since the *Seneca Warrior* had sailed for Africa. Winds and storms, of course, could vary the duration of any voyage, but even allowing for bad weather, the time had come and gone when the *Warrior* would have returned had Renno found Mingo and his family in Bastian Vanderrenner's slave fort.

The pleasant days had come to England. Flowers were in bloom wherever one looked, and the days were longer. Twilight lingered, and the birds were still awake, singing her to sleep, when she retired to her bed.

Beth had documents in her possession that were signed by a host of officials, including the minister of trade, and made binding by the royal seal of King George. Her potential for fortune was now greater than William's, in spite of his far-flung ventures. Soon her ships would range the Caribbean freely, hauling the produce of North Carolina outward and carrying the goods and produce of the islands back into the port of Wilmington. Her purpose had been accomplished, but she still lived in the town house instead of going back to Beaumont Hall to be with Estrela and little Ena Estrela Elizabeth, who, it seemed, would be called after her American aunt, Ena.

Now Beth's evenings were filled with gaiety—with grand balls and clever conversations with new people, the peers of England and wealthy merchants who vied to please her because in her hands lay the means to great riches.

Joffre was her constant companion. She owed him a great debt; he had been instrumental in securing an audience for her with the minister of trade, the meeting that had made her proposal a reality. After that one night when Joffre had stated his feelings for her, he remained silent about that issue, but she could not help but be impressed by his devotion. She was fully aware that her frequent appearances with him in public were a subject for gossip. London society was a small, elite group; the court circle, of which Joffre was a member, was even smaller.

On a beautiful, late-spring evening, Joffre called for her in a handsome town carriage drawn by two of the finest black horses Beth had ever seen. Their destination was a reception at the home of a Scot shipbuilder who had become a favorite of the court because of his charm and noble lineage—he held a respectable title and hundreds of acres of estates in both Scotland and the north of England.

"This should be a special night, my dear," Joffre told her as the carriage bounced over the rough streets. "Only the cream of society will be there."

"Then I shall be out of place, for I am only a shipping merchant," she teased.

"But the most alluring shipping merchant in all the world," Joffre remarked.

It was a subdued, dignified gathering. A string quartet played in the garden. A grand buffet of tantalizing dishes occupied one huge room. A butler announced the arrival of Sir Joffre Jowett and Lady Elizabeth Huntington. Beth, in a green gown that accented her red hair, attracted attention as she swept into the reception room. They circulated, greeting friends and being introduced to a few people Beth did not know. A small orchestra was playing in the ballroom.

The host, a tall redhead like Beth, insisted on being her partner for her first dance. As the music started, he brought up the subject of ships, guessing that she, with her new trade agreement, would be needing more vessels. She promised to have her representatives talk with him before she purchased new ships.

Beth was accustomed to discussing business during social occasions and, in fact, welcomed meeting the Scotsman. Personal contact was an advantage to her because she could prove her intelligence and good sense. Men looked at her with new respect and realized that this flame-haired beauty was capable of negotiating them right out of their profits.

In most ways it was a typical evening in London society. Joffre hovered near, sensitive to her every desire. Men crowded each other to share her attentions. Women sniffed in disapproval. It was growing fairly late when, with a cry of pleasure, Beth saw William enter the room. Although he was on most guest lists as a peer of the realm, he seldom ventured out for such an occasion. She ran to him and took his hands.

"I expected I'd find you here," he said.

She caught her breath. "You have news?"

"Yes and no."

"Don't keep me in suspense," she pleaded.

"A ship has just returned from Africa," William said. "Not our ship," he hastened to add. "But the captain had traded at three places along the Slave Coast, including native towns near the Niger delta. I questioned him. He had not heard of any English ship in the delta area."

Beth pulled her full lower lip between her teeth and bit it. William squeezed her hand. "That doesn't mean anything. Mainly I was interested in hearing that this ship had an easy passage back, with no severe storms. That bodes well for the *Warrior*. If she is returning now, as she should be, she should have good sailing."

"Walk with me," she said, taking William's arm. They went into the gardens. The string quartet was still playing, although only one or two couples were outside.

"It may have taken weeks to locate the place where Renno's friend was being held," William rationalized. "It may have taken a while to find cargo to bring back. They might have encountered bad weather on the voyage out." He sighed. "I suppose I shouldn't have mentioned the returned ship. The *Warrior* could have been upstream on half a dozen tributaries that form the delta when the man I spoke with was there.''

"William," she said, "you don't have to feign optimism for my sake. I recognize all the possibilities.''

"I should have gone with him.''

"No," she said quickly. "Your place is here.'' The words lingered in the air, for Joffre had told her the same thing.

"If the worst should happen,'' William said, "what would you do? I hesitate even to mention it, but one should be prepared, I suppose.''

"I've thought about it. I've wept, wondering how I would feel if Renno never came back.'' They walked on for a few moments as the string quartet played a plaintive, old English folk melody. "Whether or not he returns, I will have to go back to North Carolina. I have good, trustworthy people there who are capable and willing to handle our business in America.''

"Then you like it here in London?''

"I would be lying if I said no, William. Oh, I know it's brittle and sometimes artificial, but good Lord, this is where the power is. My little business venture in America is so insignificant compared to, say, the East India Company.''

"And are those the only attractions?''

"If you mean Joffre . . .''

"I had him in mind.''

"He is a very good friend to both of us,'' she said.

"Who wants to be more than a friend to you.''

"He has never overstepped the bounds of propriety.''

"He wouldn't,'' William responded. "But I suspect that he'll become more forceful as time passes.''

"You sound as if you don't think Renno is coming back,'' she said, her throat constricting.

"I have not given up hope. If he should not come back, I will mourn him as one of my greatest friends; but Joffre is also my friend, Beth, and I'd hate to see him hurt. He's very much in love with you."

"Joffre falls in love with the change of the moon," she scoffed.

"No, it's different this time."

"He's spoken to you about it?"

"He talks of you but has not touched on any intimate subject. I'm referring to his actions, the way he conducts his daily life. He's given up all his mistresses. He doesn't gamble anymore. He's a changed man, and you must believe me when I say—for I know him well—that it's because of you. All I ask is this: If there is no hope that you would have Joffre if the worst has happened in Africa, tell him so now."

Beth was silent. She knew it was not right to encourage any false expectations in Joffre, and yet she had not done otherwise. There, in that English garden scented with blooming flowers, a romantic little melody in her ears, she suspected something that did not sit well with her self-image. Had she ceased reminding Joffre that she was a happily married woman because, deep in her heart, she knew that Renno was dead? Or worse, was she being selfish, keeping Joffre hanging on his hopes, just in case? Either way she felt belittled, and she irrationally blamed Renno. It was he, and his honor and his vow of blood brotherhood to a slave, who had put her into such a predicament.

Chapter XV

At first Bastian Vanderrenner thought he was alone, hundreds of miles from any ally. He had barely managed to escape the Fulani city with his life, one musket with a limited number of balls and a small amount of powder, and a pistol. He had no food or water but was an experienced African traveler and knew that he could live off the land as he made his way back to the coast and his fort. Then, one by one he was reunited with four of his lieutenants, men who had shown quick wit by escaping rather than fighting the hopeless odds in Zaria. They would be of help in the long journey to his stronghold. He promised them great rewards, and his face dark with anger, he vowed one day to extract a proper measure of vengeance from the cause of his losses in the lands of the Fulani.

Anxious about the condition of his fort since his eyes first settled on the rescued Tano, the Dutchman drove the horses mercilessly. The animals were spent by the time his party reached the beginnings of jungle, and he shot them without remorse. Until the horsemeat got too ripe in the heat, there was flesh in plenty. The four Yorubans gorged themselves so shamelessly, Vanderrenner was filled with disgust.

Soon they reached the most dangerous stretch of their journey, passing by the small, isolated villages in the jungle. Many inhabitants would recognize Vanderrenner and thank all their gods for a chance at him when he was protected by only five muskets. The need for caution slowed their progress, but day by day the dank miles passed under their feet until the Dutchman, having pushed the men hard all day, stood on the banks of the sluggish stream separating him from his fort.

The scene of devastation across the stream shocked him into glowering silence. The jungle was in the process of reclaiming the island where his stronghold once stood. Not a single building was to be seen, and there was no evidence of the strong palisade he'd had built there. Through the rampant greenery he could see the charred remnants of the wooden buildings. He knew that he was in trouble. There was no sign of his ship, and between him and the sea were miles of sluggish water, stinking mud flats, and impenetrable masses of mangrove thickets. Perhaps the ship, too, had been destroyed and now lay at the bottom of the black waters.

Because the Yorubans clearly understood the precariousness of the situation, Vanderrenner feared that once he turned his head, the four men would melt into the jungle. "Come," he ordered. "The ship is most probably anchored downstream."

He led the way. Movement was difficult once they left the trail, and darkness forced them to camp in sodden surroundings.

Vanderrenner awakened to find a warm, thick mist hanging over the riverside jungle, and several hours passed before the sun burned it away; at last he could see well enough to continue the struggle toward the delta. His heart leaped when he saw the outlines of a ship through a curtain of creepers. As he moved closer to the water, however, he saw the thirteen-starred flag of the United States flying from the masthead of a ship that was definitely not his.

"There is nothing we can do," said one of the Yorubans, making ready to leave the Dutchman.

Vanderrenner studied the ship. It showed signs of having been on the river for some time. The furled sails were mildewed, and her paint was beginning to flake. But he could still read her name: *Seneca Warrior*. And Uanna could be seen on deck with her sons.

"They have become complacent," he said, his eyes narrowing. "They can be taken easily."

"We are five," protested a Yoruban.

"We will kill them one by one as they sleep," the Dutchman said. "Can a Yoruban warrior not move with the silence of a jungle cat?" He smiled. "Think of the riches aboard the ship. And there is the woman of Mingo. She will be yours to share."

Actually Vanderrenner had no hopes of taking the ship. While the Yorubans killed a few of the crew, however, he would find enough shot, powder, and food to enable him to make his way through the jungle to Benin. There he could get help from an old slave-trading ally, the oba Eweka. The Yorubans would be killed, of course, but he would be able to escape during the confusion—perhaps even taking a boat to make his journey to Benin easier.

He could see that the Yorubans were thinking of the woman. He smiled. "When the night is far advanced," he said, "we will board the ship and kill the crew one by one.

Now we will construct rafts of branches and reeds, so we can cross the water without wetting our weapons and our powder."

He set the example, beginning to construct a small float.

Aboard the *Seneca Warrior* Billy the Pequot was having his evening meal with Uanna and her sons, Tanyere and Little One. Conversation was limited, for they had been waiting on the river for weeks, and each was lost in thought. After the meal Billy made his rounds, shaking his head at what the sodden tropical climate was doing to the *Warrior*. He made sure the watches were set—two men, one at the bow and another at the stern, to alternate throughout the night—and then he went to his cabin.

Uanna, Tanyere, and Little One had found that they were more comfortable sleeping on the deck than in the steamy quarters below. Uanna had made one small area her family's own by hanging clothes to screen them from the crew members who also slept on the deck. She slept with a finely honed knife under her makeshift pillow. Tanyere, the older son, kept a Beni spear by his side.

The heat of the day lessened slowly, and a blessed, small breeze came down the river to offer a bit of relief. Uanna, however, did not sleep until long after the snores of the crewmen on deck made a rumbling background to the sounds from the jungle and the buzzing of insects. Her last waking thought was of Mingo.

Vanderrenner watched as the lookout at the stern sat down on the deck, leaning his head against the rail, as if there were no danger within miles. His exposed throat made an easy target for Vanderrenner's keen knife. The sailor died without knowing that danger was near.

Fools, Vanderrenner thought as he saw four other men die quickly at the hands of the Yorubans. He was creeping forward, looking for another victim, moving toward a screened area. He guessed that Uanna and the two boys slept there.

When the Dutchman heard a soft moan from his left and knew that another man had died, his hopes soared. Perhaps they could take the ship, after all. Although one ship could not begin to make up for the loss of the Fulani ivory, at least there would be satisfaction in knowing that once Renno reached the river with the ivory, he would not have a ship to transport it. In the meantime Vanderrenner could gather Beni soldiers and wrest the treasure from his enemy.

Lost in his newly born dreams, he was not as alert as he had been. His foot contacted a pewter mug left on the deck by a sleeping seaman, and it skidded toward the scuppers. Vanderrenner froze in place for long, tense moments before concluding that no one had heard.

But Uanna had heard. Her eyes had sprung open at the sound. She lay still, scarcely breathing, heart thudding. There was no repetition of the sound that had awakened her. Her eyes closed and then snapped open again at a faint rustling. She moved silently, lifting the curtain of clothing, and peered out into the black, motionless night. The ship showed no lights, but toward the stern a shadow moved. She put her hand over Tanyere's mouth and woke him. He sat up, rubbing his eyes.

"There," she whispered, pointing. "What do you see?"

Tanyere wasn't sure he could see anything, but the blackness moved, and his hand clenched his spear. And to their rear, there was the smallest of sounds. Tanyere turned his head slowly to see a black hand pulling the clothes curtain aside. There was a knife in the other hand. Tanyere, young but trained by his father, moved with one quick lunge, driving the Beni spear into a softness that only resisted when the spear penetrated deeply. A shriek of pain came from the impaled intruder as he fell.

Suddenly the deck was alive with shouting men. The three remaining attackers fired their muskets, but no one ball found its mark. Seamen closed in on the flashes to engage the men in hand-to-hand fighting.

Billy had sprung from his pallet at the sound of the dying scream. He wore only a loincloth, and his tattooed body gleamed with sweat. He broke out of his cabin on the run, his hand reaching for the heavy, long harpoon that always stood beside the cabin's hatchway. "Light," he bellowed as he burst into the darkness on deck. "Someone light the lanterns."

It seemed as if it took forever for the lanterns to glow, transforming shadows into a melee of bodies on the deck. Billy moved first to one side, then to the other, looking for a target for his harpoon. There was none; the three remaining black intruders were quickly swarmed under.

"Keep them alive!" Billy yelled, but he was too late. Knives and belaying pins had done a deadly job. "Search the ship!" he ordered, and sailors began to move about with lanterns.

Vanderrenner was cowering in the shadows of the rail. It had all happened too quickly. At his feet lay a seaman, killed by his knife. He fumbled at the body and hissed with disgust when his hands emerged wet with blood but without having located so much as a powder horn or a shot bag.

He had only seconds to make his decision. If he went over the side into the water, he would wet and ruin the last small amount of gunpowder in his possession and be alone in the jungle, with his chances of reaching Benin greatly diminished. Moreover, he was very angry. When he saw Mingo's woman moving toward Billy, her dark legs striding strongly, he moved on impulse. With one bound he was behind Uanna, his left arm around her waist, his right pressing his razor-sharp blade to her throat.

Billy saw the movement and cocked his arm, poised to loose the harpoon.

"Hold!" Vanderrenner yelled. "Or the woman dies."

"Stand easy," Billy shouted to the men who had begun to converge on Vanderrenner.

"I want shot and powder," the slaver demanded, "and food. Put them into a boat. I will release the woman when I am safely away from the ship."

"Do as he says," Billy said, his arm still cocked, the harpoon at the ready. Men moved to put supplies into a boat and started to lower it. Vanderrenner and Uanna edged toward the rail where the boat was being lowered, while Tanyere stood wide-eyed and helpless, a comforting arm around Little One.

"I take it," Billy said, "that you have encountered Renno."

Vanderrenner snarled. "You may tell the savage that he has not heard the last of me."

"So," Billy muttered, "Renno is alive." He raised his voice. "If you harm that woman, I will follow you to the ends of this becursed land."

The Dutchman was forced to cross the width of the deck, moving directly in front of the mainmast.

"I warn you," Vanderrenner said, "any false move and she dies."

"The boat is ready," a seaman called as the vessel hit the dark water of the river with a mighty splash.

Vanderrenner had paused directly in front of the mast. He was taller than Uanna, her head coming up to his shoulders. Over her dark head his contorted face and his throat were visible.

Billy knew that if he allowed the Dutchman to leave the ship with Uanna, she would not survive. He tightened his grasp on the harpoon. Many times he had thrown the heavy weapon. Many times he had won bets with his accuracy. He had to decide now, for Vanderrenner was looking toward the rail, his eyes diverted momentarily.

The harpoon made a hissing sound as it was propelled by the full strength of Billy's stocky body and his strong right arm. The deadly point touched Vanderrenner's throat at the hollow below his Adam's apple, and blood gushed. There was a thud as the harpoon penetrated, thrust through, and buried its sharp head into the stout wood of the mainmast.

Billy was on the move even as the harpoon flew, but it was unnecessary. The harpoon had severed Vanderrenner's spinal cord. His eyes went wide. He was alive, but all strength left his arm, then his entire body, and he slumped.

Uanna jerked free, falling to the deck. Tanyere ran forward, helping her to her feet.

The Dutchman's body was limp, his arms dangling at his side, his weight supported by the harpoon through his throat and neck.

As the days passed without a sign of Ena, Renna, or Se-quo-i, Toshabe's concern grew. Neither she nor anyone else in the village could know that the delay had been caused by Nora Johnson's illness and subsequent death. Ha-ace and Rusog, who had faith in Ena's ability to handle any situation, told her not to worry. Toshabe knew that the warriors were basing their opinion on Ena's past record, and it was true that Ena had excelled as a warrior and a scout. But, Toshabe knew, Ena had never before given birth.

Although she said nothing of her concern in front of Little Hawk, he, too, had been aware of the passing time. "They should be back,'' he remarked one day when he was alone with Toshabe.

"Perhaps they stayed for a visit with the Johnsons," Toshabe said, although, knowing Ena, she didn't believe it.

"Grandmother," Little Hawk said, "the weather is fine. Don't you think we should take a walk in the forests?"

Toshabe smiled. "An excellent suggestion. I think that we should walk toward the east and be in no hurry to get back. What do you think?"

"You have always been wise," Little Hawk replied.

"I think, too, that the outing should be our little secret," Toshabe added. If she announced her intention to travel toward Knoxville until they met Ena's party, she knew the men would laugh at her worries and, perhaps, even forbid an older woman and a young boy from venturing out on such an excursion.

Little Hawk nodded in understanding.

They set out early one morning under fair skies and a kind sun, traveling light. Little Hawk had his knife and his bow, and Toshabe carried food and the means of making fire.

The sun smiled on Ena and her party, as well, during the first day of their travel. The pace was slow because Renna insisted that she was no baby to be carried by Se-quo-i. That pace suited Ena; she felt very heavy, and the baby pressed upward against her diaphragm, so she was short of breath. Twice during that day she had to stop, bent from a severe cramp in her stomach. When Se-quo-i chose a place for a camp beside a cool, clear little rill, they had not covered a quarter of the distance to the village.

Ena had no appetite. She allowed Se-quo-i to make her a bed of pine boughs, then she spread her blanket and was asleep immediately. When she was awakened by a severe pain in her midsection, the moon was high. She put her hands on her belly and whispered, "Son of mine, behave yourself." The cramp passed, and she was dozing when another, more severe contraction hit her with a force that caused her to gasp. The sound woke Se-quo-i. He put dry twigs on the embers of the fire and came to kneel beside her.

"I'm fine," she assured him. "Muscle cramps from the walking." But even as she spoke, the great ache came again, and she closed her lips tightly, straining against it.

"We will get an early start and reach the village as quickly as possible," Se-quo-i told her.

"Yes."

The cramp subsided, and she went back to sleep.

Se-quo-i put more dry wood on the fire and sat for a long time watching his friend, but she was sleeping soundly. He went back to his blanket and lay down. As the sun was just rising, his worst fears were realized—he saw Ena tense and strain against a great spasm. He rose and began to cut supports for a crude shelter.

"What are you doing?" Ena called to him. "We must be on our way."

He talked as he dug holes for the supports. "I'm afraid we won't be traveling today."

"Of course we—" Another contraction cut off her words.

"That's two you've had since dawn," the Cherokee pointed out. "Was it thus through the latter part of the night?"

"Only a few."

"And now the pain comes more often," Se-quo-i stated.

Ena's eyes widened. "It can't be. It is not my time. I have a month—"

"My dear Ena," Se-quo-i said, speaking English, "you are a woman of vast experience, except in this. Your infant warrior is telling you that it is time."

"Oh." Ena gasped. "I see." She hissed as a giant contraction seized her by the midsection and squeezed.

After a chilly night the early-morning sun was hazy. High clouds were arranged in fluffy rows, like small, white chickens, bespeaking a change in the weather. As Se-quo-i worked, Ena rose from her bed to help lace pine boughs on top of the shelter.

Renna woke. "Are we building a playhouse?" she asked, looking puzzled.

"Yes," Se-quo-i replied. "And you can help. We will need more firewood, and you're just the right size to gather it."

"As soon as we have breakfast," Renna countered.

Ena stopped work on the shelter and gave Renna food from the pack that had been prepared in the Johnson kitchen. She tried to hide her discomfort when a pain came, but Renna saw her aunt's face go pale and watched her strain and reach for a horizontal member of the shelter for support.

"That's the way Grandmother Nora looked when her stomach hurt her," Renna whimpered, her eyes filling.

Ena looked at the little girl quickly. Renna's face was contorted with fright. "It's only your cousin, here," Ena soothed, patting her belly. "He's misbehaving this morning."

"You won't die?"

"Of course not," Ena said, going to take Renna in her arms. "We may, however, have to let your cousin come into the world right here. That won't frighten you, will it?"

"No . . ." Renna said doubtfully. "I guess not."

"You can help," Ena suggested. "Get wood, as Se-quo-i has asked you to do."

Another pain forced Ena to sit down. Renna had moved away and was gathering dry sticks. "Se-quo-i," Ena whispered. He came close. "I know little of this. I was depending on my mother and the midwife."

The young man smiled. "Fortunately you are traveling with an odd fellow of endless curiosity. I have watched the birth of babies. The midwives, of course, would not let a mere man assist, but it looked to be quite a straightforward process."

"That is easy for you to say," Ena said, laughing.

"You'll do all the work," he continued. "I'll be here to say 'There, there' and 'Now push,' and things like that."

"I am blessed," Ena said, still smiling until another pain doubled her over. When the contraction had passed, beads of perspiration shone on her upper lip and she blew out her breath. "That was the best so far."

"The pains are coming close together," Se-quo-i remarked. "But often, with a first baby, a woman's travail lasts for a long time."

"Manitous," Ena said, rolling her eyes. "How long?"

"A few hours."

"Thank you very much," she said.

She was lying down under the shelter when the next pain came, and it lasted longer than the others. Renna, eyes wide, had come to stand beside the shelter.

"Here, helper," Se-quo-i said. "Take off that nice petticoat you're wearing."

"Me?" Renna asked. She had only two changes of the clothing that Nora had made for her since Ena—intending to have her niece dressed decently in buckskins as quickly as possible—had left most of her clothing in Knoxville.

"Yes, you," Se-quo-i said.

"Why?"

"I want to tear it into strips so that you can then wet them in the stream for me," Se-quo-i said.

"Oh, well, then," Renna consented. Soon she was helping Se-quo-i cool Ena's brow with the damp cloths. A spasm took control of Ena.

"It hurts bad?" Renna asked, her pupils dilated.

"No," Ena said. "It's natural. It is a beautiful pain, because it will result in a son being born."

"I never want to have a son," Renna announced.

"The cloths are drying," Se-quo-i said. "Helper, take them to the stream."

"What will we do with her?" Ena asked when the child had left. "She's too young to understand. She shouldn't see this."

"Some are required to grow up faster than others," Se-quo-i said.

The sky had turned gray with the advance of a cloud mass from the west. There was a smell of rain in the air. The Cherokee busied himself reinforcing the roof of the shelter. Renna returned and sat next to Ena, wincing each time her aunt tensed, went pale, and strained. The pains were close together, but they had been since early morning.

"Renna, my love," Se-quo-i said. "More wood."

"More?" the girl complained. "There's a big pile now."

"More," Se-quo-i ordered. "I saw a few pieces of lighter wood there." He pointed. "You can tell it by its good, rich smell. It will burn well."

Renna went in the direction that Se-quo-i had pointed, and soon she was out of sight.

"Don't go too far," Ena called.

"I see the wood," Renna called back.

"I need to look at you," Se-quo-i said.

At first Ena didn't understand, but when he reached for the blanket and pulled it up from her feet, she felt a great flush begin. Only one man, Rusog, had ever seen her nakedness.

"Pull the dress up above your stomach," Se-quo-i requested, and she obeyed, her face burning. She felt his hands on her knees and, after initial resistance, opened herself to his gaze. He pulled the blanket down quickly.

"It will be soon," he said. "Already you are opening."

"How so?"

He laughed. "You should have had a long talk with your mother. The Master of Life put into your body the knowledge, the ability to change, to alter the structure of your bones, to spread them and give the baby an opening. That process has begun."

"It is taking its own sweet time." Ena gasped as muscles contracted with great force.

Toshabe and Little Hawk made camp some miles from the halfway point to Knoxville after a day during which Toshabe discovered, to her pleasure, that she was still capable of a long march at a distance-covering pace. Little Hawk, scorning the corn and the smoked, dried meat in his grandmother's pack, slew a rabbit with his small bow and took his due as a warrior, tending the fire while Toshabe roasted the meat. He had also prepared beds, building his across the fire from Toshabe's.

Toshabe went to sleep immediately, somewhat amused because she felt safe. She told herself that she should be alert; after all, Little Hawk was only a small boy. But when a deer passed close to the camp, breaking just one twig to wake her, she saw Little Hawk already sitting up, bow in hand.

"It's all right, Grandmother," he informed her. "It was only a deer."

Once more she awoke, in the coolness of early morning, to see him squatting beside the fire, feeding it branches.

"You should sleep," she said.

"Grandmother, rise and prepare yourself for travel."

"It's still dark," she said.

In the light of the fire his face was serious, too young to

wear that expression of concern. "They need us. There's something wrong."

Toshabe felt a chill. He had stated his worry with such conviction, as if he knew without question that something was amiss. She was reminded of Renno when he was younger. He had often voiced things that he could not possibly have known, unless he had been told of those things by the manitous. This was Renno's son. She got the pack ready quickly, and they gnawed on rabbit bones as they moved at a fast pace into a gray, dull morning that promised rain.

A light rain started falling just past midday. At first Renna crouched by Ena's head under the protection of the shelter's roof. The contractions came almost without respite, and it was obvious that Ena was in terrific pain. Sweat drenched her face and her hair, and Se-quo-i swabbed it away with damp cloths. Ena was gasping and breathing hard just as Grandmother Nora had done when she had had one of her "spells."

Although she didn't voice her fears, Renna knew that Auntie Ena was going to die, and she wanted to cry, to beg Ena to stop. And then Uncle Se-quo-i lifted the blanket and looked under it at Ena, and this, combined with his expression when he emerged, frightened her almost as much as Ena's panting.

Renna crawled out from under the shelter, went to the fire, drew her blanket up around her shoulders, and sat there in the light rain, thoroughly frightened and increasingly miserable.

Se-quo-i folded the blanket up to Ena's waist, looked at her, and smiled. "I can see a head of very black hair, like his father's," he whispered.

"Oh, oh, oh," Ena said, laughing through a severe contraction.

"Only a few more," Se-quo-i encouraged. "One, two, push! Now!"

To her shame Ena let out a keening wail as she pushed and felt as if she were being ripped in half. And then there was a feeling of something slipping, and vast relief as she sank back.

"It is indeed a son!" Se-quo-i enthused.

The baby was tiny, but then, he was thinking, it had been born a month early. His hands were shaking as he received the baby, and he feared that it would slide from his hands, but he held it and seized it by the heels and ran his finger into its mouth and then slapped it on the behind.

Renna put her hands over her ears. Ena's wail seemed to hang in the air, and then there was the sound of something else—a protesting, angry howl—and she could stand no more. She could not stay there and see Auntie Ena, whom she loved, die. She leaped to her feet, the blanket still around her shoulders, and plunged heedlessly into the trees. She ran aimlessly, her vision blurred with tears. Her only thought was to put distance between herself and Auntie Ena's death.

Se-quo-i tried to lay the baby on Ena's stomach, as he'd seen the midwives do, so that he could cut the umbilical cord. Her stomach was still round and huge, and a fear washed over him. Something was wrong.

"Oh, let me see him," she whispered.

He held the boy up. And then he put the baby on the blanket and severed the cord, tied it, and was about to hand the newborn into Ena's extended hands when she tensed and clutched her belly as another contraction ripped through her.

"It won't stop," Ena whispered. "It won't stop. Why won't it stop?"

He had no answer. Her pains were not like the afterpains

he'd witnessed when watching the midwives. Then he heard the sound of running footsteps and leaped to his feet. Outside the hut he felt a surge of pure joy when Toshabe came into the clearing. He silently thanked all the spirits.

"There is a son," he announced, leading Toshabe into the tiny hut. They knelt beside Ena. "But"—he pointed to Ena's stomach—"something is wrong."

Toshabe put her hand on Ena's belly. Ena was straining against a great pain. Se-quo-i was shocked to hear Toshabe burst into great laughter.

"There's nothing wrong," Toshabe declared, peering closely at Ena's opening. "The young warrior was not alone. And now the other comes."

Little Hawk had followed Toshabe closely and had come to a halt looking down onto a tiny, still-bloody baby, hands and feet moving erratically.

"Has this one been in battle?" he asked.

"Go," Toshabe ordered.

"Mother?" Ena whispered.

"I am here," Toshabe assured her. "You're doing very well. You are simply making up the time you've lost by bringing two of them into the world at once."

"Twins?" Ena gasped, laughing weakly.

"Go into the woods, Little Hawk," Toshabe said. "Catch us some lunch."

"I have never seen a baby born," Little Hawk said calmly. "Does it hurt very much, Ena?"

"Go and keep Renna company," Se-quo-i said. And at that thought he stretched to look into the clearing. The girl was nowhere to be seen. He jumped to his feet, went outside, and called her name. There was no answer.

"I'll go find her," he said, sticking his head in the hut.

"I'll need your help here," Toshabe told him. "You have

proven by one birth that you are a capable midwife. You, Little Hawk, find your sister.''

"She can't have gone far," Se-quo-i said. "Probably after more wood.''

Little Hawk, glancing back now and then through the light rain to the shelter, cast a circle around the fire. He saw tracks where Renna had gathered wood, but two or three times the tracks and signs led back to the fire. He made a broader circle out of sight of the fire and the shelter and came across a sign. Small footprints far enough apart to tell him that Renna had been running led him on an erratic course through the trees toward a densely treed rise of ground. Twice he lost the trail, for the detritus of the forest left little imprint, but each time he found it again. The trail veered away from the rising ground and became ever more erratic. Once, the tracks made a complete circle. He knew that his sister was confused, lost, and trying to find her way back toward the camp, but when the trail straightened into one direction, it led away from the camp.

My father and I will have to give her lessons, he thought.

His own sense of direction was intact, even though he had circled to find and follow the trail. Renna had been moving at a walk, and he called out, for he felt that she should be near. There was no answer. He pushed on, lost the trail, circled, and came on it again. Here she had torn her dress on a broken limb; there she had stepped in a soft spot where a squirrel had been digging for buried nuts. He had learned his lessons well, for a trail through a pine forest was among the most difficult to follow.

He judged that he was well over a mile from the camp when he heard sounds, not those made by a small girl, off on one flank. He stopped. Something was moving through the forest, crashing through brush, with great unconcern for noise.

Not a deer, he thought. A deer would be moving much more quietly.

He forged on, following Renna's path, and the sounds diminished. Here she had veered off to the left, and now she turned, moving aimlessly. The trail was making a wide circle, back toward the area whence had come the sound of something large moving in the underbrush. Little Hawk increased his speed, even at the risk of losing the trail. And then he froze in place as he heard a scream of fright, then the gusty, rumbling growl of a bear.

"Renna," he called.

His only answer was another roar from the bear. He jerked his bow off his shoulder, nocked an arrow, and ran toward the snarl of the bear and the whimper from Renna. He burst out of the thick undergrowth, covered with scratches. The first thing he saw was a black bear, rearing up, tall, his huge paws slashing angrily at the air. And then he saw Renna. She had fallen. The bear was standing tall not ten feet from her, waddling forward on its rear legs. Mesmerized by fright, she lay on the ground with her head turned, eyes wide, watching the bear come closer.

Little Hawk's first impulse was to draw his bow, but he knew that his boy-sized arrow would not even pierce the bear's tough hide. Moreover, the bear was the totem of his clan. No bear-clan member would harm his wild brother. Into his mind flashed memories of tales told over a glowing campfire. It was said that more than once his father had spoken to the sacred totem, to a wild bear, and once he had tamed a killer bear and had treated a wound on the bear's paw.

Little Hawk moved forward, his heart pounding, and extended his hands. "Brother," he whispered. He cleared his throat. "Brother," he said, louder.

The bear turned its head and gave a fearsome roar.

Little Hawk again edged forward, although his fear was great, to put himself between Renna and the animal. "I am Little Hawk, of the bear clan of the Seneca. And this one is my sister. Peace, Brother."

He considered how swiftly he might turn, scoop Renna up from the ground, and flee. But the bear, he knew, would be much faster. He had only one choice. He took a step closer and spoke soothingly in Seneca. "You are great and powerful, my brother. I sing your praises, totem of my clan."

A low growl rumbled from the bear, and slowly it lowered its forepaws to the ground.

"We beg your pardon for disturbing you in your hunting ground," Little Hawk continued. "And now, if it pleases you, we will go."

The bear shook its head but made no forward movement. Little Hawk turned, took Renna's hand, lifted her, and without looking back led her into the trees. After a few steps he took a deep, shuddering breath, exhaled in a gusting sigh, and looked over his shoulder. The bear reared and opened its mouth to loll out a tongue, then softly growled before sinking to the ground once again to turn and pad away.

Renna, shivering, clung to her brother.

"If you ever again are in the forest alone," Little Hawk instructed patiently, kindly, "try to travel downhill if there is a slope and stay in a straight line. If there is moss on the trees, it will be on the north side."

"I forgot," Renna said.

"Well, that's all right," Little Hawk told her. "We'll just have to see to it that you're not left alone again—at least not until our father and I have a chance to teach you." He closed his arm tightly around her and led her slowly back through the rain to the campsite.

Renno came out of a sound sleep to a feeling of great urgency pertaining to his children. The day had been long and eventful. Scattered fighting had continued into the late evening before Ogane's soldiers of the Order of the Hand had restored peace. For a while Renno and El-i-chi had watched in the throne room as Tano, new oba of Benin, his wife-to-be beside him, held audience for noblemen and other personages. Ogane sat at Tano's other side. The son of Eweka had willingly stepped aside so Tano could claim his rightful position. It had not been so easy to watch Sokata, Ogane's childhood sweetheart, become Tano's betrothed.

There had been a sameness to it that quickly bored El-i-chi, and soon Renno allowed one of the buxom young girls assigned to care for him to guide him to a room with a pallet covered with leopard skins. The smooth feel of the skins reminded him of Ese, and he prayed to his manitous for the departed spirit of the animal who had died while protecting him. Then he slept quickly and soundly until he woke with a nagging feeling of uneasiness.

He walked into the night. The palace was quiet, and the only sounds were insects buzzing around him and dogs barking from outside the palace walls. The strange stars in the unusually haze-free sky reminded him again of the distance separating him from his home and his people.

Time was growing short. Within days—if Billy the Pequot followed his orders—the *Seneca Warrior* would leave the Niger Delta for England.

Renno did not go back to sleep. In his room he cleaned his weapons. He had retrieved the longbow from the square and had recovered three undamaged arrows from the dead. He honed the stiletto by the light of an oil lamp and, with first light, was shaking El-i-chi into reluctant waking. The shaman had just awakened Mingo when girls came shyly to tell the great warriors that the oba requested their presence.

Tano was breakfasting in the room where he had slain

Eweka. Baro and Xeno were also present. Sokata, arrayed in finery, sat beside the new oba.

The oba jumped to his feet and, to the horror of the Beni elders who had been summoned to pay allegiance, rushed to take Renno's arm in the Seneca clasp of friendship.

"Be it known to all," Tano announced, "that this is my friend, my brother, and an honorary noble of Benin. The same is true for El-i-chi and Mingo. Their blood is my blood."

"So be it," Ogane approved.

"Bring food to these noblemen of Benin," Tano ordered, and the women immediately obeyed. He escorted the three to sit with him.

Sokata smiled, looking every bit a queen. The food was plentiful, but Renno had no hunger.

"My friend, you do me great honor," the white Indian said when Tano had finished recounting his debts to Renno and renewing his pledge of brotherhood.

"Any gift and any request within my power is yours," Tano proclaimed.

"I ask only a boat," Renno replied, "to take us to our ship near the Dutchman's fort."

"So soon?" Tano asked, greatly disappointed.

"I have been away from my people too long," Renno said, feeling a resurgence of the odd feeling that had awakened him. "Although it saddens me, I ask that you arrange for us to leave today."

"So be it," Tano consented, "although my sadness, too, is great."

The Beni knew the rivers and watercourses well. Tano had sent an escort of a dozen boats, one laden with gifts—coral ornaments, small, ancient bronze works of art, and exquisitely carved ivory. The distance was not great, but with the twisting and turning among the gloomy mangrove swamps, three days were consumed in reaching the waterway leading to the Dutchman's fort.

The *Seneca Warrior* was a sweet and welcome sight, although the sodden climate had mildewed her sails and dimmed her paint. Billy the Pequot hailed them, and soon they were aboard, Mingo trying to take all three members of his family into his arms at one time. They had arrived a full week after the deadline given to Billy by Renno, but neither man mentioned it. Tano's gifts were taken aboard, and Billy examined the treasures with great interest.

"They offered me nothing like this in trade," he complained.

"Nor will they," El-i-chi put in. "These are gifts to those who fought side by side with Tano, who is now oba."

"Good for Tano," Billy enthused. He grinned. "Those callers you sent to us arrived."

Renno, his mind far away, was puzzled and looked at Billy to elaborate.

"The Fulani," Billy said. "There's a small fortune in ivory belowdecks. I have already arranged to meet the Fulani here, at the site of the Dutchman's fort, with the rest of the muskets. Your wife and brother-in-law will turn a tidy profit from this."

"The rest of the muskets?" Renno inquired. "Then you gave them the muskets that were aboard?"

Billy nodded. "I had held them back from the Benis for some reason. Maybe because I didn't like the bloody bastards."

The Beni escort that had come with Renno had not yet started the trip back. "Tell them," Renno said to El-i-chi, "that the Fulani now have muskets. Tell them to inform Tano, so that he can be ready."

Billy's face fell. "I traded muskets to a tribe that are enemies of Benin? But they were from so far inland—"

"You did rightly," Renno assured him. "The purpose of

the trip was trade. If you hadn't traded muskets, others would have. Where the white man goes, so go his weapons, and we are powerless to stop it.''

"I guess you're as eager as I am to get out of this swamp," Billy said. "The Dutchman made his way back here, and here he'll stay. We threw his body to the reptiles—a fitting end for the likes of him."

"So," Renno acknowledged. He could not feel sympathy for the slaver. The sachem had had his fill of this savage land, and he longed for the clean freshness of the land of the Seneca-Cherokee village.

He looked back from a distance on the low, dark coastline of the Bight of Benin, then turned to feel the fresh ocean breeze on his face. He had come to that musty, steaming land only to save his friend, and now he was going home—first to England and Beth and then to America—and he could not have the good earth of his own land under his moccasins quickly enough.

Oddly, aboard ship, he no longer experienced that sense that something was terribly wrong.

Ena's ordeal ended with the birth of a second child, a girl identical to the firstborn boy. It was not an easy birth, and the day was long gone before the babies lay side by side, and Ena, much weakened, slept. It had been a tense and trying time for Toshabe, who feared for the life of the second child, who was born feet first. Indeed, the girl was not breathing and would not respond to a vigorous slap on the bottom. In desperation Se-quo-i splashed cold creek water into her face and onto her body, and then and only then did the tiny lungs fill and a weak, angry cry ring out.

Renna's misadventure was soon forgotten when she was

allowed to see the twins and, with Toshabe's help, to hold the boy. Ena was awake, her eyes bright with happiness.

"Little Hawk," Toshabe said, "can you reach the village alone?"

"Of course," he said disdainfully.

"Go, then, and bring men with a litter," Toshabe requested.

Ena objected sternly. "I will not be carried back to my village like some weak, wounded warrior."

That discussion lasted for a while, then Toshabe surrendered to her daughter's wishes. Little Hawk took Renna to the fire and gave her his blanket to add to hers.

The rain stopped before darkness came, and with the morning Ena was standing. She had to go slowly, but she walked the distance, refusing to lean on Se-quo-i's arm, and by the time they reached the village to find Rusog and Ha-ace preparing to follow Toshabe and Little Hawk, she was walking strongly and erectly and carrying one of the babies in her arms.

Rusog looked at the child in Ena's arms and gave a whoop, and then he saw the other in Toshabe's arms and began to do a wild little dance of joy before he embraced Ena and closely examined his children.

The news spread, and Ah-wa-o and An-da were appointed to help care for the babies. Well-wishers from both villages came in a steady stream to Rusog and Ena's home to share the happiness.

The sun smiled on the *Seneca Warrior,* and the winds were favorable. "Let us not linger long in this foreign land," El-i-chi said in Seneca as he leaned on the rail beside Renno to view the shores of England.

"So," Renno said. Over a year had passed since he had last trod the woodlands of home, since he had seen his mother, his sister, and all his people. And still he was an ocean and a long march away. Even under the most favorable circumstances the year would be old before he could cross the mountains and go westward to the village.

No one was waiting when the ship docked, for, of course, those who were interested in her had no way of knowing that she had completed the long voyage. Renno was eager to see Beth and to arrange for the voyage home, but he took time to find a well-armed ship that was leaving within the week for the Caribbean. He arranged passage for Mingo, Uanna, and the two boys. Their parting was brief in words but deep in feeling.

"Come again to my country, my friend," Mingo invited, clasping Renno's arm.

"Perhaps, one day," the white Indian responded, but there was sadness in knowing that he would probably never see Mingo again. Yet he felt great satisfaction that the big black man would soon be back among his own, as Renno longed to be.

The gifts from Tano were sent to Beaumont Hall. Renno and El-i-chi rented horses and rode hard, arriving at the manor on a balmy evening to a wild greeting from William and tears of happiness from Estrela. But Renno had to ask Beth's whereabouts. William spoke evenly, but Estrela's stricken look did not escape Renno.

"She's at the country house of our family friend, Sir Joffre Jowett. I'll send a messenger at once, Renno. She'd never forgive me if I didn't let her know as quickly as possible."

"No messenger," Renno said. "Direct me there."

"Good idea," William approved. "Quite a surprise for her to see you ride up."

"Very much of a surprise," Estrela said, getting for her tone of voice a severe look from William.

"Rest tonight," William urged, "and let Estrela put some

meat back on your bones. You've both lost weight. And there's a lot of news to be exchanged: New Hampshire became the ninth state to ratify the Constitution in your country, which puts that document into effect. And the new Congress will be meeting soon. Your friend George Washington will be the first president.''

"That is good," Renno agreed.

"And El-i-chi," William said, leading them into the dining room, "a certain lady has been inquiring for you. I think you remember Elaine?"

El-i-chi grinned uneasily. "It might be best to tell her that I died in Africa."

William was highly excited when he heard the news of the ivory trade and the prospect for much more. He told Renno of Beth's success with her venture. There was much, much more, and a showing of the Huntington baby, Ena, but the words seemed empty and meaningless to Renno.

He could not share William's pleasure over the success of Billy's trading. Nor did he have any desire to return to Africa, ever. In that dark land there had been a surplus of death and cruelty, heat and misery. As long as he lived he would not forget the smell of blood that had permeated the very air in the great square in Benin. He was pleased that Tano had come into his rightful place and that he had found love with Sokata, but he did not envy Tano his wealth of bronze and ivory or his power. He would remember Tano and Sokata with fondness, but he would think of the city of Benin, always, as the City of Blood.

Chapter XVI

Even El-i-chi had to admit that his brother looked impressive when dressed like an English gentleman. The shaman didn't like to see Renno in the role of a white man, but he felt a perverse sense of pride in knowing that Renno could hold his own, and more, in any circumstance.

William had offered to accompany his friend to Jowett's manor, but Renno had said he preferred to go alone and would not presume to take William away from his business affairs.

"I'll be back in no more than four days," he said after checking a map and listening to William's careful instructions. "I'll be in your debt, William, if you'd arrange immediate passage for us to Wilmington or Norfolk."

Under different circumstances it would have been a pleasant ride. The weather was generally good as he rode through a tailored countryside of miniature farms and small villages with ancient, stone houses. He was never far from some habitation, and he often met people on the roads. He understood now why Englishmen were wont to venture out to far lands, for space, for land, for simple living room. Would his own country, with the prolific breeding habits of the Europeans, look like this—manicured, every acre in use, with only token stands of forest? Would the Seneca, the Cherokee, even the wild tribes of the West, one day be living in peaceful regimentation under the rule of a central government? That he doubted. In all of the vast lands of the North American continent before the coming of the white man, only the Iroquois had made any attempt at organization beyond tribal and clan units. Regimentation was not in the Indian's nature. And yet, as he rode through a green, blooming countryside in a country that was quite small, where masses of people were compacted into an area smaller than the area claimed as hunting grounds by several tribes in America, he realized that change was inevitable.

Change would come, and his children and their children's children would perish unless they could come to an accommodation with the European style of life. The compacted masses of people in the towns and villages of England, multiplied by all the towns and villages in Europe, would send their shiploads of people hungry for land and for space. And what had happened along the eastern seaboard of the continent would gradually be expanded past the mountains and westward.

Little Hawk was Seneca, but with only a small portion of Indian blood. When he grew to manhood, what would his life be like? How would he dress? How would he earn his living? So thinking, Renno had an urge to rip away the tailored English finery, to bare his chest, to paint his face the colors of a Seneca warrior, and to strike out defiantly—but against what? Whom?

Joffre Jowett's country house overlooked the waters of the English Channel. The approach was through neatly cultivated fields, where workers halted to tip caps to the gentleman who rode past. A lane lined by huge trees led to formal gardens. A maze of hedges occupied a great space in the front garden. An outdoor party was under way on a pleasant afternoon when Renno rode up, gave his horse to a bowing servant, and stood for a moment searching among the people on the lawn who were strolling, sitting on the grass or in lawn chairs, or picking at food from a long buffet table.

Beth was not among them. He walked toward the food table where several elegantly dressed men and women stood. One face was familiar, that of Joffre Jowett. One bejeweled lady caught sight of Renno approaching and whispered to a companion, "Who is that handsome devil?"

Jowett, at first, did not recognize Renno. He stepped forward and said, "Good afternoon, sir. May I help you?" Then Jowett recognized the chiseled chin, the strong nose, the piercing, blue eyes. "My God. You're back."

"So," Renno said, his eyes leaving Joffre's face to search for Beth.

It was a moment before Jowett regained his composure. "I expect you're looking for Beth. I think you'll find her there, in the maze, with a few of the children."

"Thank you," Renno said as he moved off.

He entered the maze. Lush green hedges extended to a height of ten feet. The grass underfoot was deep and perfectly manicured. He took a wrong turn, faced a dead end, and had to retrace his steps, moving deeper toward the core of the maze. He heard young voices—a girl giggled and was joined by the throaty laugh of a woman. Beth. His heart lifted, and he ran toward the sound, nearing the voices by trial and error.

He rounded a sharp corner and saw her, tall, dressed in white, her flame-colored hair piled atop her head to expose the nape of her slender neck. Five children were gathered around her in a small square at the center of the maze. For long moments he was content to watch her, to hear the sound of her voice as she spoke to the little ones.

Then she turned and saw him. Her mouth fell open, then was closed. She swayed on her feet, and as a small girl screamed, Renno ran forward to catch Beth as she collapsed. She was light in his arms, and she smelled of violets.

Her eyes fluttered open. "Renno?"

"I am here."

"Oh, praise God! Renno, Renno, Renno." She was covering his lips, his cheeks, his nose, with sweet, warm kisses while the children giggled. "Oh, thank God you're alive."

"I feel sure of that," Renno said, speaking lightly to cover the great emotion he felt.

Then, suddenly, she went rigid in his arms. The joyful smile faded from her face. Her eyes sought his, and she burst into frantic sobbing as she tried to pull out of his arms.

"Here, here," Renno said helplessly, thinking that she was weeping for joy. "Come, let's find a place where we can talk."

"Oh God, oh God," Beth was saying as her body was convulsed by sobs. Only she knew that her tears were not the sweet tears of joy but of regret and guilt. For only last night, thinking that Renno must be dead, she had allowed Sir Joffre Jowett into her bed for the first time.

For weeks Ena was content to mother the twins, to pamper them and hold them and nurse them from breasts that once had been small and hard but were now full and sensitive.

Summer found her sitting by the swimming creek, watching the tribes' young ones cavort in the water, dreaming of the day when her two babes would be among the wild young ones who were led in their daring dives and splashes by Little Hawk.

She had named the boy Rusog Ho-ya, for he was the fruit of Rusog; the girl, since she had been born in the rain, We-yo O-no-ga-nose, Good Water.

In the manner of men, the chief of the Cherokee left the care of the babies to Ena and willing helpers such as Ah-wa-o and An-da. But in the privacy of his lodge he often held the twins, his eyes smiling as he examined the perfection of their tiny fingers, their limbs, which, from small beginnings—both were very small and born a month prematurely—had acquired a healthy chubbiness. Already Ena was giving them a taste of food, first chewing it thoroughly herself, then spooning it into the little mouths. Ho-ya was gaining weight faster than his sister, but We-yo had outgrown her weakness at birth within the first two months of her life.

It was a beautiful time for Ena. To the surprise of many, the woman-warrior maiden seemed perfectly content in her motherhood. Even her cooking improved, much to Rusog's pleasure.

Rusog found his wife by the stream, with the twins lying naked on a blanket beside her, happily playing with their toes. Ena smiled up at him. He sat next to her and watched the antics of the village children for a long time before he spoke.

"It is now the turning of the year," he remarked.

"Yes, soon the great bear in the sky will drip blood to color the leaves."

"He has been gone for over a year," Rusog continued.

Ena frowned. "He will be back before the first snow. I feel it."

"Tor-yo-ne has called council."

Ena sat up, anger in her face. "It is time that we put that young wolf in his place."

"How do you propose that such a thing be done?" Rusog asked. "The young Seneca tell me, 'Cherokee, this is not your affair.' " He shrugged. "I am not invited to the council, as I have always been."

"Then I will go," Ena said, her voice low. "I have in my veins the blood of Renno, Ja-gonh, and Ghonkaba. I have killed my enemies and matched the best warriors in the long march."

"Then go," Rusog encouraged, "for they are gathering now."

Ena left the twins with Toshabe, who, as matriarch of the tribe, was concerned about this new tactic of the young war chief from the north. Ha-ace, as a senior warrior and a pine tree of the clans, was, of course, to be present in the council with the other elders.

Ena dressed in a worn buckskin skirt and tunic, and when she entered the council longhouse, she carried bow, quiver, tomahawk, and knife. The senior warriors of the tribe were already seated, a pipe making the rounds. Tor-yo-ne sat at the far end of the circle, and his eyes widened when he saw Ena enter. She made a place for herself beside Ha-ace.

"Is it the tradition of the Seneca to have a woman present in council?" Tor-yo-ne asked mildly.

"This is Ena," an old man said.

"Is a woman, then, unencumbered by the taboo against weapons in the council longhouse?" asked one of Tor-yo-ne's followers.

"Some must have proof of my standing," Ena said.

"Ena's fame is well-known," Tor-yo-ne said expansively. "But she is a woman."

"Try me not, young Wolf," Ena cautioned, "or I will ask

that you seek your own weapons and face me outside the council longhouse.''

Tor-yo-ne barked a short laugh. ''She who was a scout for the armies is apparently an exception to the traditions. So be it. I, and those who came with me to this land of the south, have called this council to discuss the matter of naming a sachem for our people. We have been leaderless too long. The young men grow restless.''

''The young men have had a leader in this restlessness—a leader named Tor-yo-ne,'' Ha-ace pointed out. ''And now Tor-yo-ne wants to blame the friction that he has created among us on the absence of our friend, our sachem, Renno.''

''Tor-yo-ne has no ambitions,'' the Wolf denied. ''He is content to be war chief to his own. But he is discontent to see his people, those who followed him from the north, fall into ways not of the Seneca.'' He rose. He had a powerful voice that filled the longhouse, and the Seneca, who loved a fine oration, settled back to listen.

''The bloodline of your sachem boasts only a small boy, far too young to deal with responsibilities. No one questions the greatness of Renno or his right to be sachem. Moreover, if his brother, the shaman, were here, I and mine would gladly follow him. But neither is here, and the seasons pass, and we can only assume that both have gone to the Place across the River.''

''We are reminded,'' Ha-ace said, ''that the man who speaks has incited our young warriors to break the peace with the Chickasaw and thus to endanger our lands and the lands of the Cherokee.''

''In this, at least, we observe tradition,'' Tor-yo-ne commented wryly. ''For how else would our young warriors learn the skills necessary to protect our homes and our lands?''

''In times of peace and prosperity,'' an elder declared, ''the counting of coup is not in the best interests of the people.''

Tor-yo-ne ignored the comment. "We are Seneca. Our brothers to the north, in our ancestral homeland, are hard pressed. Here Seneca become Cherokee." He looked at Ena. "Your children. Are they Seneca or Cherokee?"

"My children," Ena said, "have the blood of great chiefs of both nations. They have Seneca names. They will observe the traditions of both Cherokee and Seneca."

"So," Tor-yo-ne said, as if his point had been made. "And will they live in a white-man's log cabin instead of a Seneca longhouse? Will they"—he put scornful emphasis on the words—"peacefully and in great prosperity greet the white men who will come in search of land? Stand aside in brotherhood while their hunting grounds are turned by the blades of plows?" He continued, his voice rising to cover the comments from various men. "There are decisions to be made! Decisions of great importance, and we are without a sachem to lead us. It is time that we choose a leader."

"You perhaps?" Ena asked innocently.

"I have said that I have no ambitions," Tor-yo-ne responded.

"Tor-yo-ne is of the blood of sachems," said a young warrior who had been a child when Ghonkaba led the Seneca southward. "He should be sachem."

"So your ambition is to be voiced by others," Ena said. She stood. "We welcomed you and yours as brothers, Tor-yo-ne, for we are of the same blood. Since you have arrived, you have done nothing but agitate our young men, give them doubts, and cause some of them to die at the hands of the Chickasaw. Now I, Ena, tell you this: Renno is sachem. He lives, and he will return, so we may follow his wisdom as we have followed it in the past." She put her hand on her tomahawk. "I say this, and my blade says this. If any care to test me—"

"I do not seek discord," Tor-yo-ne said. "I seek only an

answer to our needs, and our greatest need is for a wise leader to guide us, to help us prepare for the future."

"Hear me," Ha-ace said, standing. "It is true that Renno has not been with us, except in spirit, for many moons. It is true that young men need the guidance of a sachem. Young Wolf, you are strong and you are Seneca and our brother, but you are young in the ways of the world. I, the Panther, senior warrior, father-by-marriage to Renno, say this: Cease your raids into the lands of the Chickasaw. It has come to my ears that you now advocate that the Seneca travel back to the north, and this confuses me. How, if you left the north for the reasons you first stated, can you now think that it is desirable to return, with not only the people you brought but with others who have found a new homeland here?"

"Rather than be leaderless, rather than drift like an empty canoe in a flowing stream, I would rejoin our tribe. There, at least, wise men such as the sachem Cornplanter could give us counsel."

"If any want to go to the north," Ha-ace said, "they are free to go. A Seneca goes where he pleases. In the meantime, young Wolf, I ask you this, speaking in full awareness that both Renno and El-i-chi may not return: Let us wait until the snow flies, for no major changes occur in the winter. And then, if by the time of the new beginning Renno and El-i-chi have not returned, it will be time to talk of a new sachem."

Ena frowned.

"And how will the new sachem be named?" Tor-yo-ne wanted to know.

Ha-ace made a parody of puzzlement with his facial expression. "One who speaks so loudly of tradition should know the answer to that question. The sachem will be chosen as sachems have been chosen among the Seneca since the dawn of time—by the matriarch of the blood, by the wise woman who, in the time-honored method, will choose from the noble lineage. She will announce her choice to the other women, and then to the tribe. At that time there will be a discussion, and only then.''

"Is Ha-ace, then, of noble lineage?" Tor-yo-ne asked.

"I am not of the lineage of Renno," Ha-ace answered.

"Nor I," Tor-yo-ne said. "But I am of the blood of sachems, of the same lineage as Cornplanter."

"There are others who have sachems as ancestors," a senior warrior remarked. "And Ha-ace is among them."

"So then," Tor-yo-ne said bitterly, "since Ha-ace is married to the matron of the bear clan, the choice is foregone."

"Tread easy, young one," Ha-ace cautioned, "lest you insult the integrity of Toshabe. I do not lust for your death— only for your agreement to be at peace, to cease your search for coup to the west, and to hold all questions until the time of the new beginning."

"Ha-ace speaks wisely," someone said, and there was general agreement from all but Tor-yo-ne and those who followed him.

"I bow to my seniors," Tor-yo-ne said. "I will wait for the time of the new beginning; however, with the wearing of the false faces, unless I see Renno or a new sachem taking part in the ceremony, I will travel to the north with all those who want to follow me."

Later, in Ha-ace's lodge, Ena grimly told Toshabe, "If Renno has not returned, Tor-yo-ne will not be satisfied unless he is sachem. And if we oppose him successfully, he will leave, taking with him the life's blood of our clan, for he has gained the loyalty of most of our younger warriors."

On the morning after Renno's arrival at Sir Joffre's country manor, barking dogs and coats of red on a dozen riders signaled that it was to be a day of the hunt. The previous

afternoon and evening had been an odd time for Renno. After
Beth's heartrending weeping in the maze, she had introduced
him around, and there'd been great curiosity about Renno's
adventures in Africa. He had not told them the full story, for
there were more important things on his mind. When at last
he had Beth alone, it was early evening. The room in which
she was sleeping was furnished with dainty, beautiful chairs
from France and a huge, four-poster bed with carved teak
uprights and a lacy tester overhead.

Renno and Beth were both young and in love, and for a
while there was little talk. Beth, responding to Renno's need,
could forget that she had waited so long only to betray her
husband even as he rode toward her after his long absence.

Soon, however, when the heat of passion had cooled, guilt
made her wish that God had taken her before she had let
Joffre into her bed. She felt a deep, aching sadness, for there
was a feeling of something's having ended. She knew that
she must continue the enterprise she had begun.

"You'll be leaving soon," she whispered, clinging to
him.

"You, too, must be ready to go back to Wilmington."

"Not just yet," she faltered. "There are things I must do
here." She was surprised, for the words came without thought.
In fact, she did need to get back to Wilmington, to start the
flow of commerce between that port and the islands.

Renno, too, was feeling the sadness.

"But let's not talk about that tonight," Beth said. Tears
came and she whispered, "Oh, God, Renno, why didn't you
come back sooner?"

He looked into her eyes. He didn't want to hurt her. She
had been sent to him by the manitous, and he had loved her,
still loved her. "You're right. Tonight is not the time to talk
of the future. Let's enjoy the present and the fact that we are
together again."

He woke with a million birds chattering outside the windows. He turned to see that she was awake, as well. Voices came from outside, and then there was a knock on the door, and a servant told them that breakfast was being served.

"I want to leave early," Renno said.

"You can't. Today is the day of the hunt, and I want everyone to see what a superb rider you are."

"The hunt," he said, smiling, knowing very well what sort of hunt she meant. "There is no fresh meat in this house?"

"Silly," she said, grinning. "Today we're going to be very, very English and ride to the hounds."

"After a fox," he said. "Tell me, will we then skin the fox and roast it and eat it?"

Her smile faded. "Just this day, Renno. Then we'll go back to Beaumont and—" She couldn't finish.

"I kill only to eat," he said.

"Then come along just for the ride. Actually, if they catch it, the dogs kill the fox." She took his hands in hers. "I've been looking forward to it. Please?"

The horse he'd borrowed from William was a fine animal, and although he did not have the proper clothes for the hunt, he drew admiring eyes as the guests and Joffre formed up outside the stables. They rode out into the fields, and soon the hounds had a scent. With glad cries the riders began to stream away. Renno held his horse back.

"Come on," Beth said. "We'll be left behind."

"Go," Renno said.

"All right." She kicked her horse into motion.

Renno turned his horse and rode back past the house, through a grove of trees and into a scene of peaceful beauty. A rolling meadow stretched from a ridge down to the sea. He saw no people. The morning was balmy, with a light breeze from the channel. He rode toward the water, dismounted, and let the horse crop the rich, green grass. He lay on his back to look up at the sky. He was, he knew, going to have to hurt the woman he loved. He was not content to linger even one more day; there was an urgency in him that could not be denied.

He dozed in the sun, his thoughts far away, and then he sat up with a start, for he had heard the clash of battle, the cries of wounded men, and the ring of steel. He looked around, but there was only the empty meadow. And then he saw a shimmering presence, a ghostly mist that formed into a recognizable image as he leaped to his feet. There was the original white Indian, Renno—dressed as an English gentleman but unmistakably Renno, his great-grandfather.

"You have traveled far," the manitou acknowledged, "but not without purpose."

Renno felt a great surge of relief, for the spirit had addressed himself directly to the tumult in Renno's mind—his doubt, his guilt for having stayed from his responsibilities for so long.

"It was meant that you see this world in its imperfections," the manitou continued. "You have gained knowledge. In Africa you have seen savagery and the depths of cruelty to which men can sink, and here in England you have seen the forces that you will have to fight in the future. In this time of great change, you will have private sorrows and you will question, but there was a purpose for the flame-haired one, as well."

Renno noted the use of the past tense—"was a purpose." He felt a pang of loss.

"Look around you," the manitou urged, beginning to fade, and Renno tore his eyes away, shocked, for around him, in silent fury, waged a battle as bloody as any he had ever seen. Oddly dressed Englishmen on foot faced mounted, armored cavalry and died in an eerie silence. And then the scene faded, and there came to him the voice of his great-grandfather. "Do not let this happen to our people."

Beth saw him as she rode to the top of the ridge. He was standing sternly erect. She had left the hunt, at first angered, then concerned by his refusal to join her. She slowly rode toward him, and he turned, looking at her as if he did not see her, his eyes wide, staring into the distance. When he saw her, he shook his head, then came forward to help her dismount.

"You're standing on a historic spot," she told him. "The ships of William the Conqueror landed his army not far from here, and here Harold came to form a defense on that ridge, there."

"Yes," Renno said, "I have seen it. Both armies wore ring mail ending in a divided skirt, so they could mount their horses. But the English dismounted and pitted shield and battle-ax against armored light cavalry thrusting with spears and striking downward with swords."

Beth looked at him in surprise. "I have never truly known you, have I?"

Renno was looking into the distance, remembering the vision shown to him by the manitou. "I have read about it, and now I have seen it. There were no more than twelve thousand Normans, only half of them mounted. And yet they subjugated millions." He turned and walked a few paces. Beth followed him, an eerie shiver skittering up her spine.

"The English had ridden hard," he went on, "and had come from a hard fight against the Danes in the north. They fought well and bravely, but they were bound by tradition, and traditionally, the English rode to battle but fought dismounted. The longbow had not yet been developed. The

Norman archers stood there"—he pointed—"and riddled the English ranks before the charge of the cavalry."

"I *don't* know you," Beth whispered.

"Infantry against missiles and cavalry," Renno mused. And the words of the manitou echoed in his head: *"Do not let this happen to our people."* He walked on, oblivious to Beth, who shadowed him. What did it mean? Was it as simple as a warning to teach his warriors how to fight as cavalry? It was not probable, since, unlike the English who had fought so long ago on this field, in any war with the whites, his people would be outnumbered. Were the manitou's words meant to warn him that invaders would attempt to conquer, as they had conquered the eastern tribes of the coastlands?

"Renno!" Beth had been calling him repeatedly.

He turned. He was once again aware of the pleasantness of the day, the blue of the sky, the song of birds. And in him was the knowledge that he had to part from this woman he loved. He went to her and drew her down to sit beside him on the grass.

"You said you saw it. The battle," she whispered.

"No matter," he said. "What matters at this moment is this: Will you come with me not only to Wilmington but to my homeland?"

Tears filled her eyes. "I can't. You know I can't. Not now."

"So," he said. He kissed her. "The manitous gave you to me, and now, by the manitou, I must leave you."

She was weeping silently, but there was a perverse feeling of relief in her. *He* had made the decision. Now she would never have to tell him of her betrayal with Joffre. Now she would not have to hurt him by telling him that it was time that they went their separate ways.

"It would be unfair to you to be chained to me at great distances," he said. "I have often told you that your place

was in England or in a great house in America, with servant
and the fine clothes that you wear so well, with members o
your own race."

"I remember," she said. "You were trying to talk you
way out of marrying me." She was thinking, however—an
this surprised her—that the Indian ceremony she and Renn
had performed, just the two of them, in the cold, dar
northern forest was not legally binding. "In God's name,
was good, wasn't it, Renno?"

"It was good," he said.

"I'll always love you."

"I know."

"Is there some Seneca ceremony to end a marriage?"

"When a wife is captured by an enemy tribe and carrie
away without hope of being retaken, a warrior is free to—"

"And I've been captured by the enemy?"

"You have returned to your own, as I must," he said.

"Hold me just once more?"

He held her and brushed the tears from her cheeks, an
their closeness roused them as one. He loved her, once
and finally, on the grassy slope under a mild English sun, anc
neither of them, as passion burned, worried about prying
eyes.

It was the time of storms in the Atlantic, and the crossing
was a rough one. El-i-chi's seasickness returned, and he
almost fell when he stepped out onto the wharf on the Cape
Fear River in Wilmington on a cold, blustery day. The solid
wood seemed to be in motion under his feet, but he soon
recovered.

The copy of George Washington's letter was given to
Renno by Moses Tarpley. Renno read it and felt, for just a
moment, a surge of interest, but he put the letter into his pack

and out of his mind, for more and more he felt that great urgency to get home.

They rode hard. Winter came in its full fury in the mountains. Their horses struggled through great drifts of snow, and the winter winds whistled over their campsites at night. In Knoxville they found the Johnson house boarded up and were told by neighbors of Nora's death. Roy Johnson had simply disappeared.

The brothers made the trip to the village in one long ride, pushing on through the night to arrive in a cold, windy dawn. Winter was lingering, in spite of the fact that the time of the new beginning was on them.

The village slept in the predawn darkness. The horses' hooves rang on the frozen ground. "If we were an enemy. . . ." El-i-chi said grimly. "Indeed, we have been gone too long."

The longhouse of Toshabe and Ha-ace was still quiet.

"Old ones sleep late." El-i-chi grinned, looking up to the sun as it peeked over the eastern mountains.

Grinning like errant urchins, they hid their horses in the forest and crept into the longhouse. Behind a partition of skins they could hear a mighty snore, Ha-ace's. Renno's heart soared as he saw a tousled head of hair protruding from furs and blankets. He crept to the bed, put his hand over Little Hawk's mouth, and then tweaked an exposed ear. Little Hawk's eyes opened wide, and he started to struggle but soon ceased, and Renno, feeling a great, wide smile on the mouth under his hands, said, "A warrior should be more alert."

He removed his hand, and a young warrior squealed with joy as he threw up his arms. The sound brought Ha-ace bounding off balance out of his bed, to stumble and pull down the skin partition.

"Hold," Renno said, laughing, as Ha-ace checked the swing of his tomahawk in midair.

Toshabe cried out happily and threw herself into El-i-chi's arms, then embraced Renno. Renno looked around and saw a pair of pale eyes under tousled, pale hair, and his heart melted, for it was his daughter, a miniature image of Emily.

Renna looked at him solemnly, and then her face broke into a great, glad smile, and he was lifting her high to crush her to his breast while Little Hawk clung to his legs.

"Woman," El-i-chi said in a gruff voice, "when warriors return—"

Toshabe slapped El-i-chi on the rump. "I know, hungry one. Be patient."

And then it was El-i-chi's turn to be surprised when Ah-wa-o, having taken time to brush her hair and don her day clothing, stepped shyly from behind her own hide partition. He was surprised because, although he remembered her beauty, he had not remembered the true impact of it. Stunned as surely as if he'd been struck in the head by Renno's war club, he could only stare until Ah-wa-o threw herself into his arms.

"Now *that* trouble begins," Toshabe moaned, rolling her eyes at Ha-ace. She turned and caught Little Hawk's arm. "Dress quickly. Run to Ena and tell her." She smiled hugely. "And don't neglect, as you run through the village, to tell others, as well."

"Hold," Ha-ace said. He had a smile on his face that Toshabe did not often see. She recognized it as his mischief face, a face that came, usually, when they were alone in their bed. "Tomorrow we celebrate the new beginning, and I have carved a fine false face. Let Little Hawk go very quietly to Ena and tell her to be equally discreet when she comes to greet her brother. And then, tomorrow, we will have a surprise for all."

Ena came with Rusog and two adorable little ones, and by that time Renno had been informed of the troubles in the village. He agreed that Ha-ace's idea was a worthy one. So

Ah-wa-o went out into the village to tell everyone that Toshabe had come down with the winter fever and that, as a result, lest the fever be spread, Ha-ace's longhouse was to be in temporary quarantine. Inside that longhouse was laughter and enough talk to make the ears of the spirits tired.

The day of the new beginning dawned, and the most sacred ceremonies of the Seneca were under way. The Society of the False Face was much in evidence, and no one noticed that its numbers had been increased by two as Renno and El-i-chi, in silence, roamed through the village listening to the talk of the people, getting firsthand the feeling of dissatisfaction that had been fomented by Tor-yo-ne.

"How can we properly pay tribute to the Master of Life," a young warrior was complaining loudly, "when we have no shaman?"

There were dancing, songs, and a great consumption of food as the day ended and the false faces stood ready to perform their antics, which failed to frighten even the very young. Tor-yo-ne was much in evidence—a tall, proud, handsome young warrior. He plied his way around the village, speaking to supporters here and there and nodding coldly to the elders and senior warriors who had opposed him.

The entire village was in the compound when the time of the false faces came. Renno and El-i-chi, legitimate members of the society, in the faces made by Ha-ace, joined the dance. El-i-chi performed mightily, knowing that Ah-wa-o's eyes were on him.

Toshabe, miraculously recovered from the winter fever, was seated in a place of honor beside Ena. Rusog, who had come to feel like an outsider because of his allegiance to Renno and being a Cherokee, stood elsewhere, glowering, hoping that when the time came, Tor-yo-ne and the warriors who followed him would become violent.

The dance ended with laughter and calls of encouragement

and praise. Now it was time for the tribal shaman to chant the praise of the Master of Life and to invoke the new life that was his gift to his people. Once that task had been performed by old Casno. After Casno's death, the duty was El-i-chi's. In El-i-chi's absence, during the past year's celebration, the chant had been done by Toshabe, who was well versed in the tribe's tradition. Now all looked to her, expecting her to rise. Instead, a tall man in a false face leaped to the center of the compound, and hands held up toward the night sky, he began to sing the chant in a strong, young voice.

Tor-yo-ne, caught by surprise, demanded, "Who is this? Who dares take the place of a legitimate shaman?"

Ha-ace, waiting, had moved to stand behind Tor-yo-ne. "Do not overstep yourself more, young Wolf," he hissed. "Do not speak and thus show disrespect when the new beginning is being chanted."

Tor-yo-ne readied a reply, but one look at Ha-ace's face moved him to silence. He had made his plans: As soon as the chant was over, his time would come.

Whispers flew back and forth among those Seneca who had been long in the south, for the strong voice was a familiar one, and some felt that a ghost was among them. But out of respect they sat, pounding their palms in the dirt in time with El-i-chi's rhythmic chanting.

It was over. El-i-chi's voice trailed down, down, and then into silence. No one moved. It was a moment of great reverence, for now the Master of Life was instilling the magic of growth in all things, and the mystical renewal was under way.

It was Tor-yo-ne's voice that broke the silence.

"Hear me, Seneca!" he proclaimed, standing. "In solemn council of all elders, it was decided, and now the time has come: This time of new beginning would not pass without a sachem. Tonight, on this sacred occasion, I call council of the entire tribe. Before the sun, there will be a sachem.''

Renno, hidden behind the false face, walked slowly toward Tor-yo-ne and the group of young warriors gathered around him. He halted three paces away. In his grasp the war club that had known the hand of the great Renno glowed with warmth.

''Who stands before me?'' Tor-yo-ne demanded. ''Does he who hides behind the false face question a decision taken in solemn council?''

Renno rolled his shoulders back, letting the robes fall to the ground. Now he stood in buckskin trousers, his chest bare but painted in the colors of a Seneca sachem. Then, slowly, he lifted the false face, dropped it. The gasp that came from the gathered tribe was in unison.

Tor-yo-ne looked into a pair of cold, blue eyes, and he knew in his heart that he had lost. ''Do I address Renno?''

''You demanded a sachem,'' Renno said coolly. ''I am here. Do you wish to say anything else?''

''I thank thee that thou are well,'' Tor-yo-ne said, inclining his head in respect, ''great Sachem.''

An-da, sitting with Ah-wa-o, who had had a terrible time keeping such a delicious secret from her best friend, saw a face that seemed somehow familiar to her, although she had never seen it. Her breasts heaved as she thrilled to the sheer beauty of the grim face that now turned toward the assembled tribe.

''Renno,'' she whispered.

★ WAGONS WEST ★

A series of unforgettable books that trace the lives of a dauntless band of pioneering men, women, and children as they brave the hazards of an untamed land in their trek across America. This legendary caravan of people forge a new link in the wilderness. They are Americans from the North and the South, alongside immigrants, Blacks, and Indians, who wage fierce daily battles for survival on this uncompromising journey—each to their private destinies as they fulfill their greatest dreams.

☐	26822	INDEPENDENCE! #1	$4.50
☐	26162	NEBRASKA! #2	$4.50
☐	26242	WYOMING! #3	$4.50
☐	26072	OREGON! #4	$4.50
☐	26070	TEXAS! #5	$4.50
☐	26377	CALIFORNIA! #6	$4.50
☐	26546	COLORADO! #7	$4.50
☐	26069	NEVADA! #8	$4.50
☐	26163	WASHINGTON! #9	$4.50
☐	26073	MONTANA! #10	$4.50
☐	26184	DAKOTA! #11	$4.50
☐	26521	UTAH! #12	$4.50
☐	26071	IDAHO! #13	$4.50
☐	26367	MISSOURI! #14	$4.50
☐	27141	MISSISSIPPI! #15	$4.50
☐	25247	LOUISIANA! #16	$4.50
☐	25622	TENNESSEE! #17	$4.50
☐	26022	ILLINOIS! #18	$4.50
☐	26533	WISCONSIN! #19	$4.50
☐	26849	KENTUCKY! #20	$4.50
☐	27065	ARIZONA! #21	$4.50

Prices and availability subject to change without notice.

- -

Bantam Books, Dept. LE, 414 East Golf Road, Des Plaines, IL 60016

Please send me the books I have checked above. I am enclosing $_____ (please add $2.00 to cover postage and handling). Send check or money order—no cash or C.O.D.s please.

Mr/Ms _____

Address _____

City/State _____ Zip _____

LE—11/88

Please allow four to six weeks for delivery. This offer expires 5/89.